Mitch turned to the door, then faced her again. "And don't worry about missing me while I'm busy. I've arranged for us to have a private dinner here in the apartment tonight."

Lila's breath froze. Private dinner? She remembered those thirty seconds when he'd yanked ̶ ̶ ̶nst him on the dance floor. The si̶z̶z̶

And the longin̶

She fought the u̶ ̶ ̶ ̶ ̶ ̶ ̶ had a crush on this ̶ ̶ ̶ ̶ ̶ ̶ ̶er so close… Well, her ̶ ̶ ̶ ̶ ̶ ̶ of control and she'd felt so many ̶ ̶ ̶ings.

What if he'd felt them too?

Oh, boy.

The words "private dinner" took on a whole new meaning.

But he opened the door and was gone before Lila could blink, let alone argue. She straightened her shoulders. She wasn't going to fall into the trap of thinking he intended to seduce her. They'd shared one "crackly" moment the night before. He hadn't instantly fallen in love with her. He probably wanted them to have dinner alone so he could catch her up on whatever happened at the family business meeting that day.

She was, after all, his assistant…

THE BOSS'S
FAKE FIANCÉE

BY
SUSAN MEIER

All rights reserved including the right of reproduction in whole or in part in any form. This edition is published by arrangement with Harlequin Books S.A.

This is a work of fiction. Names, characters, places, locations and incidents are purely fictional and bear no relationship to any real life individuals, living or dead, or to any actual places, business establishments, locations, events or incidents. Any resemblance is entirely coincidental.

This book is sold subject to the condition that it shall not, by way of trade or otherwise, be lent, resold, hired out or otherwise circulated without the prior consent of the publisher in any form of binding or cover other than that in which it is published and without a similar condition including this condition being imposed on the subsequent purchaser.

® and ™ are trademarks owned and used by the trademark owner and/or its licensee. Trademarks marked with ® are registered with the United Kingdom Patent Office and/or the Office for Harmonisation in the Internal Market and in other countries.

First published in Great Britain 2015
By Mills & Boon, an imprint of Harlequin (UK) Limited,
Eton House, 18-24 Paradise Road, Richmond, Surrey TW9 1SR

© 2015 Linda Susan Meier

ISBN: 978-0-263-92319-3

23-0615

Our policy is to use papers that are natural, renewable and recyclable products and made from wood grown in sustainable forests. The logging and manufacturing processes conform to the legal environmental regulations of the country of origin.

Printed and bound in Spain
by CPI, Barcelona

First Published in Great Britain 2017
By Mills & Boon, an imprint of HarperCollins*Publishers*
1 London Bridge Street, London, SE1 9GF

© 2017 Linda Susan Meier

ISBN: 978-0-263-92319-3

23-0817

Our policy is to use papers that are natural, renewable and recyclable products and made from wood grown in sustainable forests. The logging and manufacturing processes conform to the legal environmental regulations of the country of origin.

Printed and bound in Spain
by CPI, Barcelona

Susan Meier is the author of over fifty books for Mills & Boon. *The Tycoon's Secret Daughter* was a Romance Writers of America RITA® Award finalist, and *Nanny for the Millionaire's Twins* won the Book Buyers' Best Award and was a finalist in the National Readers' Choice Awards. She is married and has three children. One of eleven children, she loves to write about the complexity of families and totally believes in the power of love.

CHAPTER ONE

"I THINK YOU'RE going to have to do more than show up at the wedding."

Mitcham Ochoa tossed his pen to his desk and glared at his cousin Riccardo. It wasn't exactly like looking in a mirror when he saw Riccardo, but it was close. All the Ochoa men had dark hair and dark eyes. Most were tall. The same age, Mitch and Riccardo didn't just share physical characteristics; they behaved like brothers and knew everything there was to know about each other. Both had also been dumped by a woman they thought they wanted to marry. Except Riccardo had been broken to his very core when his fiancée chose her former boyfriend over him and Mitch eventually realized he hadn't really loved Julia. Because Riccardo knew that, Mitch was not pleased with what Riccardo was hinting.

"I'm over her."

Riccardo winced. "You know that and I know that, but it isn't every day that a woman leaves her boyfriend for his brother, and then the jilted brother is asked to be the best man at their wedding. Tongues are going to wag, my friend. Everybody's going to watch every move you make. Unless—"

"Unless what?"

"Unless you have no reason to be jealous."

Righteous indignation whipped through Mitch and he bounced out of his tall-back black leather office chair. If anybody knew Mitch felt nothing but happiness for his brother and Julia, it was Riccardo. It annoyed the hell out of him that his cousin was pushing this nonissue. "I have no reason to be jealous!"

"Your brother is the oldest. He got the CEO-ship of your family's business. He stole your girlfriend."

Mitch growled.

"And let's face it. He's better looking."

Mitch tossed his pen at Riccardo, who ducked.

"It's reactions like that that will have Nanna fussing over you for the two weeks we're in Spain celebrating this wedding. Do you want to have Nanna hovering?"

Finally seeing what Riccardo was doing, he slowly lowered himself to his seat again. "No." Oh, Lord. He did not want Nanna hovering. His mother would be bad enough, but his grandmother? If she thought he was having even one iota of sadness over Julia marrying his brother, she'd do everything but spoon-feed him his dessert and make him look pathetic, when he wasn't. Finding his brother in his bedroom with his girlfriend two years ago hadn't been upsetting as much as it had been a wake-up call that rippled through his whole life. Losing Julia had put him back into the dating pool where he'd realized maybe their "love" was more about convenience than real emotion. They'd been together so long that staying together just seemed like the right thing to do. Recognizing the mistake he'd almost made in the name of comfort had jarred him. And now he was smarter, sharper, alert to the pitfalls of getting too comfortable with anything.

"Then you have to figure out a way to prove—from the

very second you step off the Ochoa Vineyards jet—that you're not just fine with this wedding. You are happy."

Unfortunately, his family didn't seem to see that his brother's betrayal hadn't really been a betrayal but a way for Mitch to dodge a big, fat bullet. They didn't see how it had spring-boarded him to the kind of success he'd always longed for. All they remembered was that the initial shock of it had thrown Mitch into a tailspin. This was what he got for moving an ocean away. They hadn't seen how quickly he'd bounced back. And when he tried to tell them, they thought he was either attempting to smooth things over or save face.

"The only way Nanna will ever think I'm happy is if I'm married."

Riccardo frowned. "You can't get married before your brother. No time." He stopped. His face shifted and he burst out laughing. "But you could bring a fiancée to the wedding celebrations."

"Right."

"No! I'm serious! All you have to do is find a woman to agree to be your fiancée for the two weeks we're in Spain. You make up a story about how you met. You create some romantic schmaltzy thing about how you proposed. You kiss her a few times in front of Nanna and—" He snapped his fingers. "You're no longer the rejected brother."

"Except I'm engaged?"

"No. No. A couple weeks later, you call Nanna. You say you had a fight and you're not engaged anymore. And you don't really have to explain too much until the next time you go home."

He had to admit there was a certain poetry to it. He'd sneaked home to propose to Julia the night he'd found her and his brother in the bedroom of their apartment. They were fully clothed, but there weren't a whole hell of a lot of reasons why Alonzo would be in her bedroom, except that they were lovers. Alonzo had vehemently denied it. He'd even told Mitch he'd walked in on their first kiss. They weren't cheating. They didn't want to hurt him. But it was clear from the way Alonzo protected Julia that Mitch's brother might not be sleeping with her, but he loved her.

He'd been gobsmacked, but the whole mess had prompted his dad to give him the go-ahead to start the project he'd been angling to try for years: put his family's wines on-line. He'd moved to New York for a change of scenery and grown to love the city. He'd also gotten so good at selling his family's wines that he'd started a second website. That site sold wines from numerous vineyards—and glasses, wine racks, corkscrews, aprons, T-shirts with funny wine sayings, books on wine, books on serving wine, books on hosting wine-tasting parties—anything and everything related to wines. That was the site where he made money. Lots of money. Enough money to bring Riccardo from Spain to New York to help him start three more specialty websites. One sold anything and everything to do with cycling. One sold cooking supplies. One sold anything to do with golf.

All he had to do was pick a topic, find the vendors who made the "best" of whatever he wanted to sell, test their products, rule out the weak, choose the good and create a site. There was enough variety in the duties that he was never bored, and Riccardo was a financial genius. Whatever money Mitch's websites brought in was invested to make more money. Though they wouldn't tell their family, they were on track to be worth more than the entire Ochoa family enterprises in as few as three years.

So losing Julia had opened the door for him to become the businessman he was today. The very fact that he wouldn't go back and change the outcome was proof that everything that had happened was for his benefit.

Still, none of those things would sway Nanna into believing he was happy, and she'd more than hover. She'd make him look pathetic. Worse, his grandmother making a big deal about him would put a real damper on his brother's wedding. This was supposed to be Julia and Alonzo's special time, two weeks of celebrating, and if he didn't do something, his presence could actually ruin it.

But if he didn't attend the wedding, refused to be best man, people would gossip that he was upset and the whole wedding would be about him not being there.

Either way, Julia and Alonzo's wedding could become all about him.

He had to fix this.

"So where do we find this woman who'd be willing to pretend to be my fiancée for two weeks?"

Lila Ross gathered the sheets of paper that flew out of the copier, stacked them neatly, stapled them and headed into her boss's office. It wasn't often that she had both Mitch and Riccardo in the same room at the same time. She had to take advantage of this opportunity to get their approval on last month's income statements, especially since they were leaving the next day for a family wedding.

Reports ready, she shoved her big-frame glasses up her nose and headed for the open door. She knocked twice to let them know she was there, then entered the room talking.

"I have last month's income statements."

Mitch said, "Great. Thanks. Come in."

Riccardo's face shifted. His eyes narrowed. His forehead wrinkled. His head tilted.

Deciding that expression probably had something to do with whatever they'd been discussing before she came in and was, therefore, none of her business, she handed one of the reports to Mitch and one to Riccardo before she sat on the empty chair in front of Mitch's huge chrome-and-glass desk. The floor-to-ceiling windows behind Mitch displayed a beautiful view of the Manhattan skyline, glittering in the bright sunlight of a perfect June morning. The big geometric print area rug beneath her feet protected hardwood floors bleached then stained a medium gray that complemented the gray paint on the walls. The ultramodern black sofa and chair sat with a chrome-and-glass coffee table and end tables that matched the desk. The room was the picture of luxury and success that didn't surprise her. Mitch Ochoa had the Midas touch.

Not to mention good looks and charm.

He glanced up at her and smiled. "Give me two minutes to peruse this, and then we'll talk specifics."

Her heart pitter-pattered. When he smiled, it was like the sun breaking over the horizon in her soul. "Sure."

He smiled again before he began reading.

She told herself not to look at his shiny black hair as he read, but that only took her eyes to his broad shoulders, white shirt and black tie. He was so urbane. Born and raised in Spain, he'd been all over Europe before he'd come to the United States. She had no idea why he'd chosen New York City to start his breakaway business, but every night she'd thanked her lucky stars that he had—

Every night until last night.

Last night, she'd finally realized that she'd been his assistant for an entire year. They'd eaten many a lunch

together. Not to mention late-night dinners when they
worked until midnight to get something online or to wait
for stats at the end of a new product day.

He could have kissed her thirty-seven times. She'd
counted.

But while she'd gazed up at him with stars in her eyes,
he'd looked down at her with the eyes of a friend. No.
Scratch that. He'd looked down at an assistant. She hadn't
even broken the barrier to become his friend.

And last night—

She fought the urge to squeeze her eyes shut as pain
and emptiness assaulted her.

Last night, she'd realized he would never see her as
anything other than an employee, and she had to start
job hunting. As long as she was this close to him day
after day, she would continue believing that someday
he'd notice her. But if he hadn't noticed her—not even
as a friend—after an entire year of late nights and weekends, he wouldn't *ever* notice her. It was time to get on
with her life.

And if she really wanted to get on with her life, she
had to find a job with a company where she could climb
the corporate ladder and eventually earn enough money
that she could start looking for her birth mom. They'd
been separated when she was ten. Raised in a series of
foster homes, she'd been without a family, a place, since
then. Finding her birth mom would give her the sense
of belonging she'd always yearned for. That meant she
had to get away from the distraction of Mitcham Ochoa.

Riccardo cleared his throat. "These numbers look fine,
Mitch." He tossed his copy of the income statement to
Mitch's desk. "So maybe we can finish talking about that
thing we were discussing before Lila came in."

Mitch's head jerked up. His gaze flew to his cousin, then over to Lila and back to Riccardo again, as if reminding Riccardo they had an employee in the room. "Now?"

"I just want you to see the opportunity you have before you. We were talking about not being able to find a certain person to fulfill a specific job, and suddenly I'm thinking perhaps that person is right under our noses."

Okay. She wasn't stupid. They were talking about her. If she was reading this situation correctly, they had a job they needed to fill and she fit the bill. For Mitch to be cautious, the new job had to be a promotion.

Her heart leaped with joy. A promotion would mean more money—maybe enough to hire a private investigator to begin searching for her mom—

Then she remembered that for her sanity and her future, she had to leave Mitch Ochoa's employ and her heart sank. Wasn't it just like fate to finally give her a chance at a promotion when she'd decided—firmly decided—it was time to move on? As hard as she'd worked to climb the ladder in this growing company, she also knew herself. Other people might think she simply had a crush on Mitch. But she couldn't work for someone for a year without getting to know him. In her heart, she genuinely loved him. And promotion or not, she had to leave this job or she'd end up living her life for a man who barely noticed her. Then even if she found her mom, she'd be a broke, single spinster. Not a mom. Not a wife. Not a woman who gave her mom grandkids. She'd be none of the things she longed to be.

She rose from her seat. "I'm not a hundred percent sure what you're talking about, but I think I should tell you that I—"

Riccardo held up a finger to stop her. "No decisions until you hear us out."

Mitch said, "Riccardo," his voice a warning growl.

Riccardo walked behind Lila's chair, put his hands on her shoulders and sat her down again. In two quick moves, he had her chopstick-like pins out of her chestnut-brown hair, and it fell to her shoulders in a curly waterfall. Then he reached forward and removed her glasses.

If Mitch had done either of those, she probably would have swooned at his touch. Because it was all-business Riccardo, she spun around and gaped at him. "What are you doing?"

He turned her head to face front. "Are you seeing what I'm seeing?"

Mitch blinked. "Oh, my God. Yes."

"*Sì.* She is perfect."

Mitch rose and rounded his desk to lean against it, in front of her. "Pale and delicate to Julia's dark features."

"Short and petite where Julia's a little taller."

"Smart," Mitch added.

Riccardo laughed. "I won't insult Julia by making the obvious comparison."

Lila looked from Mitch to Riccardo and back to Mitch again. "What comparison? And could I have my glasses back so I can see?"

Riccardo said, "You can't see without your glasses?"

She took her thick glasses from his hand. "Why else would anyone wear them?"

"Do you have contacts?" Mitch asked quietly, seriously.

Their gazes met and she swallowed hard. For the first time in a year, he wasn't looking at her as an assistant but as a woman. She wasn't sure how she knew the difference, except something in his eyes had shifted, changed, and a million fireflies glowed in her stomach.

"Yes. I have contacts. But I only wear them for special occasions."

Riccardo said, "We have a very special occasion for you."

"You're sending me somewhere?"

"*I'm* taking you somewhere."

Oh, wow. The only thing she'd heard in that sentence was *I'm taking you*. Her heart about popped out of her chest, and she knew she was in more trouble than she'd even believed the night before. She had to get away from this man or she'd be knitting sweaters for him when he was eighty as he dated twenty-year-old starlets.

"Mitch's brother is getting married," Riccardo said. "In Spain."

She frowned. "I know. I reserved the family jet for you guys."

"Yeah, well, Mitch needs more help than reserving the jet."

Mitch pushed away from the desk. "You know what? I think Lila and I should talk about this privately."

Riccardo's eyebrows rose in question.

Mitch said, "Think it through, Riccardo. The less you know, the better the ruse will work."

Riccardo laughed. "Okay. I get it." He scooped up his copy of the income statement. "I'll be in my office, but just remember I'm your detail guy. You won't want to leave me out of the loop completely."

He left the room, but in the last second, reached in, grabbed the knob on the door to the office and closed it.

The oddest feeling snaked through Lila. She'd been alone with Mitch a million times, behind closed doors lots of those times. But suddenly it felt like everything had changed.

"I really do need a favor. A big favor," Mitch said, walking around his desk and dropping into his black leather chair.

"How big?" Seriously? Had her voice just shivered? The man was not the Big Bad Wolf and she certainly wasn't Little Red Riding Hood. She'd been a foster child until she was eighteen. She'd fended for herself forever. Even in some ugly situations. How could a man she'd known a year, a man she loved and respected, send that kind of fear skittering through her?

"Riccardo already mentioned that my brother is getting married."

"Yes."

He leaned back in his chair. "What you don't know is that Alonzo's fiancée had been my girlfriend." He glanced up, caught her gaze. "I cut a business trip short, sneaked into our apartment to surprise her with an engagement ring and caught them together in our bedroom."

Her eyes widened. "Yikes."

He waved his hands. "They were fully clothed. But, really? What reason did my brother have being so comfortable in my bedroom with the woman I'd come home to propose to?"

"None."

"Exactly. They had the good graces not to even try to deny that they'd taken advantage of my many trips for our family's vineyard to…get to know each other."

She couldn't help it. She giggled. He had such a sense of humor. And he seemed fine with his brother's betrayal—or was it his girlfriend's betrayal? Oh, God. It was both.

How had he gotten over that? Maybe she shouldn't have laughed?

He sat up. "That's exactly the attitude I'd want you to have. That my brother marrying my former girlfriend is no big deal. Funny even. Because I couldn't be happier for them. Alonzo truly loves Julia. She truly loves him. Theirs is the match that should have been made all along."

Putting some of this together in her analytical brain, she said, "So you want me to come to Spain with you?"

"*Sí.*"

"As your date for the wedding." The very thought made her nerve endings do a happy dance, but she told them to settle down. There was no way she could agree to that.

"No. Actually, I'd want you to pretend to be my fiancée."

Her breathing stopped. "What?"

"My mom is okay. She has a lot of duties with the wedding to keep her busy. But my grandmother? She's got way too much free time. I swear to God," he said, raising his hands and opening them in supplication, "it won't matter what I say. She'll treat me like a wounded puppy the entire celebration."

"And everybody will feel sorry for you."

"It's not just about pride. It's about Julia and Alonzo's special celebration. I don't want the focus to be on me. I want it on them."

"True."

He leaned a little farther back in his chair. "I turned this arm of my family's enterprise into our company's biggest moneymaker. I'm branching out on my own. I don't want to spend two weeks with my dad looking at me as if I'm emotionally unstable and wondering if he should replace me, even though I'm making tons of money for him and even more money for myself."

"Never thought of that."

"Then you don't know how stubborn and thickheaded Spanish men can be."

Oh, she had a pretty good idea.

"Your presence alone will satisfy everybody's curiosity about how I dealt with my brother moving in on my girlfriend while I was traveling." He laughed. "Or maybe I should say just your presence will prove that I easily handled my brother and girlfriend falling in love. And there will be no talk, no questions. Discussions with my dad will go smoothly. My grandmother will chat you up about our future wedding plans and probably take you shopping for china patterns, not smother me with unwanted, unnecessary sympathy."

He took a breath, then added, "I'm not going to lie. This will be a long two weeks of acting for you. But I'll compensate you. In fact, right now I'm so sure this is the best way to go that I'm willing to give you anything you want."

What she wanted was him.

But that was actually what made this favor impossible. "I can't." She'd get stars in her eyes. She'd read into things and when she came home she'd be even more in love with him than she was now. So, no. She couldn't do it.

"Okay, let me be frank. The family jet leaves tomorrow. I can't go out and hunt up a woman to do this for me. Not someone whose discretion I trust. Because you truly have to keep this secret. If my family even suspects this is a ruse, it will backfire." He held her gaze. "I trust you in a way I've never trusted anyone. And I need you. I honestly don't think anybody but you could pull this off."

She said nothing, torn between agreeing simply because she was an employee who believed it was her job to do whatever her boss wanted, and recognizing this wasn't a normal boss/assistant request. It was above and beyond her duties. And potentially heartbreaking for her.

"Isn't there anything you want?"

She said nothing.

"Anything you need?"

That's when it hit her. She did have something she needed. She could ask him to use his considerable resources to find her mom, but then she'd still be working for him. She'd spend two weeks pretending to be his fiancée and come home to being his assistant again. That was a heartbreak waiting to happen.

But a new job would not only provide money for a private investigator to locate her mom, it would get her away from Mitch and her pointless crush. She really would be getting a fresh start.

"I need a new job."

He frowned. "What?"

"I want a new job." Assistant jobs, though a dime a dozen, didn't always pay well. With his connections he could find her one of those gems of a job that didn't get advertised in any of the job search websites. Plus, if she handled this right, going to Spain could be the end of her association with him. She wouldn't have to come home and pretend they hadn't kissed—albeit for the benefit of his family. She would be gone. Off to start a new job. A new life. The life she wanted.

"You have lots of friends and connections. I'd need to

get a job that would pay me more than this salary. And the job would have to lead to promotions."

"You don't like your job here?"

"I didn't say that."

"I could raise your salary."

"Mitch, if you want me to do this, *today* has to be my last day with Ochoa Online."

He didn't even blink. "Okay."

CHAPTER TWO

LILA WALKED OUT of the office building that housed Ochoa Online and toward Mitch's black limo, which awaited her on the busy New York City street.

Opening the back door, his driver, Pete, said, "Good morning, Lila."

"Morning, Pete. We'll be stopping two blocks up on the right to pick up my friend Sally."

"Very good."

She slid onto the seat. He closed the door, and she made herself comfortable as he took his position behind the wheel and eased into traffic. Two blocks up, he stopped, jumped out and opened the door for Sally.

When Pete pulled out into traffic again, pretty blonde Sally turned to Lila and said, "All right. Spill. What did you agree to?"

She sucked in a breath. "Two weeks of pretending to be my boss's fiancée. In return, he's going to find me a new job and I'm going to use the extra money I earn to find my mom."

The expression on Sally's face showed that she was trying to understand, but in the end she shook her head. "You are certifiable. Your motives are good, but pretending to be the fiancée of a man you actually like? That's nothing but trouble."

"That's why I couldn't just have him hire a PI to find my mom. Because then I'd still be working for him. I had to ask for a new job so that no matter what happens in Spain it wouldn't follow me home. Once I leave Spain, I'll never see him again. Plus, he assured me that most of the time I'd be on my own while he and his brother, father, uncle and cousin talked business."

"On your own?"

"After I agreed to do this, he told me that I'd spend most of the two weeks with his nanna shopping or running errands, or helping his mom organize the house for a ball a few days after we get there that opens two weeks of celebrations, a second ball the following week to greet latecomers, a reception the night before his brother's wedding and a party the day after."

"You are going to have to be one hell of an actress."

"Or I can just look at it as an extension of my job. I plan Mitch's yearly Christmas party. I plan the business dinners he hosts at his penthouse." She shrugged. "I'm just going to look at it like another Ochoa party."

Sally sighed. "And the other?"

"What other?"

"When you have to be his date?"

"I'll be fine."

"You'll be pee-your-pants nervous."

Lila laughed. "Maybe at first. But I've also decided to look at *that* as an extension of my job."

"Kissing your boss?"

"I'll pigeonhole it somehow."

"You're crazy."

"No. I'm getting a new job out of it. A new *life*." She

angled her thumb to point behind them. "Me walking out of that office building a few minutes ago was me walking out forever. I told him the two weeks we spend in Spain are my two-week notice and when we get back I will expect him to have gotten me a new job, one that pays more than what I make with him."

"Wow. You're really leaving."

"I have to. He was surprised when I said I wanted a new job, but when I pushed he didn't seem at all upset to see me go." And that had hurt more than she cared to think about. But it also proved he absolutely had no feelings for her. "He might as well have come right out and said that he desperately needed this favor, or that he just doesn't give a damn that I want another job. Either way, it sort of proves doing this was the right thing. If he needs a fiancée this badly, I have to help him. And if he doesn't care that I want a new job, then it really is time for me to go. It's win/win."

"Are you sure you're not going to be sorry?"

"I've had a crush on this man since the day I met him. He's never noticed me. Only an idiot hangs around forever."

"True."

"And this way I don't merely have a new job that pays enough that I can find my mom." She waved two credit cards. "I get a new wardrobe out of it."

Sally grabbed the cards. "Seriously?"

"Yep. That's why I need your help this morning. I have a hundred-thousand-dollar credit limit on each. Riccardo said use it all. Get everything, including fancy luggage. He said the wedding is formal and I'll also need a gown for the reception the night before. Not to mention the opening ball and a few cocktail parties. He said I'll need enough jeans and shorts and dresses and bathing suits never to be seen in the same thing twice."

Sally gaped at her. "You have hit the jackpot."

"Nope. Believe it or not, Riccardo and Mitch see this as absolutely necessary. I have to look like somebody Mitch would want to marry. To them it's like wardrobe for a play. So, all I have to do is endure two weeks of pretending to be in love with the man I actually do love, and I'll walk away with my freedom, a new job that hopefully pays enough that I can find my mom and enough clothes to be a whole new person."

She also had to not take any of it seriously, keep her wits about her and not end up with a broken heart.

But she didn't tell Sally that. She'd had enough trouble convincing herself she could do it. Sally would never let her go if she thought there was even an inkling of a doubt—and she desperately wanted to find her mom. She wanted the life they'd missed out on.

Oddly, pretending to be in love with the man she actually loved was her ticket away from him and to that life.

Mitch paced the tarmac at ten o'clock the next morning, nervous about this plan. Yesterday, it had seemed like a good idea. Today, thinking about Lila's unruly hair, glasses and frumpy clothes, he found it hard to believe he actually thought they could pull this off. He liked her as an assistant— No. He *loved* her as an assistant. She was smart and thorough and always at his side, ready to do whatever needed to be done. But in the entire time they'd worked together they'd never even had a good enough conversation to tip over into becoming friends.

How in the hell could he have been so desperate to imagine they could pretend to be lovers for two weeks?

His limo suddenly appeared around the corner of the hangar. He'd bought a cab to the airport, leaving Pete and the limo for Lila to make sure she got to the correct place. Seeing them pull up, though, only added to his apprehension. How was he going to pretend to love somebody he barely knew?

The limo stopped. Pete jumped out and opened the back door. One pale pink strappy sandal appeared, then a long length of leg, then the pink hem of a skirt, then Lila stepped out completely. Chestnut-brown hair had been thinned into a sleek, shoulder-length hairdo and now had blond highlights. Her lips were painted a shimmery pink. The little pink dress hugged her curves.

Holy hell.

Big black sunglasses covering half her face, she strolled up to him, a smile curving a lush mouth that he'd never noticed before.

"Do I pass?"

He fought the urge to stutter. "You look—" Unbelievable. Amazing. So different that his tongue stuck to the roof of his mouth. "Very good. Perfect."

"I took you for the sunglasses and miniskirt type."

And who knew her legs were so long, so shapely?

He covered his shock at her perception of his taste in women with a nervous laugh. "You maxed out Riccardo's credit cards, didn't you?"

She glanced back at Pete, who pulled suitcase after suitcase out of the car. "He told me to, but I didn't. You don't grow up a foster child without getting some mad skills with money. It would have killed me to pay full price for some of these things. Besides, clearance racks sometimes have the best clothes."

She made a little motion with her fingers for Pete to

bring her luggage to the plane, then she headed for the steps. Mitch watched her walk up the short stack and duck into the fuselage, vaguely aware when Pete walked up beside him.

"Who knew, huh?"

"Yeah." Mitch didn't have to ask what Pete was talking about. His Plain Jane assistant looked like she'd stepped off the cover of a magazine. Her high-heeled sandals added a sway to her hips. Sunglasses made her look like someone who summered in the Mediterranean.

Pete said, "Better get going."

Realizing he was standing there gaping like an idiot, he walked to the steps and climbed into the plane. Lila sat on one of the four plush, white leather seats that swiveled and looked like recliners. He stopped.

She peered up at him over her sunglasses. "The pilot told me to sit anywhere and buckle in."

"Pedro?" *The good-looking one?* Why did that make his chest feel like a rock?

She shrugged and pulled an e-reader out of her over-size purse. "I don't know. The guy with the great smile."

It was Pedro. He might not be a millionaire business-man who came from a family with a vineyard, but pilots made a tidy sum, especially private pilots. And the man was a flirt.

He told himself he only cared because Lila was supposed to be his fiancée, and she couldn't use this trip to cruise for dates. "When we get to Spain, you can't be noticing the great smiles of other men."

She laughed. "Jealous?"

"No." The rock from his chest fell to his stomach. He wasn't jealous. This was a make-believe situation. Great hair, sexy body, flirty sunglasses or not, this was still

Lila. "I'm saving myself a ton of grief with this ruse. Not to mention that I'm getting the focus off me and onto the happy couple where it belongs. I do not want to spoil my brother's wedding."

He sat on the seat across the aisle and buckled in. Pulling a sheet of paper from the breast pocket of his suit jacket, he swiveled his chair to face her and said, "Riccardo came up with this last night."

She glanced around as if confused. "Where is Riccardo?"

"He took a commercial flight so he could get there ahead of us to pave the way for our story. He's going to tell everyone I'm engaged. He's going to pretend to have let it slip and tell my mom and Nanna they have to behave as if they don't know because I wanted to surprise them."

She frowned. "That's weird."

"No. It adds authenticity to the story. Makes it more believable."

"Ah."

That one syllable gave him a funny feeling that tightened his shoulders and made his eyes narrow. "What's that supposed to mean?"

She laughed. "It just meant I understood." She laughed again. "You're cranky in real life."

"Yeah, well, you're..." She was a knockout in real life. How had he not noticed this? He couldn't remember a damned thing she'd worn to work, which meant it had to be nondescript—nothing worth remembering. Her hair had always been in those odd chopstick things. And her glasses? Thick as Coke bottles.

"You're different too." He finished his thought with a bunch of lame words that didn't come out as much of a comeback.

And that was another thing. When had she gotten so sassy?

He opened the folded sheet of paper. "Riccardo decided that we should stick with the fact that you're my assistant." He glanced up and saw her watching him intently, clearly wanting to get her part down so she could play it. He relaxed a bit, though it did send an unexpected zing through him that she'd taken off the sunglasses. She must be wearing contacts on her smoke-gray eyes. Very sexy smoke-gray eyes that tilted up at the corners and gave her an exotic look.

He cleared his throat. "Anyway, the whole thing started with a long chat one night when we were working late."

She caught his gaze. "We never chatted."

"Yeah, I know." And he suddenly felt sorry that they hadn't. "But this is make-believe, remember?"

She smiled slightly and nodded.

He sucked in a breath, not liking the nervousness that had invaded him. If he couldn't even read the facts off a sheet, how was he going to perpetuate this charade?

"After our long talk, we started eating dinners together on the nights we were working late."

"Hey, we did do that!"

"But we talked about work."

She bobbed her head. "Yeah, but because we actually did eat dinners together we have another bit of authenticity."

Her answer softened some of the stiffness in his shoulders. "Sí. Good." He pulled in a breath and read a little more of Riccardo's story. "Then we started going out to dinner."

She leaned her elbow on the armrest. "We certainly took our time."

He looked up, met the gaze of her soft gray kitten eyes. "I think Riccardo is trying to show we didn't act impulsively."

"God forbid."

He wasn't sure why, but that made him laugh. "Stop. Riccardo's already telling this story and we have to stick to it."

"What if we came up with a totally different set of circumstances? What if we said that one day you ravaged me at work, and we started a passionate affair but we changed the story for Riccardo because we didn't want him to know we couldn't keep our hands off each other?"

All the blood in his veins caught fire. He could picture it. If she'd come to work looking like this he might have ravaged her.

He pulled his collar away from his throat. The plane's engines whined to life.

"Let's just stick with Riccardo's story."

Lila nodded quickly, wishing she hadn't said anything about the passionate affair because with the way he'd been looking at her since she arrived, she could imagine it. If he'd ever, even once, looked at her like that, she might not have been able to resist the temptation to flirt with him—

She'd been flirting with him since he got on the plane. And that was wrong. Wrong. Wrong. Wrong. She didn't want to like him any more than she already did. Worse, she didn't want to become another one of his one-night stands. And that was the real danger in this. That they'd take this charade to the next level, with him thinking it was just a part of the game, and her heart toppling over the edge into something that would only hurt her.

So, no more flirting. She was smarter than this.

She drew in a cleansing breath, gave him what she hoped was a neutral smile and motioned for him to continue. "Go on."

"Riccardo says our dating life was fairly normal. Shows, dinners, weekends in Vegas and the Hamptons."

She nodded, liking the dispassionate direction the conversation had taken. "Your family's house in the Hamptons is pretty." When he gave her a puzzled look, she added, "Riccardo showed me pictures."

"He goes there more than I do. But it's good you know what the place looks like. That'll probably come in handy."

He sounded so nervous that she smiled again. "You don't like this charade."

"I don't like lying to my family. But this is necessary. It isn't just the fact that I don't want to be hounded by Nanna. This is Alonzo and Julia's big celebration. The focus shouldn't be on me. Not in any way, shape or form."

"You don't think your engagement will be reason for them to make you the center of attention?"

"We'll let them fawn one night. Tonight. Then after that when they get too happy or too focused on us, we remind them that it's Julia and Alonzo's celebration. Not ours."

"Makes sense." She cocked her head. "You really are over her."

He sighed. "I've said it a million times. No one seems to believe me."

"Maybe because everybody knows getting over your brother's betrayal would be harder."

He sniffed a laugh. "When'd you get so perceptive?"

"I've always been perceptive. That's how I stay one step ahead of what you need."

He nodded, as if just figuring that out, and sadness started in her stomach and expanded into her chest. He might think her pretty in the pink dress, showing off her legs and even being a little sassy with him, but in the end she was still the assistant he barely noticed.

But that was good. If she was going to start a new life when they returned, she didn't want to do it with a broken heart. A woman who needed to find her mom and fix their damaged past couldn't afford to make stupid mistakes. Though she'd always believed she was destined for something great, she also realized that that fairy tale had just been a vehicle to keep her sane, keep her working toward things like her high school diploma and eventually a degree. Lately the desire for "something great" was taking a back seat to the things she really wanted: her mom. A family. That's why her crush on Mitch had seemed so pointless that she'd decided it was time to move on.

Mitch's groan of disgust brought her out of her reverie. "That's the stupidest engagement story I've ever heard."

Oh, crap. He'd been reading Riccardo's notes and she'd missed something important. "Read it again. Let me think it through."

He gaped at her. "How would you possibly need to hear it again? It's ridiculous. I wouldn't rent a hot air balloon. I wouldn't hire a skywriter to spell out the proposal at sunset so I could get down on one knee in a balloon."

She laughed. Wow. That was bad. "Okay. So it's a bit schmaltzy."

"It's pedestrian."

"What would you have done in real life?"

He sighed. "What I'd planned for Julia was to come home early, pour two flutes of champagne, walk around the apartment until I found her, tell her she was beautiful and I wanted her in my life forever…then give her the ring."

"Oh." Her breath wobbled. His proposal idea was perfect. Elegant in its simplicity. "That would have been nice."

"Yeah, if I hadn't caught her with my brother."

She laughed, then stopped herself. How was it that he could make her laugh over something that had probably broken his heart—even though he seemed to be over it?

"Well, it was a great proposal idea."

"I thought so too. But apparently my brother did some grand gesture on the yacht."

"Oh, I get what Riccardo's doing. He's making sure our proposal keeps up with Alonzo and Julia's. But maybe he's making things suspicious by thinking you need to compete with Alonzo."

"I'm not like my brother."

"Plus, simple is better sometimes."

He met her gaze. "Exactly. He should have said something more me. Like I gave you the ring, then stripped you naked and we spent the weekend in bed."

This time her breath froze. If Riccardo had come up with that scenario for their engagement story, she wouldn't be able to breathe anytime anyone told it. Better to stick with the fake one.

"So maybe the hot air balloon idea is a good one."

"It's not me."

"We'll try not to tell it too often. We'll use the 'this is Julia and Alonzo's celebration' excuse."

He nodded. "Good idea."

He focused his attention on the sheet of facts Riccardo had written up, but stopped reading out loud. Her gaze swept the five o'clock shadow growing on his chin and cheeks, then rose to his nearly black eyes and up to his shiny black hair. Her fingers itched to run through the thick locks, and it suddenly struck her that maybe sometime in the next two weeks she could.

Just as her heart stumbled in her chest, his gaze rose and he smiled at her. "Riccardo also says this flight would be a good time for us to exchange stories."

"Exchange stories?"

"He thinks I should tell you about things like the time I jumped off the roof of one of the winery's outbuildings, thinking I could fly."

She didn't know whether to laugh or gape at him. "Why would you think you could fly?"

"I was eight and I had a cape."

A laugh burst from her. "That's hysterical."

"Didn't you ever do anything stupid?"

Her earliest memories were of her mom sleeping on the couch. She'd sit on the floor in front of the sofa and watch her mother's chest rise and fall, being scared silly because technically she was alone. Four years old and all alone. She was six or seven before she realized her mom kept sleeping because she drank too much alcohol. And it wasn't until she was ten that she understood what a hangover was.

The only stupid thing she'd done was mention that to a social worker.

CHAPTER THREE

"I LED A very quiet life."

Even as that statement came out of Lila's mouth, Mitch remembered her answer when he'd asked if she'd maxed out the company credit cards Riccardo had given her. "Weren't you a foster child?"

She brushed at her dress, as if trying to smooth out nonexistent wrinkles. "Yes. But that doesn't mean my life was exciting."

He knew little about the American foster care system, but he did understand the basics. A child was taken in by a family who was paid by the state to care for him or her. He supposed that left little room for being silly or stupid or even experimental, if you wanted to keep your home. Because if you didn't keep your home—

The picture that brought to mind tightened his chest. Not wanting to think of Lila as a child on the street, alone and scared, and not wanting to examine his motives for the emptiness that invaded his soul just considering that she might have been alone or scared, he changed the subject.

"How were your grades?"

She grinned. "I was a star."

He knew that, of course. They'd checked into her when

they'd hired her. She'd been top of her class everywhere from elementary school to university.

"Anything I should know about your love life?"

She glanced across the aisle at him, caught his gaze. "No."

"At least tell me the story of your first date."

She smoothed her hair off her forehead. "Oh. Well, I guess that depends on what you consider a date. I had a huge crush on my next-door neighbor when I was five."

He laughed. "Not that far back."

"Okay. I went to the prom in high school."

"Seriously? That was your first date?"

She shrugged. "I was busy getting those good grades, remember?"

He sighed. "All right. If we really were engaged, I probably wouldn't know every corner of your love life. But give me something I can take to Nanna that will convince her we're…" He paused, grappling for words, because now that he was getting to know her everything felt funny. He'd already pictured himself ravaging her. Her fault. She'd brought it up. But, because he'd already seen it in his head, he couldn't quite say *lovers* out loud.

Finally he just sucked it up and said, "To help her believe we're intimate."

"Oh, my gosh. Seriously? Did you just say that? You couldn't say lovers…or that we're having sex or even knocking boots?" She laughed heartily. "Mitch, you have got to lighten up. You'll do more to convince your grandmother we're engaged with your actions than you will remembering a bunch of useless information about my life."

Irritated with himself for all these weird reactions, he said, "Yeah, I guess."

She caught his gaze again. But this time the light of humor brightened her pretty eyes. "I *know*."

The awkwardness of being so informal with her pressed in on him again, and he had to get rid of it. Since she seemed to like humor so much, he went in that direction and said, "I suppose this means you're not going to tell me the story of how you lost your virginity."

She laughed. "No. And I don't want to hear about yours."

"Mine's a great story," he teased, so relieved that the tension had been broken that he decided to keep her laughing.

"I'll bet."

"I was about fifteen. A middle-aged woman came to the winery for a tour—"

"Oh, my God!" She put her hands over her ears. "Stop."

"All right. I suppose that one isn't exactly G-rated. Want to hear about Riccardo's?"

Her eyes widened comically.

But he realized something important. "If we really were engaged, you might not know about our sex lives, but you would know about Riccardo's and my antics as kids. So what do you say I tell you some of those stories?"

She slowly pulled her hands away from her ears. "Okay. If I were your fiancée for real, I would know those."

"Exactly."

He told her about skipping school, climbing trees, swimming in the lake behind his family's property before the family put in the in-ground pool. He told her about Nanna covering for him and Riccardo a time or two, then using her knowledge for blackmail.

"Your nanna's a pistol."

"You don't know the half of it."

"Thus the reason for the fake fiancée."

"Sí." He paused a second, then said, "So what about you?"

She smiled at him from across the aisle. "What about me?"

"What do I need to know about you to fool my grand-mother?"

"Nothing."

"Oh, come on, I have to tell her something."

"Nope. I'm a nonentity in this charade. I don't matter. Just as Riccardo made up stories about our getting together and your proposal, I can be anything you need me to be because two weeks from now I'm out of the picture."

"But doesn't it make more sense to use your real life?" He peeked at her. "You know...for authenticity."

"Then we'd trip over into too many details that wouldn't fit. Since we didn't actually start dating." Her eyes met his. "We never even became friends. It's easier for us to make up a background that's more suited to a woman you'd date."

Though what she'd said made sense, irritation slid through him. Why was she arguing? Evading him?

"That's just the point. For better or worse you *are* the woman I chose. So I think it would make more sense if we figured out *why* I chose you—sticking with the truth—rather than to make up a story that we'd have to remember. Riccardo's story is that we started talking and became friends." He smiled his most charming smile. "So let's become friends."

She just looked at him. Her pretty gray eyes softened

with a sort of sadness. He expected her to argue again, but she said, "I live in a walk-up in Brooklyn. I put myself through university as a barista in a coffee place. I sort of live to work." She opened her hands. "Honestly, no hobbies. Nothing really interesting about me."

"You have to have more to your life than that."

She shook her head. "Unless you want to dip into the foster child stuff—which I don't—I am as dull as watching paint dry."

He would have accepted that, except she avoided his eyes and looked away quickly, the way a person does when they are lying or hiding something.

She did live in a walk-up in Brooklyn.

She had put herself through university as a barista.

She'd told him both of those in her employment interview. So if she wasn't lying she was hiding something.

He knew it for certain when she firmly said, "Okay. Once we get over the initial introductions, I'll just keep deflecting questions by reminding everybody this is Alonzo and Julia's weekend. There's no reason to get fancy about this."

He nodded, but his gut knotted. Why would she want to keep something from him? *What* would she want to keep from him? It couldn't be a criminal record—her record had been clean when he hired her. Which meant she didn't sell drugs. Or rob banks. Or even have a permit to carry a gun. But maybe she dated losers? Or collected spiders? Or was one of those people who dressed up like a zombie and went to those weird parties—

Maybe he didn't want to know?

After all, as she'd said, this charade would be over in two weeks. And if he forced the issue, he'd know an ugly detail of her life that he probably shouldn't know.

When five minutes went by with neither of them saying anything, she pulled out her e-reader.

Trepidation filled him again. She was about to walk into the heart of his family. They would ask her a million questions. Yes, he understood that she could make up answers about their dating and her life, since this whole deal was fake, but—

No buts. She was right. They'd spent a year working together, not getting to know each other. If she had a private life she wanted to keep private, he should just accept that and trust that she could handle this ruse.

He relaxed a bit, settled back in his seat, used the remote to activate the television and nodded off thinking that his assistant had handled every job he'd ever given her. He should trust that whatever she wasn't telling him it wasn't relevant to her job—

Except she wanted to leave his employ and she'd never fully explained why.

Damn it! What the hell was up with her?

The jet landed in Spain a little after one o'clock in the morning, Spain time. The pilot's announcement woke Lila and she yawned and stretched.

"So much for meeting your family tonight."

Mitch blew his breath out on a groan that spoke of someone desperately wanting to continue sleeping. "I don't know how I got so scattered that I forgot about the time difference, but we'll get to the winery by two. I can show you to your room and you can either go back to sleep or take a shower or something to wake yourself up enough you can adjust to the new time zone."

She waved her e-reader at him. "Don't worry about me. I can always entertain myself."

He smiled tiredly. "Great."

His unenthusiastic tone sent a little jangle skipping along Lila's nerve endings. Now that they were on the ground in Spain, near his family, he didn't seem as convinced about this plan as he had in New York City. And part of that might be her fault. He hadn't been pleased that she refused to talk about her past. But, really, they'd spent a year together and he'd never once asked her what she'd done over the weekend, let alone chitchatted about her past. So maybe a little part of her had decided to hold back. But she was still right about the ruse. It would be too difficult to explain how a high-powered executive, a charmer with a killer smile and tons of money, would want *her*. He hadn't wanted *her* in a whole year. They were better off to make up an interesting past for her that turned her into a woman who would attract him and keep his interest enough that he'd want to marry her.

They exited the plane and Lila stood by Mitch as they waited for the copilot and limo driver to unload their luggage and pile it into the trunk of a big black car.

Finally finished, the driver opened the back door of the vehicle and greeted Mitch. *"Buenas noches."*

Mitch laughed. "Shouldn't that be *buenos días*?"

The driver chuckled. *"Sí."*

Good day rather than good night.

Lila had to agree with that because it was after midnight, already an hour into the new day, except her body was on New York time. Though she'd had a nap on the plane, a few hours from now when his family was waking, she'd want to go to sleep for real.

Once they were settled on the long, comfortable back seat, Mitch said, "Don't worry. My family and the entire staff speak English."

She shrugged. "I toyed around with being a social worker, so I took enough Spanish in college that I'm fluent."

He frowned. "You thought about being a social worker?"

"Everybody does." She met his gaze, throwing him a bone with a little personal information since she'd clearly insulted him before when she wouldn't tell him anything beyond the basics. "Everybody wants to save the world."

Shaking his head, he said, "Not my family." He motioned toward the window even though she could see nothing in the dead of night through the darkened glass. "We have a legacy to protect."

"I think that's kinda nice. You know—" She lifted one shoulder slightly, trying to be nonchalant, even though she envied him and his casual acceptance of not just having a mom and dad, a brother, a nanna, an aunt and uncle and a cousin, but also a legacy. "A place to belong."

"Oh, we belong all right. Sometimes I feel like an indentured servant."

She studied him, confused that he couldn't see how lucky he was. "Is that why you came to New York?"

"My father released me to more or less follow my dream of setting up a website to sell Ochoa wines online after I caught Alonzo and Julia together. There was no way Dad could have picked sides. Picked one son over the other. Especially since what I'd walked in on was basically Alonzo and Julia's first kiss. I'd more or less been ignoring her, traveling around Europe, trying to sell wine. So I didn't have to do a lot of soul-searching to realize I didn't really love her, and from the way Alonzo protected Julia the next few days, it was clear he did. Allowing me to create and head up Ochoa Online and move it anywhere I wanted, my dad put a positive spin on what could have potentially caused a huge rift in our family."

"And then you came to New York and you were successful and now it all seems to have had a purpose."

He tilted his head. "That's basically how it's panned out. Except I took it one step further, started the general wine site and headed off in my own direction. Forged my own success. I don't want this wedding to take the luster off the fact that I stepped away and started my own businesses, any more than I want to have people thinking of me instead of my brother during what should be the happiest time of Alonzo's life."

She nodded, totally understanding. But she didn't want to know too much more or to tell him too much more about herself. That would be a heck of a lot like confiding, a heck of a lot like actually becoming friends, and that was risky to her heart. Not to mention the fact that he might not think highly of a little girl who'd gotten herself sent into foster care and cost her mom a chance to pull herself together and become a good parent.

Worse, while he had told her the stories about himself and Riccardo, she'd pictured him as a devilish little boy and her heartstrings had tugged. So no more confiding. She had to stay strong.

"Oh, I almost forgot." He reached into his jacket pocket and pulled out a small black velvet ring box.

Her gaze leaped to his.

He smiled as he opened it. "Will you marry me?"

He said it casually, but her breath froze in wonderment. She remembered her first day of working with him, how he'd knocked her for a loop with his good looks and charm, remembered how much she loved that he was strong and smart. She thought of all the things that she imagined she would think about if he were asking her to marry him for real. Her heart lodged in her throat and her chest got so tight she could barely breathe, but she reminded herself this wasn't real. And that falling into this kind of emotional land mine was the very thing she had to avoid.

So she laughed and said, "Sure," as if her feelings weren't going in a million directions, and she was able to see the humor in their charade.

He slid the rock on her third finger, left hand, and instantly her hand sank along with her heart. Not only was it the biggest diamond she'd ever seen, but it was the most beautiful ring ever crafted, and it was all a sham.

Determined not to fall into any more emotional traps, she glanced up at him with a smile. "Wow. I hope you didn't pay for this by the ounce."

He laughed. "It's on consignment."

The reminder that for him this was temporary, just a means to an end, a way to accomplish a goal for his family and himself, fortified her. Especially since she was being rewarded for her part. If she wanted a new job, money to hire a PI to find her mom and ultimately a new life, there could be no more slipups. She had to make this look real. And she could do it. It wasn't like she hadn't faked her way through things before. As a child she'd had to pretend to like potatoes or peas or ham so her new foster mom wouldn't think her too picky, and plenty of times she'd had to pretend to love certain television shows just to fit in. When she left that life, she'd vowed she'd be herself for the rest of her days and never pretend again, but this was for a good cause. Two good causes. Mitch could keep the focus of this wedding on his brother and she would find her mom.

Faking to make it work made perfect sense.

They traveled through a country she couldn't see for forty minutes, then the limo stopped. When the driver opened the door, she saw the magnificent stone mansion in front of her. Two stories and clearly built centuries ago, the house stood like a sentinel, taking care of its occupants, marking the passage of time with lines and wrinkles pressed into the stone by wind and rain.

As she stepped out of the limo, she said, "It's fantastic."

The air felt different. Or maybe the knowledge that she was on a different continent had her sensing that the warm air around them was sweeter, earthier.

"The upstairs contains Nanna and my parents' residences. Winery is in the basement beside a restaurant. First floor holds business offices, tour information and gift shop."

Well, there went all the romance out of that.

"Oh."

"Don't pout." He put his hands on her shoulders and turned her to the right. "We have an apartment in the second building down."

His voice had dipped low, as if he really was talking to a girlfriend. The place where his hands rested on her shoulders felt like it was on fire. A shower of tingles rained down her spine.

More nervous than she'd ever imagined she could be, she turned, hoping to get out from under his warm fingers. "And the first building is?"

"Alonzo and Julia's home. He runs the winery. It's

only fitting he has a house." He smiled casually. "I'm just a guest now."

Had she heard a little sadness in that? A dollop of emotion?

She studied his dark, dark eyes. There was no hurt in the black orbs. No rancor. He did not begrudge his brother his success. But there also didn't seem to be an attachment to this wonderful home—this *legacy*—that she would give half her heart and most of her soul to be a part of.

She broke the connection and turned toward the two newer buildings. Her nerves eased a bit. The last thing she wanted was to find herself in the same house with his relatives. This way she had private space.

Mitch put his hand on the small of her back and guided her to the second building. In the muted glow of small lamps to light the path, she could see lush green grass that created comfortable lawns, but little else.

Vaguely aware that the driver pulled their things from the back of the limo, she allowed Mitch to lead her up the cobblestone path to a front door and into a quiet foyer with a set of stairs to the second floor. He nodded for her to climb them.

As they walked up the thin stairway, she realized his eyes were about level with her butt. That might have made her nervous, except she remembered the casual way he'd given her the ring and knew she had nothing to worry about. When they reached the second floor, he pulled keys out of his pocket, unlocked the door and gave it a nudge to open it. He granted her entry first, then flipped on a light.

"Surprise!"

The room was full of dark-haired, dark-eyed people

she assumed were his relatives. Pressing her hand to her chest to stop her galloping heart, she turned to Mitch.

He quickly caught her hand. "Mom, Dad!" he said, glancing around. "Everybody's here."

The woman around fifty, with streaks of white in her shiny black hair, raced over. When she grabbed Mitch's shoulders, went up on tiptoe and hugged him, Lila guessed she was his mother.

"Why didn't you tell us you were engaged?"

He looked around as if totally perplexed, but Lila caught his ploy. Apparently, Riccardo had done his part and "slipped" the engagement to his family and they'd planned this gathering. Mitch was reacting the way he would if he really were engaged. "I wanted to tell you in person."

Riccardo stepped forward. "Sorry, cuz. I accidentally let the cat out of the bag."

Everyone laughed, and Lila watched them in amazement. Riccardo had been correct. Pretending to let it slip that Mitch was engaged had actually made it all seem real. But, oh my goodness, he had so much family. And all of them close enough to welcome him home.

Mitch dropped her hand but slid his arm around her shoulders and nestled her against his side. "Everyone, this is my fiancée, Lila."

Mitch's mom hugged her fiercely, then burst into tears. "Both of my boys are gone now."

Mitch chuckled. "Not gone, Mom. Just getting married."

Everyone laughed. Someone in the back said, "They should make it a double wedding."

Lila held back a gasp of horror, but Mitch said, "Not

on your life. We want our own celebration and think Alonzo and Julia are entitled to theirs."

A man who looked like Mitch held his glass high. "Hear! Hear!"

Mitch turned to her and said, "Lila, that is my brother, Alonzo."

She smiled. "Nice to meet you."

Mitch quickly ran through the introductions, starting with the closest person, his mom, Marguerite, then on to his dad, his aunt and uncle, Julia and Alonzo, and finally a small gray-haired woman in the back.

"Nanna."

She eased through the small jumble of people. "So, you stole my grandson's heart."

She glanced up at Mitch. Something inside her wouldn't let her lie, so she laughed and said, "He certainly stole mine."

Mitch's dad, Santiago, the tall, dark-haired man with white hair at his temples, pulled a bottle of wine from a small wooden washtub filled with ice and many other bottles of wine. "Get me two glasses so we can toast."

Riccardo immediately produced two beautiful, intricately patterned wineglasses. Santiago took them and began to fill them.

"Oh, no need to fill a second glass," Lila quickly said, before he poured. "I'll just have some orange juice for the toast. I don't drink."

A weird hush fell over the room. Foreheads wrinkled in confusion. All eyes jumped to her.

Nanna said, "You don't drink?"

"No. But I'd love to toast with a glass of orange juice or even water."

"You're dating a man whose family owns a winery... but you don't drink?"

"Forget about that," Santiago said with a laugh. "You *work* for a winery. You did meet because you're his assistant, correct? That means you work for a winery."

Marguerite said, "How can you take a job with a winery when you don't drink?"

Because she took one look at Marguerite's son and couldn't say no?

"I'm not opposed to other people drinking."

Mitch stole a peek at Lila, his head spinning. How could he have missed that she didn't drink?

Elegant Marguerite recovered first. "Riccardo, a glass of orange juice, please."

Obviously his family had stocked his apartment in anticipation of his arrival because Riccardo went to the kitchen and returned with a pitcher of orange juice. He poured a glass and handed it to Mitch's dad, who also held a glass of wine for Mitch.

Santiago gave the drinks to Mitch and Lila. She took hers with a smile and he inwardly sighed with relief.

"To my son and his fiancée." Santiago's eyes crinkled at the corners when he grinned. "I expect a wedding this time next year." Everyone laughed. "Our family is truly blessed. *Salud.*"

"*Salud!*"

Everyone took a sip of their wine. Lila downed her entire glass of orange juice as if she was either dying of thirst or so nervous she couldn't stop herself.

"Thank you, everyone, for the toast and for meeting us." He glanced at Lila again. She didn't appear to be falling apart, but after her gulping down the juice he didn't want to risk it. He didn't want her saying something from which they couldn't recover. He wasn't entirely sure they'd recovered from the fact that she didn't drink. "But we're exhausted. Can we finish this celebration in the morning?"

Nanna said, "Of course! We will make the best breakfast ever cooked."

Mitch shook his head. "No! This is Alonzo and Julia's celebration. Not ours. We'll be back in the fall and you can celebrate properly if you wish."

His mom nodded. "Yes. You are correct. This is Alonzo and Julia's time. Now that we have toasted your engagement, we can go back to celebrating the wedding."

The family began to file out. Each stopped and took the chance to shake his hand and hug Lila, who hung in there like a trooper.

Finally Nanna stepped up. She hugged Lila, saying, "Welcome to the family." Then hugged Mitch. He could feel the tension of the first meeting ebbing away as she pulled out of the embrace.

Then she looked him in the eye and said, "While Lila gets settled, why don't you and I take a minute to catch up, *Nene*?"

His heart sank. To the casual observer, her request was the simple longing of a grandmother to spend time with her grandson. But she'd called him baby boy, the term she'd always used right before she scolded him.

"Of course."

She turned and started to the door, but stopped suddenly and faced him, motioning with her fingers for him to follow her. She wanted him to leave with her. There'd be no reprieve. No couple of minutes to pull himself together. He had to go now.

He glanced at Lila. "I won't be long."

Her smoky gray eyes clouded with fear. "I'll be fine."

The look in her silvery orbs didn't match her words. She sounded relieved. She looked totally shell-shocked.

"Oh, come on already," Nanna said with a sigh. "I'm an old woman, getting older, and I need my sleep. Kiss her goodbye so we can get going."

His heart chugged to a stop and he understood how Lila could sound relieved and look terrified. Nothing had gone as they'd planned. Once they'd landed and he remembered the time difference, he'd believed they'd sneak in under the cover of darkness, get a little sleep, then go to an ordinary breakfast in a few hours, be bombarded by well-wishers and sit down and eat eggs. Instead, they walked into a group of his family lying in wait. And now he had to kiss her.

Obviously, she didn't want him to.

His male pride took a direct hit. It wasn't like he was Frankenstein. Hell, most women considered him good-looking. Yet, this woman he'd seen almost every day for a year seemed appalled at the thought of kissing him.

Putting his hands on her shoulders, he brushed his lips across hers quickly, not even pausing when a little zap of something set his hormones humming and sent an unexpected urge to linger through him. She was Lila, for heaven's sake.

He pulled away, a bit surprised by the stunned expression on her face. It matched the weird jumpy feeling he had in his stomach. His hands slid from her shoulders, down her arms to her hands, and for a few seconds he didn't want to let go. He liked the feeling of her small, soft hands in his. He wanted to investigate the weird buzz of confusion.

But Nanna cleared her throat.

He followed her out of the apartment, closing the door behind him, still feeling a little shaky from the odd reaction to a kiss that was nothing more than a touch. When Nanna didn't talk on the way to the main house, through the high-ceilinged foyer, up the stairs and into the living room of her quarters, he was glad. He wasn't sure he could have spoken without his confusion coming through.

Nanna perched on a Queen Anne chair as if it was a throne and, out of habit, he walked behind the shiny mahogany bar and poured her a small glass of red.

After handing it to her, he sat down. Trepidation raced through him. In all the confusion of that kiss, he'd forgotten Nanna wanted to interrogate him.

Damn it! He shouldn't have let Lila get away with evading his questions about her past because now he had virtually nothing to tell Nanna.

"So, your fiancée, she is pregnant?"

Mitch's heart slammed to a halt, as his eyes bulged. "What? No!"

"The baby's not yours, then?"

"What?"

"Why else does she not drink?"

"There are a million reasons a person doesn't drink." And right now he wished to hell he'd asked her. Damn it. How could a woman who doesn't drink work for a winery—

He paused his thoughts. That was actually a very telling thing. If she could work for a winery that might mean her reasons for abstaining weren't serious ones. Like, maybe, she didn't like the taste of alcohol? Or maybe she didn't want the extra calories—

"She's so casual about not drinking that I never asked

her. At first, I was only her boss. So I figured it was none of my business." He shrugged. "Now? I just assume it has to do with watching her calories. She's crazy about keeping her figure."

There. His ass was totally covered. He'd as much as said he didn't know, yet there were valid reasons for not knowing. He had been lucky this time, but there was no guarantee he'd be lucky the next. When he got back to his apartment they were going to have to have a long talk.

"So she's not pregnant?"

"No."

Nanna set her wineglass down and laid her hands on her lap demurely. "Hmm…"

"No 'hmm,' Nanna. She's not pregnant." And even if she was, they'd be gone in two weeks, the fake engagement over, and no one in this family needed to know. Except—

What if she was pregnant? What if that was why she needed a job that paid her more?

"It's just that she has a certain glow. A happiness that women get when they are pregnant."

"Did you ever stop to think that maybe she's happy to be engaged to me."

Nanna laughed slightly.

"Now what's *that* supposed to mean?"

She rose. "You are too suspicious."

"Oh, yeah? I'm not the one who jumped to the conclusion that my girlfriend was pregnant."

"Fiancée."

He scrubbed his hand across the back of his neck. Another mistake. He should be smarter than this. On his toes. Especially with the woman he needed to fool. "She's been my girlfriend so long that I sometimes lapse."

"Really? Because according to records she's only been your assistant for a year."

"Right."

"Then you started dating right after she went to work for you?"

"Sort of, but—" He thought of Lila's suggestion that he'd ravaged her in his office one night but they hadn't told Riccardo and smiled. "Actually, Nanna, Riccardo doesn't know everything about our relationship. And it might not be appropriate for you to know either."

She laughed. "Oh, *Nene*. You are truly the bad boy of the family. But this woman, Lila. She is sweet. It will hurt me if you hurt her."

"We're engaged, Nanna. I'm not going to hurt her." The lie stuck in his throat like stale peanut butter. Not just because he didn't like lying but because it never once occurred to him that he could hurt Lila. This was a business deal. She knew that. He knew that. Why was he thinking about stupid things?

Nanna squeezed his hand. "Good night."

He said, "Good night," watching her leave the living room and head back the hall to her bedroom. When she was gone, he looked skyward and rolled his eyes. He'd certainly accomplished his purpose of taking everybody's mind off his reaction to Julia and Alonzo getting married, but he should have thought twice about where he'd chosen to put their attention.

He headed for his apartment, knocked twice, lightly, because he was an idiot, involved in a scheme with a woman he didn't know, who he was going to have to learn completely before breakfast the next morning, then he opened the door and walked into the empty living room.

"Crap." He hoped to heaven she wasn't in the shower

and wondered if he should go looking for her. Because
that was another thing he'd forgotten about this charade.
She could be stark naked behind either of the bedroom
doors.

CHAPTER FOUR

TWO MINUTES AFTER Mitch left with his nanna, the driver brought their bags to the apartment, immediately turning left and stacking them in the larger of the two bedrooms.

He made three trips and all three times, Lila had smiled and thanked him. But when he left for the final time, she darted into the room with the luggage, grabbed her bags and set herself up in the second bedroom. Mitch was gone so long she'd taken a quick rinse in the shower, put on her pajama pants and a T-shirt and crawled into bed. Just before she would have fallen asleep out of sheer exhaustion, the apartment door opened and quietly closed.

He was back.

Her breath stalled as she waited in silence, wondering if he would realize she was already in bed and simply head for the room where the driver had left his bags. He'd gone to that bedroom without any instruction from her and she'd decided that had to mean it was the room Mitch typically used. She certainly didn't think he expected her to be in his bed.

So, if she was lucky, he'd figure out she was in the other room and let her sleep.

"Lila!"

She squeezed her eyes shut. Nope. Not lucky.

"Lila! We need to talk."

Oh, she didn't think so. Her plan was to play a role so she could keep enough emotional distance between them that she didn't fall any more in love with him than she already was. So talking was absolutely out. Especially since she had the sneaking feeling his nanna might be a little harder to fool than Mitch believed, and that's why his voice sounded so edgy. Sweet little Nanna had wanted to talk to him in private. Of course she had reservations. And Lila didn't want to discuss any of them.

"I refuse to go to breakfast tomorrow with my family unable to give even simple facts about you. Not to mention the big questions dredged up by your announcement that you don't drink."

This time she winced. It had never even occurred to her that she was a nondrinker working for a winery. For her, work was a way to make a living—and her job had also been about being with him, hoping he would notice her. Ironic that she intended to avoid him as much as she could in their last two weeks together.

A long space of silence ensued. She waited, not breathing, praying he didn't open the door and find her lying in bed with covers up to her chin, hiding her worn pajama pants and New York Giants T-shirt. If he came in now, he'd be talking to the real Lila. Not the fancy girl in the pink dress and tall sandals. That girl could handle him. Real Lila would stutter.

"All right. If you're sleeping, fine."

She pressed her fingers to her lips to stop a laugh. It was just like Mitch to keep talking to someone he thought was sleeping. He never let a thought go unfinished.

Her smile faded. That meant first thing in the morning they'd be having the talk she was avoiding now.

She'd better dress pretty damned dazzling to have enough confidence to keep him at bay the way she had in the airplane.

In spite of her worry, she fell asleep almost immediately. Having set her phone alarm for six o'clock, Spain time, she got up when it sounded and headed for her closet, ready to jump into this problem and solve it. The pink dress had worked to keep him slightly off his game the day before. So she'd have to find something like that. She flicked a few hangers to the left, then realized she shouldn't get too dressed up for a breakfast. She pulled a white lace top out of the closet and matched it with a pair of skinny jeans and flat sandals. Fixing her hair the sleek way she had it the day before, she decided she had the best of both worlds. A sleek, sophisticated hairdo and contact lenses that made her look like a different person, paired with an ordinary outfit that said she was a comfortable, easygoing person, who oozed confidence.

She made a long assessment of herself in the full-length mirror. If she had to say so herself, she'd chosen well. The outfit made her appear casually sexy, as if sexy was her natural state. She looked so unlike herself that she felt like she was seeing a stranger. But that was good. The only way she would manage to keep her distance with Mitch would be to remember this was all playacting, and there was no better way to get yourself into character than with a costume.

Satisfied, she walked out of her bedroom and found Mitch in the sitting area, on the sofa, reading a newspaper, probably a *Wall Street Journal* that he'd brought with him. When she closed the door behind her, the paper rustled as it lowered.

For a few seconds, Mitch said nothing but the expression on his face spoke volumes. His eyebrows rose. His lips twitched, going from a smile to a frown and back up into a smile again.

"Do I pass?"

"Ridiculously. That's one of the reasons I think we need to talk. I can't quite reconcile you with the Lila who works for me."

"You're not supposed to connect me to who I am for real. I'm a *fake* fiancée, remember?" She motioned around herself. "All this is smoke and mirrors. Something *you need* to take the focus off you and put it on your brother and his bride."

He sucked in a breath. "All right. I get that, but last night Nanna—"

The phone rang. Mitch's face became like a thundercloud at the interruption. He grabbed the receiver. "Yes! What!"

There was a pause, then he jumped from the sofa and squeezed his eyes shut. "Sorry, Nanna!"

Wearing cargo shorts and a golf shirt, the kind he usually wore when they worked Saturdays in the summer, he was 100 percent Mitcham Ochoa. Except that his nanna really seemed to be able to push all his buttons.

"Right. I know we eat promptly at seven, but Lila and I—" He stopped. His face twisted with horror. "There was no hanky-panky, Nanna! We just slept in. We are on our way downstairs now."

He hung up the phone and Lila sucked in a breath. "She's a tough one."

"Which is exactly why we need to talk."

"No," Lila said, racing to the door. "We're late. We need to get down to breakfast and keep the conversation on your brother and Julia."

Mitch followed her. As he closed the apartment door, she ran down the steps, knowing that once they got outside he wouldn't ask questions because they'd be within hearing distance of anybody milling about on the grounds. But success right now only provided a short reprieve. After breakfast, she'd have to give him a darned good reason for not drinking. And it couldn't be foolish. It had to work.

It just couldn't be the real one.

She wanted a clean break when they got home. So he couldn't empathize or sympathize with her. She didn't want any emotion at all between them. Not even friendship. When she walked out of his life in two weeks, she didn't want either one of them looking back.

He caught up to her as she started across the empty parking lot to the sidewalk that led to the house. He took her hand and she gave him a brief smile, though her heart began to chug and all of a sudden heat infused her. Real Lila couldn't handle things like holding hands, and she realized that though she'd gotten into costume, she kept falling out of character.

She took a second to remind herself she was playing the part of a rich guy's fiancée, and she was in Spain. Gorgeous Spain! Where the sun glistened on the dew coating the leaves in the rows and rows of grapevines. Rolling hills stretched to black mountains. And the sky was such a perfect blue it almost took her breath away.

"It's beautiful here."

"It's summer. Everywhere is beautiful in the summer."

"Yes. I guess." She glanced around at the grounds. Healthy green grass and trees gave way to a plethora of grapevines that seemed to go on forever. "Your family must make a lot of wine."

He laughed. "How else do you think we support three generations of Ochoas?"

"By making a lot of wine."

He shook his head. "By *selling* a lot of wine."

He opened the door for her and she stepped into the lobby of the main house turned business premises. On the right were shelves filled with bottles displaying the Ochoa label, as well as touristy trinkets, T-shirts and corks with the vineyard's logo. On the left was a silent corridor. Mitch had told her the family's business offices were on this level, and she assumed that hall led to those offices.

Remembering the restaurant in the basement, she said, "Do we go downstairs?"

"Upstairs. To the residences."

"Okay."

Once again they climbed a flight of stairs, a circular stairway wide enough for them to walk side by side. A huge sitting room greeted them at the top of the steps with corridors jutting left and right.

"My parents' quarters are that way," Mitch said, pointing to the left. "And Nanna lives down here." He directed her to walk to the right.

At the end of the hall they entered a door that opened onto another sitting room, then Mitch led her to a dining room where it seemed the entire Ochoa family had gathered at a long cherrywood table.

The men rose. Mitch walked Lila to the two empty places at the table, pulled out her chair and helped her sit before he sat beside her.

As the men returned to their seats, Julia said, "Jeans at the breakfast table! Lila, what a bold woman you are!"

A quick glance around showed all the women were dressed up. Though the men were a lot more casual, like Mitch.

"I thought you were coming with us this morning while I pick up my gown for tonight's opening gala?"

Lila smiled at Mitch, then Julia. "Actually, I didn't know that. But I'd love to come." She wasn't sure if Julia was being catty, but she could handle a million Julias. It was a morning alone with Mitch she needed to get out of. "Give me ten minutes after breakfast and I can be ready."

Julia smiled. "So you're a quick-change artist."

That was definitely catty. But Lila wasn't really Lila here. She was Lila, Fake Fiancée. Almost like a superhero, playing a part.

"Absolutely. I'm thrilled to be here to be part of your wedding." A waiter set a glass of juice in front of her. "Actually, I'd love to hear details. It's so beautiful here. I can only imagine how wonderful your ceremony will be."

"The wedding's not here," Nanna said as she motioned for staff to serve breakfast. "It's at Julia's family's tiny vineyard."

She noted a little animosity there, but, again, none of her business. Particularly since Alonzo gazed at Julia with real love in his eyes. When he caught Julia's gaze, her lips rose in a smile filled with an equal amount of love. Julia might have dated Mitch, but she truly loved Alonzo.

Julia, Nanna and Mitch's mom, Marguerite, began to talk nonstop about the wedding. There was a gala tonight, hosted by the Ochoa family. Then on Friday night, Julia's parents would host an outdoor cocktail party. The Ochoas would host a second ball a few days before the wedding for out-of-town guests who hadn't been in Spain for the first ball. A few days later, the bride and fifty or so of her closest friends and relatives would have a luncheon as a bachelorette party. Alonzo and his groomsmen and fifty or so of his closest friends would have a bachelor party. And, of course, the Ochoas would host a rehearsal dinner the night before the actual wedding.

Lila's head spun. No wonder Mitch and Riccardo had advised her to get so many dresses and gowns. She'd thought they'd exaggerated. Now she wondered if she'd bought enough.

Mitch lost Lila for the entire day. Pacing the sitting room, waiting for her to dress for the welcome gala, he admitted to himself that he knew why. While his mom stayed behind to supervise preparations for tonight's ball, Julia, Lila and Nanna had taken one of the family limos into town to pick up her gown. Julia had kept them out all day. She also had been dropped at her family's small vineyard first. Then Nanna and Lila had spent another thirty minutes returning to Ochoa Vineyards, and that left Lila only about an hour to dress.

Why?

Because Julia wanted to be the prettiest girl at the ball and she knew Lila could give her a real run for her money.

He shook his head in disbelief. Who'd have ever thought beautiful Julia would be jealous of Lila? His mousy assistant?

He was about to laugh when Lila's door finally opened and she walked out of her room in a red dress that almost made his eyes pop. Low cut and cruising her breasts to her waist like a second skin, the gown belled out into a skirt that wasn't full, but held yards and yards of material that swished when she walked.

She glanced down at herself. "Too risqué?"

"No!" Sweet mother of God. Who was this woman? How had he not noticed his assistant was so sexy?

He frowned. He hadn't noticed because he'd never seen her anywhere but work. She'd planned every one of his parties but she'd never attended any of them. For all he knew, the office might be the only place she dressed down. And why not? They were working.

She walked over to him, the satin of her ruby-red dress swishing, the pale skin of her shoulders shiny in the glow of the lamp by the sofa, her gray eyes sparkling.

She leaned in. Speaking in a conspiratorial tone, she said, "I have to admit I love this dress."

A floral scent hit him. Her shampoo. *His assistant's* shampoo. Something he'd smelled a million times. A wave of recognition looped through him, but as quickly as the connection came it floated away.

"You look wonderful in that dress."

She reached up and smoothed the collar of his tux jacket and straightened his bow tie. "*You* look wonderful." She gave him a quick, approving once-over, then glanced up at him again. "I like you in a tux."

His breath stuttered, confusing him. Lots of women told him that he looked good in a tux. Yet for some reason hearing her say it stopped his heart and caused his nerve endings to crackle.

He stepped back, cleared his throat and shook his head slightly to force himself to return to the real world, where he had to fool his family and keep the focus on Julia and Alonzo.

Though he would have liked to ask her a million questions, this was one time they absolutely couldn't be late. He motioned to the door. "Ready?"

She smiled broadly. "Sure. I don't think I've ever been to a party looking this pretty. It's going to be fun."

What she said and her tone of voice caused the connection between the woman in front of him and his dowdy assistant to click again. If only for a few seconds, she stopped being two different people. She was his assistant in costume. Lila in a pretty dress. So, it baffled him that thinking of her chatting up a few of his friends or his dad's acquaintances squeezed his chest with jealousy.

"You're not there to have fun. You are there to pretend to be in love with me."

She said, "Uh-huh," as she headed for the door.

He reached it two seconds before she did and opened it for her. The urge to remind her that she couldn't flirt with other guests surged again but he stopped it. He wasn't the jealous type. She wasn't really his fiancée. And he could keep her at his side to make sure she didn't ruin the ruse.

He stopped just before pulling the door closed behind them, a little embarrassed by his need to be in control. This was Lila. When he gave her a job, she did it. He did not have to micromanage her. He had nothing to worry about.

Except that she had a secret that caused her to negotiate a new job as her payback for pretending to be his fiancée.

She worked for a winery, but didn't drink.

His grandmother thought she was pregnant, and would probably ask her a million questions—

Unless she'd already asked them while they were out with Julia that afternoon?

As they reached the sidewalk that led to the main

house, he took her hand. Warm and smooth, it fit nicely in his palm. "So…did Nanna ask you anything that I should know about?"

"Julia kind of monopolized the conversations."

He sniffed a laugh. That he believed. "So, Nanna didn't say anything while you were waiting for Julia to try on dresses?"

She looked thoughtful for a second, then said, "No. Nothing significant that I can remember."

"Did she ask about your past?"

"Yes." She winced. "I decided it best not to lie and I told her the truth."

Two feet away from the side door he'd been guiding Lila to, he stopped. "You did?"

She nodded. "Yes."

"And that truth is…"

"Pretty boring. Just stuff about me being in foster care." She laughed. "Which is why she accepted it so easily."

She took a few steps toward the French doors and servants opened them for her. Music from a string quartet poured out as Lila smiled at the doormen and began walking inside the house.

Mitch scrambled after her. He stepped into the private entry just in time to watch Riccardo take Lila's hands. "I see you put our money to good use."

Lila laughed and did a quick turn. "Isn't it gorgeous? Would you believe I got it on a clearance rack?"

Riccardo tapped her nose. "You're not just good-looking. You're smart. That's why we love you."

A surge of a different kind of jealousy rose up in Mitch. Lila had always been more comfortable with Riccardo.

Right now the easy way she spoke with him made Mitch angry.

"Don't toss too much praise her way. Remember she's leaving us when we get home."

Riccardo's happy, flirty expression deflated. "I forgot."

Lila shrugged. "It's for the best." She faced Mitch. "Shall we go in?"

Mitch took the few steps that separated them, caught her elbow and led her into the ballroom. They weren't late, but early guests had already begun to arrive. Julia and Alonzo would make an entrance once everyone was seated. Mitch's parents stood at the entry to the ballroom with Nanna, greeting guests.

"Can I get you a drink?" He pulled in a breath. Realizing his mistake, he added, "Orange juice? Club soda?"

She shook her head. "No," she said, her gaze slowly circling the room. "I don't want to be distracted. I want to remember all of this. It's so gorgeous."

He shoved his hands in his trouser pockets. "It is pretty. My mom has wonderful taste."

"She does." She faced him with a smile. "And she seems like a lovely person."

"She is."

"I guess I sort of knew that from the fact that you and Riccardo are such good people. Good people come from good parents."

Now he was talking to real Lila. Not the woman who was a mix of his assistant and his fake fiancée. But just plain Lila. The woman who was as loyal as anyone could be. The hard worker. The woman who'd grown up in foster care. He'd never thought much about her personally.

But tonight, watching her reaction to his luxurious home, disgrace at his bad behavior with her enveloped him.

She got along so well with Riccardo. Why had he and Lila never become friends?

He quietly said, "I do know that I was lucky."

"In spite of the fact that my life is dull, I was pretty lucky too. Not every foster kid finds a way to make it through university." Her smile grew. "And after a day with your former girlfriend, I also think you dodged a big bullet with Julia." She leaned in close. "But if you tell anyone I said that, I'll deny it."

A laugh burst from him. Up until this trip, he'd never seen her sense of humor but clearly she had a great one. So maybe the serious way he attacked his work had kept her from getting comfortable with him?

As more and more guests filed into the ballroom, Lila said, "Okay, here's the way I see this. You are the best man, second son, who probably has to make one or two obligatory comments or maybe a toast or something, then for the rest of this event your job is basically to have a good time."

He hadn't thought of it like that, but the assistant in Lila had looked at the situation and summed it up perfectly.

"*Sí.*"

"Okay, so that means no more serious talk. If you want to drink, go ahead. I'll make sure you don't say anything too far out of line or put a lampshade on your head."

"A lampshade on my head?"

"It's an old American expression for when somebody drinks too much and has such a good time they do foolish things."

He nodded but all the good feelings that had been

welling up in him disappeared in a puff of smoke, as the truth poked its way into their good time again. She was funny here but he'd never seen her sense of humor in the office. She didn't drink. She wanted another job. She was leaving him. How was he supposed to be happy around her when there were so many unanswered questions?

Nanna swished her way over. Wearing a pale blue gown and long diamond earrings, she looked like the wealthy matriarch that she was. She greeted Lila first. "Darling, you look fantastic."

Lila said, "Thanks. You look amazing."

Nanna bowed slightly. "Thank you." She peered around. "So? What do you think?"

Mitch said, "Everything's beautiful."

Nanna batted a hand. "You're a man. Of course you say that." She faced Lila again. "What do *you* think?"

"I'm bowled over."

Nanna frowned. "And that's good?"

Lila laughed. "Yes. Very good."

"Sweetheart," Nanna said, laying a hand on Lila's forearm, "I left my small beaded bag on the table behind the receiving line. Could you sneak over and get it? I'd ask Mitch but he'd get drawn into the conversations with arriving guests, and we wouldn't see him again until dinner."

Lila said, "I'll be glad to."

The second she was out of earshot, Nanna turned to Mitch. "So did you ask her?"

"Ask her?"

"If she's pregnant."

Mitch groaned. "I haven't really had two minutes alone with her. Besides, you're the one she talked to today."

Nanna batted a hand. "She told me about the foster

child experience. Very sad. But it made her resilient. She's a wonderful girl, but if she's pregnant you need to know."

"Maybe she's waiting until after the wedding to tell me, so she doesn't steal any of Julia's limelight."

The lie rolled off his tongue easily. But inside Mitch felt odd again. What if Lila *was* pregnant? She wanted a new job. Because she thought he wouldn't support her through her pregnancy? Because he was a business-man who only thought of work? Because he hadn't even known that beneath those glasses and dowdy clothes was a really beautiful woman, who was also very nice?

She returned with Nanna's bag. Nanna took it, leaned in and kissed Lila's cheek. "Thank you."

Lila said, "You're welcome."

Nanna turned and began talking to another guest, be-side them.

Mitch stole a peek at Lila's flat tummy. She couldn't be pregnant… Could she? And if she was, did she intend to raise a child alone? In New York City, where every-thing cost a fortune? Would not having a dad for her baby bring up bad memories of her own childhood?

Wait. There had to be a dad. That was just plain biol-ogy. And Mitch couldn't assume the guy didn't want to be in his baby's life. He could want to be in the baby's life but for some reason Lila didn't want him there. Maybe he was a loser? Maybe he was a thug—

Mitch groaned internally. Now he was making up stories about an imaginary father for an as yet undocu-mented baby.

He had to get some answers.

Nanna redirected the couple she was speaking with to Mitch and Lila, introducing Lila as his fiancée. She played her role, leaning toward him so he could put his arm around her waist.

They spent the next twenty minutes talking to guests that Nanna directed to them. Julia and Alonzo arrived to a blare of trumpets—undoubtedly Julia's idea—then dinner was served. He and Lila sat at a long table with Alonzo and Julia, his parents, her parents and the entire wedding party. There wasn't a second of privacy to ask the questions nagging at him, but even if there had been, Mitch had the sudden, uncomfortable feeling that he couldn't ask for such personal information from somebody he barely knew.

He wasn't bold to the point of almost being ill-mannered like Nanna.

He wasn't friendly with Lila the way Riccardo was.

He wasn't anything.

She might be in trouble, real trouble, and though Mitch had worked with her for a year, he didn't know her well enough to help her.

He wasn't sure if he should be ashamed of himself or mad at himself.

His father made the first toast. Julia's father made the second. Then Julia's mother declined a toast, dabbing tears from her eyes and saying Julia's dad had said it all. Mitch's mom was ready with a fabulous salute to her older son, then everybody looked at Mitch.

He rose. He'd been thinking about this for weeks before this trip, so he very casually picked up his champagne glass and said, "To Alonzo and Julia, the perfect couple. May they have a long, happy marriage. *Salud.*"

Everyone said, *"Salud!"* and took a drink of champagne.

When he was seated again, Lila touched his arm. "That was perfect."

"I decided to think of myself as just an ordinary best man for my brother and gave the toast that way."

"Well, you were brilliant."

His father announced dancing, and Alonzo and Julia immediately took to the floor. After a first dance for the about-to-be-weds, Mitch rose. "Our family goes out onto the dance floor immediately to signal to the other guests that they can dance."

As he helped Lila stand, she said, "Sounds great."

They danced the first dance a little stiff and awkward but by the second, they were much more attuned to each other. His hand on the small of her back relaxed. The hand she had on his shoulder shifted to be more comfortable.

His nervousness settled. Lila was a great dancer. Very light on her feet. Very easy to guide around the dance floor.

When the second song started, Riccardo cut in. Polite, Mitch smiled and excused himself, but he stood on the sidelines watching her as Riccardo whirled her around in a huge, looping circle to the music of the waltz that floated around them. She tossed her head back and laughed, and the weird jealousy rolled through him again.

As soon as the song ended, he was at her side. "Thanks, cuz. We'll see you later."

Riccardo excused himself and walked away, but the second the music started Lila was in Mitch's arms again.

"So what were you laughing about with Riccardo?"

"He offered to give me his condo if I'd stay with Ochoa Online."

The possibility that she wouldn't leave filled him with bubbly joy. "And you said?"

"No!" She laughed and he whirled her around again.

"Why don't you want to work for us anymore?"

"Maybe the better question to be asking yourself is where am I getting Lila a job?"

"But Riccardo and I want you to stay."

"Really? Because if I stay then all bets are off and I'm not your fiancée anymore and you've got some explaining to do to your nanna."

"I know you think you're very clever at confusing me. But I've caught you every time, and you've just been lucky with the plane landing, or Nanna insisting I chat with her or being late for breakfast."

He yanked her close, tight up against his body to show her that he was in control, and instantly regretted it. She felt wonderful. How could he make a point when he was tongue-tied?

"Don't forget Julia keeping us out all day."

Her soft, breathless voice did something to his soul. She was as turned on as he was. Though she used her wit to try to divert his attention, he could feel the quiver that ran through her small frame.

He smiled. This was a game he could play. "Julia thinks you're beautiful."

She caught his gaze. "No, she doesn't."

"Why else did she keep you out all day except to limit the time you had to prepare for the gala?" He whirled them around again. "But you fooled her. You didn't need three hours of prep work to be beautiful."

The song ended. He kept her pressed against him, staring into her eyes. "You are beautiful tonight. More beautiful than she is."

Her eyes shifted, softened. But she said, "Music has stopped."

"So? We're in love, remember?" He dipped his head

slowly, desperately wanting a kiss, desperately curious about what she'd do if he kissed her for real, not a quick brush of a goodbye kiss.

Everything around them melted away. She studied his eyes, her own pale gray orbs curious, but wary. She wanted the kiss as much as he did, but something held her back.

She pulled away. "I think I need a club soda."

He released her, but took her hand and headed for the bar. As much as he wanted to kiss her—really kiss her—the fact that she'd stepped away told him that he couldn't until he knew what was going on with her. Was she pregnant? Was that why she wanted another job?

He already knew he couldn't ask her something so personal, so private until he really got to know her. She'd slid out of every chance to have a conversation, but she wasn't wiggling out this time. There were no parties, no galas scheduled for Thursday night. Tomorrow, there'd be no one to save her.

CHAPTER FIVE

LILA WOKE THE next morning with plenty of time to spare before the family breakfast. She showered, fixed her hair, put on makeup and slid into a comfortable skirt and silky top. When she stepped out into the sitting room, Mitch was at the table in the small kitchenette, his tablet in front of him. He was probably online, reading the morning news. The delicious aroma of fresh coffee permeated the small space. So did the scent of toast.

"Good morning." She carefully walked through the seating area to the little round table with four chairs. She wasn't exactly sure what had happened the night before, but her heart tripped over itself when she remembered that minute on the dance floor when she was absolutely positive he was going to kiss her. She'd called herself all kinds of crazy for even thinking he'd wanted to kiss her. But she couldn't discount the fact that something had sizzled between them, and now the mood in their apartment felt different.

He smiled at her. "Good morning."

He wasn't just smiling. There was a weird gleam in his eyes.

Her heart bumped against her ribs. Something absolutely, positively had changed.

"Nanna called. No family breakfast this morning." He pointed to a silver coffeepot. "The cook sent up coffee and a tray of cheeses and breads for toast."

"Oh."

"Nanna has an appointment with her stylist today to figure out her hairdo for the wedding."

Lila couldn't help it; she laughed.

"What?"

"It's funny to hear you talk about girl things."

"I know about girl things."

Oh, she would bet he did. But she wasn't opening that door. Instead, she picked up a coffee cup and poured herself a mug of the hot, dark liquid from the silver carafe. She set the cup on the table and was about to pull out a chair, but hesitated when she saw the wicked gleam in his eyes again. That's when she put two and two together and realized that no family breakfast and Nanna leaving for hours on an errand meant she would be alone with Mitch. Maybe all morning.

"So what's your mom doing?"

The light in his eyes intensified. "Worried you'll have to spend time with me?"

Heat rose to her cheeks.

"Well, don't. We have a board meeting at eight. My mom has to attend, so Nanna invited you to go with her and help her decide on a hairdo."

The breath returned to her lungs. "I can do that."

His head tilted as he looked at her, studying her hair. "Last week, I might have wondered if you could." He smiled again. "Today, I know you can."

The way he kept looking at her, smiling at her, sent a ripple of unease through her.

He rose from the table. "These meetings frequently

last all day." He headed for the door. "I'm assuming you and Nanna will have lunch in town and probably shop. Riccardo said you still have the credit cards." He glanced over at her. "Use them. And don't bargain hunt. I want Nanna to see you spending my money as if you're accustomed to it."

"Okay."

"Okay." He turned to the door, then faced her again. "And don't worry about missing me while I'm busy. I've arranged for us to have a private dinner, here, in the apartment tonight."

Lila's breath froze. Private dinner? She remembered those thirty seconds when he'd yanked her against him on the dance floor. The sizzle. The confusion.

And the longing.

She fought the urge to squeeze her eyes shut. She'd had a crush on this man forever. When he'd pulled her so close—well, her thoughts had spun out of control and she'd felt so many wonderful things.

What if he'd felt them too?

Oh, boy.

The words *private dinner* took on a whole new meaning.

But he opened the door and was gone before Lila could blink let alone argue. She straightened her shoulders. She wasn't going to fall into the trap of thinking he intended to seduce her. They'd shared one "crackly" moment the night before. He hadn't instantly fallen in love with her. He probably wanted to have dinner alone so he could catch her up on whatever happened at their family business meeting that day.

She was, after all, his assistant—

No, she wasn't. She'd quit his employ. Anything his

family decided for the company today made no difference to her.

There was only one reason left for his wanting private time with her. One logical, part of the charade reason: he wanted her to tell him things about her past.

After the way he'd looked at her the night before—

The way he'd smiled at her all morning—

There was something going on in that Ochoa brain of his. He definitely had a plan for getting her to spill the beans she'd kept to herself for an entire year in his employ. And he seemed pretty cocky about it. Which meant he had an idea that he genuinely believed would work to get her to talk.

The phone in the sitting area rang. She set her coffee on the table and raced to get it, hoping it was Mitch telling her he'd only been teasing about the private dinner, or he'd changed his mind, or something had come up that meant they wouldn't be alone.

Because the one thing she hadn't factored into this charade was that they'd be alone. Somehow she'd always pictured them at parties and family dinners, or dressing for parties and family dinners.

The phone rang again and she picked up the receiver and cautiously said, "Hello?"

"It's me. Nanna. I'm just calling to let you know I'm already in the limo. Breakfast by myself takes a lot less time than with family."

Lila squeezed her eyes shut. She was not getting out of a private dinner with Mitch. "I'll be right there."

After grabbing her purse from her bedroom, Lila raced down the stairs and outside where she found the family limo sitting in front of the duplex. A driver opened the door for her and she slid inside.

Smiling at Nanna, she said, "Good morning."

"Good morning." Nanna squeezed her hand. "We're going to have such fun." She leaned in and whispered, "You got a credit card from Mitch, right?"

She laughed. Two minutes in Nanna's company and she already felt better. "Yes. And he said to use it."

"That's my boy."

The driver started the limo and pulled out.

"Once we get this hair nonsense out of the way, we'll have lunch—then we can shop."

Lila laughed again. She should have felt guilty about using Mitch's money or maybe her pride should have stopped her from buying a skirt, two blouses and a new pair of shoes, but Nanna made it very easy to get into the role of playing fiancée to her grandson. Nanna was inordinately happy that Mitch was happy. All in all, they had a great day.

But ten minutes into the drive back to the vineyard, Nanna said, "So, aside from what you told me yesterday about your childhood, what else do I need to know about you?"

"Actually, I pretty much told you everything." Lila shrugged. "There's not much to know about me."

Nanna turned her rich, dark eyes on Lila. "Really?"

"I have an uncomplicated past. I grew up, went to university, got a job." She smiled at Nanna, but Nanna didn't smile back. "Honestly. There's not much to tell."

"I believe there is much to tell," Nanna contradicted. "But I think you look around and see a world beyond yours and assume we wouldn't be interested."

Now *that* was perceptive. No wonder Mitch worried about her figuring out the ruse. "That's part of it."

"And maybe you compare yourself to Julia?"

Lila winced. For as much as she knew Nanna was digging for something, she also couldn't lie to her. She doubted anyone could lie to her. The woman should work for the CIA. "I try not to compare myself to Julia. We're clearly two different people. I think comparing us would be a big mistake."

"Yes. Mostly because New York changed Mitch. For the better. His taste in women certainly improved."

"That's not really fair to Julia."

"Julia is a lovely woman." Nanna straightened the pleats in her skirt. "But she is also complicated." She met Lila's gaze. "I'm sure you can figure that out from the switch in choice of brothers. She loved Mitch, but she also loved the fact that his older brother would someday run the family business."

"Ah."

"Ah, indeed." Nanna took a quick breath. "But I have no doubt now that she loves Alonzo." She shook her head. "Complicated."

"Love usually is."

"And you believe Mitcham is over her?"

Lila laughed slightly. "Absolutely. In fact, he's happy for Julia and Alonzo. You should see the lengths he was willing to go to to make sure the focus of these two weeks was on his brother and future bride. This is their time. He wants them to enjoy the celebrations."

"He told you that?"

"Yes, he did."

Nanna studied Lila's eyes for a few seconds. "He trusts you."

Those terrible feelings about deceiving Nanna rose in Lila again, but she wasn't really deceiving her. Mitch really did trust her. That's why they were in this charade. Talking about trust wasn't lying.

"Yes. He trusts me with a lot more than you'd ever believe."

Nanna squeezed her hand. "That's good. After the mess with him finding Alonzo and Julia, he needs to be with someone he trusts."

That nudged a little bit of guilt into her thoughts. But when Lila weighed the pros and cons, and considered how this one little charade really had assured this celebration would be about Julia and Alonzo, she couldn't feel too guilty.

The limo pulled up to the apartment building first. Nanna kissed Lila's cheek before Lila slid out of the car. The driver handed her purchases to her, and happy after the fun day with Nanna, she all but skipped up the stairs. Until she remembered she was having a private dinner with Mitch.

Damn it.

She walked up the rest of the steps slowly. They were a good hour away from dinner. Mitch could still be at his family's meeting. She could use the time for a bubble bath and to dress.

And then—

Then she would do what needed to be done. It wasn't like they would be out in public where she had to play a role. Actually, that was the first sane thought she'd had about this time alone. Technically, she was working out a two-week notice. In fact, with this dinner being private, she shouldn't be Lila, Fake Fiancée. She should be Lila, Mitch's assistant.

The very thought that she should be herself put a spring back in her step. Mitch wasn't curious about that woman—his assistant—or attracted to her. She'd spent tons of time alone with him as his assistant and he'd barely looked at her.

She raced into the apartment, tossed her new things on her bed and got into the shower instead of a bubble bath. She washed her hair, intending to let it frizz out again, but the straightener the beautician had used was doing the job it promised to do for the next sixty days. Her hair, even after using a blow-dryer, was sleek and shiny.

She really shouldn't have put on makeup, but she liked the way she looked with a little mascara and eyeliner. And a dab of lip gloss wasn't a sin.

Luckily, she did have a pair of her old jeans—but, darn it, she really wanted to wear one of her new blouses.

But she wasn't putting on shoes.

And she wasn't wearing her contacts.

A few minutes after she entered the sitting room, a member of the kitchen staff arrived with dinner. She was about to tell him Mitch hadn't come back from his meeting when he stepped out of his bedroom, pulling a polo shirt over his head, looking freshly showered. He also wore jeans. His feet were bare. He intended to be as comfortable as she was.

"Thank you, Tomas," he said, indicating that Tomas could roll the cart containing dinner and wine into the kitchenette area, near the table.

Tomas did as he was told and exited with a smile and a quick nod.

Amazed, Lila watched him go, then faced Mitch again. "You have some wicked good staff."

"We pride ourselves on knowing how to pick excellent employees. It's why we don't usually expect them to ask us to find them a new job."

Wow. Direct hit. Right for the jugular.

She sucked in a breath. "These are special circumstances."

"I gathered that."

He motioned for her to join him at the table, then he took the two covered dishes off the cart and set them at the two place settings. He removed the lids, revealing steak and potatoes.

"Smells good."

"It should be. Our chef trained all over Europe before he finally settled in to work for our restaurant."

"Nice."

She took her seat and he sat across from her. "I expected to see more surprise from you at how we live."

She shrugged. "You forget that I see how you and Riccardo live in New York. Plus, I'm playing your fiancée. I'm supposed to know you enough that how you live doesn't surprise me." She paused for a second, then said, "Nanna and I had another bit of a conversation today. She appreciates that you trust me."

"I do trust you." He plunged his fork into his steak. "Did you tell her anything I need to know?"

"No. I've pretty much been able to keep the conversations neutral and simple, focused on a few main facts."

Frustration rolled through Mitch. If direct and outspoken Nanna couldn't get Lila to talk, he wondered if he'd be able to. Still, the purpose of this dinner was to get to know her so that eventually she'd tell him why she wanted to leave his employ, why she didn't drink and if she was pregnant.

The best way to get her to open up would be to talk to her, to let a personal conversation evolve naturally. Let it ebb. Let it flow. Let a little trust in him build for her—the way he trusted her.

"So in spite of the fact that you were able to keep your secrets from Nanna, I take it you had fun with her."

"The woman's a shopping machine."

He laughed. "And you spent money?"

She pointed at her blouse. "This shirt's new. And it set you back more than my part of the month's rent."

"That's right. You share an apartment. With your friend Sally?"

She glanced up, surprised.

"I heard you telling Riccardo you would be taking a friend shopping with you the day before we left."

The way she could talk to Riccardo rankled, but he smiled. After all, he was trying to get this woman to trust him the way he trusted her. He couldn't get mad that she was closer to his cousin. That's what he was trying to fix.

"You mentioned her name was Sally."

"Actually, Sally got a promotion about a year ago and can now afford her own apartment."

"Oh." And maybe that was the reason for her sudden interest in a new job?

Before he could ask, she said, "My roommates are Joselyn and Jennie." She laughed. "I call them the two jays. Like blue jays only two jays." She shook her head. "I have a weird sense of humor."

He cut into his steak. "No. I just think your mind is always working."

"That's one way to put it."

The conversation died as they began to eat. She took a bite of her steak and groaned. "Holy cow."

He leaned in. "The chef's secret ingredient is butter."

Her eyes rose to meet his. That's when he noticed she

was wearing her glasses. He was making the connection between her as his assistant and her as his fake fiancée so completely that he hadn't even noticed her glasses. Right now, she was just Lila. Something of a cross between the two.

"Your chef adds butter to meat that's already loaded with fat?"

"I know. Decadent, isn't it?"

"Yeah. But it's also probably ten million calories."

He cleared his throat. Knowing what he was about to ask her was personal, and she'd probably shut him down, he nonetheless said, "You don't look like the kind of woman who has to watch her weight."

She laughed. "All women watch their weight."

Her laughter thrilled him. She'd laughed with him before. Especially when she was dressed up and pretending to be somebody else. But this woman was the real Lila and she was laughing with him.

"Hell of a cross to bear," he said, teasing her, hoping she wouldn't disappear back into the protective shell of the character she was supposed to be playing.

"Yeah, especially when your fiancé serves you steak slathered in butter."

He liked the way she very casually called him her fiancé. Maybe he was getting accustomed to that too?

"Tell me a bit about growing up in foster care."

"I already told you I don't care to revisit all that. Why don't you tell me more about growing up here? Now that I've seen your home and met your family, I'll have a better perspective."

He set his fork down. This dinner was supposed to be about getting to know her and she'd already turned the tables. But what if part of getting her to trust him was respecting her wishes? She didn't want to talk about her years in foster care. Who could blame her? And she did want to hear about his childhood.

"All right. When my dad and his brother inherited the vineyard, they also bought the adjoining vineyard, not just to increase the business enough to support two families, but also to have a second residence."

She put her elbow on the table and her chin on her fist, watching him as he spoke. "That's how you and Riccardo became so close? You grew up next door to each other."

"We grew up together. My mom and my aunt basically ran the business office, and the stories go that Riccardo and I were in the same play yard between their two desks."

She smiled. "Your moms didn't want to be away from you or have you raised by a babysitter. That's kinda nice."

"I never thought of it that way before, but, *sí*. It probably was nice."

He could see a shadow of sadness in her eyes and ached to ask her about her own childhood, but knew it was nowhere near as pleasant as his, and suddenly he understood her hesitancy to talk about it. Who would want to relive loneliness? Pain?

"So," he said, picking up his fork again, deciding to continue talking about himself, about good times, so that maybe she could live them through him. "By the time we were six or eight, we behaved more like twins than cousins. We worked alongside each other in the vineyards when we were teens, and had desks in the same room when we began our internships in the office."

As he took a bite of steak, she said, "That makes sense. And also explains how well you click for Ochoa Online."

"Technically, we've been working together for decades."

Her smile warmed. "That's wonderful."

"Or you could say our dads took advantage of slave labor."

That made her laugh. "It was good to be together so much. It bonded you. Made you the great team you are today."

"Yes." And he could see that she envied that. Or maybe longed for it. He felt the empty hole in her life as surely as if it were a living, breathing thing.

"What about Christmas?"

He glanced over at her. "What about Christmas?"

"With all this togetherness, your family Christmas must be happy." Her smile grew. "Wonderful."

He pulled in a breath. He'd never really thought about it. But he supposed that to an outsider, someone who was totally alone, being surrounded by so much family must be wonderful. "Riccardo's family and our family have separate celebrations for some things. But everybody likes to be with Nanna, so Christmas Eve is in her quarters. Christmas dinner is in my parents'."

She nodded. "Nice."

"Really. It is." And he now regretted whining about having to fly to Spain for the holidays last year when she might not have had anywhere at all to go.

Knowing he had to get them out of this weird mood, he said, "Okay, so you don't want to discuss your childhood... and I respect that. But surely you've got a good story or two from university."

She thought about that. "The whole reason I made it through was that the coffee shop I worked for paid well and had great benefits. They also paid a big portion of my tuition."

His heart lifted a bit for her. "That was a lucky break."

"Yes. That was when I began to see that in some respects I was lucky."

Being a foster child did not make her lucky. Having one good life break also did not make her lucky. Yet her tone of voice said she believed she was.

His curiosity rose and he peeked at her. "How so?"

"No matter where I worked or who I roomed with, I was able to make friends. I was always able to find friends."

He leaned forward, across the table, putting his elbow close to hers and his chin on his fist, mimicking her. "Why am I not surprised?"

"You should be surprised. In an entire year this is our first real conversation. You obviously think I'm a real dolt."

"Maybe I'm the dolt who never thought to ask you anything personal?"

"Personal things don't belong in the workplace."

"Yes, but you went out of your way for me. A lot." He leaned a little closer; the desire to kiss her once again swam through his veins. This time it was stronger, more powerful. She wasn't just Lila, his confusing assistant. She wasn't Lila, his fake fiancée being sexy. She was both of those wrapped up in one cute little package with sleek hair and big glasses. And he liked her. He really liked her.

He leaned in a little closer. "I did notice what a good worker you were."

"But you never noticed me otherwise."

He leaned in a little more. "I'm noticing now."

Her tongue darted out and slid along her lips, but she didn't move. Maybe being together in a different situation than boss and assistant had changed her opinion of him too? Maybe it made her notice him as more than a boss?

He erased the final inches between them and pressed his lips to hers. Soft and warm, they melted under his touch. Desire slammed through him, but so did an aching frustration. How could he kiss her properly sitting down, with a table between them? Without breaking the contact of their mouths, he slid his hands behind her upper arms and pulled her up with him as he rose, taking the step that put them as close as they had been when they were dancing.

Then he deepened the kiss and unexpected awareness spiraled through him. This wasn't a woman he'd met in Central Park, at the theater or in a coffee shop.

This was Lila.

A woman he genuinely liked.

And he was kissing her.

It was the most different, most wonderful thing.

CHAPTER SIX

LILA'S HEART HAMMERED in her chest. She had been Real
Lila all through dinner, hoping to deter him. Instead, the
opposite had happened. He seemed interested in her, bare
feet, glasses and all. She had absolutely no idea what had
happened, what *was* happening between them, but she'd
had enough boyfriends, flirtations and relationships to
know the man was interested in her.

The man she'd had a crush on for the past year wasn't
just noticing her. He was interested.

Kissing her.

The warmth that filled her was part joy, part need.
Then he deepened the kiss a second time, opening her
mouth and sliding his tongue along the rough texture of
hers, and her knees about buckled.

He was definitely interested in her.

The oddest thought drifted into her brain, wound
around her nerve endings and whispered through her
consciousness.

What if this was her chance?

What if fate had set her up as his fake fiancée not to
get her a new job but to have a real chance with him? Yes,
she wanted to find her mom, but she could do it as easily as his girlfriend as she could some nameless assistant

working for another company. Maybe more easily. If she could get up her courage and tell him the truth about her past, maybe he could use his connections to help her?

Her breath stalled. But he pulled back slightly.

Raising his hands to the stems of her glasses, he said, "Let's get rid of these."

"Okay." Her voice came out a mere whisper, as horrible pain tumbled through her.

He'd asked her to take off her glasses. He didn't like *her*. He liked Fake Lila. He'd taken off the glasses to bring her back. If he wanted Fake Lila, she couldn't tell him the truth. She couldn't tell him anything.

Unless…

She looked down at the tortoiseshell frames on the table. Unless he was about to take them into no-glasses territory? The big romantic place. The place for which she wasn't prepared…

His bedroom.

All the wonderful warmth floating through her turned to the ice of fear. If he was only toying with her, or having some fun with Fake Lila, it would kill her to make love with him, and then be nothing to him when they got home. But even if he was getting feelings for her, this was too soon. She wasn't ready. But he wasn't either. He didn't know her. Not all of her. And unless she could say with absolute certainty that he was interested in Real Lila, not Fake Lila, she couldn't tell him. She most certainly couldn't go to his bedroom with him.

She took a step back, cleared her throat and looked him in the eye, as much as she could without her thick glasses.

"We have a big day tomorrow with Julia's parents' garden party." She took another step back. "So I'm going to go." She picked up her glasses and motioned to her bed-room. "I want to make sure I get enough sleep."

His head tilted as if she'd confused him.

Okay. They were even then because he'd sure as hell confused her.

She turned and walked back to her bedroom with as much grace and dignity as she could muster. Behind the safety of her closed door, she slipped out of her skirt and blouse and into her Giants T-shirt and pajama pants.

But sleep didn't come.

She tried for an hour, wishing she had someone to talk to, then realized that she did. She might not have a close friend in Spain, but she had plenty of friends in New York. And it was still daytime there.

Grabbing her cell phone, she hit contacts and dialed Sally's number. Though she was probably at work, she answered in three rings.

"So how's life in the fast lane?"

"A lot faster than I thought it was going to be."

Sally sighed greedily. "Tell me everything."

Lila sat up in bed, plumped her pillows and plunged into a discussion of Nanna and Julia, balls and shopping.

"Oh, my gosh!" Sally's voice dripped with incredulity. "That's unbelievable."

"Okay, then. If you think that's unbelievable, you're gonna faint at this."

"I am on the edge of my chair."

"He kissed me."

"He? Mitch? Isn't he supposed to kiss you to make the ruse work?"

"Yes. But that's only in public. He kissed me in pri-vate tonight."

"What in the heck is happening between you two?"

"That's the big question." She paused, bit her lower lip. "I kinda dressed like Real Lila for dinner tonight, except that I like the way mascara looks and a little lip gloss never killed anyone. So I was a cross between Real Lila and Fake Lila."

"You're enjoying this! You don't want to be a mouse anymore."

"I just… I don't know. I guess I never realized mascara and pretty blouses could make such a big difference. Especially with my hair all sleek."

"And you like new Lila."

"I'm not really new. It's still me, except pretty."

"You were always pretty. You just hid it."

She sighed. "I suppose."

"So if you're enjoying this and the guy you swoon over kissed you, what's the problem?"

"He took off my glasses when we were kissing."

"And?"

"And it makes me feel that either he doesn't like to be reminded of the real me or he was going to take us a little further than I was ready to go."

Sally's "Oh…" came out slow and strangled. "You're in the big leagues."

"I guess."

"And it happened too fast?"

"We've only been here a few days."

"I get that. But technically you've known him for a year."

"I know him, but he doesn't know me."

They were silent for a few seconds, then Sally said, "You can't tell him about your mom?"

"I could… I *would* if I knew he was interested in me.

For real. But I won't humiliate myself by telling the story to someone when it doesn't really matter."

"So what are you going to do?"

Lila laughed. "Call you?"

"For advice. Hmmm." Sally paused, obviously considering how to answer. "I think that if he only likes Fake Lila you're right to back off."

"That's my thought too."

"Now, don't be ready to jump ship yet. There's another side to this. If you really are sliding into a combination of Fake Lila and Real Lila, then you just have to make sure he slides with you. Then you can tell him. Then he'll know you, and everything else is going to depend on whether or not he's genuinely interested or just being a player."

"I forgot what a serial dater he is."

"Yeah," Sally said, obviously still thinking. "But all men date around until the right girl catches their attention."

"You think I'm the right girl for him?"

"You don't?"

She had. From the first moment she laid eyes on him, she had. She sighed heavily, almost afraid to admit it, afraid to jinx what was happening between them. "I do."

"Then keep wearing your glasses. Not all the time, but in your downtime. If it's you he likes, he'll adjust to Real Lila, and you'll know it. Then you can tell him about your mom. And if he doesn't adjust? Then maybe *you* don't want *him*."

The following evening, Mitch sat in the sitting area of his small apartment, waiting for Lila. He knew she'd talked to his grandmother about what to wear to this outdoor cocktail party, but he didn't think she had to worry. She seemed to have impeccable taste. Or at least the knowledge of what looked good on her because she'd been stunning him since the day she got out of the limo at the airport.

And that kiss? It had been amazing.

But he had no idea what he was doing with her. First, she didn't really talk to him. She very well could be pregnant, yet she hadn't felt the need to tell him and he still didn't feel comfortable asking. Then there was the matter of her wanting another job. All along, he'd had a ping that something was terribly wrong with that. If she was pregnant, maybe a new job had something to do with affording a baby. But he and Riccardo could provide both money and moral support. So why was she leaving them?

Still, the biggest reason of all to be careful was that he didn't want to hurt her. He'd been horribly surprised by Julia falling in love with Alonzo. True, it all sorted out for him very quickly, but there was no place in a Spaniard's life for weakness. And with the abundance of potential dates in New York City, he'd happily realized he never had to get serious about a woman again.

Which meant, if he got involved with Lila, their relationship wouldn't last. It would end. And he would hurt her.

He shouldn't have kissed her.

She had been right to step away and go to her room.

So how did he get this charade back on track and still nose into her personal life—on the chance that he could help her if she was pregnant?

He wasn't sure he could.

Her bedroom door opened. She stepped out wearing a yellow dress and light-colored sandals, not quite white but not quite yellow either. Her hair had been pinned up on one side.

She pointed at it. "This is my nod toward the fact that the party is outside."

"You look—" Perfect. Fantastic. Unreal. So wonderful he wanted to bite her neck, and make her laugh and moan at the same time.

He sucked in a breath, reminding himself that if she was pregnant, he wanted to help her, and he couldn't help her if he romanced her then dumped her. But pregnancy aside, they were here to ensure his brother and future sister-in-law were the stars of this wedding celebration.

They had a charade to pull off. And he had to make sure she would do her part.

"You look very nice."

She peered at him. "That's it? Very nice?"

He laughed. "All right. You look spectacular. You've been surprising me every day of this trip." He suddenly realized the one thing that would get her totally on board again. Her reward. The reason she'd agreed to do this. "In fact, you're helping me so much that I can't even tell you how grateful I am. So I think it might be time you and I talk about the new job you want."

"Now?"

He pointed to the door. "I'll need details on things like the kind of work you want to do, how much salary you want, benefits—" He said that, then paused, giving her the chance to say, "Yeah, I'm going to need good benefits with a baby on the way." But she didn't take the bait. "So that I can take a look at my friend list and call their HR departments to see who needs someone."

"Okay."

He caught her gaze. "You know. This is the kind of task I'd normally give to you."

She looked down. "I'm kind of busy right now."

The urge to put his finger under her chin and lift her face was nearly irresistible, and he was glad he'd started this conversation. Leaving him made her as unhappy as the thought of her leaving made him. There was hope that he could persuade her to stay in his employ—with a raise—and then he could help her. He just had to tread lightly.

They had the limo to themselves because his parents and Nanna had gone to the vineyard an hour earlier to spend time with Julia's parents to discuss last-minute details of the wedding.

He said very little on the drive, satisfied that he had her thinking about how she would miss working with him and Riccardo. If he gave her some space to really ponder that, she might recognize keeping her current job was the right thing to do.

They arrived at Julia's parents' vineyard, and as she stepped out she gasped. "Oh, my goodness. It's so homey."

He laughed. "Is that another way of saying small?"

"You may not notice this, mister," she said, following his lead when he gestured with his hand that she should walk around the side of the stately stone house to the back patio. "But your family's estate is a little commercial."

"We do sell wine there."

"And I think that's all you ever think about."

"Sometimes I think about selling golf balls."

She laughed and shook her head. "You're incorrigible."

"But you like me."

She stopped. Her gaze crawled up to his. "Yes. And I'm not sure what that says about me."

He started to laugh, but he remembered he wasn't supposed to flirt with her when they were alone. It was so easy to romance her that he had to remind himself to fight the impulse.

Then her words soaked in and his mouth turned down. *She didn't want to like him?* That was more than a little insulting. Especially since he wasn't sure if she was talking about liking him romantically or liking him as a boss.

She walked away and he scrambled to catch up with her.

"Why did you say that?"

"What?"

"That you didn't know what it said about you that you liked me."

"You're a very demanding man. Yet that doesn't seem to bother me."

Good. Sort of. He didn't want them to be flirting, but how insulting was it that she didn't want to like him as a boss? Especially when he was trying to keep her as an employee.

"You're my assistant. You're supposed to do what I ask." They walked into the crowd of about a hundred well-dressed people, milling around a beautiful blue pool. Waiters served appetizers and drinks. He hailed one who brought a tray of champagne.

He took a flute and said, "A glass of club soda for my fiancée, please."

Lila turned to him with a smile. "Let's not fight about how bossy you are. Let's enjoy the evening."

She was back to being logical Lila, ace assistant, who didn't like him.

He studied his champagne, brooding because he'd

never guessed she didn't like his bossiness—because he was her employer. He was supposed to be bossy.

Apparently, none of this bothered her because she studied the crowd like Cinderella at her first ball.

"So is that why you want to leave Ochoa Online?"

She faced him. "No. Not really. There was never a time when I didn't think I could handle you."

The waiter came with her club soda. Mitch took it from the tray, handing it to her just as Julia's parents spotted them and raced over.

Rosa kissed his cheek first, then homed in on Lila. Taking her hands, she said, "I am happy to see Mitch has finally met his match."

Lila smiled gracefully, then glanced up at him lovingly. "I am too."

The joke wasn't lost on Julia's dad, David. He laughed and hugged Lila. "I've heard you're a firecracker."

From Julia, no doubt, who'd already criticized Lila's choice of clothes for breakfast and kept her away from home so long she barely had time to dress for the first gala.

"Where *are* the bride and groom?" Mitch said, not caring if either of her parents caught that he knew it had been Julia who'd been talking about Lila.

"Milling about," Rosa said. A flood of people had accumulated behind them, so she added, "Go. Have fun. We'll work our way back to you once all the guests have been greeted."

He smiled and nodded, but as he directed Lila away, he said, "You know what? I should be thanking my lucky stars Julia picked Alonzo. I never had the warm fuzzies for her family."

Lila laughed. "Warm fuzzies?"

He waved his hand. "Or whatever it is you Americans say."

"We say *warm fuzzies*. I've just never heard it coming from *you*."

"Maybe I'm changing." Or maybe he needed to. She'd said her reason for wanting to leave his employ wasn't his bossiness, but it certainly couldn't hurt to be a more diplomatic boss.

She shook her head. "You don't want to change."

He looked into her eyes. Soft, gray orbs that were always filled with emotion. Right now, they oozed warmth. Why had he never noticed that? "Really?"

"No. You're good just the way you are."

Then why do you want to work for someone else?

He wanted to ask her. He really did. He wasn't afraid of the answer until he realized that he would fix whatever she said. He'd totally change the way his office ran—

To keep an assistant?

Or to keep Lila?

Because he was beginning to like her?

Really like her?

They finally reached the table where his mom sat with Nanna while his dad stood beside them, talking to another vintner.

Lila immediately walked to Nanna and leaned down to hug her. "You look stunning." Nanna's pale blue dress enhanced the gray in her salt-and-pepper hair but somehow made her look years younger.

"Doesn't she?" Mitch's mom said.

Nanna batted a hand. "With money, even an old coot can look good." She motioned for Lila to take the seat beside her, and she did.

Then Nanna glanced up at him. "Oh, Mitcham. I'm sorry. I didn't see you."

He would have teased her, except he sort of understood. This new version of Lila seemed to always steal the show. Not because she was exceptional, but because she was kind and warm. She didn't overdress, wanting people to notice her. She didn't laugh too loud, edge her way into conversations.

She was just easy to be with.

He suddenly realized why the charade was working so well. She fit. She fit into his family. She fit with him.

He took a step back. The collar of his white shirt got unbearably tight.

Oh, dear God.

Had he actually met his match?

He didn't want a match! He liked being single. Being free.

Julia and Alonzo strolled over. Wearing a pale pink cocktail dress, with her black hair piled on top of her head in an array of curls, Julia was stunning. When she reached Mitch, he hugged her, but the familiarity of the hug drove a tsunami of memories through his brain. The strangest truth rumbled through him, surprising him. Julia had been his girlfriend forever, but Alonzo had been able to swoop in and steal her because he'd been the crappiest boyfriend under the sun. He'd gone on business trips, leaving her behind. He'd constantly canceled dates because of work. Eventually, she'd had it with him and had taken up with his brother. A man who treated her very, very well. Who didn't put the business before her. Who wasn't trying to conquer the world. A man who wasn't selfish.

A man who only had to run one vineyard—he didn't have to assure the financial security of his entire family.

The thought brought him up short. He wasn't a bad boyfriend because he was inconsiderate. He'd been a bad boyfriend because as Alonzo, Riccardo and he grew into adulthood and had a right to a share of profits, he'd seen the family finances first strain, then begin to fail. He'd worked his tail off to sell more wine, but he hadn't fixed their money troubles until he got the go-ahead from his dad to sell the family wines online. And he would continue to work his tail off to make sure the family would never have to worry about money again.

All this time, he'd been thinking he would be the one to break up with Lila if they got involved. But Lila was a hundred times smarter than Julia. She'd figure out he wasn't a good bet as a boyfriend the first time he put work ahead of her. He would always put work ahead of everything because no one else in his family did.

Then *he'd* be dumped.

Again.

Because he'd deserve it.

Julia caught Lila's hand. "Boys," she said, looking first at Alonzo, then at Mitch. "You're going to have to excuse me and Lila. There are a few people I'd like her to meet."

Mired in his own confusion, Mitch absently said, "Sure. I'll wait here with Mom and Nanna."

"Great." Julia slid her hand beneath Lila's elbow to guide her away. "You look lovely, Lila."

Mitch's brow furrowed. It was rare for Julia to give a compliment. Though another person might have thought it was nice that she had, Mitch knew it wasn't. The urge to drag Lila away from Julia roared through him, but they were already walking across the grassy lawn.

"Isn't that last year's gown?"

And there it was. That compliment Julia had given Lila had only been a way to get her guard down so she could insult her.

The very second before he would have raced across the yard to rescue her, Lila laughed. "You actually care about those things?" She batted a hand. "I don't have time." She glanced down at her pretty yellow dress. "Besides, beauty is beauty." She smoothed her hand down her skirt. "I think it's a sign of someone who doesn't really have her own style when a woman likes something based on a calendar year or a designer." She smiled at Julia. "Don't you?"

Julia's mouth opened, then closed, then opened again. For once she had absolutely no comeback.

Smothering a laugh behind a fake cough, Mitch glanced at Nanna, who winked.

His bad feelings about Julia's motives morphed into warmth of approval for Lila. She was so much more than he would have ever guessed she was.

Still, being with Julia might bring out the best in Lila, but hugging Julia had not brought out the best in him. It had reminded him of what a bad boyfriend he was, right after Lila had told him he was a demanding boss. But he also suddenly saw what had been right in front of him all along. He didn't have a choice. Though everyone in his family worked, it seemed no one but him knew how to make money. And they needed money. Lots and lots of money to keep up the lifestyle to which they'd become accustomed.

That meant no getting involved with Lila. If he wanted to keep her as an employee—wanted to help her if she was pregnant—he couldn't hurt her. If they took this charade into reality, she'd figure out she came second, and she wouldn't stay on as his assistant. Then he wouldn't be able to help her.

No matter how sassy and strong and really, really fun she was, he had to keep their relationship strictly professional.

Looking at her in the sexy yellow dress, with her sleek hair and her bright smile, he held back a groan. When it came to pretty girls, he was not known for his self-control. Plus, he still had to play the part of loving fiancé—hold her hand, kiss her.

This was not going to be easy.

CHAPTER SEVEN

LILA NOTICED THE minute Mitch changed. When he'd hugged Julia, the expression on his face had flattened, as if he'd thought of something terrible. He didn't say anything, but he didn't have to. She could read him very well and she had a bad feeling about this. He was finally noticing her—Real Lila—and they were communicating with her being her. Then he'd hugged Julia and gone quiet. He'd shut down. He'd even let Julia sweep her away from him.

He might be attempting to be a good best man, a good Ochoa, who gladly accepted Julia into their clan and didn't mind her spiriting Lila away. But maybe when he'd hugged Julia he'd remembered how much he'd loved her—

No. He'd said a million times that he was over her. She'd seen him happy. He did not still love Julia.

Then what had caused that horrible expression to come to his face?

Julia walked Lila across the gorgeous yard of her family's home. The stunning view of the mountain backdrop was enhanced by rows and rows of grapes. A warm sun beat down. Smooth, sweet air enveloped them.

As they headed toward a grove of trees, Julia said,

"So how did you meet Mitcham… Oh, wait, that's right. You're his assistant."

Lila smiled, wishing they'd get to the people Julia wanted her to meet so she could go back to Mitch and figure out what was going on with him. "Yes. We work together."

"Long nights together caused you to talk?"

That certainly wasn't a lie. Though they'd been discussing work, they'd still talked. "Yes."

Julia stopped walking and pressed her fingers onto Lila's forearm. "Come on," she cajoled. "No one's really heard details, and I for one am curious."

She supposed she should have expected this. The former girlfriend wanted the scoop. She'd seen the way Julia gazed at Alonzo. She didn't have feelings for Mitch. She was just snooping for some juicy gossip.

"Don't be curious," she said with a laugh. "We're sort of boring."

When Julia smiled triumphantly, Lila's heart thumped. That wasn't the expression of a woman looking for gossip. It was the victorious glow of someone who'd caught her in a lie. As a woman who'd dated Mitch, Julia would know time spent with him would never be boring. Lila's flip answer had just taken the first step to ruining the charade.

Thinking quickly, she added, "If going to restaurant openings, clubs and New York's wonderful theaters are to be considered boring."

Julia frowned. "Oh. So you were…teasing me?"

Relief skittered through Lila. She took a second to compose herself before she said, "Not teasing. Making a joke. Of course our courtship is exciting. We live in the most wonderful city in the world." Even though she knew she was digging her and Mitch into a pit, one she'd have to explain to him so he could confirm everything she said, she realized it was necessary. If Julia was poking around to find something wrong in Mitch's engagement, they would have to step up their game.

Julia took her arm again and led her in the direction of a gaggle of women clustered by the trees. She introduced them as her bridesmaids. Lila happily said hello, accepted congratulations on her engagement and then excused herself.

Because there was no reason for Lila to meet the bridesmaids, it was abundantly clear Julia had used that excuse to get a private minute with her. She was definitely looking for a crack in their relationship. She had to talk to Mitch. Now.

But the conversation at Nanna's table was bright and lively as most of the party guests came over to greet Nanna. There was never an opening for her to ask Mitch to walk around the grounds with her so she could tell him about Julia. When Julia's parents offered a congratulatory toast for Julia and Alonzo, Lila tried leaning into Mitch to make it look like she was love struck, in case Julia was watching, but it was as if he didn't notice. He didn't put his arm around her, pull her close or even talk to her. Later, when Alonzo and Julia came over to chat with the people at the table next to Nanna's, Lila tried holding Mitch's hand, but he slid it away to use it to make a point.

And she clearly saw what Julia saw. Two people who really weren't in love. She had no idea why Julia thought she had to expose them, but if they didn't fix this, Lila had no doubt that she would.

It was almost the end of the evening before she could lure Mitch away from the table. She deliberately led him to an empty spot under two huge shade trees. Glancing around to make sure there was no one near enough to overhear, she whispered, "Julia is onto us."

He laughed. "Are you kidding? You've been handling her beautifully. I think we're fine."

"We are not fine," Lila began. The last thing she expected was that he wouldn't believe her. How could she explain that he never looked at her with love in his eyes? Or touched her automatically? Or, worse, that he'd pulled his hand out of hers when she tried to make the charade look realistic?

The only thing she could think to say was, "It wasn't merely what she said. It was the way she used a weird excuse to get me alone, as if she was angling for a chance to find something wrong."

"Did you ever stop to think that that's because she doesn't like you?"

Lila gaped at him. "If that's true, then you're making my point. She's watching us. We need to make this engagement more believable."

Mitch awkwardly stepped closer. "Okay."

Lila's heart jumped to her throat. His awkwardness made things worse.

But her nervousness about being so near didn't help either. Cuddling up to each other was exactly what they needed to do—look like two people in love, stealing a private moment. Except after this past twenty-four hours of ditching her persona and being only Real Lila, it wasn't quite so easy to be Lila, Fake Fiancée. Especially not when she wanted this to be her moment, her chance to get him to like *her*. But he was awkward. As if he'd forgotten he'd kissed her—for real—the night before.

She resisted the urge to shake her head. He could not have forgotten that kiss. The man was interested.

She gingerly put her hands on his lapels. Regardless of what Julia said, Lila loved this man. And he had begun to more than notice her. There were a million reasons he could be nervous now. A million reasons he could have gotten a weird expression on his face when he hugged Julia. Including the fact that he might not like her. The woman *had* betrayed him.

"If we were really engaged, you'd probably look more comfortable doing that."

She wasn't surprised it was easier to touch him when she knew it wasn't real. Fake Lila could do any darned thing she wanted with no consequence. Real Lila knew how much was riding on this. She *wanted* to flatten her hands on his chest. To run them up to his collar so she could ease her fingers through the hair at his nape. Then she could easily pull his head down for a kiss.

That's what she'd do if they were really engaged. That's what she'd wanted to do since the day she'd met him.

That's what she would do now.

She eased her palms along the smooth material of his jacket, enjoying the decadent richness of the fabric, but it still didn't feel right. And she finally understood why. She was trying to take this relationship into reality because she could see he was getting feelings for her— but he didn't know her. She'd already realized that until she told him the truth about her life, her childhood, he couldn't really fall in love with *her*. She didn't know why she was trying to seduce him now, without telling him.

She sucked in a breath, pulling her hands away. "There is something important I should tell you about me."

His face changed. The fun-loving expression left and was replaced by a look that somehow combined seriousness and expectancy. He put his hands on her shoulders supportively. "I think I know what it is."

That was the last thing she expected him to say. It confused her so much she said, "You do?"

He stiffened. "Yes. You're pregnant."

She had no idea there were levels of shock, but her head jangled with something so incomprehensible she might have created a new one.

"What? No! I'm not pregnant!" All thoughts of her mother and the horrible childhood she'd brought on herself fled. She swatted his upper arm. "What's wrong with you? Why the hell would you think that?"

"When you said you didn't drink, Nanna sort of jumped to conclusions."

She gaped at him. "Nanna thought I was *pregnant* because I don't drink?"

"Well, that and because she said you had a certain glow."

If she had "a certain glow" it was because she was thrilled to be at his home, *with him*, just plain spending time with him.

She pulled her hands away from his and dropped her head into her palms. "Does your whole family think that?"

"No. Just Nanna."

She glanced up sharply. "And you?"

He shook his head. "I didn't know what to think."

"But you weren't sure?"

"Well, you never tell me anything."

And now she knew why. Real Lila absolutely, positively didn't fit into his world. She was awkward and simple. She wouldn't in a million years have thought his family would assume she was pregnant because she didn't drink. She wasn't a sophisticated thinker. She'd been foolish to even consider she belonged here. She had no place with these people.

And she was done embarrassing herself. She most certainly wouldn't tell him the truth about her life now. From here on out, she would only be Fake Lila.

Spotting Riccardo walking toward them, Lila nudged her head to the right so Mitch would look over and see him.

As he got closer, Mitch said, "Hey, what's up?"

Riccardo didn't reply until he was almost on top of them, then he lowered his voice. "I had a conversation with Julia tonight. I'm pretty sure she's onto you."

Glad to be thinking of anything other than how Mitch's family thought she was pregnant, she shifted back into her role as his coconspirator. "I told you."

"*Sì*. You did." He caught her gaze, his eyes filled with remorse, but he turned to face Riccardo. "So what do we do?"

"You're going to have to start looking a little more like two people who want to get married."

Mitch's gaze crawled back to hers. She swore he was silently seeking forgiveness for thinking she was pregnant. But she was the one who was sorry. If she hadn't wanted a real shot with him and hadn't considered telling him the truth about herself, none of this awkwardness would have happened.

Including the fact that Julia wouldn't be onto them. Fake Lila was a much better fiancée choice for Mitch than Real Lila.

Riccardo said, "If it somehow gets out that your engagement is fake, this charade won't have saved your butt. It will have made matters worse."

Mitch sighed. "No kidding. Lila and I need to go back to the apartment and regroup. Luckily, the show's over for tonight." He glanced around. "Half the guests have gone home." He held out his hand to her. "Come on. Let's say good-night to our hosts, get the limo and go."

She took his hand, brightened her smile, leaned into his arm.

Fake Lila was alive and well and ready to take over. And Real Lila wasn't coming out again—at all—unless she was alone in her bedroom. Because of trying to be herself, she'd almost ruined this whole damned charade.

They found Julia and Alonzo. Alonzo kissed Lila's cheek, while Mitch kissed Julia's cheek.

"Thank you for coming."

Lila smiled fondly at Julia. "Thank you for having us. It was a lovely party. Your parents have a beautiful home." Then she gazed lovingly at Mitch, snuggled into his arm. "I'm ready to go when you are."

Mitch shook Alonzo's hand. He said, "We'll see you tomorrow," and they walked around to the front of the house to the limo.

The moon had risen to a glorious height and cast a heavenly glow on everything. Even the grapevines gleamed surreally, and Lila realized it was all so perfect, so beautiful that she should have immediately recognized she didn't belong in this place with this family. From here on out, every time she looked at the perfection around her, every time she slid into a limo, or put on clothes she couldn't afford in her real life, it would fortify her resolve to stay in character and protect herself.

CHAPTER EIGHT

MITCH HELPED HER into the back seat of the limo, then climbed in behind her. She'd thrown him for a loop when she'd said she had to tell him something about herself. It was clearly so difficult for her that he'd tried to save her some agony and incorrectly guessed she was pregnant. But that didn't mean the conversation was over. He needed to know her problem, her secret, so he could figure out how to keep her in his employ and how he could help her. Now that he had his head on straight about not getting involved with her, it would be much easier.

"Let's go back to talking about what we were talking about before Riccardo came over."

She smoothed the skirt of her pretty yellow dress. "It's not important."

"Really? Because the very serious look on your face told me that it was. Plus, you said it was something you had to tell me."

She laughed and batted a hand. Her fake fiancée persona fully in place, she casually said, "I was just going to say I should tell you a couple of stories about my roommates that would help us to continue to be more familiar with each other so there'll be no more slipups."

His heart twisted a bit. He'd embarrassed her so much

by asking if she was pregnant that she wasn't going to tell him. No matter how much he pushed. In fact, pushing might be the worst thing to do. Which meant the best thing to do would be to back off until he found another time to bring it up. Maybe after a day or two she'd get comfortable with him again and be able to open up.

Tabling the conversation for the moment, he relaxed on the limo seat. "Okay. Have at it."

She started with a story about one of her roommates illegally keeping a cat in her room that made him laugh. Then she moved on to a story about pooling their money once a week to get one order of Chinese takeout that they split, and he felt like an idiot.

"Why didn't you ever tell me that you needed more money?"

"Because I checked around. My salary is average for what I do for you. If I want more money, I need to be doing more important things. Things I know how to do. But you don't need."

He thought about that. "Is that why you want another job? To get to do those more important tasks?"

"Yes." She glanced down at her dress again.

That was something she did when what she said was difficult for her—or when she was telling him only half the truth. His heart softened again. "You want your job to be challenging?"

She peered over at him. "Who doesn't?"

There was more. He knew there was more, but he could also see she wasn't going to spill it. If he really wanted to help her, he had to work with what he had. "Riccardo and I could probably create a new job for you. Something that wouldn't just be more challenging, it would also pay enough that you could get your own apartment."

She shook her head. "If you'd created a new job on your own because you needed someone, that would have been great. Doing it now, it would feel like charity."

Frustration rose in him and he sat up. "You want a more challenging job that could pay more. Riccardo and I could probably make one for you, but you won't take it because it would be charity?"

"Wouldn't it?"

"No! It would be more or less like you making us aware of a need and us filling it."

"The need is mine. Otherwise you would have already created the job."

"Your circular logic is going to explode my brain one of these days."

She laughed. "Aren't you glad we never talked before this?"

"No. I'm thinking that if we'd talked before this I'd have been more ready."

"You have to take the heat for that one."

That made his eyes narrow. "Why me? Why not you? Why couldn't you have come into the office and said, 'Hey, Mitch, how was your weekend?'"

"I did."

That surprised him. "You did?"

"Every Monday morning for a year. You'd always answer 'fine' without looking up from whatever you were reading."

"Yeah, well, every Monday morning, we also get weekend sales reports. So I was preoccupied."

"So you take the blame."

He put his fingers on his temples to stop the throbbing that had begun there. Luckily, the lane for Ochoa Vineyards came into view.

They got out of the limo, stepping onto the grounds for his family home where anyone could be milling about, meaning the conversation was over until they got behind the closed doors of his apartment. They climbed the steps. He unlocked the door and they walked into the sitting room.

He stopped.

He'd kissed her here the night before. She'd told him that she wanted to think things through, that she wasn't ready, and tonight she'd probably been about to tell him why and he'd blown it by asking her if she was pregnant.

She headed directly to her room, but she paused. Facing him, she politely said, "Good night."

But she didn't wait for him to return her good-night. She all but raced to the open door and scurried to get herself behind it.

Shrugging out of his jacket, he strode toward his bedroom. The weirdest sensation enveloped him. Something like a pounding need. She'd been two seconds away from telling him something very serious and very important, and trying to help her, he'd rushed in, making a guess that was wrong. His usual arrogance had cost him a chance, but by God he was not letting this drop. No matter what hoop he had to jump through, she would tell him.

"How were your meetings today?"

Lila stepped out of her bedroom talking. Because of more Ochoa Wines business, she hadn't seen Mitch all day and had enjoyed an afternoon by the pool with Nanna, who was incredibly apologetic for thinking Lila was pregnant.

Mitch's grandmother was also hosting a private family dinner that night. Careful now that Julia was clearly watching them, Lila had once again asked Nanna what she should wear, and Nanna had suggested a flirty floral skirt and white tank top because the evening was supposed to be casual. Family being family. Not socializing.

Resigned to going back to being Fake Lila and fairly pleased with the way she looked in the happy skirt, she smiled at Mitch. "I almost felt guilty sitting by the pool for hours knowing you were working."

He walked to the apartment door. "Don't. It's good for you to keep Nanna company. Besides, I love my job."

Something about the way he said that struck her oddly. He opened the door for her and she stepped out into the small hallway.

"I know you love your job."

He motioned for her to go down the stairs. "I *created* my job. I searched around, looking for something I loved, something that made me as much money as I wanted, and I didn't stop until I found it."

Walking down the steps, she frowned. She hadn't missed the way he'd emphasized the word *created*. Obviously, he wasn't going to drop last night's conversation, but that didn't mean she had to take the bait. "Well, you did great figuring it all out."

At the bottom of the steps, he stopped her before she reached the door. "*Sí.* I did. And I don't ever pretend that I'm not proud of myself."

Still not taking the bait. "You should be."

"So last night I also realized that that thing you almost told me yesterday—when I stupidly asked you if you were pregnant—is probably part of the reason you won't let me create a job for you."

Wow. He might be a little slower than Nanna, but he was pretty damned perceptive too. Still, she'd hit this wall the night before. She was not in the same league as these people. No matter how much she liked Mitch, she wasn't the right girl for him. Pretending she was or might be or could be would only make a fool of her. So no matter how much he pushed or hinted, she would keep her secrets to herself.

"Seriously, it was nothing. And it's not related to our pretending to be engaged."

He studied her for an agonizing twenty seconds. Twenty seconds that had never felt so long. She knew he didn't give up on anything, but maybe he hadn't ever been in a tug-of-war with a person who'd basically been taking care of herself since she was four. Because there was no way in hell she was telling him about her past. After the mistake she made with her mom, she could keep a secret, hold her tongue, pretend everything was fine better than anyone. Particularly after how he'd reacted last night. Raised in a mansion with tons of money and even more love, Mitch had no idea how her side of the world ran.

When she'd had her raging crush on him, she'd always envisioned that when she told him about her past, he would be sympathetic. She'd pictured him telling her she was brave for wanting to find her mom and make up for the blunder she'd made at ten. But when she'd thought it through the night before—ensconced in the bedroom that spoke of the wealth of his world, the privilege, the love that he and his family took for granted—she suddenly realized he wouldn't see it that way. What would a man who adored his parents think if he knew she was the one who'd called Child Services on her mom? She'd been a little girl, a cold, hungry little girl. Her only food was the free lunch she got at school on weekdays. She'd spent most of her first ten years alone and scared.

So she'd forgiven herself for taking the step she naively thought would solve her problems. But what would Mitch think? For her to have been taken away from her mom, he had to know her childhood hadn't been good. But he didn't know the extent of it. How could a guy who'd grown up with such perfection understand such poverty? Such pain? Not just her own but her mom's?

He wouldn't.

So she wouldn't tell him.

"You're sure it's nothing? Because we still have an entire week of this charade. You and Riccardo both think Julia's onto us. We can't afford to have any slipups."

She nodded. "I'm perfectly capable of keeping up the charade until we go back to New York."

He said, "Good," and the expression in his eyes said he believed her, but he continued to search her gaze.

She stared into his dark, dark eyes, holding her ground, almost daring him to push for more, knowing he didn't have another angle into the conversation about her job or her secret, and she'd satisfactorily handled the one in he'd had.

Finally, he looked away. He caught her hand and turned toward the door, but he stopped again. "If this thing falls apart, it's going to be more than embarrassing. It will look like I had something to hide or a reason to go to the extreme of pretending to be engaged."

"You did. You were trying to keep the focus of this wedding on your brother."

"True."

"But we're not going to fail."

He opened the door and she stepped out into the soothing evening sun.

They were quiet for a few seconds, then he casually said, "You're so sure of yourself."

She laughed. Sure of herself was the last term she'd use. What she was was protective.

"No. I'm sure of you. You don't lose, Mitcham Ochoa. I've been watching you win for an entire year. If I have confidence, it's in you."

He sniffed a laugh. "Right."

"It is right. You're a winner. You're one of those people who just has to crook his little finger and things fall into place."

He frowned. "That's how you see me?"

"Isn't that the way your life is?"

"I lost my girlfriend to my brother. That same brother will inherit the top position for the vineyard. I looked around when I was twenty-four and realized I would be a footnote in Alonzo's tenure as vintner for Ochoa Wines if I didn't figure something out."

She shrugged. "And you did."

He sighed. "Sí. I did."

"I would think you would be a little more proud of that."

"I am proud. Very proud." He sucked in a breath. "Ochoa Online pulled the vineyard out of the jaws of bankruptcy."

They were only a few feet away from the main house, so she almost stopped walking. But the grounds were unusually quiet, and she suspected that's why Mitch spoke openly. So she did too.

"I thought Ochoa Vineyards was very successful?"

"It was, but we weren't selling enough wine to keep

three families. My dad couldn't see the potential of e-commerce, but I wanted a shot at selling wine online and when I got it, I made it work."

"See. There you go. Back to being a winner."

"In everyone's eyes but my family's."

She frowned at him, totally confused, and he laughed. "I don't want to sound like I need credit for what I did. I just want you to see that sometimes success is in the eyes of the beholder. You look at me as if you think I was born under a lucky star, and in some ways, I was. But my life is far from perfect and a person doesn't just fall into the category of winner. Most of us work for it."

She knew all that, of course. When she compared her life to his, he did look like a guy who had it fairly easy. But she lived the truth. She was with him every day at his office. "I know how hard you work. I'm sorry."

"It's okay. Truth be told, I liked saving my family."

She laughed. "You're such a guy."

He chuckled and shifted his grip on her hand. "I know. There's a lot of male pride in a Spanish family."

"No kidding."

"So you can see why I didn't want my dad connecting Julia dumping me to the work I did with Ochoa Online. I virtually saved my family. I found a position of authority for me and Riccardo in a situation where we might not have had one. I don't want people saying I only did that because Julia dumped me, when exactly the opposite is true. Julia dumped me because I was too busy for her. And what I was busy doing was figuring out how to sell more wine so that we could all continue to live like kings."

"You think she dumped you because you were too busy?"

He sighed. "If you look at this from her vantage point, I wasn't a good boyfriend. I wasn't around. I was always traveling, searching for new ways to sell wines because my dad wouldn't give me permission to build a web-site. In her eyes, she shifted to a man who paid atten-tion to her."

"Wow."

"For a good five years, I had known the family was headed for trouble financially. But it wasn't until she dumped me that I got permission to do the one thing that would save us."

"And this," she said, waving her engagement ring at him, "is sort of your way of distancing yourself from Julia so your family doesn't feel sorry for you. They see what you did?"

He shrugged. "I really do want Alonzo and Julia's wedding to be theirs. But I also wish my family could separate our breakup and the creation of Ochoa Online."

"So let's get in there and make them believe we're the happiest couple on the face of the earth."

He laughed and opened the door to the vineyard's main house. They hurried up the stairs and back down the hall to Nanna's quarters.

As they stepped into the living room where everyone was enjoying a cocktail, Lila watched Julia's expression shift and confirmed—again—that Julia was suspicious.

But for once, she didn't care. Not only was Julia a jit-tery bride, looking for trouble, but also the two-minute conversation they'd had walking to the house had infused her with new energy for the ruse.

It had also given her the weirdest feeling about Mitch. She'd only seen his successes—and, yes, there were many. But she never considered that his family expected this of him and that it would bother him that they didn't seem to appreciate the wonderful things he had done.

Dressed in simple pink trousers and a white top, Marguerite walked over. She handed Mitch a glass of wine and Lila a glass of club soda before she kissed both of their cheeks. "I'm glad Nanna wanted dinner to be informal. It's good to relax after a day of meetings."

Mitch laughed. "Except some people sat by the pool while we worked."

"Yes, we did," Nanna chimed in, totally unapologetic. Wearing white capris and a navy-blue-and-white-striped T-shirt, she looked casual and comfortable, like a woman about to go out for a sail.

Mitch directed Lila to the gray sofa and as she sat, Mitch's father, Santiago, said, "So, Lila, you and I have barely said two words to each other. Are you enjoying your stay here?"

Surprised to have Mitch's father pay attention to her, she said, "I'm enjoying my stay very much. Your vineyard is beautiful. And Nanna's pretty good company."

Everybody laughed.

Julia said, "She's just glad to have someone to hang out with."

Nanna shook her head. "No. I *choose* to be alone sometimes." She reached out and squeezed Lila's hand. "I only give up my privacy for special people."

Her eyes shining, Marguerite said, "We could start talking about your wedding while you're here."

Knowing this was exactly the opposite of what Mitch wanted, she said, "We just got engaged. I haven't really thought much about it. Besides, this is Julia and Alonzo's special time."

Julia shrugged. "I have no problem talking about your wedding. In fact, I'm curious."

Of course she was. This was one of those moments Lila had to make sure everything between her and Mitch looked real.

Lila glanced at Mitch, who smiled as if to say, "Go ahead. Say what you want."

She faced Marguerite again. "I think having the wedding here would be wonderful."

Santiago grinned. "Really?"

Marguerite clapped her hands together. "I was so afraid you'd say you want to be married in the States."

"No. It's beautiful here. Perfect."

Mitch said, "Yes, it's perfect here." He took Lila's hand and kissed the knuckles. The intimacy of his lips touching her skin filled her with warmth. Mostly because, like the kiss in the kitchen, it felt real. Tonight he'd shared something with her that his assistant Lila never in a million years would have gotten the chance to know. Her heart expanded almost to overflowing. It was the first time he'd ever been so honest, so normal with her. If nothing else, they were becoming friends.

So… Yeah. The touch of his lips on her skin felt different.

Genuine.

Then he shifted the discussion in the direction of tuxes and Alonzo's bachelor party. And she watched him as he talked. It was clear he loved his family and she could understand his pride at saving Ochoa Vineyards. She glanced at Julia, thought of her not as annoying but the first woman who had loved Mitch. She studied his mom, his dad, Nanna and even Riccardo and his parents and realized it probably wasn't easy to keep ten people happy.

Yet Mitch did it. Every darned day. Day in and day out. And he did it without any credit. His brother ran the vineyard. His dad ran the business. And Mitch was the one who actually made them money by selling the wines. Mitch would always be second to his brother—who was second to their dad.

Of all the people in this room, Mitch was probably the smartest, and craftiest, yet you'd never know it from how he behaved. He deferred to his dad, loved his brother, doted on his nanna and his mom.

And somehow it made him all the sexier.

The staff announced dinner. Mitch's dad waited for her as they all walked into the dining room. Taking her hand, Santiago slid it onto his forearm as he escorted her to the table. "So you like it here? You like Spain?"

Temporarily shelving her thoughts about Mitch, Lila smiled at him. "I love it here."

He walked her to her seat and pulled out her chair. In her peripheral vision she saw Mitch scramble to get his mom's chair. She also saw his eyes narrow as his dad said, "We have incredible weather year-round."

Marguerite said, "The best."

Mitch walked to the seat beside Lila. "We'll have to visit later in the year so Lila can see for herself."

"That would be wonderful," Santiago said. Facing Lila, he added, "And you can bring your family."

"Oh." She glanced at Mitch, then at Riccardo, whose eyebrows were raised the whole way to his hairline. She wasn't sure if his panicked expression meant he'd told somebody she'd grown up in foster care, or if his panicked expression meant he hadn't. But that was the problem. If she said, "Sure, that'll be great. I'm sure my family would love to meet you all," somebody at this table could say, "I thought you were a foster kid."

Actually, Nanna could say that. The first day she was here she'd told Nanna she'd been raised in foster homes.

She had to stick with the truth.

She glanced back at Santiago. "I'm sorry. I just assumed Mitch would have told you that I was raised in foster care."

Marguerite said, "Oh, no! You have no family? No one to invite to the wedding?"

A quick glance around the table showed eight very sad faces. Except for Nanna, who gave her a smile of encouragement.

"It wasn't as bad as everybody thinks it is." She peeked up at Mitch, who studied her intently, as if hoping she'd finally fill in some of the blanks for him. Her heart somersaulted in her chest. After the way he'd been so honest with her on the walk over, she almost felt she could. Or maybe she *should*. But this wasn't the time or place. "Plus, I have a lot of friends."

Obviously eager to get beyond his faux pas, Santiago boisterously said, "That's wonderful! You can invite them all. You and Mitch will have a big, happy wedding."

Lila said, "That'd be great," satisfied that she'd smoothed over that potential bad spot. But a tiny bit of guilt suddenly pinched her chest. She wanted to tell Mitch the truth about her life. So why hadn't she corrected the Ochoas when they assumed she had no family? She might not have brothers and sisters or a dad, but her mom was still alive. It would have been an easy way to open the door to have the discussion about her past when they returned to the apartment.

So why hadn't she?

She shook her head to clear it.

It didn't matter. This was a ruse. Not real.

If she were getting married for real she would want her mom there. She would move heaven and earth to find her. There was no reason for her to feel as if she'd somehow disrespected her mom by not mentioning her.

But she still felt guilty. Wrong.

She'd dealt her mother the ultimate insult when she'd called Child Services and gotten herself placed in foster care. Now she was pretending she didn't exist—

Before she could finish that thought, another, stronger truth ruffled through her, like the first blast of wind from an oncoming storm.

The two times she'd finagled enough money to locate her mom, her mom had taken off. Disappeared as if she'd never existed.

What if she didn't want to be found?

What if she didn't want Lila in her life?

What if that was the real fear Lila had always had but couldn't admit because it was just too horrible to contemplate?

And what if that was why she'd created the big fairy-tale crush around Mitch as soon as she'd started working for him? The past year, she'd been quietly content, thinking she was staying with Mitch, hoping he'd pay attention to her. Her crush had kept her from looking for a job that paid more, so she'd have money to search for her mom, but most of all it had kept her from admitting the brutal truth...

That her mom didn't want her.

CHAPTER NINE

MITCH GLANCED OVER at Lila. Her face had gone white. She didn't look like she was even breathing. Talk of her foster care experience had all but paralyzed her.

They made it through dinner because the conversation shifted away from them and over to Julia, but the walk back to his apartment was made in complete silence. A slow ache built in his chest. He knew if she'd just talk about this, he could somehow make it better. He always could.

In the apartment entryway, he said, "I told you my biggest secret on the way over. And you repay me with silence?"

She started up the stairs. "Your dad suggesting I invite my family sort of threw me for a loop."

He followed her. When she didn't elaborate, he said, "I thought we'd made a connection. You know—"

She reached the apartment door and waited for him to catch up with her.

Pulling out his key, he added, "I'd tell you something about me. You'd tell me something about you."

"Is that why you told me about the bankruptcy? And you saving them? So I'd talk?"

He opened the door. "No. I did that so you would un-

derstand the importance of our mission being successful. I might not be the one who gets credit for being the
leader but I am the leader in this family. I'm the one
making the money that holds us together. I cannot be
perceived as weak."

She turned to him with one of her fake smiles. "I get
it. I do. And we will be successful." Without waiting for
his reply, she headed for her bedroom.

She didn't say good-night.

Every other night, no matter how confused or angry,
she'd always said good-night.

The strangest urge to follow her raced through him.
He wanted to grab her arm and stop her from walking
away. Not because he was angry that she wouldn't talk.
But because it broke his heart that there was something
that made her unbearably sad. He wanted to tell her that
whatever was wrong, he would fix it. It was what he did.
His brother loved his girlfriend; he stepped aside. Ochoa
Vineyards was in trouble; he created Ochoa Online. *He
fixed things.*

But he couldn't fix whatever was wrong in Lila's life
if she didn't tell him.

The next morning, she came out of her room dressed in
jeans and a shirt. As she walked to the kitchen table, she
said, "Nanna called. She said you guys have some sort
of vintners meeting?"

Her comments were offhand, almost light, but when
he looked into her kitten-gray eyes he saw the sadness
she couldn't quite cover up.

"Yes. My dad hopes to drum up a little more business for the website that sells wines for other vineyards.
He's invited them here so he can tell them about Ochoa

Online and see if we can get their wines on the multi-producer site."

Her head tilted. "But that's your company. Ochoa Vineyards is a client of Ochoa Online. *You* own Ochoa Online."

"My dad still sees it all being under the same umbrella. Besides, he's helping me." He rose from his seat. She looked tired and worn, as if she hadn't slept the night before. "Can I get you some coffee?"

She waved him off. "I'll get it."

He lowered himself to his chair, feeling weird again. She'd been perfectly fine. Feisty even. Until his dad mentioned her family the night before, and she'd had to admit she'd been in foster care. Now her face was drawn. Her usually warm gray eyes had dimmed.

He couldn't stand to see her this way. But he also didn't know what it was about being a foster child that tore her up. He knew the basics of her life. To be a foster child, she didn't have any family who could raise her. But she'd been dealing with this her entire life. Why did admitting it to his family make her so sad?

She poured a mug of coffee and walked to the table with the tray of bagels and pastries the chef had sent up.

Pulling out a chair, she said, "So your dad likes being involved in *your* companies too?"

"My dad's a Spanish man. He's a family man. He believes he has the right to comment on, interfere with and downright run anything that belongs to anyone he loves."

She laughed. "That's funny."

He sat back in his seat, glad her mood seemed to be improving. "It's not so funny if you're the one running the business he's interfering in."

"He can't interfere a lot. I'm your assistant. I'm in

the office every time you are, and I've never seen him do anything."

"That's because nothing he's suggested has ever made it to our idea meetings. He makes phone calls. Suggests shifts. Gives ideas. And Riccardo and I listen, but don't take action on anything he says."

"Sounds like he's just being a good dad."

He shook his head. "Lila, I'm thirty. I don't want my daddy telling me what to do."

She laughed again and his heart lifted, but they'd sort of run out of conversation. Unless they were talking about the ruse or his family or Ochoa Online, she didn't really talk to him.

Something had made her sad. She wanted to leave his employ and he was powerless to help her. He had never had this feeling of helplessness before.

He rose from his seat. "I guess I'd better run."

She nodded. "Yes, Nanna will be around for me soon."

He stood by the table, not quite wanting to leave, too awkward to stay. The urge to press her for answers shimmered through him, but in over a week he hadn't been able to get her to talk to him. Last night she'd totally shut down. Maybe it was time to admit defeat?

"Enjoy your day."

She smiled slightly. "I will. Nanna's always fun."

"Spend money."

She laughed. "Oh, I'll do that too."

He finally turned and walked to the door, a strange thought weaving through his brain. Her laughter had been real, and he liked hearing her laugh, making her laugh, almost as much as he'd liked sharing a confidence with her.

He knew she'd had a hard life. Now he knew that

working for him hadn't been the joy he'd always thought it was. Being in Spain, with his family, was fun for her. So maybe instead of trying to get her to tell him her secrets, what he should be doing was making sure every step of this charade was fun for her.

Wednesday night, the second welcome ball began almost the same way the first had. Lila came out of her bedroom in a cobalt-blue satin gown, looking good enough to eat. Mitch adjusted the cuffs on his white shirt before sliding into his tuxedo jacket.

"You look amazing."

She smiled. "Thank you."

He motioned to the door and Lila preceded him out of the apartment and down the stairs.

They hadn't had a chance to have another private conversation since the one on Monday morning. Still, he'd accepted that she wasn't going to talk, and he had a new plan. Julia could be the crowned princess of the world that night, and hog up all the family attention to her heart's delight, because he was a man on a mission. He was going to make sure Lila enjoyed this evening.

They walked out into the warm night air and she looked up and sighed. "Oh, my gosh! Look at those stars."

He peeked at her. "You've seen stars before."

"Not like this. Not in the city."

He took her hand. The gesture had become as natural, as easy as breathing. "Don't you get out of the city much?"

"I've never been out of the city. I mean, except now. Being here is my first time away from New York."

That shocked him, then he wondered why. Her life was compact, filled with purpose. She had to work to support herself. Work was the key to everything for her. His life was filled with purpose, too, and he also believed work was the key to fulfilling his responsibilities. But he had releases, options that she didn't have. Tonight he would make up for that.

"Then I'm glad I'm with you when you see the stars."

She stopped walking. It looked as if she was going to say something, but she shook her head as if to clear it and started walking again. Disappointment rattled through him, but he was growing accustomed to that now.

When they stepped onto the sidewalk that led to the back entry to the main house and the corridor that would take them to the ballroom, she did the thing where she pressed herself up against his arm and disappointment turned to disgust.

At first when she'd cuddled against him, he'd realized she was trying to give people the impression they were close. Now that he was getting to know her and now that they'd held hands and even kissed for real once, it felt fake to him. Really fake. So fake he wondered if that wasn't the thing that made Julia suspicious about their relationship.

"What are you doing?"

She gazed up at him.

Confusion flickered through him. That adoring expression wasn't "her" either.

With other guests milling about the grounds, he couldn't say anything. But the looks of adoration she gave him as they wove through the crowded ballroom, saying hello, and through dinner only frustrated him. She'd been doing this all along and it had seemed perfect. But tonight it set his nerve endings on edge.

He didn't want to entertain *this* woman. He didn't want to dance with *this* woman.

He wanted to entertain Lila. His assistant. He wanted to make her laugh. He wanted to make her forget whatever problem she had. He wanted *her* to have some fun.

As dinner concluded and the lights on the dance floor dimmed and the lights on the stage lit, Lila struggled to keep her smile in place. For the past two days, she'd managed to avoid Nanna and stay away from Mitch, spending most of the time in bed.

The pain of admitting she'd secretly suspected her mom didn't want to be in her life pressed down on her. She'd tried to tell herself it wasn't true. That her mother wanted her. Then she asked herself why? Why would her mother want the child who'd turned her in to the authorities?

And she knew there was no reason.

Alonzo and Julia danced the first dance. Both sets of parents joined them for the second song. And Lila knew what was coming. When the music started for the third dance, Mitch rose, and she held out her hand to him, like a good fiancée.

His smile was warm, loving. "Shall we?"

She matched his sweet smile. Though Julia was far away, there were a hundred other guests to fool, and now more than ever she knew the importance of this ruse. Not only had Mitch saved his family but he wanted to be able to continue to do so. Even without credit. Like a strong Spanish man. In some ways, she thought his sentiment outdated. In other ways, she thought it very cool that he could let his brother have all the attention and his dad meddle to his heart's delight.

Her smile for him grew a notch. With everything she learned about Mitch, she liked him a little more. She wanted to help him. "I'd love to dance."

He walked her to the dance floor and pulled her into his arms. Lila smiled up at him adoringly, making sure the ruse was in place, and he paused.

"What do you say we forget about our engagement for one night?"

She hurriedly glanced around to make sure no one was listening. "You want to break up?"

He laughed. "No. I want to be us tonight."

Her brow furrowed. "Us?"

"You. Me. Real us. A few times we've let our guard down and had a lot of fun. I think I'd like to do that tonight."

She tried to answer but her tongue stuck to the roof of her mouth. He'd had fun with her? Not Fake Lila?

The slow dance finished, but the band immediately began playing another tune. A song she'd never heard.

He grinned. "Samba."

"Oh. Bad timing." Or good timing for the Lila who was on the dance floor totally confused. She understood him wanting to have a good time. If they did that, they'd look like a real couple, enjoying each other's company. But she wasn't in the mood to have real fun. She'd much rather pretend her way through this. "I don't know how to samba."

He caught her hand. "Don't worry. I do. Just follow me. We start with a box step, then when I push back, you step back. I'll twirl you a few times. Then we're back to the box step. Then when I let go of your hand, you just do what I do…turn one way then the other."

She gaped at him. "I once tried a Zumba class and had to quit because I have two left feet."

He laughed. "Come on. It will be fun."

As he pulled her into the typical hold, she noticed everybody was dancing, having fun, and no one was paying any attention to them. She relaxed a bit, especially through the box steps, which were easy.

Then he lifted his hands from her waist and he took both of her hands. He stepped back and she stepped back. He pulled her close again, then nudged her back again.

She laughed. She supposed it was fun. And a lot easier than Zumba since he was guiding her.

He pulled her into the typical dance hold. They did the box step again. Then he twirled her, and laughter bubbled up from a place so deep inside her, she didn't even know it existed.

All right. Samba was a lot of fun.

He twirled her a few more times, then he let go of her hand and he turned in a circle. She followed his lead.

When he pulled her back into the box step she was laughing. He smiled down at her. "Fun. Right?"

"Yes," she admitted reluctantly, worried she'd spend the whole night dancing if he thought he was entertaining her.

"So relax." He caught her hands again and did the step back, step forward, step back thing. He brought her into the hold for the box step, then he twirled her.

Though the dance floor was full of festive dancers, the rest of the world began to disappear.

She was just plain having fun until he pulled her into the box step hold again and said, "You know, you can swing your hips a bit."

She winced. "Swing my hips?"

"Fun, remember? You're in Spain. Let go a bit."

She'd never, ever, ever had anyone tell her to let go a bit, but why not? She was with people who would never see her again. With a boss who was about to find her a new job. No one would remember this.

She relaxed, glanced at the other female dancers, saw that the hip swaying ranged from his mother's conservative swing to Julia's unabashedly sensual sway, and she started off with a sway more like his mother's.

But then the music sort of took her. It wasn't an easy dance, but it was predictable and the notes flowed through her. Her sway shifted from hip movement to something that encompassed her whole body.

And it was really fun.

The music stopped and the band began to play a flamingo. He quickly explained the steps and they began dancing again.

When he pulled her in close, he looked into her eyes and said, "You're a natural."

She laughed. "I've never been a natural at anything."

"How many things have you tried?"

"Not many." Because she was always preoccupied with her mistakes, her failures, her longing for her mother to be in her life.

"So maybe it's good that you're here in Spain."

"Maybe."

"And maybe it's good we let go again, *si*?"

She smiled. *"Si."*

This time he laughed. "I will make a Spanish dancer out of you yet."

She pulled out of his hold, raised one hand and danced away from him. "Or maybe I'm such a natural at this that I'll make you look good in front of your friends."

"You've already managed to make me look like a smarter man to Nanna."

"That was easy."

"She likes you."

"I like her."

Suddenly the world felt as if it opened up to her. Without the burden of finding her mother or an unrequited crush on Mitch pressing down on her, she was just herself. Not Real Lila or Fake Lila, just Lila.

They danced until the band took a break, then they walked to the open bar. She watched the bartender pour wine into a beautiful etched glass flute.

"Wine is actually very pretty."

"Agreed. It's why there are lots of pictures on our website."

She smiled at him. The bartender walked over and he ordered a glass of club soda for her and a beer for himself.

They strolled around talking to a few family friends, and though Lila didn't cling to him or hang on to him, she had the sudden impression they were actually more believable than they ever had been as a couple.

The music began again and they danced to everything the band threw at them. At the end of the set, the music slowed and Mitch pulled her into his arms. She couldn't stop the urge to melt against him and close her eyes.

She'd always wondered what life would feel like when she could stop worrying about having her mom in her life. She'd just always thought she'd stop wondering because she would have found her mom and made peace. She'd never once considered the other side of the coin—that she should give up.

But dancing with Mitch, so close they couldn't get a strand of yarn between them, she was very aware of everything she'd given up all the years she'd searched for her mom. She had absolutely no idea what she would do when she got home—how things would change. But being done with her quest suddenly felt right.

When the song was over, he pulled back, studying her face. "You look tired."

"The last three days have been a little trying."

"Let's get something to drink, then walk back to the apartment."

"But the party's not over."

He shrugged. "We're also not the guests of honor or the hosts. Alonzo and Julia are having a blast. My parents love entertaining." He searched her eyes. "And you're tired."

Tears welled in her eyes. Oh, she was tired. So, so tired.

He took her hand. "Come on." They walked to the bar where he ordered a club soda for her. Then he paused before saying, "You know what? I'll have club soda too."

"You don't have to do that."

His head tilted as he looked at her. "What if I want to?"

"You own a winery. If you're not going to have a beer you should have a glass of wine."

"Unless I want water?"

She laughed. "Now what are you up to?"

"Being with you." He turned when the bartender arrived and took the two club sodas.

The strangest feeling bubbled up in her. He was sharing her experience. Maybe considering what she felt drinking club soda while everyone else drank wine? It was the oddest way anybody had ever connected with her, yet that's what she felt—that they were connecting.

They drank their club soda listening to another samba.

When they were done, he set the glasses on the bar, took her hand and led her outside.

But as soon as they were out of the crowd, on the sidewalk, he let go of her hand, loosened his bow tie and sighed. "That feels better."

Nerves flitted through her. "You're really into being yourself tonight."

He chuckled. "Yeah. I am."

"Well, in that case." She stopped and slipped out of the four-inch-heel sandals. When her feet met cool cobblestone, she sighed. "Now *that* feels better."

"So, you are liking being yourself?"

"A hundred percent."

He took the sandals from her, hooking them over the index finger of his left hand. She expected him to catch her hand, if only to keep up the charade. Instead, he strolled along beside her.

Butterflies filled her. For all the times he'd hugged her, kissed her cheek, put his arm across her shoulders, danced with her, held her hand, *this*—not touching her— seemed a hundred times more romantic.

Because he was with her. Not Fake Lila. Not his pretend fiancée. But *her*.

They reached the duplex and he opened the door, but before she stepped inside, he scooped her up. "I'm not letting you walk on that floor, those steps, without shoes."

Held against his chest, with their faces a few inches apart, she tried to think of something to say but nothing came. The feeling of being held against his chest— of being held, being cared for—shot attraction through her. He was so handsome. So smart. So wonderful. And he was growing to like her.

His eyes narrowed. "What? You think I can't make it up the stairs carrying you?"

She was so busy buzzing with attraction that it had never occurred to her that she might be too heavy to carry up a flight of stairs. Before she could say anything, he laughed and started to run up the steps.

"I don't have a gym membership for nothing." He nodded at the door. "Reach into my jacket pocket and get the keys."

Still a little shell-shocked, she found the keys.

"It's the one with the green tab."

She inserted it into the lock, twisted, and the doorknob turned. With a light shove the door opened.

Inside the apartment, he caught her gaze and whispered, "Maybe it's not a good idea for you to walk across this carpet without shoes."

"We both did it the other night."

He said, "I don't remember."

She knew that he did. That was her first night as Real Lila with him. That was the night she was just about certain he wanted to lure her into his bedroom.

Her heart thumped in her chest. She could demand that he set her down. But right at this moment, with everything in her life gone—every hope, every wish, every dream—she just didn't want to be alone anymore.

He dipped his head and brushed his lips across hers. She tightened her hands around his neck, shifting in his arms, getting closer.

His mouth lifted, then smoothed across hers again before his tongue darted out and she opened for him. Their tongues danced and entwined. Her heart rate slowed to a crawl. Everything about the world slimmed down to him and her. And the fact that this was real.

Actually, the only times he'd kissed her were when she was herself.

She felt the connection growing. A click of rightness so very different than the click she'd felt when she'd gotten her crush on him.

This was real Mitch kissing real Lila.

This was real.

And for as much as she didn't want to be alone anymore, she also didn't want to be hurt.

Worse, she didn't want to screw things up with him. She'd ruined her relationship with her mother. She might have been a child, but she'd spent a lifetime paying for that mistake. She didn't want to spend a lifetime paying for another.

She pulled away. A lock of his hair had fallen to his forehead. His lips glowed with dew from their kiss. His dark, observant eyes met hers.

"I think you better put me down."

Her voice came out soft and fragile. She knew that was why he instantly heeded her request. When her bare feet met the floor, she almost turned away, but stopped herself and gazed up at him. "If nothing else, I'm going to take some really great memories home with me."

Then she left him standing in the sitting room, the way she had the last time he'd kissed her.

She closed her bedroom door behind her and leaned against it. A night with him might be worth the broken heart she knew would follow. But this wasn't the moment to choose. She wasn't sure when the moment would arrive, but she was fairly certain she'd know it when it came.

CHAPTER TEN

THE NEXT MORNING Mitch woke Lila with a brisk knock against her door. "Wear something really comfortable today. After our meetings this morning I'm taking you on a tour of the vineyard."

He had absolutely no idea what was happening between the two of them. He only knew that he hadn't had that much fun with a woman in his entire life. And he hadn't even slept with Lila.

And he wouldn't. Oh, sure, they'd been in the preliminary round the night before with that steamy kiss. But something was going on between them. Something special. He wouldn't ruin it by sleeping with her before she was ready. He also didn't think he could sleep with her until he knew why she was so sad.

Part of him wanted to disagree with that strategy. He had no intention of a permanent relationship with anyone. He had a family to support. He also did not make a good boyfriend, which probably meant he'd make a worse husband.

So he couldn't be thinking thoughts of permanency with Lila.

Still…

He didn't want to stop the natural flow of what was

happening between them. Sleep together. Not sleep together. It didn't make any difference. What mattered was
that everything evolved naturally. Then there'd be no
mistakes. There'd be no hurt feelings.

If he had to choose, he wanted her more as a lover
than an assistant. But that was another bridge they would
cross when they came to it. He would never let her go
empty-handed. When whatever they had fell apart, he
would make sure she had another job. A better job. He
would make sure she wasn't sorry that she had loved him.

Satisfied, he left the apartment, walked up the cobblestone path with a silly smile, attended a dull, dry meeting with Alonzo, who presented a study on grapes, then
begged off lunch. In the restaurant, he grabbed the basket of food he'd ordered that morning and headed back
to the apartment.

He opened the door but didn't see Lila, so he called,
"Are you ready?"

She came out of her room dressed in skinny jeans and
a big, sloppy T-shirt, wearing her glasses.

"That's different."

"These are my own clothes." She caught his gaze.
"Too casual?"

The tone of her voice told him that for some reason or
another wearing her own clothes was important to her.
He presented the basket. "We're having a picnic in the
grass. I'd say you're just right." He smiled and held out
his hand. "Let's go."

She led him down the flight of stairs, the same stairs
he'd carried her up the night before. Crazy sensation
spiraled through him and he let it. Whatever was happening between them, he liked it. She did too.

Outside, she stopped on the cobblestone path, gaping at the vehicle before her.

He laughed. "That's my ATV. We're going out." He pointed at the vineyards. "Way out. I want you to see the vineyard, the grapes."

She peeked back at him. "The whole deal, huh?"

"*Sí.*" He walked to his all-terrain vehicle and set the picnic basket in the bin in front. "You've worked for a vineyard for a year. I think it's about time you saw it."

He climbed on and patted the seat behind him. "You're here."

She looked a little nervous but that only made him all the more determined. She'd probably felt out of her league this entire trip, yet she'd held her own. She'd tried everything he'd asked of her—including a samba and flamingo. She wouldn't wimp out now.

She climbed on behind him. Though he could have shifted forward, he liked the feeling of her small body nestled against his. She gingerly slid her arms around his waist, and because she was at his back and couldn't see his face, he smiled. He simply loved the way she felt. In his arms. Wrapped around him. Dancing with him. It didn't matter.

"Shouldn't we have helmets?"

"You are about to take a leisurely drive along some of Spain's most beautiful land. You should just enjoy."

She pulled in an unsteady breath. "Okay."

He started the engine with a quick flick of his wrist and eased them over a short path that took them to a dirt road that led to the vineyards. The movement of the ATV created a cool breeze that billowed through the heat. They passed rows and rows of grapevines. Wanting her to see everything, he took a few detours, winding between the rows, past ponds and along tiers of new plants.

She didn't say a word. He probably wouldn't have been able to hear her over the roar of the engine, but he sensed that she wouldn't speak. She would want to take it all in. If there was one thing he'd realized about his assistant, it was that she was curious. And when it came to Ochoa Vineyards, he was happy to indulge her.

After they had looped around the entire original vineyard, he brought the ATV to a stop beside a grove of trees that had at one time been the boundary marker for the two vineyards that his father and uncle had combined.

He turned off the engine and it took a few seconds for his ears to adjust to the sound of silence. Soaking in the peace and quiet, he gave them all the time they needed before he turned on the seat to face her and found her eyes shining.

"It's pretty, *si*?"

"*Pretty* doesn't even begin to describe it. It's huge and open." She shook her head as if bemused. "It's fabulous."

He laughed before motioning for her to climb off the ATV. "I don't think anybody's ever called the vineyard fabulous."

"Well, somebody should, because it's remarkable." She didn't make a move to dismount, just looked around as if unable to get her fill. "It's so green."

"What did you expect?"

"I thought I'd see purple." She laughed. "You know. Grapes. Purple."

"Actually, you'd see red—in July and August."

"Your grapes are red?"

"Most of them. Right now everything is green. Sucking up minerals from the soil."

"How very technical of you."

She got off the ATV, still gazing around.

He shifted his weight to the side and hoisted himself off, then grabbed the picnic basket. "We're at the spot that at one time separated the two vineyards." He pointed to the rows of grapes on the other side of the trees. "That's the second half of Ochoa Vineyards. About a half mile away is the house Riccardo's parents live in."

She stared in the direction as if trying to see the house and finally turned to him. "This whole setup is designed to support two families."

"Exactly."

"And your dad doesn't see the flaw in that?"

He set the basket on the ground and opened it, pulling out a blanket. "He didn't. He does now."

"Hmm…"

With a quick whip, he unfurled the blanket and let it drift to the rich green grass. "A question?"

She helped him straighten the edges. "No. Probably more of an observation. I wonder if sometimes you don't scare your dad."

He pulled a bottle of grape juice out of the basket and two wineglasses. "Scare my dad?" He chuckled. "I doubt it."

"Oh, I'm sure he wouldn't let you see it. But he'd have to be blind not to realize how much you do…how far ahead you can think."

He shrugged, placed the basket in the middle of the blanket and motioned for her to sit. "Perhaps."

She lowered herself to the spot across from him. "No *perhaps* about it. I'd be willing to bet a year's salary he's waiting for the day you boot him out of the head chair at board meetings."

"Then he doesn't know me well. I respect his position as eldest in his family. As long as he is alive he will be head of our household."

"And you'll run everything discreetly in the background."

He laughed. "It's what I do."

She shook her head. "So maybe it's not as easy having parents as I've always thought."

She made the comment so casually he might have missed it if he hadn't been working to figure out her secrets. Knowing she was a foster child, it wasn't a stretch to understand that she probably longed for a place. So maybe she wanted another job, one with more employees—or maybe fewer employees—where she could build a "work" family. God knew he and Riccardo weren't the two friendliest guys. They were driven. Work oriented. He'd never even as much as asked her to have a drink with him at the end of the day.

Which would have been fruitless anyway, since she didn't drink.

He picked up the bottle of grape juice. "We make this in limited quantities."

She peered at it. "It's not wine?"

"Nope. Just rich, delicious juice."

She laughed. "Always selling."

"That's the other thing I do. I sell. I know how to get people to want what I have."

Her face scrunched. "I never looked at it that way."

"How else do you think you sell? By badgering people?" He batted a hand. "That only turns people off." He caught her gaze. "You need to entice them. Seduce them."

She stiffened ever so slightly and shifted back.

She'd pulled away from him the night before. Not because she didn't want to be seduced, but because she did. He could feel it in her kiss. So now he would go back to selling himself—selling *them*. They might not be a forever match. He had too many responsibilities to be a husband. But there was no reason they couldn't spend time together now. Especially if becoming her lover earned him enough of her trust that she'd tell him her secrets and let him help her.

He took out roast beef sandwiches, cheese and fruit and set them on the blanket between them, then he leaned across his offering, took her small chin in his fingers and brushed his lips over hers quickly, briefly, teasing her.

"I hope you like roast beef."

"I do."

He swore he could feel the trembling of her heart in her shivery whisper. Now that she was getting to know him, she liked him. She could no longer hide it and he intended to take full advantage of it.

He handed her a napkin and a plate.

Her eyebrows rose. "The good china?"

He shrugged. "Maybe. I just told the chef to put in nice plates."

"They're pretty."

He laughed at her attempt to change the subject and brought it back to where he wanted it. "A man doesn't seduce a woman with paper plates." He motioned to the cheese and fruit platter. "Go on. Eat."

She ran her tongue along her lips and the thrill of victory raced through Mitch's blood. He could take her right here. Right now. But he wanted to do this correctly. Short term didn't mean shortchange. Their affair would be passionate. Perfect.

He poured the juice, handed a glass to her. "Have you ever tried wine?"

* * *

Her gaze shot to his. Everything he'd done that day had begun to weave a connection between them. So he could seduce her. She wasn't so inexperienced that she didn't see that, and a hum had started in her heart and radiated out to every part of her. Not because the man of her crush suddenly wanted her. But because the Mitch she was getting to know—the nice guy, the strong man who took over his family business without deposing his dad, the man who loved his nanna and went to extraordinary lengths to make sure the brother who stole his girlfriend had a good wedding—because *that* guy wanted her.

"No. I've never tried wine."

"Maybe tonight?" He smiled. His lips tipped up. His eyes filled with warmth. He wanted her to share something that was important to him.

Temptation crept up on her. Not in a bad way, but as a curiosity. Her entire life had been lived waiting for the day she would find her mom, rebuild her family. Now, realizing that dream wouldn't happen, everything was open to her. Was it so wrong to want a real relationship with Mitch? To share his world? The product he was so proud of? If she tried all the things she'd stayed away from, would she actually find herself? Her real self?

She closed her eyes, pulled in a breath. She'd never been more real than she was in that moment. She was on a blanket with a man she was growing to love. Not for his looks. Not for his money. Not for some stupid daydream. But for him. And like it or not, she had a past. She couldn't pretend she didn't. Couldn't pretend she could drink wine and act as if nothing mattered.

Who she was at this very second was real Lila. And if he wanted her, he had to take all of her.

When she opened her eyes, she said, "I don't drink because my mother is an alcoholic."

Mitch's face scrunched in confusion. "Your mother was an alcoholic?"

"My mother *is* an alcoholic. She's alive, I think, living in New York City. I was taken away from her when I was ten. Before I started working with you, I'd been trying to find her."

"*That's* why you don't drink?"

She nodded. "Alcoholism can be inherited. I spent too many horrible days and nights as a child to risk it."

Even though she made it all sound so simple, a million things bombarded Mitch's brain. She'd been raised by foster parents, taken away from her mom, probably because of her mom's drinking. He knew that had to be part of why she didn't want to talk about her time in foster care. Other kids in her situation didn't have parents. She'd had one who hadn't been able to care for her and had lost custody.

Had she longed for her mom? Wished her mom would sober up? Been disappointed a million times?

What a horrible childhood that must have been.

His heart hurt for her. He balanced his glass on the lid of the picnic basket so he could put his hands on her shoulders. They drifted down along her arms, soothing her. "I'm so sorry."

"You asked me once if I'd ever done anything stupid. Well, I have. When I was ten I told the social worker that my mom slept a lot. I showed her an empty whiskey bottle I'd pulled from the trash. She put it all together and within twenty-four hours I was in a foster home."

And she blamed herself.

He didn't believe it was possible to feel any worse
for her, but here he was stunned and aching for her. His
hands slid from her forearms to her fingers. He caught
them up and squeezed.

"That must have been awful."

She met his gaze. "Do you know how horrible it is to
feel like you did something terribly, terribly wrong when
you were only trying to protect yourself?"

His feelings worsened. Not only had she lost her mom
and blamed herself, but there was an ache to it. She had
been a scared, maybe hungry child, trying to protect herself and instead she'd lost her mom.

He shook his head. "I'm so sorry you went through
that." He tried to reconcile beautiful Lila sitting beside
him with mousy Lila who had worked for him for a year
and little Lila who had lost her mom, and suddenly everything about her made sense. She didn't accent her
beauty or call attention to herself in any way because the
last time she had, she'd lost the most important thing in
her world. Her mom.

But even as he thought that, he realized something
else. She might have been taken away from her mom, but
she hadn't actually lost her permanently.

He squeezed her hands again. "So your mom is alive?
In New York?"

She pulled in a breath and caught his gaze with her
pale gray eyes. "The last I heard, she was alive. But I
don't know where she is. Private investigators cost more
than I can afford for a sustained period of time. It seems
that when I hire one who finds her, she somehow disappears."

He almost couldn't bear to hear that, didn't want to
process it, but he had to. While she was talking to him, he

also had to be brutally honest. "Do you think she doesn't want you to contact her?"

"I didn't think that." She caught his gaze. "Until I came here. Met your family." She shrugged and looked away. "I don't know. Somehow it all came together in my head. That a mom who wanted me in her life wouldn't run every time I found her."

And it was killing her. Grasping for straws, he said, "Maybe she's still drinking? Maybe she doesn't want you to see her like that? Or maybe she believes *you* wouldn't want *her* in your life?"

Her spine stiffened. "She might have trouble acclimating or she might be finding better jobs, better places to live, pulling herself up by her bootstraps. Improving her life. I know that's not easy. But when someone spends money to find you, you have to know she wants you in her life."

His chest filled with sadness. "I suppose."

She said, "Don't feel bad. It took me three days before the truth sank in. But it's in and I'm okay with it."

She might be resigned, but he felt awful. Well and truly awful. *This* was why she hadn't wanted to talk about her past. It was also why she wanted a job with more money. She'd wanted to find her mom. But being with his family had forced her to face the truth that maybe her mom didn't want her.

He looked around at the two vineyards that made up his family's estate. Rolling hills. Grapevines. Houses. Limos. A jet.

She probably thought the entire Ochoa clan was spoiled, selfish, except for Nanna. She probably also had no idea how her story had affected him. Broken his heart for her.

But he suspected that if she knew he felt sorry for her it would make her angry.

The sound of an ATV drowned out the *swish, swish, swish* of the grapevine leaves shivering in the breeze. His head snapped up and he peered at the vehicle, trying to figure out the driver. When he realized it was Julia, he had to stifle a groan.

She roared her ATV up to their blanket. "Here you are!"

Tired of her antics and bad timing, he said, "What do you want, Julia?"

"I think your fiancée forgot the bachelorette party I planned."

"For yourself? You planned your own bachelorette party?"

She smiled prettily. "I had to make sure I got what I wanted. So I told the girls to leave it to me." She looked at Lila. "But you were gone when we came to pick you up."

Mitch started to say, "She's busy right now."

But Lila touched his arm to stop him, as she addressed Julia. "Drive me back. Give me ten minutes to change and we can go."

Always happy to get her own way, Julia beamed.

Lila gave him a sad smile. "You don't mind gathering all this stuff up by yourself."

He studied her face. Knew she was leaving because what she'd told him had been difficult for her and the outcome hadn't been what either had expected.

Because whether he liked admitting it or not, her past had a bearing on their future. When he boiled it all down, what he wanted from Lila was a few months, maybe a year of fun. Selfish to be sure. But that's who he was.

As pretty as she was, as fun as she was, as much as he

was attracted to her, she was wounded. Truly wounded. She'd endured a level of pain, hurt and emptiness that a man like him would only intensify.

He couldn't have her. Not even for a few months. Not even once.

He reached for the wineglasses. "Go. Have fun." Then he smiled at her. "Spend money."

CHAPTER ELEVEN

MITCH DIDN'T KNOW where they had gone for the bachelorette party, but at six he showered to get ready to go to his brother's bachelor party. If he looked at the situation with Lila closely, she'd been warning him off all along, and he'd been too stupid or maybe too arrogant to heed her.

Because he was a fixer, he believed he could fix anything.

But how could he fix a lifetime of loneliness and guilt? A mom who probably didn't want her?

He couldn't.

It was no wonder she didn't want him in her life.

Still, a little after seven, when he heard his apartment door open, he raced out to the sitting room hoping it was her, only to find Riccardo.

"I thought we were meeting at seven?"

Mitch glanced at his watch. Twenty after. "I wasn't quite ready." He'd been stalling for time. Hoping she'd come back. Why? He had absolutely no clue. There was nothing he could say to her. Nothing he could do to make her life better. He should stay out of it. With his track record with women, he'd undoubtedly end up making her pain worse.

Ducking into his bedroom, he grabbed his wallet. "But I'm ready now."

He, Riccardo, Alonzo and six of Alonzo's friends piled into the limo and headed into town. Mitch had no idea where they were going. If this were New York, they'd go to a strip club. But it wasn't New York. It was rural Spain. Their choices were limited.

Alonzo opened the limo bar, which had obviously been stocked for the occasion.

Riccardo hooted with laughter. "Shots?"

A general cry of agreement from Alonzo's friends followed.

Mitch cringed. But when they handed him a shot glass, he took it. He was, after all, the best man. "What is this?"

Riccardo raised his glass in a toast. "The finest tequila money can buy."

"So we're not going to take our time getting drunk? We're going straight to the trouble."

Alonzo playfully punched his arm. "This is my last hurrah. I want it."

Riccardo said, "To Alonzo. And a long, happy marriage after a wicked night in Monaco."

Mitch raised his shot to drink, but what Riccardo said settled in at the same time that he realized they weren't going to town when the limo turned left. He squeezed his eyes shut. "We're going to the airstrip."

Riccardo laughed. "Well, we're sure as hell not going to drive to Monaco."

No. He supposed they couldn't.

And he should also stop being so morose. This was his brother getting married—to Mitch's ex-girlfriend. Did he want to ruin all the progress they'd made with the cha-

rade and have Alonzo's friends think he was upset about
Alonzo marrying Julia?

He grabbed the tequila bottle and refilled everyone's
glass. "One more. A toast to my brother and his bride-
to-be that they will have a houseful of kids."

Alonzo laughed. "Julia might not be on board with
that."

Mitch shrugged. "So?"

One of Alonzo's friends said, "And *that's* why you
lost her."

Everybody laughed, but Riccardo quickly picked up
the charade and said, "But he found an even more beautiful woman."

Chuck Martin, one of Alonzo's childhood friends,
said, "Lila is something."

Alonzo nodded. "At first, I thought she was a bit stiff.
But she really loosened up when you were dancing the
other night. And I totally saw why you love her." He
winked. "Besides her good looks."

Uncomfortable, Mitch held up his hands. "Are we
going to sit here and talk about my fiancée like a bunch
of old women? Or are we going to drink?"

They downed the shot Mitch had poured and Chuck
grabbed the bottle, pouring another round. They toasted
Alonzo and Julia again and again, until the next shot
Mitch secretly spilled into a nearby wastebasket.

With a designated driver and probably hotel rooms
booked, he shouldn't have cared if he got drunk. But
as the feeling of the alcohol taking him began to slither
through Mitch, he thought of Lila. About how she didn't
drink. About how her mother had been a drunk. And the
whole ritual of getting plastered seemed wrong. He could

see the value of a nice glass of wine. Maybe a sipping whiskey. But to drink for the purpose of getting drunk...

It had more than lost its luster.

The drive to the airstrip took forty minutes. By the time they got there, the light of the sun was weak and shimmery, and Alonzo, his groomsmen and his friends were singing off-color songs. They rolled out of the limo and, arms on each other's shoulder, they headed for the stack of steps leading into the Ochoa family jet.

Mitch stared at them as they disappeared into the plane. A minute passed. Then two. But he couldn't seem to get his feet moving toward the steps. He glanced at Fernando, the family's longtime driver. One of Fernando's eyebrows rose, then he opened the limo door again.

Mitch laughed.

"I'm sure, Señor Ochoa, that they won't even notice you aren't there."

Another laugh burst from Mitch. "You're probably right."

"So go home. Go see the pretty girl they talked about."

He shouldn't. Lila probably wanted a break from him. And he now felt odd being around her. Spoiled. More selfish than he'd ever thought he was.

"She's at the bachelorette party."

Fernando shrugged. "So maybe you just take a little time to yourself."

That sounded amazing. Since he'd gotten to Spain he'd attended ten meetings about the family business. He'd entertained Lila, watched out for Lila, kept Lila on track. And then there were the family dinners, family breakfasts, balls, garden parties...

He was tired. Not just tired of being on, but maybe he was tired of being all things to all people.

He got into the limo.

He spent the forty-minute drive back to Ochoa Vine-yards with his eyes closed and his head resting on the seat. When the limo pulled up to the duplex, he felt marginally better. He got out, joked with Fernando a bit, then climbed the stairs to his apartment. He would get out of this suit, into something comfortable, and read a book.

But when he opened the apartment door, he stopped dead in his tracks. Lila sat on the sofa in the sitting room. Wearing sweatpants, her big shirt and her glasses, she sat cross-legged, watching television.

He tossed his wallet to the door by the table. "Television?"

She flicked off the TV. "I was bored."

"So what happened to Julia's bachelorette party?"

"We went to a spa in town. Got massages. Got makeovers." She presented her fingernails to him. "And manicures."

"At least you didn't have eight shots of tequila."

She winced. "They were about to go barhopping when I bowed out."

"Smart."

"Yeah."

The conversation died a natural death and Mitch glanced around nervously. He wanted a minute to himself, and instead he found the one person he didn't want to see. The one person he should stay away from. Because he didn't want to hurt her.

"I guess I'll go to bed."

"At nine?"

"I was going to read."

"That makes sense."

Awkward silence filled the room again.

She pulled in a breath. "You know what? I think I'm going out to the balcony to look at the moon."

The urge to join her fluttered through him. There was nothing like the sight of the moon rising over the mountains and above the vineyard. He struggled to keep himself from saying, "I think I'll come too."

When they weren't knee-deep in the charade, he liked being in her company. She was normal. Funny. And so easy to be with, she was exactly what he needed after ten days of talking business and forty minutes with friends getting drunk.

But, in the end, he reminded himself that she was a nice woman. And he was—well, him.

He walked into his bedroom, slipped out of his shirt and trousers and into sweatpants and a T-shirt, very much like what she was wearing.

He opened the drapes on the French doors in his room, telling himself it was an easy, nonintrusive way to get a glimpse of the moon. But he knew it was actually his curiosity about Lila that had him looking at the balcony. Seeing her out there alone, watching the great yellow ball, his heart filled to bursting. He might not be right for her. She might not be right for him to have a fling with, but she was alone and he couldn't stand seeing her alone.

He walked out, sat on the chaise beside hers, stretching out his legs and relaxing on the long chair, and silently watched the moon with her.

"I've seen the moon in New York City."

He laughed at the easy way she started a conversation. "Yeah. I figured you had."

"I'm not totally deprived, you know. In fact, I'm normally a very happy person."

He glanced over at her. Moonlight picked up the yellow in her hair and made it shine. Her gray eyes were serious, intent, so he answered seriously. "Yeah. I get that."

"I don't want you feeling sorry for me."

"I know *that* too."

"Don't get snooty. I'm allowed a little pride."

He sniffed. "Huh. You have a lot of pride."

"Coming from the king of pride, I'm not sure if that's an honest observation or just you trying to find similarities between us."

"We have a lot in common."

She glanced around the estate, then burst into giggles. "Right."

He sat up on the chaise, facing her, and forced her gaze to his. "You think we don't? We're both driven. We both respect family. You might not have your mom in your life, but you respect her. And we don't go out of our way to make ourselves the center of attention like Julia and Alonzo. We're happy in the background. Doing things. Making things happen."

Her head tilted. "Wow. We're practically twins."

"Is that how you handle life? When something pops up that you don't want to discuss you make a joke of it?"

She shrugged. "I don't know. Maybe."

He blinked. "I expected you to dodge that question."

"Ech. I'm not in a dodging mood."

His heart flipped. The moon illuminated the vineyard. The gentle *swish, swish, swish* of grape leaves blowing in the breeze sang through the air. And the woman he was growing to believe he might love wasn't in the mood to dodge his questions.

He turned and settled on the chaise again. Relaxed. Closed his eyes, wondering what he should ask her.

What he should tell her.

And wondering why the very thought of an honest conversation with her made him happier than he'd been in years.

Lila settled on her chaise. All along Mitch had been showing her pieces of the real him. Especially dancing. Just the thought of how much fun they had shot a thrill of memory through her. They'd danced. They kissed. They'd told each other secrets. After ten days, she was probably closer to him than she'd ever been to anyone. Even Sally. Because there were things she didn't think Sally could handle that she knew Mitch could.

"My first summer vacation was actually a shopping trip."

He glanced over at her. "Really?"

"Most foster families provide things like clothes but don't take you shopping. So this one year, my foster mom could see I was bored. I tried to hide it. I tried to pretend it wasn't true. But she saw right through me. I'd never said anything but I think somehow she knew I'd never been shopping for real. I'd looked in store windows and walked up and down the aisles of stores just to see what was there. But I'd never shopped." She smiled. "She taught me about clearance racks."

He laughed.

"She also took me shopping every other month. There wasn't a lot of money to spend on clothes. But it was nice—special—not just that she spent the time with me but that she let me have choices."

He nodded. "I would have shot myself if my mom had expected me to pick out my own clothes."

She laughed. "We're not sounding so much the same anymore, are we?"

He batted a hand. "We're still the same in the things that count."

"You don't think being raised in the lap of luxury and being raised to count pennies makes us different?"

"No. Because I think we ended up with the same core values."

"Interesting."

"Not really. I was in university when I began to see there were too many of us to be supported by the vineyard. In a way, that was my first experience of counting pennies."

"Except your pennies were dollars."

"It's still money."

They were quiet for a minute, then he said, "Julia never got that."

"I don't think Julia wanted to get it."

He shrugged. "Maybe."

"How'd you ever end up with her anyway?"

"My relationship with Julia was almost an accident. We went to the same school as kids, went to the same parties. We just sort of evolved."

"So you were with her for *years*? You'd never dated anybody else?"

"There's a lot to be said for convenience and comfort."

She winced. "I'll bet Julia would love hearing that."

He laughed. "When we broke up, I went a little crazy dating in New York."

"You don't have to confess all that to me."

"You need to know who I am. That I'm a bit selfish. And I have tunnel vision. I will do whatever I have to do to keep my family safe, happy, pampered."

He was telling her not to make anything of this. Maybe because the conversation had given him the same warm feeling of connection that it was giving her and he didn't want it? Whatever the reason, she respected his wishes and wouldn't force him to say the obvious. She knew, as all good foster kids knew, how to turn the conversation in a neutral direction.

"They're very lucky to have you."

He waited a beat. Then he shifted on his chaise again so that he was facing her. "And your mom would be very lucky to have you. God only knows what kinds of demons she's facing, what kind of life she has. You can't judge her or assume any of her motivations. You can only make your life the best it can be."

Tears welled in her eyes, but she stopped them. What kind of guy warns you off in one breath and soothes your soul in the next.

"Spoken like a man who's figured the same thing about himself."

"I have to keep my family solvent." He rose.

Tired, ready to give up her star/moon gazing for the night, she rose too.

"And I have a good life."

Standing in front of him, a little shorter than he was without her three-inch heels, she whispered, "I have a good life too."

"Then neither of us has anything to complain about… *Si?*"

Right at that moment, she could think of at least one thing. His dedication to his family would keep him on a solitary path. At the same time that she envied him for his family, his destiny, she suddenly felt cheated. That moment she'd been thinking about since she talked to Sally… This was it. And he was telling her he didn't want it.

She rose to her tiptoes. She wasn't trying to change his mind. She wasn't trying to make a point. She just wanted to kiss him. If this ache of understanding and connection was love, no matter if he was turning it down, she wanted at least a kiss.

She touched his mouth with hers, softly, gently, as she slid her hands up his arms and to his shoulders. At first, she thought he'd refuse her, but suddenly his hands came to her shoulders and slid to her nape, forcing his fingers into the thick locks of her hair, sending tingles of joy down her spine.

She stretched higher to deepen the kiss and he bent a bit so that their mouths could meet and merge, as if he was unable to stop himself.

And that was the moment she didn't just know she loved him. She also knew he loved her.

CHAPTER TWELVE

MITCH FELL INTO the kiss. Drowning in sensation, he pressed his mouth to hers, even as he grazed his hands down her back, forcing her body as close to his as he could possibly get it. She was warm. She was wonderful. But more than that she was the first person to really know him. Him. Quirks. Foibles. Destiny and all.

Knowing someone completely was the only way anyone could really love anyone else. Now she knew him. And he knew her.

And it was pointless.

Because he really didn't want to hurt her. As pretty as she was, as fun as she was, as much as he was attracted to her, she came with baggage. Real pain and hurt and emptiness. At some point, he'd only make her life worse.

He pulled away, slid his hands up her back to her shoulders and to her face, as he stared into her eyes. For one blistering minute, he longed to throw caution to the wind. To tell her she was perfect and he wanted her. Then he heard the sounds of the limo returning. He heard Julia's laugh as she got out of the limo so she could clamber to the house she shared with Alonzo, and he pulled back. Julia had dumped him because he was never there for her.

Lila needed somebody who would be there for her.

She didn't need him.

A few years from now she would thank him for stepping away from her, saying "Good night" and returning to his room alone.

The next morning, Mitch had himself all together. He hadn't spent a sleepless night. He'd thought it all through and fixed it.

He'd always known he had tunnel vision. After Julia, he'd realized he wasn't made to be a one-woman man. But what he had forgotten was that he'd promised Lila a job. When he remembered that, the fixer in him had perked up like a bull seeing a red flag. He might not be able to love her, but he could help her.

So he'd made a few calls to friends in New York, and because it was still afternoon in the States, within hours he had the perfect job for Lila.

Then he realized that there was an even better way to repay her for helping him with this ruse. For being a good sport. For being a nice person. She needed a job, but she also wanted to find her mom. She wanted the chance at a family that he'd always had and maybe taken for granted.

Because it wasn't quite five o'clock in New York City, the town was still open for business. He pulled a few strings and got the name of a private investigator. With the promise of a bonus for quick work, he hired a firm that began looking for Lila's mom. He didn't ask what websites they'd checked, if they'd hacked things that shouldn't be hacked, but two hours later he not only had her mom's employer; he had her address and phone number.

Then he slept like a baby.

*** * ***

Sitting at the far end of the conference table, listening to his dad convene the final meeting of his stay in Spain, he felt pretty damned proud of himself. His family was solvent. The woman he might be coming to love would have a secure future once he told her about the job he'd found for her. She'd also have another shot at talking to her mom.

And he was back to being who he was. Not the needy man standing on the balcony wondering if he should take a risk.

He hated risk. Even considering taking a risk was foolish. Not him. And he was glad to be back to normal.

"As most of you have probably guessed, we have no agenda for this final meeting because there's nothing left to discuss."

Though everyone else in the conference room laughed, Mitch struggled to keep his facial expression neutral. He could be in his apartment right now, telling Lila she had a high-level administrative position in an investment bank and handing her mom's personal information to her. Instead, he would sit here and listen to his dad rehash decisions that had already been made.

But he could do it. He was Mitch Ochoa, fixer, background guy who made other people happy.

"But there is one thing we haven't discussed."

There might be. But Mitch honestly had no clue what it was.

"I'd like to acknowledge my son…"

Alonzo. Who was getting married.

"Mitcham."

For a few seconds his name didn't register. When it did, he glanced up sharply.

"You think the family doesn't see that you rescued us. But we do. Alonzo will be a great vintner. Your mother and aunt love managing the restaurant and gift shops. I'm okay with overseeing everybody. But, you, Mitch, fill in the final piece of the puzzle. The big piece. You sell us. Without you, we'd be broke."

He sat back in his chair. Not quite sure what to say.

Riccardo laughed. "He hates praise."

"I don't hate praise. I simply don't need praise."

"It's a foolish family," his mom said, "who doesn't acknowledge the person who's holding it all together."

"I wouldn't say that I—"

Riccardo snorted. "Oh, please. Modesty? Take the praise and run."

"Better yet," his dad suggested. "Take a vacation. We've looked at the books and we've never seen that you take time off."

Because he didn't.

His mom reached across the conference table and patted his hand. "We also worry that you don't have a life."

"I have plenty of life."

"True, but I wonder if Lila feels that way." His mom caught his gaze. "Riccardo tells me you've never even taken her to the house in the Hamptons. Your dates are all in New York City. You need to give this woman more."

Oh, boy. Dating advice. From his mom.

Here's where he had to stop things.

He rose from the table. "Okay. Good talk. I'll just be going back to my apartment now." He started to turn away, but shifted back. "In fact, I'll take your advice, and Lila and I will have lunch in town."

Before he could make his escape, his dad walked over to him and gave him a stiff, all-businessman hug. "I'm still the boss, but I wanted you to know that we see what you do." He pulled away and caught Mitch's gaze. "I know you saved us financially, but we've all agreed this week that we're on solid ground now. You can go and have some fun."

Mitch left the conference room and all but ran out of the main house. But when he got to the sitting room of his apartment and saw Lila on the sofa reading, he stopped dead in his tracks. His family had given him the green light to slow down, take time off.

What if he did?

What if, after the wedding, he and Lila got into the family jet and toured Europe?

The possibility was so tempting his breath almost caught. He could have or do anything he wanted and what he wanted was time with this woman.

Except he wasn't a guy who could make commitments. And he would hurt her.

She looked up and saw him. "Hey."

"Hey."

She turned off her e-reader. "Sorry, I was a little lost in my story. How'd the meeting go?"

She rose from the sofa. Her long legs seemed to go on forever beneath her short shorts. Her hair swayed as she walked over to him. And her soft eyes called to him.

"The meeting was fine."

"So what's on the agenda for today?"

He fingered the slip of paper in his jacket pocket. The name and address of the company for her new job. The address and phone number for her mom.

"My dad told me today, in front of everyone, that he realizes I saved the family."

Her eyebrows rose. "That's cool."

Now that he was past the dating advice and remembering the things his dad had said, it was cool. Warmth bubbled up in his chest. All the weird feelings from the unexpected praise disappeared like a puff of smoke. The sense of accomplishment that rippled through him made him laugh.

"It was great. A surprise, but great. I think my dad might be making a road for a new way for the family's company to do business."

He fell to the sofa, happily confused.

"And that's good too, right?"

"Absolutely."

No feeling had ever come close to the emotions rolling through him at that moment. Another man might have looked at Lila, with his family's instructions for him to have some fun floating through his brain, and seen his chance. Mitch remembered that he wasn't a good bet as a boyfriend and Lila needed more.

And suddenly everything felt off. Wrong.

They had three more days of this charade. Three days of getting to know her, laughing with her, longing for something he couldn't have.

Maybe it was time for this ruse to end? His family respected him. He'd found her mom. They both had what they wanted.

Except he wanted her.

But he couldn't have her. It annoyed him that his usual self-control was deserting him. When he decided against something, he never thought of it again. He didn't torture himself. He took action.

He rose from the sofa. "I found you a job."

Her eyes widened. "You did?"

The excitement in her voice strengthened his resolve.

He hadn't even told her about her mom yet, but she was so thrilled with the job it was clear she wasn't invested in this, in him, the way he was beginning to feel about her.

He reached into his pocket and pulled out the little slip of paper. "Your mom's address and phone number are on there too."

Her mouth fell open. "Oh, my God."

She was just about to jump in his arms and tell him she loved him, when he said, "I found your mom because I don't like to do things halfway. I realized last night that you wanted your mom, not a job. So I did what I should have done in the beginning—I hired a PI and found her. The new job is like a bonus as a thank-you for being so convincing as my fiancée."

She stepped back, away from him so she could see his face. He'd said the words as if he was happy, proud of himself, but she saw deeper. She saw the flicker of uncertainty in his eyes.

"You found my mom last night?"

He nodded. "It was only afternoon in New York City, even after our chat on the balcony."

When she'd kissed him.

And he'd pulled away.

He'd immediately gone to his room and found her mom.

She took another step back.

He might have feelings for her. She'd sure as hell felt them the night before. But he didn't want to love her.

Her heart felt crushed. Not smashed into a million pieces, but flattened into a thin red line.

And she still had to go to the rehearsal dinner that

night, pretending everything was okay. Then the wedding. The day-after party.

She had to. He'd done his side of the deal. Found her a job. Then gone the extra mile and found her mom.

She had to.

Her heart tried to swell back to life, but couldn't. She was right at his fingertips. He loved her. But he wouldn't say it. Didn't want her.

When the chips were down, when commitments had to be made, no one really wanted her.

She cleared her throat to ease the tears out of her voice. "You do remember that my mom always disappears right after she's found." The right thing to do would be stay and finish this. But with every ounce of her being she knew she couldn't.

Gathering her courage, she raised her eyes to look at him. "I can't wait on this." She waved the paper. "I have to return to America today."

For one blessed second, he hesitated. Hope swelled, but he dashed it. "I don't think we have to go through with the rest of the charade."

She blinked, the tears a little harder to hold back this time.

"My family respects me." He nodded at the paper in her hands. "We found your mom. We accomplished everything we wanted."

Nodding, she swallowed hard to hold back the emotion flooding through her. *She'd* wanted her association with him to be over when she returned to New York. She'd known it was the only way she could handle this.

But now that the time was here…

Her chest shuddered with unshed tears and she pressed her lips together to settle herself before she said, "You're right. Give me an hour or so to pack. You can think of a good breakup story for your family."

He nodded.

She straightened her shoulders and walked into her bedroom.

CHAPTER THIRTEEN

LILA ARRIVED IN New York feeling like a new person. Unfortunately, it wasn't the new person she'd thought she'd be when she agreed to the charade with Mitch.

She thought she'd come back with four suitcases of beautiful clothes, a sophisticated knowledge of Spain and how the other half lives and a new job she could sink her teeth into. Though she had those, she'd brought home something else with her.

She was truly in love with Mitch. And she knew he loved her too. But he'd nudged her out because he didn't *want* to love her. Who knew why? On the flight home she'd wondered if he didn't think her good enough, but recognized that wasn't true. He wasn't that kind of guy. She'd considered that what had blossomed between them had happened too fast. But he didn't have to ask her to marry him. They could have dated.

He didn't even want to give them a chance.

And she had to deal with that. Straight up. No pulling punches. The man had had her at his fingertips, and he'd given her the one thing he knew would push her away—her mom.

But somehow having her mom's address felt empty. Worse, it was frightening. She'd turned her mom in. Who knew how she'd react? What would she do if her mom didn't run this time, but stayed and talked with her, and flat out told her she didn't want her in her life. Then she would have been rejected by her mom and the man she loved.

Then it would be official. There would be no one in the world more alone than she was.

The next morning, Mitch woke and stumbled into the kitchen of his apartment. The one bad thing about being with a woman who had a good reason not to drink was he now couldn't get drunk to drown his sorrows. He looked at alcohol a totally different way now.

So he'd barely slept. And he hadn't had the sweet release of alcoholic oblivion to get him through the night. Instead, he'd gone back and forth between thinking he was an idiot and knowing he'd had to do the right thing.

His wedding tux hung on a rack in his sitting room—obviously delivered by staff. He wasn't shaved. He didn't feel like showering. He drank coffee but he'd just as soon throw the bagel at the wall as eat it.

A knock at his door surprised him. Thinking it was someone here to annoy him with some detail about the wedding, he barked, "Come in!"

The door opened slowly and Julia entered. "A best man is supposed to attend all wedding functions, including the rehearsal dinner, so where were you last night?"

"Taking my fiancée to the airstrip." He tossed the bagel to the table. "We broke up." And it felt real. And it sucked. And it confused the hell out of him. All the time he'd been trying to avoid hurting her, and he was the one hurting.

Julia's face fell in confusion. "You broke up?"

"Don't pretend you're not happy. Now you're back to being queen bee. I know you didn't like her."

"I adored her. She was the first person to hold her own with me in a long time. But honestly I knew something was up when she left the bachelorette dinner. I knew you were going to do something stupid."

"Yeah, well, the stupid thing I did was find her mother."

Julia fell to the seat across from his at the small, round table. "Her mother?"

"She wasn't in foster care because she was an orphan. Her mother is alive. She lost custody when Lila was about ten. Lila hasn't seen her since. Every time she finds her mom, she disappears. It seems she likes her mother more than she likes me. Because as soon as I gave her her mom's address she was out of here." That wasn't quite the truth. Though she'd been the first to mention leaving, he'd agreed.

"And she gave you back the ring?"

He ran his hand along the back of his neck. "No."

"Maybe you misinterpreted? You did say her mom disappears every time she's found. Maybe Lila didn't think she could wait."

"That was part of it, but I... Never mind."

"Never mind like hell. You love this woman! Are you just going to let her go?"

"She's better off without me."

"No. She's not! *I* was," she said, then she grinned. "But that's because you didn't love me. You could drop me for a business meeting any day of the week. But you're different with her. You sometimes can't take your eyes off her. She knows enough about business that you talk for real." She smiled. "You take her seriously, Mitch. And she makes you laugh. You love her."

Julia rose and took his tux off the rack. "You need to go after her."

"After her?"

"Are you deaf or daft? First off, you're sending her to meet her mom alone. My goodness, Mitch. Seriously? She hasn't seen her mother in over fifteen years and you sent her into that emotional land mine alone?"

He'd never thought of that. It should have shamed him that self-absorbed Julia had. "I'm not sure what I'm supposed to do."

"Nothing…just support her. Be moral support." She tapped his forearm. "She needs you, Mitch. And you love her. Go."

"What about your best man?"

"Riccardo will fill in." She waved the tux. "Luckily, you're the same size."

Lila sat at her kitchen table, staring at the piece of paper with her mom's address and phone number on it. Mitch had found her mom. She had the information about her new job. She'd already called and learned that she could start the following Monday. She had three closets full of clothes and a ring the size of a small town on her finger. She was going to have to return the ring—in person— only a fool would put a ring this valuable in the mail. But she couldn't seem to move from the table.

Oh, she wanted her mom. She longed for the chance to say she was sorry, to make things right, but she also wanted Mitch. Everything she'd resolved to avoid when she'd made this deal had happened. They'd gotten close. She'd fallen in love for real. He'd fallen for her too, but that stubborn Spanish businessman could not let go and say he wanted her.

So maybe she was better off with a fresh start.

Really.

She showered and put on a pair of jeans and one of her new blouses, along with new shoes. She took the subway to the part of town where her mom lived, but walking up the sidewalk, she saw a limo.

She almost laughed. A limo. In this part of town. She thanked God for the laugh since she was shaking in her new shoes. She'd already been rejected by Mitch. Now her mom would probably reject her too. She was the stupidest woman in the world to put herself in these kinds of positions. But if there was even a chance her mother wanted her in her life, she had to do this.

Trembling knees and all.

As she approached the limo, the back window lowered…

"Hey."

Her heart stumbled. Her breath stopped. All thought of her mother disappeared. "Mitch?"

"*Sí.*"

What the hell? The surreal feeling of everything being out of place washed over her and made her dizzy. Then her ring caught the light and bounced it back at her and she understood what was going on.

"You forgot to take back the ring. Is that why you followed me?"

"I know you still have the ring. But that's not why I'm here. Julia doesn't think you should see your mom alone."

Confusion bubbled up again. The whole situation felt like one of those crazy dreams where nothing made sense. "Julia?"

"Julia and I." The limo door opened. He stepped out.

"We had a small chat the morning of the wedding and she reminded me how hard this might be for you."

"You talked about me on her wedding day?"

"She let me out of my commitment to be the best man. But we both forgot I'd have to wait for the jet to return to Spain." He laughed. "So I got my tux back from Riccardo and did my duty. And now I'm here. With you." He pointed at the aging town house door. "To meet your mom."

It still didn't quite sink in. "You're coming with me?"

"Yes. Lila, this is a huge deal for you." He shook his head. "I can't imagine how I'd feel right now if I hadn't seen my mom in over a decade." He caught her hands. "I know the story. I know you feel she hates you. How could you think you can face this alone?"

The thought that he could do something so sweet and yet refuse to love her filled her with unbearable sadness. "I've faced everything in my life alone."

"Not this."

Tears pooled in her eyes. How could he not see that having him pop into her life, even for something important, only hurt her? "You don't have to do this."

"That's the beauty of love."

Her head snapped up.

"I get to do all kinds of things I wouldn't ordinarily do." He paused, smiled. "Because I love you."

Her lower lip trembled. She had the sudden, urgent sense that this couldn't be real. That she had to have misinterpreted. Or that he'd qualify his statement by saying something like "I love you as a friend." "You love me?"

"Apparently more than I ever loved Julia because she sees it."

That she hadn't misinterpreted. She laughed through her tears.

"Come here." Holding her close, he whispered, "I thought I wasn't good for you. That I'd hurt you. But when I thought I was fighting feelings for you, what I was really fighting was changing. Falling in love with you was changing me. I didn't see it until Julia said it." He laughed and hugged her close. "You don't have to worry that I'll hurt you."

She believed him. Everything else in her world suddenly seemed easy.

"If your mom doesn't want you—we will deal with it. Because you will have me...and my mother and dad and Julia and Alonzo, Riccardo and his parents...and Nanna. Especially Nanna."

Tears filled her eyes as indescribable joy filled her heart. She pulled back, caught his gaze. "I love you too."

"It certainly took you long enough to say it."

"Two weeks is hardly—"

But he cut her off with a kiss. A slow, heartfelt *I am in this for real* kiss. She melted into him, knowing that absolutely everything in her life had changed.

All because she couldn't resist him when he'd asked for a favor.

He broke the kiss. "Just one thing, though."

"One thing?"

"Ochoas work for Ochoas. I'll expect you in the office on Monday."

She laughed.

He caught her hand and turned her toward the door of her mom's town house. "Shall we?"

She nodded. "I'm ready."

EPILOGUE

THE WEDDING TOOK place on a beautiful August day. The vineyard looked spectacular. The sun beat down on vines bursting with red grapes ready to be harvested.

Fixing Lila's veil, Julia sighed. "Alonzo and I should have had an August wedding. It's so pretty today. So special."

Lila turned to her with a smile. "I heard your June wedding was just gorgeous. And I saw the pictures."

"I don't think the pictures did justice to my gown." She turned Lila to the full-length mirror where they both could see the elegant bodice and full georgette crepe skirt of her exquisite gown. Julia turned Lila right then left as Sally fussed with the long train that flowed behind Lila.

"I think you need to stand angled just slightly to the right to make sure the camera picks up the sparkly embellishments in the skirt."

Sally rose and rolled her eyes. "You're too picky, Julia."

Julia shrugged. Sally and Julia wore identical one-shoulder dresses but Sally's was blue and Julia's a vivid shade of coral.

"I like things to be perfect."

"Well, I think Lila is perfect, just the way she is."

Lila caught Sally's hand. "Thank you."

"I think she's perfect too."

Lila, Julia and Sally all turned toward Lila's mom, who closed the dressing room door behind her. A short woman with strawberry blond hair and a dusting of freckles, she looked so much younger, so much happier than when Lila and Mitch had called on her the year before. Not only had Mitch found her a good apartment, he'd given her a job as the receptionist for Ochoa Online and paid her a large enough salary that she could support herself. Lila had lived with her mom off and on in the past year and they'd gotten to know each other.

Today, dressed in a pretty pink gown, Francine would give her daughter away.

Lila walked over and took her hands. "You look wonderful, Mom."

Francine leaned in and kissed Lila's cheek. "You are amazing."

"No. Just finally figured out who I was."

"Well, Mitch helped," Julia said, fluffing her black hair to make sure it was perfect.

Sally sighed with disgust and put one hand on her hip. "Really? How?"

"Well, he is the one who talked her into pretending to be his fiancée, forcing her to come out of her shell."

Sally caught Lila's gaze. "How much do you tell this woman…and why, for heaven's sake?"

Lila walked over and gave Julia a squeeze. "Because she's my sister-in-law, and she's a lot smarter than you think."

"Thank you!" Julia said, returning Lila's hug. She glanced at her watch. "We need to get going. The ceremony starts in five minutes. We'll need at least two minutes to get to our staging area."

Sally led the way out the door, followed by Julia. Lila took her mom's hand and together they walked to the small tent behind the rows of seats set up to face the vineyards and the setting sun. Lila and her mom had been instructed at the rehearsal the night before to stay in the tent until they heard the first notes of "Here Comes the Bride."

Lila took a deep breath.

"Nervous?"

Lila grinned at her mom. "Not even slightly." This had been the best year of her life. A year to make amends to her mom, who also made amends to her. A year to really fall in love and be in love with the most wonderful man in the world.

How could she possibly be nervous?

Then the first notes of "Here Comes the Bride" sounded and her stomach filled with butterflies. She pressed her tummy. "Well, I'll be darned. I am just a little nervous."

Her mom laughed. "Come on. Once we get started up that aisle and you see Mitch, you'll be fine."

They exited the little tent and all eyes turned toward them. Lila sucked in a breath and walked down the aisle, smiling at her guests. People she knew very well now. Family.

They got to the end of the aisle, her mom handed her over to Mitch and the ceremony began.

She promised her life and her fidelity to a man who could be as stubborn and exasperating as he was handsome. He promised his life to her, then he grinned. And she remembered all the reasons she loved him.

The minister announced that he could kiss the bride

and he did. With one arm supporting her back he dipped her and kissed her like a man so happy he couldn't get enough. Then he brought her back to her feet, pulled her into a dance hold and together they did a bit of a samba.

The crowd laughed. Mitch grinned and Lila soaked it all in.

Family.

Silliness.

Love.

That was all there really was in life.

All she really wanted.

* * * * *

If you've enjoyed this book,
then you won't want to miss
A MISTLETOE KISS WITH THE BOSS
by Susan Meier.
Available now!

If you want to read another fake fiancée romance,
then be sure to indulge in
CONVENIENTLY ENGAGED TO THE BOSS
by Ellie Darkins.

"What about you, Marissa? What would make you happy?"

"When my crew is happy, I'm happy." She smiled. "I guess it's hard to separate one from the other. It's been a long time since it's been just me, you know?

"What would make me happy?" She paused and looked at him, and she was pretty sure her answer was written all over her face.

He sucked in a breath and leaned close and kissed her. She kissed him back, grateful for their secluded corner.

"Just for tonight," she said.

"Just for tonight."

She kissed him again, her hands on his face, everything she felt going into the fierce kiss. "No strings attached," she whispered.

"That's always been the case," he said.

No strings. She'd shake on that again, but not on being friends. She couldn't be casual friends with Autry, not after this, and certainly not after they made love.

"Maybe we should take this conversation upstairs," he said.

"I think we're done talking," she whispered and kissed him again.

* * *

Montana Mavericks:
The Great Family Roundup—
Real cowboys and real love in Rust Creek Falls!

"What about you, Marissa? What would make you happy?"

"When my crew is happy, I'm happy," She smiled. "I realise that he seems like one man after another. It's been a long time since I've taken one seriously."

"What would make us happy," she paused and looked at him, and the way her eyes met his gaze was written all over her face.

He sucked in a breath and leaned close until he raised her. She kissed him, made grateful for these seconds together.

"Just for tonight," she said.

"Just for tonight."

She kissed him again, her cheek nestling his chest. Deep, till she felt the heat beneath. "We'd just missed," she whispered.

"There always been life, easy," he said.

He smiled. "She'd wake up that night and not on these threads out there. She would herself with sorry the other hand just after they made love."

"Maybe we should take this slowly and serious," he said.

"I don't want to take this one else wanted and joined us one again."

MUMMY AND
THE MAVERICK

MEG MAXWELL

First Published in Great Britain 2017
By Mills & Boon, an imprint of HarperCollins*Publishers*
1 London Bridge Street, London, SE1 9GF

© 2017 Harlequin Books S.A.

Special thanks and acknowledgement are given to Meg Maxwell for her contribution to the Montana Mavericks: The Great Family Roundup continuity.

ISBN: 978-0-263-92319-3

23-0817

Our policy is to use papers that are natural, renewable and recyclable products and made from wood grown in sustainable forests. The logging and manufacturing processes conform to the legal environmental regulations of the country of origin.

Printed and bound in Spain
by CPI, Barcelona

Meg Maxwell lives on the coast of Maine with her teenage son, their beagle and their black-and-white cat. When she's not writing, Meg is either reading, at the movies or thinking up new story ideas on her favorite little beach (even in winter) just minutes from her house. Interesting fact: Meg Maxwell is a pseudonym for author Melissa Senate, whose women's fiction titles have been published in over twenty-five countries.

In memory of my beloved grandparents.

Chapter One

Autry Jones stood on the sidewalk in front of Just Us
Kids Day Care Center, trying to process that his family's corporation, the venerable Jones Holdings, Inc.
was in the day care business. And that he was about
to walk inside the building.

Autry and children didn't mix. Joneses and children
weren't *supposed* to mix, but somehow, two of his four
brothers had not only settled down with wives in this
small Montana town, but were heavily invested in a
day care franchise.

Autry took off his aviator-style sunglasses and
tucked them in his pocket. He sucked in a breath and
pulled open the front door.

There were babies everywhere.

Well, little humans, Autry amended, as he stepped
inside and glanced around the main room. And only
a handful of them, now that he actually counted. A
big-cheeked baby was in a woman's arms. A toddler

wearing a shirt decorated with a cartoon monkey was building a tower of cardboard blocks. A little girl with bright red pigtails sat at a pint-size table, drawing a picture of a house and the sun with a smiley face in the center.

The middle-aged woman holding the baby smiled at him and walked over. He read her name tag: Miss Marley.

"Hi, Miss Marley," he said, extending his hand. "I'm Autry Jones. My—"

The woman grinned and shifted the baby in her arms. "No introductions necessary, Autry. You're Walker and Hudson's brother. I'd know a Jones brother anywhere. They mentioned you were flying in today. But you just missed them. They left for Ace in the Hole. Everyone in town is getting together there for a viewing party."

Ace in the Hole? Was that some kind of golf tournament? He could see Walker on the course, but Hudson? No way. "A viewing party?"

Miss Marley looked at him as if he'd been living on Mars for a while. "To watch *The Great Roundup*, of course! I plucked the short straw, so I'm on duty with this lil cutie and the Myler siblings until their parents get off work, but three people promised to record the premiere for me."

Ah, a TV show, Autry figured. He didn't watch much TV. As president of Jones Holdings, an international company involved in real estate and manufacturing—and lately, a day care franchise—Autry was focused on negotiating deals and making money. Having time to watch TV was beyond him, despite the stretches he spent in airport lounges and on flights to everywhere from Dubai to Australia. Free time was about preparation—which was practically his family's motto. Well, his father's. Not that that had always been the case for Autry. Something he didn't like to think about.

Now, though, Autry had found himself with an entire three weeks, twenty-one days, to himself. No necessary meetings. No deals to broker—not until late August, when he'd have to be in Paris for the Thorpe Corp. negotiations. He could be spending these much-needed vacation weeks on the beach in Bali or southern California. Appreciating the view, including sexy women in bikinis. But two of his brothers had shocked him—and the rest of the Jones family—by settling down with wives in the boondocks of Montana.

Rust Creek Falls. If he looked one way there was a building—barely. Another, Montana wilderness. Walker hadn't been kidding when he referred to Rust Creek Falls as something of the "Wild West."

Speaking of his oldest brother, Walker Jones the Third, who didn't have a speck of small town in him, the company CEO had not only built a Jones Holdings, Inc. office here, but had built an actual log cabin for him and his new wife, Lindsay Dalton Jones, to live in. Autry wouldn't have believed it, but he'd seen the cabin with his own eyes at their wedding, back in May. Granted, it was pure luxury, but still. Logs. A cabin. Montana wilderness. Autry expected that of his brother Hudson, who loved ranch life and the open spaces of Wyoming and Montana. Hudson operated the business of the day care for Walker, and had fallen for the manager, Bella Stockton, and now the happily married couple lived together at the Lazy B Ranch.

Two Jones brothers down. None to go. Well, three, but Autry, despite being thirty-three years old, wasn't the marrying kind, and though he wasn't close with any of his brothers, he couldn't see Gideon and Jensen getting hitched. But if Walker and Hudson had, anything was possible.

He had these three weeks, zero relationships with his brothers and a chance to change that.

There was discord between his father, the domineering, controlling Walker Jones the Second, and his brother Walker the Third; their father had given up years ago on "wayward" Hudson following in the family footsteps. If Autry didn't take this time to try to bond with his brothers a little, maybe smooth over things between them and their father, the family would disintegrate. Unfortunately, his dad didn't seem to care, nor did his mother, so it was up to Autry. Why he cared so much, he wasn't sure. But he did. He wanted to know his brothers. Especially now that they'd done something so...unexpected, like falling in love and getting hitched. Making lifetime commitments.

"Whose daddy are you?" the little red-haired girl asked suddenly, her big eyes on Autry, her crayon poised in the air.

Autry froze. *No one's. And that's the way it's going to stay.* "No, sweetheart, I'm not anyone's daddy. I'm just visiting."

Miss Marley smiled at the girl. "This is Mr. Walker's and Mr. Hudson's brother, Mr. Autry."

"Mr. Walker and Mr. Hudson are nice," the girl said, then went back to coloring.

What? Walker was nice? Hudson has his moments, but Autry wouldn't go so far as to characterize him as nice. What had Rust Creek Falls done to the Jones brothers?

And what had his family done to *him* if he thought the words *nice* and *Jones* could never be paired in the same sentence?

Autry looked around the colorful space with its square foam mats with letters of the alphabet, its bean-bags and rows of cubbies in primary colors. Kid-size tables and chairs dotted the room. He could see door-ways leading into classrooms, a nursery with cribs, and what looked like a break room. The area above the re-ception desk, with *WELCOME* spelled out in blocks, was full of photographs of babies and watercolors by "Sophia, age three" and "Marcus, age seven"

How his brothers spent so much time around kids, Autry had no idea. Autry liked kids just fine. As long as he wasn't having them or raising them. In fact, Autry had a rule for himself when it came to dating: no women with baby fever. And under no circumstances would he date a single mother.

Lulu's sweet face came to mind. A face he hadn't let himself think about in months. Another big-cheeked baby, but with silky dark hair. Lulu, short for Louisa, had been a package deal with her single mother, beau-tiful Karinna. Autry had fallen in love with Karinna and soon felt like Lulu was his own flesh and blood. Suddenly the jet-setter had been changing diapers and wanting to stay in and listen to the woman he loved sing lullabies, instead of disappearing for weeks at a time on Jones Holdings business. But a few months later, when she left him for someone even richer, Autry lost not only his heart but the child he'd come to love.

So single mothers: never again.

"Ace in the Hole is on Sawmill Street," Miss Marley said, interrupting his thoughts. "Just past the gas station. Can't miss it. Oh, and order the ribs. Trust me. Best in town."

Ah. Ace in the Hole was starting to sound like a bar and grill. The kind with a big screen TV. Ribs and a good craft beer sounded pretty good. Plus, he was looking forward to seeing his brothers and getting to know their wives. Autry had flown in for the weddings, but had had to leave the next day. Now, he had weeks to solve the mystery of his brothers' complete turnarounds.

"Thanks for letting me know, Miss Marley," Autry said. "I'll be sure to order the ribs."

"Go, Brenna and Travis!" Marley said, giving the baby a little pump in the air. "Imagine that, two of our own on a reality TV show. So exciting!"

Autry had no idea who Brenna and Travis were, but a reality TV show called *The Great Roundup* probably had something to do with cattle. Maybe horses?

"Da," said the baby in Miss Marley's grasp, reaching out his arms toward Autry.

An old ache gripped Autry, catching him off guard. He'd thought he was done with the sudden stabbing pain over what had happened.

Marley smiled. "That's not your daddy, Dylan, but yes, he does look like your father with his blond hair and blue eyes."

Autry forced a smile. "It was nice to meet you," he said, extending his hand, then he headed out the door.

The one thing you could count on in this life was that there would be no babies or children in a bar.

Ace in the Hole, here I come. And not a minute too soon.

* * *

"Wow," Marissa Fuller said as she and her nine-year-old daughter, Abby, walked into the Ace in the Hole. "Standing room only tonight." Good thing she'd decided to leave her two younger daughters at home with their grandparents.

Abby's face lit up. "This is so exciting, Mom! The first episode of *The Great Roundup* is *finally* going to be on TV! Did you ever think a reality TV show would film right here in Rust Creek Falls? I could totally pass out from the anticipation! All those cute cowboys competing in teams for a zillion dollars—in Western feats and wilderness survival…and two who we actually know! I can't wait to find Janie and watch!"

How her daughter got that all out in one breath, Marissa would never know. While Abby scanned the crowd for her best friend, Marissa looked around for two empty seats. There was *one*—right next to her good friend Anne Lattimore, Janie's mother.

"Marissa!" Anne called, waving her over. "I've been saving you this seat for twenty minutes and have gotten a bunch of mean looks by folks who want it. One guy even offered to buy me the sirloin special if I let him have the chair."

"Was he cute?" Abby asked as they approached. "Blond or dark haired? Did he have dimples like Lyle in 2LOVEU?"

Marissa smiled and shook her head, then gratefully sat down next to Anne at the table for two that was wedged between two others. Her daughter's favorite subject was 2LOVEU, a boy band she listened to on repeat for hours. Marissa had heard the songs so often they'd grown on her, too.

"He was cute," Anne told Abby. "But around fifty. And no dimples, sorry."

"Abby, you can sit on my lap, like old times," Marissa said, squeezing her daughter's hand.

Abby's eyes widened. "Mom, I'm *nine*," she whispered in horror.

"No worries," Anne said, smiling at Abby. "Janie's over there, sitting on the floor in the kids section. She saved you a spot, too."

"Bye!" Abby squealed and ran over to the area, where Marissa could see around thirty or so children sitting on foam mats, talking excitedly and munching on the free popcorn the Ace staff was handing out in brown paper bags. There was a good view of the two giant screen televisions on stands on either side of the bar. No matter where you sat in the room, you could see them.

"You're the best, Anne," Marissa said, scooting a bit closer to her friend to avoid being elbowed in the ribs by the woman at the next table. A divorced mom with a full-time job as a receptionist at the veterinarian's office, Anne had her hands full but her act completely together. Something Marissa was working on. "I meant to get here twenty minutes ago, but Kiera couldn't find her favorite doll and had the tantrum of all tantrums just as I was leaving. I thought tantrums were supposed to stop by five years old."

Anne smiled, pushing a swath of her wavy blond hair behind her ear. "One of my neighbors threw a tantrum this morning over someone's dog walking on the edge of her property. I don't think there's an age limit, sorry."

Marissa laughed. "And then Kaylee managed to

smush a green bean in her ear at dinner, so I had to deal with a three-year-old sobbing that this means she's going to turn into a green bean."

Anne squeezed Marissa's hand. "Oh, to be three years old."

But finally, Marissa had made it. Her mom and dad, doting grandparents, had shooed her out the door, assuring her they'd help Kiera find the doll, and calm down Kaylee. But even when Marissa needed a night out so badly she could scream, she never felt comfortable leaving her parents to deal with sobs and tantrums. That was Marissa's job. She was the parent. She was the *only* parent.

She may have moved back in with her folks for the sake of the girls—and yes, her sake, too. But she wasn't about to take advantage of her parents' kindness and generosity. They'd been there for her two years ago when her husband, Mike, had died. They'd been there when she was struggling to make ends meet. They'd been there when she'd surrendered to the notion that she needed help, and had accepted their offer to move home. But her three daughters were *her* responsibility, and no matter how tired she was from her job at the sheriff's office, or comforting a sick child at three in the morning, Marissa was their mom. Despite that, though, living under her parents' roof sometimes made her feel like one of the kids instead of a twenty-seven-year-old widow, a grown-up.

A cheer went up in the room and Marissa glanced at the TV. It was showing a teaser promo for *The Great Roundup*, which was about to start in a few minutes, and there was Brenna O'Reilly, hometown girl, giving an interview, reality-TV-style, to someone off camera about how she never thought she could do this, but here she was, a hairstylist from Rust Creek Falls, participating in the competition with her hot fiancé, and she was going to give it her all.

You go, Brenna. Marissa knew all about finding herself in uncharted territory. You gave it your all or... There was actually no alternative.

"Brenna O'Reilly and Travis Dalton?" Anne said. She smiled and shook her head. "The cowboy no one ever thought would settle down and the flirty hairstylist always up for adventure—engaged. Crazy."

Marissa had gone to high school with Brenna, who'd been a year behind her. They'd been only acquaintances, but she had to agree. Plus, hadn't Brenna always talked about getting out of Rust Creek Falls? Granted, she had for the TV show, which had filmed for what must have been six very exciting weeks at the High Lonesome Guest Ranch. Rumor had it that Brenna and Travis would be coming to the viewing party, even though they'd been invited to watch the first episode with the producers and some of the other competitors.

"Chemistry works in mysterious ways," Jamie Stockton said, his arm around his wife, Fallon O'Reilly Stockton—Brenna's sister.

It sure was nice to see Jamie Stockton out for a change. Before he'd fallen in love with Fallon, the widowed rancher had been raising his baby triplets on his own. If anyone needed a night out, it was Jamie.

Fallon smiled and nodded, raising her beer mug. She had visited her sister on location during the filming of the show last month. But Fallon wouldn't say a word about what had gone on behind the scenes. Apparently, she'd had to sign confidentiality papers not to ruin any surprises.

What the whole town did know was that originally, Travis, the ultimate showman cowboy, was the only Rust Creek Falls contestant on the show, which was about cowboys—men and women—competing in Western-style challenges. But when the producers were in town last month to film some hometown segments and saw what amazing chemistry Travis had with his girlfriend, Brenna—and how camera ready Brenna was—they'd invited them both on the show. No one had even suspected Travis and Brenna were dating, but the next thing everyone knew, Travis had proposed and they were competing as *The Great Roundup*'s "engaged couple." If Marissa could binge watch the whole season in one night, she would. But she, like everyone else, would have to wait for every episode over the next several months.

"Now, that sounds like Travis," said Nate Crawford, who owned the general store and a hotel in town, "Asking a woman to marry him for good ratings." He grinned and shook his head.

Anne laughed. "I saw them a bunch of times together last month during the filming here. When the cameras weren't rolling. No way were they faking anything for ratings. Those two are in love for sure."

"Still, I can't imagine proposing to a woman on a whim," Zach Dalton said, adjusting his bolo tie as though it were squeezing his neck. Marissa glanced at Zach at the table on their other side. The handsome newcomer to town and his four brothers were cousins of Travis's.

"Well, no matter what happened behind the scenes,"

Anne said, "everything sure worked out for Travis and Brenna. They're engaged."

Marissa sighed. It sure had. All the romance in the air had left her a little wistful. Last month, her daughter Abby had talked nonstop about how "dreamy" their new town "star" Travis was, almost as dreamy as Lyle, the lead singer of 2LOVEU. And Marissa had always admired Brenna's free-spirited ways, especially back in high school. Brenna had had lots of dates, while Marissa had dated only one boy throughout high school and always expected they would get married. When she got pregnant after prom night, she'd married Michael Fuller at age eighteen. But Brenna had sown her wild oats and found love when she was ready for it. *Good for you, Brenna.*

Just as Marissa was about to try to flag one of the very busy waitresses, who were all racing around with platters of steaks and appetizers and ribs and trays of beer and soda, Abby ran over.

"Mom!" her daughter said, her brown eyes all dreamy. "That's the one you should pick. For sure."

Pick? Huh? Marissa looked in the direction her daughter was staring.

Ah. Three very good-looking men—two the Jones brothers and a third, who looked just like them—stood at the bar, talking, smiling, whispering. Marissa couldn't take her eyes off the one she didn't know. She was pretty sure she'd heard that Walker and Hudson, who owned Just Us Kids, had other brothers. And the tall Adonis between them, with his thick dark blond hair and sparkling, intense blue eyes, his designer shirt clearly costing more than her three kids' wardrobes for a year, had to be a Jones. They were millionaires, yes, but also rare men who looked like they belonged both in Montana and a big city. There was something about the cut of the Western shirt, the premium leather cowboy boots, the belt buckle on which was carved the initials AJ and the trim fit of low-slung dark jeans. Since her daughter knew who Walker and Hudson were, the girl had to be talking about the one in the middle. Abby was right. He was sexy.

"They look like they should be in an ad for men's cologne," Marissa quipped. "Or on a movie poster. But pick for what?" she asked her daughter.

Abby grinned and leaned close. "To be your boyfriend." The girl giggled and ran back to her seat next to her best friend.

Anne burst into laughter, but Marissa sighed. This was not the first time Abby had brought up the *b* word.

"Isn't she a little young to be this boy crazy?" Marissa asked her friend. "I mean, it's one thing for Abby to be putting up posters of 2LOVEU on her bedroom wall. It's another for her to be sizing up every man she sees as a potential love interest for her own mother."

Anne smiled but sighed, too. "Janie's the same. I hear her say good-night to the lead singer of 2LOVEU before bed. We weren't much different with our posters when we were kids."

"Except we can't remember being kids because we're a hundred years old," Marissa pointed out.

Anne laughed. "Exactly."

Marissa found herself staring at the gorgeous stranger again. She had to hand it to her daughter—the girl had amazing taste. Marissa loved the way his blond hair swooped up and back like a Hemsworth brother's. The few crinkles at the edges of his blue eyes suggested he was a bit older than her. Early thirties, she'd say. And those shoulders. Those arms. The way his waist narrowed down to those delicious jeans, which—

Oh my God.

He raised his beer glass at her and winked.

He'd caught her staring!

Mortifying!

"Can the floor open up and swallow me?" Marissa said, wishing the woman at the table in front of her had bigger hair so she could block Marissa and her cheeks, which had to be bright red.

"And miss the start of *The Great Roundup*?" Anne said with an evil grin. "Go talk to him! Hurry. You only have a few minutes."

"What? Talk to *that*? That absolute gorgeous specimen of man? He barely looks real he's so hot."

Anne laughed. "The waitresses are so busy we'll never get served before the show starts. Go get us two drafts and order a platter of something yummy. Perfect excuse to meet His Hotness. I heard Lindsay mention that her brother-in-law Autry was due in town this week and that Autry has been to just about every country in the world. How exciting is that? The man is a jet-setter. And gorgeous. Go get him."

A tiny bit of Marissa, who was trying to be more "in the moment," per a magazine article, wanted to do just that.

But come on. Marissa was a widowed mother of three young daughters and living with her parents. She might seem attractive across a room when he knew nothing about her, but she had no doubt that the man would run all the way back to Tulsa, where she'd heard the Jones brothers hailed from, the moment he discovered what her life was.

"I can just see that very expensive-looking man plucking green beans out of Kiera's ears," Marissa said. "*Not.* He's nice to look at, but come on. I'm going to be on my own until Kaylee's out of high school." Which was only, *gulp*, fifteen more years.

"Marissa Fuller!" Anne chastised her with a smile. "What did Brenna and Travis's crazy whirlwind romance teach us? That you just never know. If you're open to it, if you're *there*, love just might show up."

Marisa was so touched by how positive Anne always was—and Anne was the divorcee who'd never, ever gotten over her first love, Daniel Stockton. She wrapped her friend in a hug. "Maybe we'll both find love again," Marissa said.

"Well, if I were you, I'd march over to the bar before some other single woman does."

But Marissa stayed put, an eye on Abby and her thoughts back home. Yes, a night out was sorely needed, but Marissa missed putting her little ones to bed and wishing them sweet dreams. That was her life. Not hot men in thousand-dollar cowboy boots.

But this particular one sure was nice to fantasize about.

Chapter Two

Autry watched the brunette with the dark eyes try to snag the waitress's attention at least five times. She wasn't having any luck. Which gave him his perfect in. He asked the bartender for two of the finest craft beers and got an eye roll and two drafts on tap.

"I keep telling you, Autry," his brother Walker said. "This is Rust Creek Falls. And a dive bar *in* Rust Creek Falls. We don't do twelve-dollar bottles of beer here." His brother's wedding band glinted in the dim lighting.

"And *two* beers?" Hudson asked with a grin. "You got here, what? Five minutes ago? And you already have your eye on someone?"

Autry smiled. "I'm in town for three weeks. That's a long time. And you two have wives now and lives outside Jones Holdings. I need something to fill the hours."

"Careful, brother," Walker said, running a hand

through his dirty-blond hair. "There's something in the water here. It got me. It got Hudson. It's gonna get you."

"Not a chance," Autry said, his gaze on the luscious brunette beauty. Had a woman in jean shorts and a yellow T-shirt ever been so stunning? "End of August, I'll be in Paris. As single as ever."

"If you say so," Hudson said, raising his beer glass at Autry.

Autry caught the smirk Hudson gave Walker. No matter what, it sure was nice to see Walker and Hudson together. Joking, laughing, sharing a beer. Once, back when they were all kids, Walker and Hudson had been close. But they hadn't been for years. Looked like being neighbors had changed that some.

A woman standing next to them with a baby in her arms turned to Walker. "Hey, Walker, will you hold Jackson for me for a moment while I go hug my aunt and uncle?"

"You bet, Candace," Walker said, taking the baby as if he did this sort of thing all the time.

Walker Jones. The Third. With a baby in his arms. Bouncing it a bit and making baby talk. "Who's a cute one?" Walker said, nuzzling his nose at the tiny tot.

Good Lord. What planet was Autry on? Was Rust Creek Falls in another dimension?

And there really were babies everywhere. Even in bars. Though, granted, tonight was a special occasion. From the looks of the place, the entire town had turned up to watch *The Great Roundup*. With all the buzz Autry had heard about the show in the ten minutes he'd been in the Ace in the Hole, he was excited to watch. Cowboys competing for a million bucks? Hell yeah. That was his kind of TV. The Jones family might be millionaires, but they were cowboys at heart. Autry's first memory was of being on the back of a horse. And the first gift he'd ever gotten? A "piggy" bank in the shape of a stallion. Money and horses were two hallmarks of the Jones family.

The baby's mother returned and held out her arms for little Jackson. "You're a peach," she said to Walker.

Walker, a peach? Autry couldn't help himself. He laughed.

Hudson grinned. "Trust me. If peachhood got Walker and me, you're next. You're here."

"I'm immune," Autry said.

"*Sure*, bro," Hudson said with a knowing nod. He glanced toward the tables. "Bella's waving us over to our seats. Our rib platters arrived."

Autry glanced at their table—two entire tables away from the brunette beauty. Way too far.

"Let's all go sit down," Walker said, nodding at his wife, Lindsay, who sat next to Bella. "I'm really glad you're here, Autry. We barely got to talk at the weddings. After the show we'll all head over to Maverick Manor for a nightcap." Walker clapped Autry on the shoulder, then followed Hudson across the room.

The bartender placed the two beers Autry had ordered on the bar. "Be right there," Autry called.

Beers in hand, he wove his way through tables and the standing room–only crowd. There was no way in hell he could resist meeting this woman. Just as there was no chance in that same hell they'd have anything other than a few amazing weeks together before he jetted off to Paris. If she was game, what was the harm in letting something happen between them for twenty-one delicious days? And something *would* happen. The closer he got to her table, the more her brown eyes and her unenhanced pink-red lips drew him in. He had to know her. Well, on a superficial level.

"Hello," he said, nodding at the brunette and the blonde beside her. "Here you go," he said, handing a beer to each woman. "Autry Jones, at your service."

"I knew you had to be a Jones brother," the brunette said. "I'm Marissa Fuller and this is my friend Anne Lattimore. Thanks for the beers. That was very thoughtful." She smiled and took a sip, then set down the glass and looked around. Not at him.

Huh. Where was the flirtatiousness? Where was the fawning? Where was the sidling up to him and pressing herself against him like most women did?

"Are you in town visiting your brothers?" Marissa asked, taking another sip of beer.

He nodded. "For three weeks. I'm used to Tulsa, so Rust Creek Falls is a nice change."

"Are you staying with Walker or Hudson?" Marissa asked. "I'll admit, sometimes I drive by Walker's house just to look at it. It's amazing. A mansion made entirely out of logs."

He smiled. "A log mansion for Walker and a beautiful ranch for Hudson. I visited both homes after their weddings back in May and June. But I'm staying at Maverick Manor."

Surprise crossed her pretty features. "For three weeks?"

"I like room service," he said. The truth was that he wasn't close enough with either brother to feel comfortable staying with them that long. And he did like room service. Besides, Autry had gotten so used to luxury hotels that anything too homespun would feel...wrong and claustrophobic.

She laughed. "Don't we all."

Her smile had him so captivated he almost forgot where he was. But then the lights dimmed and he noticed Walker waving him over. "Autry, I'm gonna eat your share of the ribs," his brother called.

Marissa glanced at Walker and laughed. "Better get over there before there's nothing but a plate of bones."

"Nice to meet you, Autry," Anne said. "And thanks for the beer."

He. Could. Not. Make. His. Legs. Move. Away.

"Uh, buddy, you're blocking my view of the TV," a man said, and Autry snapped back to attention.

"Sorry," he said to the guy. He smiled at Marissa and her friend and headed over to his seat.

Autry glanced back at Marissa shortly after, but instead of ogling him with a sexy look on her face, letting him know she was up for meeting later, she was chatting with her friend.

Well, well, he thought, biting into a succulent rib with the best barbecue sauce he'd had in years. A challenge had just presented itself. And *challenge* was Autry Jones's middle name.

Hmm, Marissa thought as the credits began rolling on the two big-screen TVs. The man was in town for three weeks. Might be nice to go out to dinner or a movie with a very good-looking man, a nice change of pace from watching *ET* and *Frozen* for the thirtieth time in her parents' family room, then cleaning up errant popcorn kernels.

"There's Travis!" Anne said, as the cowboy's handsome face filled the screen. They were showing a promo video he'd shot last month in Rust Creek Falls, talking about his love of horses and his fiancée. Then there was Travis and Brenna on horseback, riding along with the other contestants to the "canteen" where the host, Jasper Ridge, a middle-aged cowboy all in black with a black handlebar mustache, awaited. The Ace in the Hole erupted in cheers.

Jasper explained the rules—the last cowboy or cowgirl standing would win one million dollars. *Whoa boy.* That was a lot of money. The contestants would be paired for some challenges, but each was competing on his or her own. So alliances could be made, but it might not get the contestants anywhere but tricked and eliminated. Marissa watched as the twenty-two contestants were introduced in little snippets. There was the Franklin family—widowed Fred and his twin sons, Rob and Joey. A grizzled cowboy named Wally Wilson in his late sixties. A fortysomething divorcée named Roberta and a handsome former soldier, Steve, with a prosthetic leg. Marissa's attention was snagged by one contestant in particular—a sexy blonde rodeo star named Summer Knight.

From just the first five minutes it was clear to Marissa that Summer had a huge crush on Travis. She kept trying to sidle up to him, but Brenna, never one to sit quietly by, sidled right up between them, nudging Summer away. Marissa had to smile. And it was clear that the divorcée, Roberta, was very interested in the war hero, who was at least a decade younger. From the way Steve looked at Roberta, the man was smitten with her, too.

The host, Jasper, explained how the main challenges

would work—contestants would be paired in teams and the events would involve everything from building a lean-to to cow roping to hay-bale racing. The winning contestant in each challenge would receive immunity for the next one, and after the day, one contestant would be eliminated.

Marissa sipped her beer while the contestants made "immunity" bracelets of braided leather and beads and put them in a carved wooden box with much ceremony. Then the group set up a tent camp and built a community fire in front. Finally it was time for the first challenge, freeze branding cattle, and Travis and Brenna were paired together. When neither was eliminated at the end of the episode, everyone cheered.

Suddenly an even bigger cheer erupted in the bar, folks standing and clapping. The Ace in the Hole was so crowded that Marissa couldn't see what was going on. She turned to Anne. "What are we missing?"

Anne shrugged, and they both glanced around. A crowd had formed by the door. Marissa craned her neck. She could just make out a pink cowboy hat. Marissa knew of only one woman who wore a pink hat.

"It's Brenna and Travis!" someone shouted.

As word spread across the Ace in the Hole that the hometown stars had shown up, everyone started clapping and wolf whistling.

"Hot wings and a round for everyone!" Travis called out. "On me."

"Lemonade for the kids!" Brenna added with a grin.

The cheers got even louder as the waitresses headed into the kitchen to make good on Travis's generosity.

"Thank you all so much for coming to cheer us on," Travis said, lifting his Stetson.

"Ya'll *were* cheering for us, right?" Brenna added with a grin.

Marissa didn't have a good view of the pair, but she could see Brenna's long red hair in a loose braid under the pink cowboy hat. Handsome Travis was in jeans and boots, his arm slung over Brenna's shoulder.

And glinting on Brenna's finger was a diamond engagement ring.

As Brenna and Travis answered questions about the episode, careful not to give away anything about episode two, Marissa couldn't help but notice the way the pair looked at each other as each spoke. They were truly in love. Travis gazed at Brenna with such warmth and respect in his eyes. And Brenna had never looked so happy.

Good for them, Marissa thought. Feeling just slightly jealous. In a good way. Maybe being a little envious meant that one day she'd want that for herself.

Of course, she couldn't imagine having some big romance. She was a widowed mother of three young children. That was her life. That was her full-time job, despite her part-time job at the sheriff's office. How on earth could she even have time for a hot love affair?

"Love is in the air in Rust Creek Falls," Anne whispered. "If it happened to them, it could happen to us."

Marissa watched as Travis dipped Brenna for a dramatic kiss, covering their faces with his cowboy hat. Sigh. Had she ever been kissed like that? Even in the brief window when she and Mike had been just a couple and not parents?

"Please," Marissa said. "They're TV stars. I'm just regular old me in my jean shorts."

"Well, someone who's anyone but 'regular old me'

sure seems to like those jean shorts," Anne said, wiggling her eyebrows with a sneaky grin.

"What?" Marissa asked but her gaze slid over toward where Autry Jones was sitting.

He was looking right at her, his expression a mix of warm, friendly and downright…flirtatious.

He raised his glass to her and she smiled, then turned back to the TV. She took another peek, and Autry was deep in conversation with his brother Hudson.

Well, here's your chance to be a little more adventurous, Marissa told herself, admiring the way his hunter green shirt fit over his broad shoulders. *If the man asks you out, you will say yes. It's just a date. He doesn't have to want to marry you. He doesn't have to want to be father to your kids. You're not looking to get married again, anyway. It's just dinner and a stroll or a movie, culminating, hopefully, in an amazing kiss. Times twenty-one days,* she added. Yes. She decided it right then and there. If Autry asked her out, she'd accept.

But then she glanced up at the sight of Brenna on TV in an ad for next week's episode, her diamond engagement ring sparkling, talking about how gallant and romantic Travis was even while freeze branding cattle. There was no way a man like Autry—single, as far as she knew; childless, as far as she knew; jet-setter, as far as Anne knew—would want to date a widow with three kids, a demanding part-time job, and parents with eagle eyes and a comment about everything.

Sure was nice to think about, though.

Well, so much for sticking around the Ace in the Hole to squeeze through the crowd to congratulate

Brenna or be tapped on the shoulder by that inhumanly hot Autry Jones and asked out on a date.

Not five minutes after the episode officially ended and the television channels were changed to sports analyses, Marissa's mother had called. Kiera was convinced there was a monster in her closet and a half hour of trying to make the five-year-old believe otherwise had only exhausted Marissa's parents. She'd said goodbye to Anne, who was ready to leave herself anyway, and headed home with Abby, who'd talked nonstop on the way about how dreamy Travis was and wasn't it amazing that he was as dreamy on TV as he was in person and it only proved that Lyle from 2LOVEU was probably a regular nice guy in real life just like Travis was.

Marissa was grateful for the chatterbox beside her as they headed into the house. The more Abby talked and required nods and "Oh yes, I agree" from her mother, the less Marissa could think about a certain six-foot-plus, muscular, gorgeous blond man.

She hadn't been able to catch his eye as she'd left. All for the best.

And so Marissa had gone upstairs with her monster-blaster super sprayer, which doubled as her spray bottle of water for fixing her hair and ironing clothes. Roberta Rafferty had tried the monster blaster, but apparently only Mommy had the superpower of vanquishing the monster in the closet.

Armed with the spray bottle, Marissa burst into her daughters' room, tiptoeing so as not to wake Kaylee, who'd managed to sleep through Kiera's tears and Grandma and Grandpa's attempts to prove there was no monster.

"Mommy! The monster is going to get me," Kiera said, holding her pillow in front of her as a shield between herself and the closet on the other side of the room.

Marissa sat down on her middle daughter's bed. "Sweets, I'm your mother and I'll always tell you the truth, no matter what. I promise you that even though you believe there's a monster in the closet, there really isn't. Sometimes our minds tell us something and scare us, even though it's not true."

Kiera tilted her head. "But I saw him! He opened the door and made a mean face at me! He had three eyes!"

"Well, let's see," Marissa said. With Kiera biting her lip and looking nervous, holding out her shield-pillow, Marissa walked over the closet. She opened the door. No monster. Just a lot of pink and purple clothing. "There's no monster, Kiera. I promise."

"Can you spray inside just to be safe?"

Marissa pumped the water bottle, the fine mist landing on the girls' suitcases.

Marissa closed the door and walked back over to Kiera's bed. "There will never be a monster in that closet. You can count on that."

"I feel better now, Mommy."

Three seconds later, Kiera was snoring, her arm wrapped around her stuffed orange monkey. Meanwhile, her mother was completely exhausted.

"You're such a great mom," came a little whisper.

Marissa whirled around.

Her nine-year-old daughter stood in the doorway, looking like she might cry.

"Abby? Are you all right?"

"Yeah. I'm just—"

"What?" Marissa asked, her heart squeezing.

"I'm really glad you're our mom. You always know what to say and do."

Marissa held out her arms and Abby rushed over. Sometimes she forgot that Abby was just nine, right in the middle of kidhood. She was the eldest Fuller girl and took her role as big sister seriously.

"Thank you, Abby," Marissa said. "I love you to the moon and back."

"Me, too, Mom." With that, Abby got into bed. She said good-night to her poster of 2LOVEU above her bed, then grabbed her own favorite stuffed teddy bear that her father had given her when she was born. Within five minutes, Abby was fast asleep.

Marissa watched her daughter's chest rise and fall and pulled up the pink comforter, then kissed her cheek and tiptoed over to Kiera to do the same. Kaylee was on her tummy in her big-girl toddler bed. Marissa bent over to kiss her forehead, then sat down on Abby's desk chair and looked at her girls.

This was her life. And this was everything. Yeah, it might be nice to fantasize about having the attention of a handsome man. A hot man. A gazillionaire, no less. Pure fantasy.

Marissa Fuller had everything she needed and wanted right in this room. Her heart was full and her life was blessed, despite the hardships.

Her head screwed on straight, she got up, said good-night to her parents and thanked them both again for watching the girls while she'd enjoyed a night out with Abby, then went into her bedroom and changed into a T-shirt and yoga pants and finally slid into bed.

Where she immediately thought of Autry Jones.

What it would be like to kiss him. To feel his hands on her.

She smiled. Just a fantasy. Nothing wrong with that, right? Their paths would likely not cross while he was in town. Her life was here and work and grocery shopping and taking the girls to the doughnut shop for an occasional treat.

But again, no reason she couldn't dream about a TV-style romance with Autry Jones in the privacy of her own bedroom.

Chapter Three

"Kaylee, no!" Marissa called, but it was too late. Her three-year-old had pushed her little doll stroller, with a yellow rabbit tucked safely inside, into a huge display of cereal boxes in Crawford's General Store. They came tumbling down, narrowly missing her.

"Oopsies," Kaylee said, her face crumbling. "Sorry." The girl hung her head, tears dripping down her cheeks.

Oh God, Marissa thought, shaking her head. After waking up twice during the night to comfort Kaylee, who had a tooth coming in, she'd had a crazed morning looking for Kiera's other red light-up sneaker and then Abby's favorite shirt, which had "disappeared" from the folded-laundry basket—it turned out it was never put in the hamper. That was followed by a three-hour shift at the reception desk of the sheriff's office, ending with getting yelled at by Anne Lattimore's neighbor for not sending an officer to deal with the dog-being-allowed-to-walk-on-the-edge-of-my-lawn-issue. Marissa didn't need one more thing. But here it was. And it was only eleven in the morning.

"Kaylee, it's—"

She swallowed her *okay* as the girl ran sobbing down the aisle, running so fast that Marissa had to abandon her cart and leap over the boxes of Oat Yummies littering the floor.

"Ah!" Kaylee said. "A giant!"

Marissa dodged a few more cereal boxes and glanced up into the amazing blue eyes of Autry Jones.

The man she'd been unable to stop thinking about. After soothing Kaylee back to sleep last night, Marissa had been so tired she'd squeezed beside her on the toddler bed, imagining Autry's long, lean, muscular physique beside her before she'd finally drifted off to sleep.

"Oh, thank God," Marissa said. "She sure is fast. A human roadblock was just what was needed."

Autry laughed. "Should we find the runaway train's mother before another display of cereal boxes comes tumbling down, this time on top of us?"

Marissa tilted her head. Was it strange that he didn't assume the little getaway artist was hers? "You're looking at her. She pushed her doll stroller a smidge too far and that was that. This is Kaylee. She's three going on ready for the Olympics."

Kaylee continued to stare up at "the giant." Marissa was five feet six and a huge supporter of comfy flat shoes, and Autry towered over her at at least six foot two, so she could understand why Kaylee thought she was dealing with a fairy-tale giant. He was much better looking than giants usually were, though.

"Yours?" Autry said, staring at Marissa.

"Are you a giant?" Kaylee asked, craning her neck.

Autry knelt down in front of the girl. "Nope. I'm an Autry. Autry Jones. And it's very nice to meet you, Kaylee. You know, when I was a kid, I would race my brothers up and down the aisles of supermarkets until the manager marched over to yell at us."

Kaylee tilted her head, understanding only about half of that. "Did you win?"

"I won every now and then," Autry said. "But with four brothers and me right in the middle, there was always one bigger and faster or lighter and faster."

"No fair," Kaylee said. "Guess where we're going now."

"Grocery shopping?" Autry asked.

"But guess why we're here," she said.

"To buy groceries?" Autry suggested, covering his mouth so he wouldn't laugh.

"We're getting picnic stuff," Kaylee said. "Sandwiches and fruit and cookies. You can come, too."

Marissa watched Autry stiffen. Yup, there it was. He now knew she was a mother, likely figured she was divorced or widowed and so had taken a literal and figurative step back.

"Sweetie," she said to her daughter, "Autry is in town to visit his family and I'm sure he has plans for the day." Marissa waited for him to jump on the out she'd just given him.

"What kind of sandwiches?" he asked Kaylee, still kneeling beside her.

"Peanut butter and jelly—my favorite," the girl said.

Autry smiled. "That's my favorite, too. I'd love to come. I have two hours before I have to meet my brothers at my hotel."

Marissa stared at the man. Did he just say he'd love

to come? That peanut butter and jelly sandwiches were
his favorite?

Huh.

"Yay!" Kaylee said.

A millionaire executive cowboy was coming to their
picnic. Why did Marissa have the feeling this would
not be the first time Autry Jones would surprise her?

Whoa boy. What the hell was he doing? When Marissa had told him the cute little girl was hers, for a
split second Autry had almost gone running out of the
grocery store. No single mothers. That was his rule.
And he didn't have many rules. But instead of racing
out the door, he'd said yes to going on a family outing. And that was after Marissa had given him a perfect and easy out.

So why hadn't he taken it?

Because he'd been unable to stop thinking about
Marissa Fuller since he'd first laid eyes on her yesterday at the Ace in the Hole. He'd been hoping to talk to
her after *The Great Roundup* ended, but by the time
he'd woven his way through the crowd, she was gone.
He and his brothers had met up at his hotel and they'd
talked for a while over good scotch in the lobby bar.
He'd wanted to ask Walker and Hudson if they knew
Marissa, and surely they did, since Rust Creek Falls
was such a small town. But Autry realized he didn't
want to hear anything about her secondhand; he wanted
to get to know her himself.

You can still run, he told himself as he carried
the grocery bags containing their picnic and walked
alongside Marissa, who held her little girl's hand. They
were on their way to a park Marissa had mentioned

that was just a bit farther down Cedar Street. He could make up a forgotten appointment. Someone to see. And book the hell away.

But he kept walking, charmed—against his will—by cute Kaylee's light-up sneakers and the way she talked about the puppy that stole her sandwich the last time she went on a picnic with her mom.

"Well, this time, I'll guard your sandwich from every puppy in the park," Autry said.

He felt Marissa's eyes on him. Assessing him? Wondering if he was father material? He wasn't. He was in town temporarily, end of story. As long as he kept his guard up, his wits about him and his eye on the prize, which was to drink in the loveliness of Marissa Fuller for a few weeks, he'd be A-OK.

He glanced at Marissa, surprised again at how damned alluring she was. The woman wore jean shorts, a short-sleeve blue-and-yellow-plaid button-down shirt and orange flip-flops decorated with seashells. Her toenails were each polished a different sparkly color, and something told him she'd let Kaylee give her the pedicure. She wasn't wearing a stitch of makeup, and her wavy, long dark hair fell past her shoulders. She was as opposite the usual woman who caught his eye as possible. Autry met most of the women he dated in airport VIP lounges, alerted to their presence by their click of polished high heels on the floor and the smell of expensive perfume.

"Guess how many sisters I have?" Kaylee asked him, holding her free hand behind her back.

Autry froze. There were more?

"One?" he asked, trying not to visibly swallow.

Kaylee shook her head and giggled.

She let go of Marissa and held out both hands, palms facing him. Ten? She had ten sisters? He was going on a picnic with a mother of eleven?

Earth to Autry, he ordered himself. *The girl is three. Calm down.*

Kaylee giggled again and held up two fingers like a peace sign.

There was nothing peaceful about this. He might not be dating a mother of eleven, but he was dating a mother of three. Not that an impromptu picnic counted as a date. This was just a friendly little picnic. After all, three-year-olds didn't accompany their mothers on first dates.

Autry felt better. Not a date. Just a peanut butter and jelly sandwich and some fruit.

Still, he pulled at the collar of his polo shirt. It was strangling him. And granted, it was August, but was it a thousand degrees suddenly?

"There's the park," Marissa said, pointing down North Buckskin Road.

Autry glanced at the sign as they passed it. Rust Creek Falls Park. He didn't spend a lot of time in parks or going on picnics. But it was eighty-one degrees and sunny, with a delicious breeze that every now and then blew back Marissa's wavy hair, exposing her enticing neck. Perfect park weather. And it wasn't very crowded. A few people walked dogs, a couple joggers ran on the path and a group of teenagers were sunbathing and giggling in the distance.

"Here's a perfect spot," Marissa said. "Right under a shade tree."

"Hi, Mr. Autry," Kaylee said, for absolutely no reason as she stared up at him. *Gulp.* She was looking at him with pure adoration in her twinkly brown eyes. She slipped her little hand into his.

Oh God. He wasn't supposed to be charming the three-year-old! It was the elder Fuller he wanted to have looking at him that way. Instead, Marissa was focused on laying out the blanket she'd brought.

"Hi," Kaylee said again. "Hi." She rested her head against his hip.

"Hi," he said, forcing a smile.

Yes. He had definitely entered another dimension of time and space. Where Autry Jones was in a park with a single mother and her three-year-old, about to eat sticky peanut butter and jelly sandwiches, which, granted, *were* his favorite.

Make your escape. Any ole excuse will do. Bolt, man! Bolt.

But Autry's feet stayed right where they were, his gaze transfixed on Marissa's lovely eyes and a beauty mark near her mouth. Now he was staring at her lips. Wanting to reach out and—

"Mr. Autry, you're lucky," Kaylee said, snagging his attention as she sat down.

"Because I'm here with you guys?" he asked, tapping the adorable little girl on the nose as he sat at a reasonable distance. Did she have to be so stinking cute?

She tilted her head as though that was a dumb answer. "Because you get to eat dessert first if you want. You're a grown-up."

"Ah," Autry said, smiling at Marissa. "But I always eat my healthy sandwich first. Then dessert."

Kaylee shrugged, turning to look in the bags. Marissa pulled out a jar of peanut butter, strawberry jam and a loaf of bread, then some paper plates and plastic utensils.

"Allow me," he said, taking the knife and peanut butter.

She raised an eyebrow. "I'm sorry, Autry, but you really don't strike me as a man who eats a lot of PB and J."

"You've never seen me at midnight, hungry for a snack while going over fiscal projections."

Her cheeks grew pink. Hmm. That could mean only one thing. That she was imagining him at midnight, naked, eating peanut butter in his kitchen. Not that that was remotely sexy. Maybe she was just imagining him at midnight. Naked or not. She still wasn't giving him any signals either way. She didn't flirt. She didn't laugh at every little thing he said, funny or not. She didn't brush up against him to try to turn him on. He really had no idea if Marissa Fuller, mother of three, was interested in him in the slightest.

They ate. They had sandwiches. They had oranges. They had chocolate chip cookies. By the time Autry almost finished his sparkling water, Kaylee had fallen fast asleep on the blanket, using her little monkey backpack as a pillow.

"Three kids, huh?" he said. "That can't be easy."

Marissa took a sip of her water. "It's not. But loving them is. Plus we live with my parents. In the house I grew up in. So I have backup 24/7."

He noticed she kept her gaze on him, as if waiting to be judged.

"*You're* the lucky one," Autry said. "If you live with your parents, you must be close with them. And your kids and folks must be close. That's gold, Marissa."

She tilted her head. "I guess I've never really thought of it that way. But you're right, we are close. Maybe too close!" She smiled. "Not you and your family?"

He looked up at an airplane high in the sky, watching it jet over the clouds. "No. We were never a close family. The Joneses were about business. Everything is about Jones Holdings, Inc. Interestingly, not even that managed to bring us closer. But I was never close with my brothers growing up. And there are five of us."

"But you're here," she said. "Visiting Walker and Hudson."

"I'm trying," he said. "My father, the imperious Walker Jones the Second, feels like his namesake eldest son defected. Walker moved here. Opened a Jones Holdings office here. Is doing what he wants—here. And Hudson always marched to his own drum, which never involved the family business."

"And you?" she asked. For a moment he was captivated by how the sun lit up her dark hair.

"All about business. But I try very hard not to be a workaholic. I never want to be like my father, who put the company above everything—family, birthdays, special occasions. He missed everything and still believes business comes first."

"You just said you're all about business," Marissa pointed out.

"Because I don't have other commitments or responsibilities. For a reason. No wife. No kids. When I work around the clock or fly off to Dubai for a month, I'm not hurting anyone. In fact, I'm making someone happy—my father."

"But surely you want a family someday," she said, popping a green grape into her mouth.

He reached for his water and took a long sip. Did he? If he were really honest, he didn't know. He'd had his heart smashed, his trust broken, and all his tender feelings for that sweet baby he'd come to think of as his own had hardened like steel.

"So you're divorced?" he asked, glad to change the subject. He wanted to know everything about Marissa Fuller.

"Widowed," she said, taking a container of strawberries from the bag. "Two years ago in a car accident. My five-year-old, Kiera, has very little memory of her father. Kaylee here has none at all."

"And the third daughter?"

"Abby. She's nine."

Nine? Marissa couldn't be older than twenty-seven, maybe twenty-eight. She'd been a mother a long time, practically all her adult life.

He watched her bite her lip, seeming lost in thought. "Abby was seven when her dad died and remembers him very well. A few times a week, when Abby is saying her good-nights to her little sisters, I'll overhear her telling them about their daddy."

Marissa's life was very different from his. What she'd been through. What she did on a daily basis.

"She sounds like a great kid," he said.

Marissa nodded. "And one who had to grow up too fast. She mothers her little sisters all the time. Sometimes I even forget that life before their dad died wasn't quite like the paradise Abby paints for her sisters."

Her cheeks turned red, as though she hadn't meant to say that aloud. She held out the container of strawberries and he took one.

"Well, I might not be married," Autry said, "but I

have no doubt that marriage is hard and takes work. And you clearly got married very young."

"I got pregnant on prom night. Married and a mother at eighteen. Four years later, Kiera came along. And Kaylee was a surprise—a nice surprise, but maybe not the boy Mike ho—" She turned away. "I guess sometimes I start talking about all this and end up saying too much."

He reached out and moved a strand of hair from her face, the slightest touch against her cheek, and yet he felt it *everywhere*. "Best way to get to know someone is to listen to them talk when they're not guarded."

She smiled. "You're trying to get to know me?"

"Well, I only have three weeks in Rust Creek Falls, but yes. I want to know you, Marissa Fuller."

"Marissa Fuller, mother of three. With baggage. With live-in parents. With a really busy schedule."

"I'd like to steal up your free time," he said.

She laughed. "Do I *have* free time? If I ever have time to myself, I always think I should spend it one-on-one with one of the girls. Or I should scrub the bathroom tub before my mother does, and she always gets to it before I can. My life isn't exactly Italian restaurants and dancing and walks in big-sky country."

He moved a bit closer to her. "But maybe you'd *like* to go to dinner at an Italian restaurant. Go dancing. Take a walk in big-sky country."

"I'd love all that, Autry. But I've got responsibilities. Three young kids."

He nodded. "Of course. But do you know who you sound a little bit like? My dad. He never felt comfortable taking a day off. He never relaxed or had fun. The business was everything, just like your home life is. As it should be, Marissa. Home and family—that's everything. But you need some time to yourself, too. To recharge."

"I wish," she said. "But I've been doing this since I was eighteen, Autry. You're what? Thirty-two? Thirty-three? I can't even relate to that kind of freedom. I hear you jet all over the world for Jones Holdings."

"Thirty-three and, yes, I do. Our corporate headquarters are in Tulsa, Oklahoma, where I grew up. I live in a skyscraper on the twenty-fifth floor. But I'm never there. I have a whole atlas of destinations in mind to build our corporate profile and assets."

"And no woman has ever tempted you to settle down? Like your brothers?"

He frowned and turned away, hoping his expression didn't match what he was thinking. He didn't want to talk about Karinna or Lulu. "I don't have the luxury of that," he said. "Not if I want to keep Jones Holdings expanding globally. Just like you don't have the luxury of going to a movie whenever you feel like it. In three weeks, I'll be in Paris, likely for a year." He paused and looked directly at her. "Maybe until I leave, we can keep each other company."

"Exsqueeze me?"

He laughed. "I don't mean in bed. I mean I'd like to spend time with you."

"I'm a package deal, Autry. Even for three weeks in August."

"Kaylee likes me," he said. "I've already passed the Fuller daughter test."

Marissa smiled. "I suppose you have. She's not easy to charm." She took a long sip of water. "Look, Autry.

You're tempting. Very tempting. But my life isn't about fantasy or what I think about before I drift off to sleep."

"Doesn't mean you can't have a little romance in your life."

"Romance? I think I'm done with that, Autry."

"Marissa—"

She took a deep breath. "My marriage wasn't perfect. Many nights, Mike and I went to bed angry. It wasn't easy for me to juggle working full-time with having three little kids and trying to take care of a home, so I became a stay-at-home mom. Money was tight, and Mike worked longer hours at the office to secure a promotion and a raise. We argued at times, the stress made it impossible not to, but we both agreed the sacrifices were worth it. Thing was, with so many added responsibilities, romance went out the window. That's just the way it was and I wasn't about to complain. I knew I had a blessed life. A home, a good husband, three healthy children. Till that one day when a drunk driver took Mike away."

"I'm so sorry."

She nodded. "I was so overwhelmed by grief and panic. I wasn't really sure how I'd keep things going, but I just kept putting one foot in front of the other for the kids. The meager life insurance policy that Mike had helped for a while, but I worried about money constantly. So when my parents suggested we move in, I said yes. Ralph and Roberta Rafferty are wonderful grandparents, but I'm a twenty-seven-year-old woman living at home with Mom and Dad."

"I admire you, Marissa. You did what you had to do at every step."

He thought about how tough her life was—rewarding and full of love, yes, but tough. He didn't date single mothers, but if he couldn't break his own rule, what good was it? For the three weeks he had in Rust Creek Falls he wanted to give her the world. Her and her kids. It wasn't like he'd fall in love. Marissa was a single mother of three. There was already a great barrier built right in.

"Well, I'd like to get to know you while I'm here," he said. "I'd like to treat you and your daughters to a little fun. Good clean fun like this picnic. Hot-air balloon rides. Baseball games. You name it." He paused. "But clearly, I'm very attracted to you, Marissa. I think you're drop-dead gorgeous. I like spending time with you. I like *you*. So romance is definitely on my mind. I just want to put that out there."

He'd enjoy his time with Marissa, cement a bond with his brothers, repair things with them and his dad, then he'd jet off to Paris—no heartache for either of them.

She stared at him with those brown eyes, and again he could see her thinking. Assessing. Considering. "You're not looking for commitment and I'm not, either," Marissa finally said. "So…friends. No strings attached."

"No strings," he repeated.

But their agreement left him a bit uneasy. It was one thing to say no strings and another to really mean it. And hurting Marissa—or her kids—was unacceptable.

Chapter Four

At dinner that night, when it was Kaylee's turn to share something special that had happened that day, a Fuller-Rafferty tradition going back generations, the three-year-old couldn't stop talking about the nice man who came on their picnic and did magic tricks.

Yes, Autry Jones did magic tricks. The man was full of surprises. Big ones and little ones. At the two-hour mark of the unexpectedly long picnic, Marissa had had to wake up Kaylee so Autry could meet his brothers and Marissa could go pick up Kiera and Abby from their playdates, but Kaylee had been a little grumpy and still tired. Autry had plucked a clementine from the bag and made it magically disappear and reappear atop Kaylee's head, which had brought forth belly laughs and "do it again, Mr. Autry."

"Who was it?" Abby asked, reaching for the bowl of mashed potatoes.

Marissa slid a glance at her mother, who was pretending great interest in passing the platter of roast chicken to her husband, but was really hanging on to every word. Marissa didn't often spend time with any men. Nice or otherwise.

"While we were shopping for our picnic in Crawford's," Marissa explained, "we ran into someone I met at the viewing party last night. So we invited him to join us. No big deal."

"Who was that, dear?" Roberta Rafferty asked, so nonchalantly that Marissa smiled.

"Autry Jones."

Fifty-five-year-old Ralph Rafferty paused with his fork in midair. "Autry Jones? Is he one of the millionaire Jones brothers?"

Marissa knew Autry was rich. Filthy rich. And he looked it. But somehow, the man she'd gotten to know a bit last night and today was a bunch of other things before millionaire. Kind. Thoughtful. Patient. A good listener. And so insanely handsome that just thinking about his face—and yes, that amazing body—gave her goose bumps. "Yup. He's in town for three weeks visiting his brothers."

"Wait," Abby said, her brown eyes the size of saucers. "Do you mean to tell me that the man I saw with Walker and Hudson at the Ace came on your picnic?"

Marissa bit her lip. It was one thing for her daughter to notice a cute man for her mother to "date," never having known her mother to date. It was another for that to become a reality.

Abby frowned and stared at her.

Uh-oh. This was new territory for Marissa. Though technically, she and Autry weren't dating. They were

friends. Who might kiss, maybe. Probably. Marissa
sure hoped so.

"I can't believe I missed the picnic!" Abby's expression turned all dreamy, and if Marissa wasn't mistaken, cartoon hearts were shooting out of her chest.
"So you're dating him? That's so exciting!"

Marissa glanced at her mother, whose expression was its usual granddaughters-are-watching-and-
listening neutrality. Roberta Rafferty would let Marissa
know her opinion loud and clear later, when the girls
were in bed.

"Abby, Autry Jones and I are not dating. We're…
friends. New friends, at that."

"He does magic tricks," Kaylee said. "Grandma,
Grandpa, Mr. Autry made a little orange appear on
my head!"

Her parents laughed, and mentally, Marissa thanked
Kaylee for breaking the tension.

"So everyone knows him but me?" five-year-old
Kiera asked, pushing her long brown hair behind her
ears. "No fair."

"Well, Mr. Autry did offer to come over tomorrow
night and make a special dinner," Marissa told her middle daughter. "Steaks and potatoes on the grill. Who
wants to help make dessert for after?"

"Me-e-e!" a chorus of three trilled.

Again Marissa felt her mother's eyes on her. She
added potatoes to her plate, despite not having much
appetite. "Tomorrow is your night to cook, Mom, so
it'll be nice for you to have a night off." Marissa, her
mom and her great cook of a dad took turns feeding the
family of six every night. She tried to imagine Autry

Jones wearing an apron. Flipping steaks on the grill. Sitting down to a meal with her entire family.

"Oh, I'm very much looking forward to grilled steak and potatoes," Roberta said. "And meeting Autry Jones."

Roberta's chin was a bit high, her eyes a bit narrowed, her expression a bit…motherish. A millionaire Jones brother in town for three weeks and mysteriously making dinner for the whole family tomorrow night? Marissa could read her very smart mother like a good book.

There was only one reason why such a man would do such a thing. Because he was physically attracted to Marissa. If and when the notch on his belt was made, his grilling days for the Fuller-Raffertys would be over.

Her mother did have a cynical streak that she defended as "reality," and quite frankly, so did Marissa. She was no one's fool. She knew when a man was attracted to her, and Autry Jones clearly was. But unless she'd suddenly turned naive—and after all she'd been through in life, she doubted it—Autry Jones wasn't a user, wasn't a wham-bam-thank-you-ma'am kind of guy. Her gut said so, anyway, and any time Marissa stopped listening to her gut, she paid the price.

Yes, indeed she, too, was looking forward to Autry coming over tomorrow. Maybe a little too much.

The next afternoon, Autry sat in a leather club chair in the lobby bar of Maverick Manor. He wished there were a Maverick Manor in all the destinations he found himself in. Autry had always been a glass and marble guy, appreciating clean lines and craftsmanship. Who knew he'd love a log-cabin-style hotel, albeit one that was pure luxury, bringing in big-sky country with great architectural detail and all the amenities? Maverick Manor soothed something inside of him, something he hadn't even been aware of. Out the windows was a breathtaking view of the Montana wilderness, and across the room a massive stone fireplace that almost made him wish it were winter. He glanced up at the mural above the reception desk featuring residents of Rust Creek Falls. The focus on community and family appealed to Autry, which surprised him. But then again, the call of family unity was really why he was in town in the first place instead of scuba diving at an Australian reef or working on his tan on the French Riviera.

He kept his gaze on the mural, uncomfortable with the scene a foot away from him. His brothers and their wives sat across from him with three babies. Little Jared sat on Hudson's lap, Katie on Bella's and Henry cuddled up against Walker and his wife, Lindsay, clutching a little monkey he was chewing on. The triplets were Bella's brother's children, and the Joneses were on babysitting duty while Jamie and his wife had a quiet lunch for two at the Ace in the Hole. The only reason Autry was able to tell which baby was which was because their names were stitched across their T-shirts. And Katie had a sparkly purple barrette in her dark blond hair.

"Talk to Dad lately?" Autry asked both brothers, watching their expressions.

He could tell by Walker's slight sigh that it wasn't a topic he was comfortable discussing. Hudson barely seemed interested at all.

"We have a scheduled call every Monday at ten thirty to go over business," Walker said.

Autry knew that. Autry had the eleven-o'clock slot with the Jones Holdings chairman. But he was referring to personal stuff. Family. Interests. Life in general. "Ever talk about anything besides business?"

Walker practically snorted. "With Dad?"

"Mom's as interested as Walker the Second," Hudson said. "Bella called Mom to ask for an old family recipe for the cheesecake we had every Sunday growing up. Mom said, 'Really, dear. The cook made that. I could look up her number if you'd like.'"

Bella smiled. "I was trying so hard to find some common ground that I said, 'Sure, give me the cook's number.' But she left it on a voice mail and that was that. No family bonding."

Autry threw up his hands. "What's it going to take?" His parents had come to the weddings and had been cordial and made the rounds, but all Autry's attempts at getting his mother or father to reveal some kind of hidden depth of joy that two of their sons had found love and happiness had been a waste of time. His mother had gone as far as to say Bella and Lindsay "were lovely young women," while his father had merely looked around and asked, "Where's the rest of the town?"

"Dad's still upset that he can't control me," Walker said. "I was the dutiful CEO, but when I said I was settling here and opening a Jones Holdings office, he never got over it."

Hudson shook his head. "I've been used to that for years. He'll never accept that I 'turned my back' on the family business and roamed the country. But if Mom and Dad want to be stubborn and spend the ten minutes a day they actually speak to each other talking about how we let them down, that's their business. I wish they could be happy for us. I wish they could be *happy*."

"Well, you did kind of shock us," Autry said. "No one expected either of you to settle down, let alone in a small Montana town."

"Sorry," Bella said, kissing her baby niece on the head. "Love struck."

"Sure did," Hudson said, reaching over to squeeze his wife's hand.

"And love is wonderful," Lindsay said. "To think that when I met Walker, we were on opposing sides of a courtroom, battling over a case involving Just Us Kids. Now, we're happily married."

Walker inched closer to his wife and gave her a kiss on the cheek.

Bella smiled. "When Hudson became my boss at the day care, I thought we'd be on opposing sides, too— the manager wanting things one way and the big boss insisting on things his way. But here we are, united."

"And thanks to Bella, I have the cutest nephews and niece in the world," Hudson said.

That was not in dispute and for a moment, the five of them just gazed at the adorable triplets.

"To be honest, Autry," Walker said, "I'm surprised Dad let you come here. Hudson and I figured he'd be afraid to let you anywhere near the town that so horribly influenced two of his sons."

"I'm my own man," Autry said. And he was. His father actually had spoken up against Autry spending such a long time in Rust Creek Falls.

Just don't drink the water, dear, his mother had said. *Or the punch, actually. I overheard a group joking about how someone spiked the punch at a wedding in*

*Rust Creek Falls with some kind of magic love potion.
It's no wonder your brothers fell prey.*

Fell prey. To love.

Don't you want your sons to be happy? Autry had
asked her. *Because they are.*

Of course I do, she'd said. *But my goodness, Autry,
there are surer paths.*

Autry had almost said "How on earth would you
know?" but he'd held his tongue. He hadn't been about
to start an argument at a charity fund-raiser.

"I'll toast to that," Hudson said, lifting the baby on
his lap. "To being your own man, little guy," he said,
then blew a raspberry on the one-year-old's tummy.

"And to being your own woman," Bella said, giving Katie a little lift above her lap. Baby Jared cooed.
Everyone laughed, which broke the tension that had
gripped the air.

"Oh—I see my friend Tom over by the bar," Hudson said, upping his chin at a tall man across the room.
"Excuse me for a minute to go say hi. Take this little
guy, Autry?" his brother asked, and without waiting
for a response, handed him over.

Autry swallowed. He couldn't exactly thrust the
baby back to him, not with his sisters-in-law and
Walker watching. Even if that was exactly what he
wanted to do.

Jared sat on his lap, looking up at Autry with giant
eyes while holding out his little chew toy.

"Thanks for being willing to share, but I have all
my permanent teeth," Autry said.

Lindsay laughed, pushing her long brown hair behind
her shoulder. "I give you a C-plus in toddler talk, but an
A-plus for trying."

Bella nodded. "Jared sure seems to like you."

Autry forced a smile at his sisters-in-law, then glanced down at the sweet-smelling baby. Lulu had sure seemed to like him, too. She was three months old when he fell in love with Karinna, and for the six months their relationship lasted, Autry had felt like a father. He hadn't thought he had it in him to be a dad until Lulu taught him that it came naturally. You loved. You showed up. You cared. You committed. You took responsibility. That baby girl had sneaked her way into his heart within hours. But she wasn't Autry's. She wasn't his daughter, didn't have his DNA, and Autry had had no claim on her when Karinna had broken up with him. He'd tried to see Lulu, asked if he could stay in her life, take her to the zoo once a week, anything, but Karinna had coldly reminded him he wasn't her father, and he'd never seen the little girl again.

That old bite of anger poked him in the heart and he shifted on the seat, his collar getting tight, his heart rate speeding up. Luckily, Hudson came back just then and scooped up his nephew, and Autry excused himself to go to the bar for a club soda he didn't want. He needed to get away, needed air.

But in just a few hours, he was due over at Marissa Fuller's house to make dinner for her, her three kids and her parents. His idea. He and Marissa had been about to part on Cedar Street, Autry going one way, Marissa the other, and he couldn't bear the thought of leaving her without having a plan set up to see her again. He couldn't ask her on a date with Kaylee's big ears listening. And he wasn't sure she'd agree to a date after their conversation. So in the middle of the intersection, he'd found himself suggesting he grill for the

Fuller-Raffertys—safe, family friendly, romance killing. He'd also figured he could get a sense of what her
life was like while living with her parents and raising
three kids on her own, just how chaotic it was. Maybe
by the time he'd flipped the steaks he'd be ready to run
screaming for his hotel. He was kind of hoping that
would be case, that something would obliterate his attraction to Marissa.

But despite knowing she had three kids, he couldn't
wait to see her, couldn't wait to meet her other two
daughters. Which made no sense. He wasn't supposed
to be so interested in her as a *person*, just as a sexy
woman. A very enticing, sexy woman.

What the hell had he done?

And how was he going to get out of it?

Chapter Five

While Abby read a novel on her summer reading list and the two younger Fuller girls played "school" with stuffed animals in the family room, Marissa and her mother made a salad. Dessert, a chocolate cake that everyone had helped with, was cooling on the windowsill.

Marissa glanced at the clock on the wall. It was five forty-five. Autry was due at six. Her toes tingled. For real. And her heart was beating a bit too quickly. She couldn't stop picturing Autry's face, those gorgeous blue eyes, his strong jaw and sexy tousle of dark blond hair. And all that height, and the muscles, the deep voice with the Oklahoma drawl.

"Marissa, you're mauling the poor lettuce," her mother said beside her.

Marissa glanced down at the big wooden bowl. "Just a little preoccupied, I guess."

Roberta Rafferty glanced into the family room to make sure big ears weren't listening. Between the *Fro-*

zen soundtrack playing softly on a speaker and her mother whispering, it seemed safe. "*Is* this a date?"

"No." An honest answer. This was a new friend, temporarily in town, coming over for dinner. To make dinner. She said as much.

Her mom chopped tomatoes and added them to the bowl. "Well, a single man is coming over to a single woman's home to make dinner for her entire family. I'd say it's not only a date, but that you skipped a few steps. He's meeting your children *and* your parents."

"Because it's not a date. We're just friends. A date would imply the possibility of a future. Autry is leaving town at the end of August for Paris. I think he'll be there at least a year. This is only about friendship."

"I just don't want to see you get hurt," Roberta said, slicing a cucumber. "Three weeks is enough time to fall head over heels in love, Marissa. And get your heart broken."

"Mom, come on. When have you known me to be anything but pragmatic?" Okay, fine, she'd gotten pregnant on prom night. But by the man she'd always intended to spend her life with. She hadn't let Mike Fuller unzip her fancy pink satin prom dress on a whim or impulse.

"I'm just saying be careful, honey. Autry Jones is from another world and if he looks anything like his brothers, a very handsome other world. You could get very hurt. And so could the girls."

Marissa stopped adding croutons to the salad and faced her mother. "How would they get hurt?" she whispered.

"Look, I don't know Autry Jones. I haven't even met the man. But that he's coming here to cook dinner for us says he's kind and gallant and charming and who knows what else. A millionaire businessman who does magic tricks? Kaylee already adores him. He'll have Kiera talking about him nonstop next. And Abby? She's nine and already talking about you dating Autry. Then, just like that—" she snapped her fingers "—he'll be gone and completely out of their lives."

"I told Abby he's just a friend and that's the truth. We are not dating. I know he's leaving town in three weeks. I'm not stupid, Mom."

Marissa's cell phone rang. Autry. They'd programmed their numbers into their phones at the end of the picnic. Was he calling to cancel? She answered quickly, eager to escape this inquisition.

"Hi, Autry," she said, walking toward the other side of the kitchen for a little more privacy. Of course she felt her mother's eyes boring into her back.

"Hi," he said. And then he paused.

He was canceling. He must have realized how crazy it was to start a friendship—when they were both clearly very attracted to each other—given that he was leaving in three weeks. Well, one of them had to be wise about this, and if she was rationalizing, at least he wasn't.

"Autry, are you there?"

He cleared his throat. "I just thought I'd make sure you had briquettes or gas for your grill," he said. "I could pick them up otherwise."

Not canceling. Neither of them was being wise.

"We have all that," she said. "You really do think of everything."

"Not always." He didn't elaborate.

"Me, either," she said.

He laughed, warm, rich and real, and her heart pinged just enough to let her know she was stepping into trouble territory. Shared worry over their situation was one thing they had in common.

Ten minutes later, the doorbell rang, and her younger daughters leaped up excitedly and raced to the door. Abby hung back a little out of shyness, Marissa figured.

Her mother raised an eyebrow.

Okay, maybe she was being a little stupid about this, in terms of ignoring the very gentle warning bell that said she was being reckless. Because this might not be a date, but she thought of herself in Autry's arms, kissing him, his hands on her, and that meant she didn't think of him as only a friend. But she'd have to. And Marisa Fuller was the queen of "have to."

Well, he'd *tried* to cancel.

But when he'd heard Marissa's voice, all thought had gone out of his head. He'd stopped thinking about how scorched he'd felt holding Hudson's baby nephew. He'd stopped hearing his motto, Do Not Date Single Mothers. He'd stopped picturing himself sitting in Marissa's backyard, three kids surrounding him.

All he'd heard was Marissa's melodic voice. All he'd seen was her face, her dark eyes. And all he'd thought about was her story, everything she'd gone through, how strong she'd been. And he was going to cancel on making her dinner because he was a one-hundred-eighty-pound weakling? No. They'd shaken on friendship and he was going to be a friend to her. Friends didn't cancel because they ran scared. Friends came through. And Autry had promised a delicious steak dinner, grilled by him, and the Fuller-Rafferty clan was not going to be let down.

The door opened and three girls beamed at him.

"Hi, Mr. Autry!" Kaylee said, waving at him.

He smiled at the adorable little girl. "Hi, Kaylee." He turned to the five-year-old with wavy, shoulder-length brown hair. "And you must be Kiera. It's very nice to meet you." The two younger girls ran onto the porch, and he could see Marissa and her parents behind Abby, who stood in the doorway.

"Do you know who I am?" the nine-year-old asked.

"Hmm," Autry said, putting down one of the two large bags he was holding. "Are you the Fuller girl who likes a band called 2LOVEU?"

The girl's face lit up. "They're my favorite!"

"Then you'll probably like this," Autry said, handing her a small wrapped box.

"What's that?" Marissa asked, looking from the gift in Abby's hand to him.

"What is it, Abby?" Kiera asked, as both younger girls rushed over.

Abby opened it and gasped. It was a small snow globe with the 2LOVEU band members inside, "singing" into a shared microphone.

"And look," Autry said, turning the snow globe upside down in Abby's hand. "Twist that and see what happens."

Abby twisted the little metal prong. A 2LOVEU song began playing. "It's a musical snow globe! Oh, thank you, Mr. Autry!" she exclaimed, wrapping her arms around him.

"You're very welcome," he said. "Wait, what's this?"

he said, pulling something else from the bag. "This one has Kiera's name on it."

Kiera grinned. "For me?" She opened her present and hugged it to her. It was a remote control miniature robot puppy. Marissa had mentioned that Kiera was obsessed with puppies, and since getting one wasn't in the cards, a robotic version seemed a good choice. "I love him! I'm naming him Fluffers."

"I see one more gift in the bag," Autry said, kneeling down and pulling out the small wrapped box. "This one has your name on it, Kaylee."

Kaylee jumped up and clapped. She tore off the wrapping paper. "Yay! Mommy, look! It's a stuffed monkey! I love monkeys!"

Autry smiled. "And when you press its tummy, the stars on his belly glow in the dark." He remembered Marissa mentioning at the picnic that Kaylee often woke up in the middle of the night. Maybe the glowing monkey would help soothe her back to sleep. And her mom could get a better night's rest.

A chorus of thank-yous from the girls had him smiling. "You're welcome."

"You didn't have to get them gifts," Marissa said. "But that was very kind. Thank you."

"It was my pleasure," he said.

"Autry, this is my mother, Roberta Rafferty. Mom, Autry Jones."

The older woman standing beside Marissa did not look particularly happy, but she had a pleasant enough smile on her face. She looked a lot like Marissa. "Very nice to meet you."

"And this gentleman here is my father, Ralph Rafferty," Marissa said.

Her father shook Autry's hand and positively beamed. "It's an absolute pleasure to meet you, Autry. It's like meeting a celebrity. I read the business pages of the newspapers and often hear about the interesting deals and investments Jones Holdings, Inc. is involved in. I hear you're headed to Paris next—I read about the Thorpe Corporation negotiations."

"Hopefully all will go smoothly," Autry said. "It'll be one of our biggest deals." As he talked business with Ralph Rafferty for a bit, he couldn't help noticing that Marissa's mother seemed even more uneasy. "I'd better get this bag of groceries into the kitchen. Warm day today."

He picked up the brown bag and pulled out a bouquet of yellow tulips. "And just a little something for the lady of the house," he said, handing them to Marissa.

"Lovely," she said. "Thank you."

Marissa's father ushered the way into the kitchen, and Autry set down the bag. He could see the grill on the patio through the sliding glass door.

"I'll help Autry," Marissa said to her parents. "You two go relax."

"Dinner in one hour," Autry called. He pulled steaks, potatoes, asparagus, a small bottle of olive oil and a bulb of garlic from the bag. "All I need is the salt and pepper."

She brought over the salt and pepper shakers. "Do you always make this grand of an entrance?"

"I'll be very honest here, Marissa. I do when I want to. I have the means, and right now, I have the time. So I went shopping."

"But you couldn't have gotten those gifts in Rust

Creek Falls," she said. "We don't have a toy store. And Crawford's General Store doesn't sell those items you bought."

"Like I said, I have the time. Plus, driving to Kalispell gave me a chance to sightsee a little."

"And what do you think of the area?" she asked.

"It's beautiful," he said, seasoning the steaks. "Gorgeous open country. You can think out here. There aren't a million distractions. Just fresh air, nature, land, sky. I could have driven around for days."

She smiled then picked up the potatoes. "I like to brush the potato skins with olive oil before grilling them."

"Me, too," he said. While she put back the salt and pepper shakers, he stole a good long look at her. Tonight she wore a light blue tank top with ruffles along the neckline and a white denim skirt and flat silver sandals. Her hair was in a low ponytail, showing off her long, lovely neck. She was so beautiful and very likely had no idea. The only jewelry she wore was a silver watch on one wrist and a macramé bracelet that one of her daughters likely made on the other.

They headed out to the grill with the potatoes, to get those going, since they'd take the most time. Then they sat on the low stone wall separating the patio from the yard. He couldn't stop looking at Marissa's long, tanned legs.

The girls burst into the yard, Marissa's parents behind them. He pulled his attention from Marissa to the five people now crowding around them.

"Play it again, Abby!" Kiera said, twisting her little body into some kind of strange pose.

Abby turned the prong on the bottom of the snow

globe and the 2LOVEU song filled the backyard. She set it down and all three girls started dancing.

"I like how they dance without moving their feet," Autry whispered to the grown-ups.

Marissa laughed. "That's how it is now. It's all about the arms."

He was about to ask Marissa if she'd like to dance, but again he felt the weight of Roberta Rafferty's presence, her…disapproval, if that was the right word. Not of him, necessarily, but of them: him and Marissa. Millionaire Playboy Courting Single Mom of Three Who Lives with Her Folks. It did seem an unlikely headline. But he wasn't courting Marissa. He was going to be her friend—a friend of the family. And a good one. The Fuller-Raffertys had been through so much and if he could ease their burden and bring smiles, why not?

Except Marissa's mother wasn't smiling. She looked worried.

Because she probably thinks you're going to crush her daughter's heart and leave her kids asking what happened to Mommy's nice, generous boyfriend.

God, he was an idiot. Of course. He had to be careful here. He and Marissa had an understanding—a strings-free friendship—but her children were young and impressionable. He needed to take care with their feelings and expectations. No wonder Marissa had commented on the "grand entrance." He'd come to town with housewarming gifts for his brothers and sisters-in-law, a few toys each for Hudson's nephews and niece, and even some things for Just Us Kids. Five long, colorful beanbags that contorted into chairs and little beds, which had arrived yesterday. It was natural for Autry to come bearing gifts. He wasn't throwing his money around; he just enjoyed giving.

As the crew decided to play charades in the yard, Autry finally put the steaks on the grill. He couldn't help laughing at the kids' antics. And the way their grandparents accommodated their various ages, making each feel understood, smart and special, was something to behold. He could see Marissa's love for her daughters in her face, in her actions, in her words, and he hoped this family knew how lucky they were. They'd had their share of sorrow, but what they had here was priceless. And Autry knew it. Growing up, Autry's family life revolved around competition. Not love.

Fifteen minutes later, he announced it was chow time, and everyone sat around the big round table under the umbrella, digging into their steaks and baked potatoes and asparagus.

"Who wants to share first?" Marissa asked, looking around the table.

Autry raised his eyebrow and Marissa explained that it was family tradition at dinner for everyone to share something about their day—something that made them happy or sad, made them laugh or cry.

The Jones family had never done anything like that. In fact, they'd rarely eaten dinner together. His father had seldom been home, spending most of his time either at the office or traveling. His mother was on every board and charity imaginable. And his brothers had various team sports and clubs, so it wasn't often anyone was home at the same time. The family housekeeper and cook always had individual portions for any of them to heat up. But Autry had become a regular at his favorite pizzeria in Tulsa. The same-age teenager who worked behind the counter had become a close friend.

"Me!" Kaylee said, raising her hand. "I saw a butterfly. It was white. But I couldn't catch it. So I was happy and sad."

Roberta smiled. "I love butterflies. I'll share that I came home from having lunch with an old friend to find my dear husband reading *Jack and the Beanstalk* to his granddaughters, who were all curled around him on the couch. That made me very happy."

"Hey, that was my share," Ralph mock-complained.

"What about you, Mom?" Abby asked. "What's your share today?"

"I'll share that it's nice to make a new friend," Marissa said carefully, looking at her daughters. Then she smiled at Autry.

"I made a new friend, too," Kiera said. "A beagle named Maddy. When Grandpa took us to Crawford's today for ice cream after lunch, Maddy was outside. I asked if I could pet her and the lady said yes."

"I pet the dog, too," Kaylee said, beaming.

"Your turn, Autry," Abby said.

All eyes swung to Mr. Jones.

"I'll share that it's really, really, really nice to be here with all of you," he said. "You're a great family."

That even got a genuine smile out of Roberta Rafferty.

"Want to know my share?" Abby asked. "This," she said, taking her musical snow globe from her lap and placing it next to her plate. "I love this so much I could totally burst."

Autry smiled. "I'm glad."

With all the sharing done, the group dug in again,

eating, chatting, laughing. Why had Autry thought spending time with this family would be difficult? It wasn't. Kaylee, Kiera and Abby were fun to be around. They didn't remind him of what had happened with Lulu and Karinna, but then again, they weren't babies. And he wasn't romantically involved with Marissa. As long as he kept a reasonable emotional distance and didn't cross a line, he could enjoy Marissa's company and share in her life for the next few weeks. If he could bring a smile to the family, all the better.

But as plates were cleared and a delicious-looking chocolate cake was brought out, Autry realized he could stay here all night, quite happily. Despite being asked four times in the past twenty minutes by Kaylee why his shirt was blue. Despite having Kiera tell him a very long story about how beagles have three colors and how her grandpa helped her do research on beagles online after meeting Maddy. Despite listening to Abby talk about the lead singer of a boy band, a "totally dreamy Lyle," who had dimples and the greenest eyes ever and did Autry know that Lyle's favorite food was cheeseburgers and how, according to *Kidz Now* magazine, Lyle couldn't decide between ice cream or cupcakes as his favorite dessert.

It was a novelty, that was all, Autry realized. He'd avoided single mothers for a while now, so this kind of get-together was new and fun. Ah. Now that it made sense, Autry relaxed. Of course. He liked novelty. It was why he enjoyed his job so much. Flying to new and different destinations a couple times a month. Brushing up on foreign languages and learning about different cultures. He loved it. And the Fuller-Rafferty family was as different a culture as Autry could get.

"Well," Ralph said, looking at his granddaughters. "Since Mr. Autry was kind enough to make this amazing dinner, let's go into the kitchen and clean up."

There were groans of "Can't we stay out here with Mr. Autry?" But the girls dutifully followed their grandparents inside.

"Thanks for all this," Marissa said. "You made them feel special."

"Good," he said.

"And potentially not so good. Come September, you'll be long gone. But they'll still be here, living in this house, living the same lives. Maybe it's better that you don't set up too many expectations. So no more gifts, okay? You're Mommy's new friend and they're not used to my friends bringing over presents except for the occasional bagels and cream cheese on Sunday mornings."

"Understood," he said. "I'm not used to wanting to kiss my friends." And, man, did he want to kiss her.

She stared at him, biting her lip. Maybe he shouldn't have said that.

"Me, too," she said.

But kissing was out. Even if they'd sort of okayed it, okayed a "let's see" with no strings, no expectations. There were always expectations of some kind or another.

"Are those your initials?" he asked, gesturing at the big oak tree at the end of the yard.

She glanced at the tree, at the two sets of initials carved into a heart—MR+MF—and if Autry wasn't mistaken, a mix of sadness and relief crossed her pretty face. "We carved that with a key when I was sixteen." Sadness that Mike Fuller was gone, he guessed. Relief that the reminder of MR and MF took her away from this "whatever" with the man standing beside her. Him.

Autry headed over, touching the initials. "You have such an amazing sense of history and family here," he said.

She tilted her head at him, and he got the feeling she was surprised by his high regard for family, despite what he'd told her about his own. She took his hand and led him around the big tree, then pointed at a spot on the ground. "I tried to climb this tree when I was five, but fell out and broke my ankle. Twenty-some years later, Kiera made the attempt and sprained her foot. We're keeping it off-limits to Kaylee."

Marissa needed a hug, he thought. But the way she was looking at him, right into his eyes, he knew she wanted more than a hug. She wanted the man she was interested in to pull her close and kiss her, hold her tight. He could be wrong, but he'd bet his Tulsa condo on it.

He stepped closer, reaching a hand to her face, and tried to read what he saw in her expression. Desire. Conflict of interest. Exactly what had to be in his.

With the big old oak shielding them from view, he stepped even closer and kissed her—warm, soft, tingling. He could smell her shampoo. His lips opened slightly as she deepened the kiss, and it was all he could do not to lay her down on the grass and explore every inch of her.

At the sound of the sliding glass door opening, they each took a step back. "Until next time," he said.

"Should there be a next time?" Marissa asked.

"Probably not. But I hope there will be."

"Me, too," she whispered.

* * *

Later that night, after a long hot shower and a re-laxing drink in his room, Autry called his father. He wished the Jones family could be different. That they could be close. That they could share what was going on in their lives—and not just whatever was related to business. Talk, vacation together, be…a family.

"Glad you called, Autry," Walker the Second said. "I was about to call you, actually. Convinced those two brothers of yours to move back home? Surely their wives would prefer a city like Tulsa over some backward small town. Not a high-end shop in the entire downtown. Your mother can't even imagine where they buy their clothes. Online, she figured. Did you know Rust Creek Falls doesn't even show up on a map of Montana?"

Well, the bad news was that his father was still fo-cused on Autry convincing his brothers to move back to Tulsa. The good news? Walker the Second sure was chatty. That meant he was in a good mood and might be open to new ideas. Like that Autry's brothers were happy here.

"Dad, Walker and Hudson love it here. Lindsay and Bella love it here. They both have deep family ties in Rust Creek Falls."

"Well, Walker and Hudson have deep family ties in Tulsa. Where they belong."

"I don't think I've ever seen Walker so relaxed," Autry said, taking a sip of his Scotch.

"A relaxed Walker means a relaxed CEO," his fa-ther snapped. "And a relaxed CEO is the last thing any corporation needs."

"Jones Holdings is up this quarter," Autry reminded

his father. "He's doing something right. From Rust Creek Falls."

"Well, while you're there, talk up Tulsa with the wives. I'll even throw in a moving-home bonus—a world cruise for the four of them. Surely anyone could run the day care."

"They're very emotionally invested in Just Us Kids. The whole franchise," Autry said. Last night, Walker had told him how much it meant to him that kids had a safe, happy place to go while their parents worked, a place where loving, supportive caregivers and teachers met their needs. Autry had stared at him in astonishment, again amazed by the change in his eldest brother. *We were rich and had bored nannies who ignored us*, Walker had reminded him. *I want every kid who attends a Just Us Kids Day Care to feel happy and loved when they're in our care.* Autry tried explaining this to his dad.

He could just see his father, waving dismissively and groaning in his home library, where he liked to take family calls. "Look, Autry. A good business model has to account for what makes the company work. Cared-for kids is the point. I get it. But for God's sake, what the hell is Jones Holdings doing in the day care business? Rhetorical question at this point—I've had this conversation with Hudson and Walker for over a year and the answer never makes sense to me. Sure, it's profitable as a franchise. But it doesn't fit with our corporate profile. I dare say, it's almost a little embarrassing."

And Autry "dared say" that his father was a lost cause. But he wouldn't. Because he didn't believe it. Right now, the man was going through a shock to the system. Granted, it had been months since the "defection" of Walker and Hudson. He'd had plenty of time to adjust but still thought his sons would "come around."

They wouldn't. Autry had been in Rust Creek Falls a few days and could see that. This was home to Walker and Hudson. In every sense of the word.

"At least I don't have to worry about you, Autry," his dad said. "Can you imagine yourself falling for some local gal and settling down there?" His father snorted. "Ah, your mother is holding up her phone to show me the time—we have a benefit tonight. Look, Autry, I appreciate your trying to talk some sense into Walker and Hudson, but with you as president, traveling the globe, I know Jones Holdings won't lose its edge."

I have fallen for "some local gal," he wanted to say. But settling down here? That, he couldn't imagine. "Dad, it's pretty great here. I can see why Hudson and Walker moved to Rust Creek Falls. It's a special town and the people are friendly and welcoming. It's the kind of place that feels like home."

"Oh, good Lord," Walker the Second said. "You've got to be kidding me. Maybe I do have to worry about you now."

His father had nothing to worry about where Autry was concerned, but he didn't bother saying so. Walker Jones the Second wasn't really listening; he was talking. And what the person on the receiving end had to say didn't matter.

Autry wasn't sure he'd ever get through to his dad. As a strange sensation fluttered in his chest, he realized something had tightened, closed up, shuttered in his heart. All that family togetherness and sharing at the Fuller-Raffertys was nice, but it wasn't his life or his family. And he had to remember that. He wasn't here for love.

Stick to the plan, he told himself. *Show Marissa and her family a nice time while you're here. Make things easier for them.*

And the next time you feel the urge to kiss her behind an old tree with the whole history of her life in it, don't.

Chapter Six

Over the next few days, Autry was a regular visitor at the Fuller-Rafferty house. He made big country breakfasts of pancakes and bacon, grilled hot dogs and served his secret-recipe potato salad. He fixed two lopsided tables, sanded a door that stuck, talked the stock market with Marissa's dad and politics with her mother, listened to Abby go on about her favorite band and charmed the little Fuller girls with more magic tricks and stories about the exotic foods he'd tried in the different countries he'd traveled to. When all three girls wanted to try Indian food and spicy curry, he'd hired a personal chef to drive in from Kalispell and whip up a special feast.

"Must be nice to have so much disposable income," Roberta Rafferty had whispered with an edge of disapproval in her voice.

"Oh, for heaven's sake," Ralph had whispered back.

"The man is a millionaire. This is chump change to a Jones. I, for one, like Autry."

So did Marissa. So did her daughters.

Marissa had noted Autry was careful to limit their time together to family activities. They didn't go for solo walks. They didn't stand behind the big oak tree in the yard, where they could kiss in private.

They didn't have a second kiss.

But every night since their one and only kiss, Marissa had lain awake in her bed, staring at the ceiling, imagining herself under the covers with Autry. Sometimes she couldn't imagine it; she'd been with one man only, since she was sixteen. But then she let her fantasies take over and all thought poofed out of her head, instinct and desire running the show.

The other evening, when Autry had made them dinner and they'd gone around the table, sharing things, Marissa had really meant what she'd said—that she'd made a new friend. She'd let someone into her life. A friend, yes, but someone new. In the two years she'd been widowed, she hadn't done that. The first year, the single men of Rust Creek Falls had let her be, but by the second year, she'd found herself asked out quite a bit. In Crawford's General Store while picking up paper towels and milk. While waiting for Kiera and Kaylee at the day care both attended. Not that men were tripping over themselves to take her out, but at least twice a week she very politely declined invitations, and slowly, the asking had trickled down to a near stop. *She's not ready to date* was the echo Marissa sometimes overheard about herself if gossip came her way. And that was fine with her. She wasn't ready to date.

She knew she needed an Autry-free day so she could

collect herself, have a good talk with the practical, smart side of herself. If they were just friends—and that was what they were both trying so hard to be— she had to stop the nightly fantasies of him kissing her, making love to her, asking her to marry him.

It was that last one that had slapped her upside the head. What? Marry him? Where had the thought even come from? She couldn't possibly be subconsciously dreaming of marrying Autry Jones, could she? Maybe in some Cinderella-like fairy-tale sense. But Autry Jones was about global travel and would be gone in less than three weeks. And that would be that.

So today, with Grandma and Grandpa taking Kiera and Kaylee to a pottery painting class for three- to five-year-olds, Marissa was spending the morning with Abby, getting a trim for the nine-year-old at Bee's Beauty Parlor and then taking a trip to Daisy's Donut Shop. But as they were about to pass Crawford's General Store, Marissa noticed a crowd gathered in front of a table. There was an easel with a poster board on it, but too many tall men were blocking her view. Leah Ganley, president of the Rust Creek Falls K–8 PTO, sat behind the table with a clipboard.

"What's going on?" Marissa asked Haley Peterman, mother of a girl in Abby's class last year. Haley's daughter and two other girls were holding hands in a circle, talking excitedly about something. Marissa noticed Abby looking over at them shyly. Her daughter had her best friend, Janie, and a few other friends, but this clique of girls always seemed to have a sobering effect on her.

"The PTO came up with the idea to hold a kids' version of *The Great Roundup*," Haley said. "Isn't that precious? Young cowboys and cowgirls competing in Western challenges. The teams are going to be mothers and sons versus fathers and daughters. Ticket sales will benefit field trips for the coming school year."

When a group who'd just signed up moved away, Marissa could now see the poster. *The Great Roundup Kids Competition! Teams of mothers and sons vs fathers and daughters! Based on the TV show and for ages 8–12, The Great Roundup Kids Competition will feature our town's young cowboys and cowgirls and their folks in Western-style challenges on the town green, such as an obstacle course, ringtoss, three-legged race, piggyback rides and more!*

Marissa's stomach plummeted. Abby didn't have a father.

Haley Peterman seemed to remember that Marissa was a widow and turned around fast.

"Oh, look, it's Abby," one of the girls from her school said, and they inched closer. "Oh my God, it's so sad that you can't participate. Are you okay?"

"Why can't she?" another girl asked.

The ringleader turned and whispered something in her ear. Marissa thought she heard the word *dead*.

Abby's cheeks turned bright red and Marissa could see tears poking at her eyes.

"Aww, I think she's crying," a third girl said, before they turned and walked away.

"Sweetheart," Marissa said, kneeling down beside Abby.

But Abby's expression suddenly brightened and she raced off in the opposite direction.

Huh?

Marissa stood up and shielded her eyes from the

bright August morning sunshine to see who Abby had run to.

Autry Jones. Walking right toward her in sexy jeans and a brown Stetson.

"How are two of my favorite pe—" he started to say, before Abby flung herself against him, wrapping her arms around him.

Marissa headed over, watching Abby wipe away tears.

"Hey, what's wrong?" he asked, tilting up Abby's chin.

"There's going to be a kids' version of *The Great Roundup* and I really want to be in it. But it's mother-and-son teams and father-and-daughter teams. And I can't do it because—" Tears streamed down her cheeks.

"Abby," Marissa said. "I know it hurts. And I'm very sorry."

"But maybe Mr. Autry can be my partner," Abby said, wiping away her tears and looking up at him hopefully.

"Sweetheart, Mr. Autry has to prepare for his big business trip to Paris," Marissa said. "And The Great Roundup Kids Competition is an entire Saturday."

Marissa watched Autry glance over at the poster on the easel.

"I understand," Abby said, her expression crest-fallen. "It's okay. Grandma always says we have to accept what we cannot change. Accept what I cannot change," she repeated. "Accept what I cannot change," she said again, as though trying to will the words from her head into her heart. And then she walked away and sat under a tree, her head down on her arms over her knees.

"If it's all right with you," Autry said, "I'll sign up with her."

"Oh, Autry," Marissa said. "You don't need to do that."

"Yes, I do. Because while her grandmother is right, you always have to have hope and believe in possibilities."

Marissa's eyes welled with tears. How was this man so kind? Why was he making it so impossible for her not to fall in love with him?

"If you really want to do it, it's more than okay with me," she said.

He smiled and squeezed her hand, then jogged over to Abby. Marissa watched as he told her daughter the good news and then Abby's face lit up. The girl jumped and flung herself at him and he wrapped her in a hug.

And Marissa caught his expression—uneasiness. A bit of sadness. She wondered what was behind it. Maybe he was just thinking that he was starting to like the Fullers and would be leaving soon, and would see Marissa and her daughters every now and then on trips to visit his brothers. Or maybe he really didn't want to do the kids competition but felt sorry for Abby and had spoken up before he thought too much.

Except from what he'd said, he didn't feel sorry for Abby. He wanted her always to know there were magical possibilities in life, even when it seemed there weren't. Yeah, her father was gone. But that didn't mean Autry Jones couldn't sign up in his place. And he had.

Marissa watched him head over with her daughter to the sign-up booth, saw the dropped jaws of Haley Peterman and the three mean girls from Abby's class.

"Mr. Autry is going to be my partner in the competition," she told the girls. "He rode his first horse when he was just three years old."

"Two, actually," Autry said, tipping his Stetson at Haley. Marissa watched the woman practically swoon.

"Actually, it's father-daughter," one girl said. "Right, Mrs. Ganley?" she said to the woman at the table.

"Well, that's just a label," Mrs. Ganley said. "But any adult can stand in for a parent or guardian. Aunt or uncle, family friend, that kind of thing. So Mr. Jones is welcome to sign up as Abby's teammate."

The girls' faces fell. Abby beamed. And Autry signed his name next to Abby's, making him her official partner for The Great Roundup Kids Competition in two weeks.

Autry took a flyer listing the challenges, like tug-of-war and an obstacle course, and handed one to Marissa. "We'll have to practice so we have a shot at winning the big prize." Free doughnuts for a month at Daisy's and a brand-new bicycle, compliments of the town mayor.

That meant Autry would be spending a lot of time at her house.

Uh-oh.

After a good ride on Hulk, one of his brother Hudson's mares, on the fields of the Lazy B ranch, Autry felt somewhat restored, a bit back to himself. He now stood under the shower spray in his suite at the Maverick Manor, the hot water coursing over him.

His mother was right. There had to be something in the goddamned punch. Not that he'd had any punch. But there was something in the water here in Rust Creek Falls, something that made previously normal people like himself turn inside out and sign up as the "dad" in a parent-kid competition.

Thing was, the minute he'd seen Abby Fuller's crumpled little face, the pain, the disappointment, the willing herself to accept what was, he'd remembered himself as a nine-year-old, a big house full of brothers he barely knew, his parents never around or interested in any of them as individuals. And he'd had both his parents alive and well. Abby had lost her father as a seven-year-old. If he could make things better, if just for a Saturday, hell yeah, he would.

He grabbed a thick, fluffy white towel and dried off, then wrapped it around his waist. Just as he stepped into his bedroom, there was a knock at the door.

He opened it, expecting to see Hudson or Walker. But Marissa Fuller stood there, cheeks pink, mouth slightly open.

"I..." she began, then turned away, and he remembered that he was just in a towel.

"Come on in," he said. "I'll go get dressed."

She stepped in and shut the door behind her, looking everywhere but at him. He smiled and held up a finger, then went into the bedroom and put on a navy T-shirt and jeans.

"I was just about to order room service," he said. "I'm craving a BLT and the Manor's peach iced tea. Join me?"

"That does sound good," she said.

He smiled and picked up the phone and placed the order.

"I can't even remember the last time I stayed in a hotel or ordered room service," she said, looking out the window at the gorgeous Montana wilderness.

"Actually, I can. It was my honeymoon when I was eighteen. We drove down to the Wyoming border and stayed at a motel in a tiny town even smaller than Rust Creek Falls. We just wanted to say we'd left the state." She smiled and turned to him. "It was just a plain room with dated furnishings and a lopsided bed, and there was no room service, but we were on top of the world for those three nights."

"I'll bet," he said. "You had each other and what else did you need?"

She tilted her head. "Exactly."

"Now here I come, wining and dining you with BLTs and peach iced tea and kid competitions involving a ringtoss and piggyback rides."

She laughed. "Well, when you put it that way, you don't sound like a millionaire jet-setter who's going to…" Her smile faded and she turned away.

He walked over to her and lifted her chin. "Who's going to what?"

"Leave."

He took a breath and nodded. "We always knew that, though, Marissa."

"Right. And we also shook on being friends. But…" She paused and dropped down on the love seat across from the fireplace.

"But things feel more than friendly between us," he finished for her. "There was that kiss, for one. And the fact that every time I see you I want to kiss you again."

"Ditto. See the problem?"

He smiled and sat down beside her. "Marissa, why did you come here? To tell me that doing the competition with Abby is a bad idea? That she's going to get too attached to me?"

"Yup."

"Except you didn't say that."

"Because I don't want to take it from her. I want her to be excited about the competition. To not lose out on something when she's been dealt a hard blow in life so young. But yeah, I am worried she's going to get too attached. All three girls. But especially Abby."

"Abby knows I'm leaving for Paris at the end of August. That's a given. Goodbye is already in the air, Marissa. We're not fooling anyone."

"Why do I keep fighting it, then?" she asked. "Why do I have to keep reminding myself that feeling the way I do about you is only going to—"

"Make you feel like crap when I go? I know. I've had that same talk with myself fifty times. I wasn't expecting to meet you, Marissa. Or want you so damned bad every time I see you."

It wasn't just about sex, but he wasn't putting that out there. If she kept it to sexual attraction, surface stuff, maybe he'd believe it. Then he could enjoy his time with Marissa and go in a couple weeks without much strain in his chest.

"So what do we do?" she asked. "Give in to this or be smart and stay nice and platonic?"

He reached for her hand. "I don't know."

"Your hair's still damp," she said. "I can smell your shampoo. And your soap."

He leaned closer and kissed her, his hands slipping around her shoulders, down her back, drawing her to him. He felt her stiffen for a second and then relax. "I don't want to just be friends, Marissa. I *want* you."

She kissed him back, her hands in his hair, and he could feel her breasts against his chest. He sucked in a breath, overwhelmed by desire, by need. "You're sure?" he asked, pulling back a bit to look at her, directly into her beautiful dark brown eyes.

"No, I'm not sure," she whispered. "I just know that I want you, too."

"Only when you're sure," he said, moving back a couple inches on the love seat. "You've got a lot going on, Marissa. I don't want this—" he wagged a hand between the two of them "—to mess up the order in your life. You have three girls to think about. You have a job. You have your parents."

"I know," she snapped. She took a deep breath. "Sorry. I guess sometimes I just wish I could have everything."

"Let me buy you a house," he said. "I could fund a bank account for you. You could quit your job."

She bolted up. *"What?"*

"To make things easier on you," he said.

"I have no interest in being anyone's kept woman," she said through gritted teeth, then marched to the door and left before he could try to explain that wasn't what he meant.

Dammit. He just wanted to make things easier. Really. Her own home. No need to work. After all she'd been through, why shouldn't she be able to relax a little?

Because she'd worked hard her whole life and had worked for everything she had. That's why. And she didn't grow up with the Jones millions.

He was about to run after her. Apologize. But maybe it was better that there was some friction between them. She wasn't sure about moving their "friendship" into the bedroom. And he knew it would only lead to problems when he'd have to say goodbye. So a little emotional space between them was probably a good thing.

So why did it make his chest ache?

Chapter Seven

Marissa hated when her mother turned out to be right, which was…always. "Mother knew best." Except when it came to Marissa the mother, who'd had a terrible lapse in judgment in allowing *that man* to sign up in The Great Roundup Kids Competition with her very impressionable nine-year-old daughter. A man who had zero scruples, obviously.

Buy her a house. Quit her job. He had to be kidding! That wasn't how life worked. You didn't make a wealthy man's acquaintance—one who'd be leaving very soon—and accept a free house and a padded bank account. And in exchange, he wouldn't have to feel bad about leaving Rust Creek Falls and the woman he'd dallied with. *But I bought the poor single mother a house and threw her some money!*

Marissa was so furious she could scream at the top of her lungs, but she was marching past Crawford's General Store, where groups were still signing up for the competition. What was she going to tell Abby? *Your knight in shining Gucci thinks he can buy me?*

By the time she got home, she'd worked out a plan. She'd tell Abby that something had come up and Autry Jones would not be able to do the competition with her. Some plan, she chided herself. Her daughter would be devastated. Tears poked her eyes.

"Marissa?" Roberta Rafferty asked as she came out of the kitchen.

Marissa stood by the front door, willing herself not to cry. "Where are the girls?"

"Your father took them to the park. Marissa, what's wrong?"

"Why would you think anything's wrong?" Marissa said. Then, with the kid-free okay to burst into tears, she couldn't stop herself.

Her mother pulled her against her and hugged her tight, then took her hand and led her into the living room—the "fancy" living room where no one ever went because the family room was the main hub of the house. Her mother sat her down on the brocade sofa and sat next to her. "Okay, tell me."

"It's nothing, Mom, really." Tears streamed. So much for nothing.

"Marissa, I know it's not easy living with me. You're a grown woman and a great mother and you have Mom overseeing everything you do and commenting. But I love you, honey. And you can always talk to me and expect me to give you advice that serves you—not me."

Marissa considered that. Her mother was fair. And she did often look the other way and bite her tongue when she didn't agree with how Marissa was handling something. The entire story poured out. How she and

Autry had shaken on being friends. How they'd kissed. How he'd signed up to be Abby's partner in The Great Roundup Kids Competition. How she'd gone to his hotel to tell him he could still get out of it, that Abby would understand he'd been pressured in the moment, and how they'd ended up kissing again and talking about how they had this mutual attraction. And then whammo, cold water on her head. He'd proposed buying her a house. Told her she could quit her job and he'd set her up for life.

"In exchange for?" her mother asked.

"Nothing," Marissa said. "He said he has the money, and after everything I've been through, he'd like to help and make all our lives more comfortable."

"Your dad would say to take that at face value."

"*You* wouldn't," Marissa pointed out.

"Maybe I would. I've been watching that man like a hawk the past week, Marissa. I've always prided myself on being a good judge of character. I don't think he meant anything…sordid by it. I think he meant exactly what he said. He does live in a different universe, Marissa. One where you jet off to foreign locales and spend money without a second thought. He grew up that way. But I'd judge him more on the fact that Abby was hurting and he stepped in—and up. That's a sign of who he is, Marissa."

Huh.

"And your reaction to his offer showed him who *you* are, honey," Roberta added. "I'm sure he's known women who would've jumped on it."

No doubt. And maybe, just maybe, Marissa was looking for anything to help her distance herself from Autry. But as her mom's words pushed past Marissa's defenses, she realized Roberta was right—as usual. Marissa wrapped her arms around her mother. "How did I get so lucky to have such a wise mother?"

Her mom squeezed her tight. "I will say this, though. I am worried that Abby is going to get very attached to Autry. She was already, and now, with practicing for the competition, she's going to worship him. She knows he'll be leaving, yes, but in her nine-year-old heart she may not understand that he'll still have to go—and isn't likely to be coming back. I do think you need to keep boundaries there."

Marissa nodded. The door opened and her father and the girls came in.

"Look who was walking up to the house when we got here!" Abby said. "Mr. Autry!"

Autry looked at Marissa, his gaze seeming to plead with her to give him a chance to explain. Little did he know her mother had done his work for him.

"Girls, I need to talk to Mr. Autry, so why don't you head into the family room for reading time?"

Abby ran over with a big smile. "Mr. Autry, after you and Mom talk, can we practice walking two hundred yards backward?"

Before Autry could respond, Roberta said, "Abby, you heard your mother. Right now it's reading time." Roberta then ushered the younger girls and a wide-eyed Abby into the family room. *Phew.*

Autry took a deep breath. "Marissa, I didn't mean—"

"I know. Now," she said. "My mother set me straight."

"You told your mother?" he asked, staring at her as though she had five heads.

"I guess we've gotten closer than I even realized.

I've been living here for two years. My mom has been my rock more than I ever knew."

"You're very lucky," he said. "No matter how hard it is sometimes to live with your parents, you're very, very lucky. I wish I were that close to my parents. I wish my father were my rock."

She nodded. "I forget sometimes." She squeezed his hand. "I shouldn't have thought you meant anything more than what you said. Everything you've done since you came into my life has been aboveboard and kind. I shouldn't have jumped to conclusions. But I've always worked for what I have, and providing for my family is my responsibility."

"You have no idea how much I admire you, Marissa Fuller."

She smiled. "Well, in that case, maybe you *can* spoil me a little bit. Take me out on the town tonight." She said it before she could think it through. But she would love a steak or seafood dinner in Kalispell, maybe some line dancing at the Ace, a drink in the fancy lobby of Maverick Manor. She would even put on her sandals with heels and a little perfume.

"You've got it. One night on the town coming up. But I need to ask. Right before our conversation went south, we were talking about the possibility of being more than friends. So is this a date or..."

This gorgeous, wonderful man was standing before her, wanting to give her a little highfalutin fun before he left in two weeks. Marissa knew he liked her, wanted her, but he'd be leaving regardless at the end of August. She could give in to the fantasy of being with him for these two weeks—with no strings. As long as she held on to reality, she'd be fine and maybe even better for it. He'd leave, but she'd have experienced something magical for a few weeks that would leave her in a good place mentally and emotionally.

Was she rationalizing an affair with Autry Jones, millionaire cowboy businessman? Maybe.

But so be it.

"I think we should let the evening decide where it goes," she said with a sexy smile she didn't even know she had in her.

The smile he returned went straight to her heart and her toes.

Just what would happen tonight?

Autry was getting ready for his date with Marissa when he heard a knock on his hotel room door. Marissa had wanted to meet him at the hotel instead of him picking her up, so that Abby, particularly, wouldn't see her mom clearly going out on a date with Autry.

But it wasn't Marissa standing in the doorway. It was Alexandra Lamoix, director of new business development at Jones Holdings, Inc. His father had hired her six months ago and she'd proved to be a valuable asset. She was a shark like his dad, which was useful in the boardroom. But she was so angelic looking that no one realized it until after her negotiations got her everything she wanted. Autry kind of admired her. And kept his distance.

"Alexandra?" He froze. If she was here, in person, something must have happened to his father. He felt the blood drain from his face and he grabbed the edge of the door to steady himself.

"I make you weak in the knees, I see," Alexandra purred in her raspy voice. She smiled, trailing a finger with a pale pink nail down the side of his cheek. "I always knew it."

"What?" he said through the fog in his head. "Is my father okay?"

"Your daddy's as fine as ever, darling."

His heartbeat returned to normal. "And you're here because?"

"Well, I was passing through Montana on my way to Seattle to research the Kenley Tech start-up, and how could I not stop by and see you?"

Rust Creek Falls wasn't exactly a stop en route from Tulsa to Seattle. She was here for a reason.

Alexandra stepped inside the room and glanced around. Her long auburn hair fell, sleek and straight, past her shoulders, and the very formfitting sleeveless dress she wore with four-inch heels accentuated every curve, including unusually large breasts. Delicate gold jewelry decorated her neck and wrists. Yeah, he'd noticed her in the office back in Tulsa. It was impossible not to, especially because she always stood very close to him. That she wanted the chairman's son and CEO's brother, the president of Jones Holdings, wasn't lost on him. But tempted as he was once, Autry's trust meter no longer let him down. *No, thanks, Alexandra.* She might be attracted to him, but he'd be a stepping-stone to her. And as enticing as she was on the outside, he had zero attraction to what was inside.

"Sweetie, your daddy is worried about you," she said. "We all are, on the executive floor of Jones Holdings. First we lost Walker the Third. Now you're here in this two-bit town for weeks? Walker the Second is worried you won't come back. So am I." She slid her arms around him, her incredible breasts pressed against him. "You know I've always had a soft spot for you, Autry. And I've come all this way to make my claim."

Unbelievable. He knew exactly what this was about. "My father sent you?"

"It was both our idea," she said, trailing a finger down his neck and pressing herself more firmly against him. "Come home where you belong. I'll take off the next two weeks and show you what a vacation *really* is, Autry Jones." She lifted her chin and puckered up her glossy red lips.

He heard a gasp.

It hadn't come from Alexandra. Or himself.

Autry looked behind Alexandra. Marissa stood in the doorway of his hotel room, shock on her face. She seemed frozen in place for a moment, then ran.

"Aww, is that a sweet lil local you picked up here?" Alexandra said. "What a quaint sundress."

"Go home, Alexandra. Now," he growled, and raced out. At the reception desk he quickly told the desk attendant to have the woman in his room escorted out and the door locked, then he rushed out of the hotel.

He looked in every direction. There she was. Marissa was running—slowly, in her heels—up the sidewalk. He caught up to her fast.

"Total honesty," he said, taking her arm. He'd just earned her trust back—thanks to help from her mother. There was no way in hell he was letting his father and his minions undo all that.

She wrenched it away from him.

He held up his hands. "Hear me out. Please. I may be a lot of things, Marissa, but I'm not a liar. Or a cheat."

She let out a breath, but at least she remained still and didn't bolt. Her hands were on her hips and she looked like she might snap a branch off a tree and conk him over the head with it.

"I was in my room—alone—getting ready for our date. Which I've been looking forward to more than anything for a very long time. Someone knocked and I thought it was you, but it was the director of new business development at Jones Holdings. Alexandra Lamoix. Turns out my father sent her to entice me out of Rust Creek Falls."

"Why?" she asked, dropping her hands to her sides. That was a good sign.

"Because he lost my brothers to this town. Or at least that's how Walker Jones the Second sees it. My brother Hudson always did his own thing, but Walker the Third was a company man, just like my father. Walker came here to handle the lawsuit against the day care and presto-chango, he now lives here. Built a Jones Holdings office building here. First Hudson settled down in Rust Creek Falls, then Walker. Now I'm visiting and my father is worried whatever's in the water will get me, too."

Marissa smiled. "Well, maybe he *should* be. Town legend says that because Homer Gilmore spiked the punch at Jennifer and Braden Traub's wedding, inhibitions were loosened and that started a love and baby bonanza. Some say the magic love potion has been in the air ever since."

"Well, there's no way that would affect me," he said. "I'm immune."

She raised an eyebrow. "Immune to love?"

"To babies," he said, turning away. "Family life isn't for me."

"To babies? But how? Why? You're great with kids. My kids adore you."

"Well, it's easy to be nice to everyone when I know there are no strings," he said. "I'm leaving in two weeks."

"And if you lived here?" she asked, narrowing her eyes. "You never would have come up to my table at the Ace in the Hole with those beers?"

"I would have because I didn't know you were a single mother."

He could see a flash of hurt cross her expression. "And if you'd known?"

"I wouldn't have approached you."

She stepped back as though he'd struck her. "Well. Like you said, you're not a liar. And now that this is all out in the open, there's no reason for you to continue your...our...ridiculous acquaintanceship." She stomped off in her heels, then bent over, took off both sandals and marched away barefoot.

"Marissa, please wait," he said.

She turned around. "For what? So we can be 'friends'? We tried that. It didn't work. We tried setting up a date. It's turned into a disaster before it could even happen."

"You always knew that I'm going to leave town. Tonight, the rest of the time I'm here, why can't we just enjoy each other's company? We know what we know."

"Because I don't want to get hurt. Because I'm not a dummy. Because I won't let my kids get hurt by your grand gestures when they'll never see Mr. Autry again after August."

"I don't want to get hurt, either, Marissa. It's why I—" He turned away.

"Why you what?" she asked.

He shook his head. He didn't want to tell her about Karinna and Lulu. Why dredge up all that pain when he'd buried it deep? Talking about it would make him feel like a fool, the supposed business whisperer who couldn't see a hostile throw-over coming when it had been in bed with him the night before.

"Autry! Marissa!"

Autry turned to see Hudson wheeling his triplet nephews and niece in their choo-choo train of a stroller. He held up a hand.

"Jamie and Fallon are on a date night, so Bella and I are babysitting. Bella's making some complicated recipe for dinner, so I thought I'd take these three little climbers over to Daisy's to play in the toddler playhouse while I had a double shot of espresso."

Marissa smiled. "They are so precious. I know you're Katie," she said to the adorable little girl. "And one is Henry and the other Jared."

"Jared is in the middle," Hudson said. "The one chewing on his favorite teething monkey toy."

"You don't freak out handling all three yourself?" Autry asked.

"I'm an expert at babysitting triplet one-year-olds now. The trick is to keep them all in your field of vision. Not easy, but that's how you keep everyone safe and alive."

Marissa laughed. "Well, if you could use some hands, we're available."

"We are?" Autry asked. Maybe there was some kind of baby magic thing happening in this town if just the sight of these three cuties had worked on Marissa's mood. Not only was she not running off, she had volunteered them both to help out. That was a good sign.

Oh, wait. No, it wasn't. She'd volunteered them to help because of what he'd said about being immune to babies. She wanted to prove to him that he wasn't.

Because she didn't know why he drew the line at single mothers—or had until he'd met her. Because she didn't know what the sight of a baby did to his head and heart, reminding him of a loss that had scorched every bit of tenderness inside him.

"I would love some extra hands," Hudson said. "Thanks, Marissa." He turned to Autry. "Guess you're on baby duty, brother."

He'd get through the half hour or however long this would be. Because it was saving his relationship with Marissa. Saving their date.

Huh. His date had been saved by teething babies. But that still didn't mean he was changing his antibaby stance. The adorable small creatures got inside your heart—and could break it.

Chapter Eight

As they entered Daisy's Donut Shop, Hudson saw a good friend and asked if Marissa and Autry would watch the triplets while he took a breather with his buddy. Marissa was thrilled to say yes. It wasn't that long ago that her own brood were babies, but Marissa would always cherish the feeling of holding a baby against her, breathing in that delicious baby-shampoo scent and remembering another time in her life.

The first time she'd held a baby to her chest, she'd been just a teenager, and she'd been so scared that she would mess up, not know what to do. She'd picked up half of "how to be a mother" from a book on parenting and "your baby's first year," and the other half came from instinct. And from her own mother's help, even though sometimes she'd wanted to tell Roberta to stop hovering.

So while she took one triplet out of the stroller—Jared's little hands were raised, showing he wanted to be picked up—she felt all the warm, happy feelings in the region of her heart.

Autry approached the stroller for baby number two, looking slightly sick. The supposed immune-to-babies thing. Right. She'd give him ten seconds to fall under the "baby spell." Henry held out his arms, and Autry flicked open the five-point harness like a pro to lift him out. But he simply picked him up and set him down over the railing of the toddler play area. No cuddle, no kiss on the cheek, no baby talk.

He wasn't smiling. He wasn't watching the little guys. He was staring out the window at…nothing, as far as Marissa could see.

Huh. Maybe he truly wasn't interested in babies. Marissa took Katie out of her seat and couldn't resist holding her close and giving her silky blond hair a little caress.

"You're so precious," she cooed to the little girl. "You and your brothers. What a gift."

Autry looked at her then turned away completely, his hands jammed in his pockets.

She frowned, surprised that the triplets hadn't worked their magic on him. No spiked punch was necessary for a baby to have even the most reserved grown-up fawning and fussing and cooing; that was a baby's superpower. They were simply irresistible.

But Autry Jones did seem oddly immune.

She'd figured this would be a great opportunity for him to see how special babies and toddlers were, that they had a way of getting inside your heart and making you remember, making you dream, making you think about the future and possibilities. Babies were the future and they were the now.

The triplets crawled around in the toddler zone, kicking brightly colored plastic balls and crawling through little tunnels.

"I can't do this," Autry whispered. "I can't. I'm sorry." He turned away and headed across the shop, away from the tables.

Can't do what? Marissa wondered. What was going on?

Hudson came back and thanked her for watching the triplets, then told her to take a break and get herself a drink and a treat on him.

She headed over to where Autry stood. He stared down at the floor, not acknowledging her.

"What's wrong?" she whispered.

He turned to face her, then took her hand and led her over to the window. "The reason I'm no strings… The reason I don't date single mothers… The reason I'm never going to be a family man—" He stopped talking and ran a hand through his hair. "Last year I met a woman in New York City while on business. Karinna had a three-month-old baby. I fell for both of them pretty hard. I loved Lulu like she was my own child. She felt like mine."

Marissa's heart clenched, sensing from his tone that his story did not a have a happy ending.

"I went to a baby store and had a room in my condo decorated as a nursery," he continued. "Crib, mobile, swing, rocking chair. I had a stroller, a bookcase full of board books with edges Lulu could chew. A changing table stocked with diapers and baby ointment. And I, Autry Jones, changed more than a few diapers on that table."

Marissa smiled. She could imagine it, actually. From

the way he was with her kids, from the way he was with her.

"That baby girl, everything I felt, made me realize how wrong my parents had it. I was going to propose to Karinna, settle down and put family above business. I'd still do my job and do it well, but family would come first. But the night before I planned to ask Karinna to marry me, she told me she'd met someone else, a CEO of a famous corporation in New York and, sorry, but it was over."

"Oh, Autry, I'm so sorry."

"You want to know something? I realized pretty quickly that I was more upset about losing Lulu than I was about losing her mother. I tried to arrange some kind of visitation with Lulu, but Karinna reminded me that I wasn't Lulu's father and hung up. I never saw Lulu again. And it hurt like hell, Marissa."

She reached out a hand to him, and he looked so… conflicted that she wanted to wrap him in her arms and never let go.

"I've dated only single women since. No single mothers allowed within five feet."

"I'm closer than that right now," she said, offering a bit of a smile.

"I know. And sometimes, it's like all the blood in my veins has just stopped flowing."

"You feel this way and yet…you still accepted Kaylee's offer to come on that picnic the day after we met. You offered to be Abby's partner in The Great Roundup Kids Competition. There's a part of you that doesn't want to let go of what you once felt, Autry."

"Maybe. I tried to stay away from you, Marissa. I

can't. And your kids have made it even harder because they're so great."

She smiled. "Well, I think I understand you a little bit better now, Autry Jones."

"Let's go help my brother out," Autry said. "Now that I actually said all that out loud, those babies don't look so intimidating at the moment."

"You can always talk to me, Autry."

"I'm beginning to realize that. And that goes for you, too."

She squeezed his hand and held his gaze, and again she wanted to fling herself into his arms. But they were in the middle of Daisy's Donuts.

They walked over to the toddler zone and watched the triplets play. Marissa stepped over the railing and sat down to play catch—or almost catch—with little Jared, while Henry toddled around the busy wheel and Hudson played peekaboo with Katie. Autry stayed just outside the play zone, but facing it and watching them. A good sign. She noticed his expression was less tight. Not that it was relaxed—not by a long shot.

"Where's Uncle Hudson?" Hudson cooed at Katie, covering his face with his hands. "Here he is!" he said, opening his hands to show his face.

Katie giggled and threw a little plastic ball at him. Hudson erupted in laughter.

"You've really changed, bro," Autry said, a wistful look on his handsome face. "Rust Creek Falls agrees with you."

Hudson smiled and scooped up a runaway nephew, blowing a raspberry on his chest and then setting him back down to chase his brother. "I'm not sure I changed so much as this town brought out parts of me I didn't know existed."

"I know what you mean," Autry said and glanced at Marissa.

"Ooh, it's that way, is it?" Hudson said, wiggling his eyebrows.

Two spots of red appeared on Autry's cheeks and Marissa tried her best not to burst into laughter. "I'm going to get myself a latte. Autry, what can I get you?"

"Aren't I supposed to be taking *you* out on the town?"

She smiled. "I think I can handle one three-dollar beverage."

"I like the real thing, just coffee, black—a dark roast. And thank you."

When Marissa headed over to the counter, she heard Hudson say to Autry, "Told you this place would get to you."

She wanted to let them know she could hear them loud and clear, just in case they thought she couldn't. But then again, she was standing only ten feet away.

"It hasn't got me," Autry said. "I'm leaving in two weeks. I'm still glad I met the very beautiful Marissa, though. But Paris awaits. I'll be there at least a year. And then another destination, then another."

Autry glanced at her then, as if he wanted to underscore that. As if she didn't *know*. Really, it was as if he walked around with it in capital letters on his shirts: LEAVING AT THE END OF AUGUST.

Hudson eyed Marissa with a raised eyebrow. In his expression she read: *Yeah, we'll see, brother.*

"Dad's worried, though. He sent Alexandra from the

Tulsa office to lure me home. In fact, the timing was so bad it almost ruined things between me and Marissa."

"Or maybe the timing was good," Marissa said as she walked over with their coffees. "Because I did see that little display, we ended up here. And you ended up opening up to me."

"Well, that is definitely good," Hudson said. "But dear old Dad needs to mind his own business. Unfortunately, that's exactly what he thinks he's doing."

"Part of the reason I came to Rust Creek Falls was to try to smooth things over between Dad and you two. Not only haven't I achieved that, but now I've made things worse between Dad and me."

"You mean *Dad's* made things worse," Hudson said.

Autry glanced at his brother and seemed to consider that. He nodded.

"We all have to live our own lives," Hudson added. "What feels right to us. We can't live the life someone else maps out for us. Even when it's our own stubbornness that maps it out."

"Meaning?" Autry said.

Hudson scooped up two of the triplets and set them in the stroller, then went back for the third. "The meaning is different for everyone. Just think about it."

From Autry's expression, Marissa wasn't sure Autry wanted to think about that one.

"Well, time to get these tykes home for dinner. Thanks for lending a hand."

"Anytime," Marissa said. "I've become a master at keeping an eye on three kids."

Hudson grinned. "See you. Oh—and Bella and I would love to have you both over for dinner at the Lazy B sometime soon."

As though they were a couple, Marissa thought, her heart squeezing.

Autry clapped his brother on the back and held the door open for the enormous stroller, and they both watched Hudson navigate the stroller up the sidewalk. The guy could barely get two inches before he was descended on by a passerby stopping to peer in at the triplets.

"Uncle of the year," Autry said, shaking his head with a smile. "The guy who'd been the lonest of the lone wolves."

"So maybe change is possible," Marissa said, before she could stop herself. "Or like Hudson said, people and places bring out sides of you that you just never knew existed."

"Or you know they exist and you try to forget," Autry said.

She glanced at him, and his expression was a bit too neutral. Trying to forget hadn't worked with Autry; that was clear. But what was that Hudson had said about stubbornness? Autry's battle was with himself. Not babies. Not love. Not her.

They finished their coffees, and then she wrapped her arm around Autry's. "Let's go have that date," Marissa said. "It might be the only one. Who knows. But you agreed to take me out on the town tonight and I want it."

He took her hand, and this time his expression told her he was glad for the change in subject. "At your service."

As she and her gorgeous date walked up North Broomtail Road, Marissa imagined herself sitting in any number of restaurants, whether here in Rust Creek Falls or over in Kalispell, and she suddenly just wanted Autry Jones all to herself. She wanted to be alone with him. To talk to him about anything that might come up, and if they were having dinner somewhere in town, who knew who might be inadvertently eavesdropping?

Yes, Marissa was going to say it. *Do it now before you lose your nerve*, she told herself.

"Autry, I just remembered that Maverick Manor has room service."

He glanced at her, waiting.

"I'd like to have dinner there. On the balcony facing the wilderness."

He grinned, his beautiful blue eyes sparkling. "A private dinner for two. Nothing I'd like more."

"Unless that woman is still there, waiting for you," Marissa said. She really hoped not. A flash of Autry's coworker came to mind. All sleek and sophisticated in her four-inch heels. She wondered if that was Autry's type. Probably. But then again, when they'd met, Marissa was in a T-shirt and shorts and flip-flops, so maybe *she* was his type, too.

"I instructed the manager to escort her out and lock up behind her. If there was any issue, Nate Crawford himself would have called me. No worries."

"Your father won't be happy," she said.

"My father is never happy. Unless he's making money."

"Do you think you'll be able to smooth things over between him and your brothers?"

"I'd hoped so, but now I'm not so sure. My father doesn't seem to care about their happiness or what they want. Only what he wants for them and for himself. I can't imagine being a parent and feeling that way."

"Me, either. All I want is for my daughters to be happy. It's my job to raise them to be good, responsible adults—not to dictate their paths or futures."

He squeezed her hand. "Those three girls are very lucky to have you for a mother, Marissa."

She smiled and squeezed back, and then there it was—Maverick Manor, the luxurious log-cabin-style hotel looked so welcoming. She'd never had cause to be in here before today.

"Hope tongues don't wag," she said as they passed the reception desk. "Marisa Fuller seen entering Autry Jones's hotel room will spread like wildfire in this small town."

"I'll make it clear to the right big mouths that we're discussing business."

She laughed. "You know three people in this town. Your brothers and me."

"Au contraire. I've been here a week and have met a lot of folks. I spent an hour at the Ace in the Hole watching a reality TV show. I met the entire town."

"Oh yeah," she said. "I guess you did." Plus he was warm and friendly and talked to people everywhere he went.

He slid his key card into the lock on his door. Earlier, when she'd arrived to find that very sexy, well-dressed woman with her arms snaked around Autry's neck, her lips puckered for a kiss that, thankfully, Marissa had interrupted, she hadn't gotten a chance to look around. The room was masculine, clearly meant for a man on his own. Leather and wood and marble. The windows were huge and faced the gorgeous Montana wilderness in the distance.

"The room service menu is on the desk. Take a look. Anything you want will be yours tonight, Marissa."

"Filet mignon," she said, perusing the menu, grateful there were no prices. Everything was a fortune, no doubt. "I had that once at a wedding. Melted in my mouth."

He smiled. "Filet mignon for two and a bottle of red wine sounds good to me."

"Me, too."

He picked up the phone, made friendly small talk with Mariel, the front desk clerk, and then ordered, adding, "Mariel, Ms. Fuller and I are having a business meeting and shouldn't be disturbed beyond room service. Thanks." He hung up and smiled. "Done. Mariel is a bit of a chatterbox. The staff is instructed in discretion, but if she hears anyone gossiping about seeing you come in with me, she won't be able to resist telling them what she knows. 'Oh, it's nothing—they were just having a business meeting.'"

She grinned. "What business are we discussing?"

"Us," he said. "Our business." He stood very close to her and tilted up her chin. And then he kissed her.

"No discussion there," she said with a smile.

"Sometimes, Marissa, I operate best by not talking too much."

She kissed him back, wrapping her arms around his broad shoulders. And then he picked her up and carried her into the bedroom. In the dimmest recesses of her mind, she knew that room service would knock soon and that they could go only so far here. Safety net in place, she let him lay her down on his bed, let him cover her with his body, his hands in her hair, his mouth fused with hers. He pulled up a bit and slid his hands under the straps of her sundress, then lower to her lacy bra and the flesh underneath, which elicited a groan from him.

She felt the hard planes of his chest, the muscles of his arms, of his neck. She put her hands on either side of his face and looked into his eyes, his gorgeous, intelligent blue eyes. And she saw everything there she needed to know. That he didn't want to hurt her, but he would.

Marissa had been through loss that had knocked her to her knees, thrown her world into a tailspin. Sent her girls howling in grief.

Granted, Autry Jones would just be leaving town. Not dying. *A little perspective, Marissa.* But he'd break her heart nonetheless.

The question was would it be worth it? To experience him for these weeks. To make love. To *feel* love. Would it be worth it even though losing him would hurt like hell?

"Autry, do you agree with that old saying that it's better to have loved and lost than never to have loved at all?"

He leaned back a bit and trailed a finger along her neck. "I might have thought so. Before."

"Well, I think the answer has to be yes. That it's better. If I hadn't loved Mike, I wouldn't have those three precious girls. We lost him. But we had him. And we have some wonderful memories."

He nodded and sat up. Guess she'd killed the mood. But it was for the best. And she knew he knew it.

"I would rather not have known Karinna or Lulu,"

he said. "But I'm the only one who got hurt. And the memories I have twist my stomach in knots. Not so much anymore. Now there's just a void, but if I think about it, I feel bitter. And sometimes an old ache."

She turned all that over in her mind. His situation was very different from hers. But his experience with loving that little baby had taught him that he *could* love, that he could be a father figure, that he did believe that family should come first.

She started to tell him that, but a knock at the door let them know it was dinnertime.

A waiter wheeled in the cart and set everything up on the table on the balcony. Then they were alone again.

He gestured to the balcony. "So maybe we *should* discuss the business of us. How this is going to work so we do the least harm."

"I think we should go back to friendship, Autry. No kissing. No carrying anyone to a bed."

"I'll miss that," he said. "Especially that."

She smiled. "Are you okay with being Abby's partner in the competition?"

He nodded. "I won't break a promise, especially not to a kid. I told her I'd be her partner and I will be. I think tomorrow night we should all watch the second episode together, and then Abby and I can make a practice schedule. Sound good?"

"Sounds good."

But while she ate the melt-in-your-mouth filet mignon and sipped her wine, all she could think about was the man sitting across from her and what it had felt like to be in bed with him, even for all of five minutes. If she could enjoy his company, clothed and naked,

without falling in love, she'd give herself this glorious fling before settling back down to everyday life.
But how could she not fall in love with Autry Jones?

Chapter Nine

In the Fuller-Rafferty kitchen the next night, Autry was making his specialty: homemade pigs in a blanket. His three helpers were next to him, Kaylee and Kiera on step stools. Kaylee was rolling the dough to smithereens, but Autry believed that pigs in a blanket were un-mess-up-able. They were just too delicious. Kiera cut a wedge of dough for each mini hot dog, and Abby rolled them.

"How are the chefs?" Marissa asked, coming into the kitchen.

"A-plus for everyone," Autry said. "These are about to go in the oven."

"I can't wait to eat them!" Kaylee said.

"Me, too," Kiera said.

Abby licked her lips. "Me, three!"

As Autry moved to the oven with the tray, he heard Abby whisper to her sisters, "This is what it's like to have a dad."

Kaylee tilted her head and stared at him.

Kiera ran over and hugged his leg.

Marissa had lost her smile, her complexion going white.

His heart lurched.

"I remember," Abby whispered to her sisters. "And it's just like this."

"It's nice," Kiera said.

Kaylee nodded.

Marissa forced a smile and backed out of the kitchen, presumably to give her daughters privacy, to have this moment for themselves.

As uncomfortable as the whole thing had made him, he learned right then everything he needed to know about Marissa Fuller. That she would put her kids first. Always. As she should. More than ever, he wanted to give her the world. The universe. The stars. But she wouldn't take anything from him, nothing more than a filet mignon dinner.

"Autry, are you anyone's daddy?" Kiera asked.

Poke. Heart. Stab. Autry turned to face the sweet five-year-old. "Nope. I don't have any children of my own."

"But you're so good at being a daddy," Kaylee said.

"He really is," Abby whispered to her sisters.

"You girls know I'm leaving town in a couple weeks. Leaving the country, actually. I fly all over the world for my job. A dad would need to be around for his kids. So that's why I'm not a dad."

"You could stay here," Kiera said. "In Rust Creek Falls."

"He can't," Abby said. "He's the president of his company."

"Oh," Kiera and Kaylee said at the same time.

The good news was that Abby understood. She didn't look sad. Or wistful.

Just as the four of them finished cleaning up the kitchen, the oven timer dinged.

"Looks like our pigs in a blanket are ready!" Autry said. "Why don't you gals head into the family room and get good seats? I'll be in in a minute."

When he was alone in the kitchen, he sucked in a breath. He and Marissa had come to the right conclusion last night. If they were romantic, they'd act romantic, and Abby, especially, would notice immediately. Suddenly she would look at him as a potential father figure instead of as a family friend. And he couldn't risk that, for the girl's sake. He cared about her and her family too much for that. He'd focus instead on being a good cowboy.

Pigs in a blanket on a platter, he brought them into the family room. Marissa's dad had made his famous three-bean dip with a side of crackers, and her mom had lime rickeys in a pitcher. Everyone loaded up their plates and cups and they sat down to watch episode two of *The Great Roundup*.

Marissa was next to Autry on the love seat. He could feel her glancing at him now and again, clearly trying to assess how he felt about Abby's comment.

"I think it was sweet," he whispered to Marissa.

"I think you're sweet," she whispered back.

He squeezed her hand and helped himself to a lime rickey, a drink he'd never had before. The lime juice, sugar and club soda concoction with its lime garnish was sweet and tart and refreshing.

"Yay, it's starting!" Abby said, her attention glued to the TV.

Just like last week, the contestants rode up to the canteen site on horseback to where the host, Jasper Ridge—once again decked out all in black—awaited. Autry recognized Brenna and Travis, the pair from Rust Creek Falls, who leaned over for a romantic kiss, which got some claps and calls to get a room from the other contestants.

"Aww, they're so in love!" Abby squealed.

Summer Knight, the rodeo star who'd made it clear she had her eye on stealing Travis from Brenna, sidled up close to him and winked at the camera. Autry wondered how much of this was staged for ratings and how much was real. It was hard to tell. From Brenna's narrowed eyes at Summer, it could be either. Travis had something of an aw-shucks look on his face, as though he couldn't help it that women were throwing themselves at him.

The first challenge involved cutting and baling hay. Travis sure was good at that. Brenna—not so much. But then again, she was a hairstylist not a cowgirl.

"Will Brenna be eliminated?" Marissa's mom asked.

"Oh, I doubt it," her dad said. "Others are doing even worse."

"I'm rooting for Brenna not to get eliminated!" Abby said.

Autry glanced around at the roomful of relatives enjoying the show over a home-cooked meal. This sure was…nice. And comfortable. He tried to imagine the Joneses ever doing something like this. Well, once in a blue moon over the years there was Thanksgiving football, but that never lasted long, since his dad would invariably get a business call and one or two of his brothers would have a date or other plans, including himself. None of them particularly wanted to hang out.

The Fuller-Rafferty clan was very lucky, and one thing he admired so much about them was that they knew it. Some folks took this kind of family closeness for granted, but this crew didn't. Maybe because they'd lost so much? Regardless, they knew what they had and they treasured it.

A chill snaked up Autry's back. In just a couple weeks he'd be gone and this would be nothing but a memory. A nice memory, at least.

As the show wound down and the girls decided who they thought would get eliminated, Autry thought about the kids competition and the events listed on the entry form. He took out his phone and started typing notes about the challenges he and Abby would practice.

"Mr. Autry, you might not know this," Abby said during a commercial break, "but our house rule is no cell phone use in the family room."

Autry glanced up at her. His family could have used that rule when he was growing up. "And it's a good rule. But I'm actually using it as a paper and pencil to come up with ideas for the challenges we should practice for. I haven't walked backward while holding a cowboy hat with a raw egg in it in a long time. Maybe even never. Probably never."

Marissa laughed. "What else was on the poster?"

"I remember a three-legged race while trying to rope a robotic calf," Abby said.

"I have a robot dog," Kiera said. "Mr. Autry gave him to me. You can use him if you want."

Abby flung her arms around her sister. "Kiera, did I ever tell you you're an awesome sister?"

Kiera grinned.

"I want to give something," Kaylee said.

"How about if we borrow your jump rope and use it for a lasso?" Abby asked.

Kaylee shrugged. "Okay."

"You're all awesome," Marissa said, smiling at her daughters.

"Roping a robotic dog while three legged," Autry said. "No problem."

The commercial ended and they all turned their attention back to the *The Great Roundup*. "Yay!" Abby cheered. "Travis won immunity! And Brenna wasn't eliminated!"

There were high fives around the room for the hometown contestants. A guy named Dean ended up getting eliminated at the end of the show.

When the show ended, Abby popped up. "Let's practice our roping skills!"

"It's late enough as it is," Marissa said. "Way past every Fuller girl's bedtime."

"Aww," the girls said in unison.

"Autry, can we practice tomorrow?" Abby asked. "Please? Pretty please with bacon on top?"

Part of him wanted to run for the hills. The other part wanted to stay with this family forever. But since he'd made a promise to Abby, coming back tomorrow and being there for the competition was as far as he had to think about right now. "You bet," he said. "We only have one week."

"Double yay!" Kiera said. "Mr. Autry will be coming over tomorrow, too!"

He glanced at Marissa, who seemed to be taking a deep breath and a step back.

You're so good at being a Daddy...

As the five-year-old's words came back to him, he knew he was the one who should be taking deep breaths and a big step in the opposite direction. But how did you do that when your heart kept you coming back, anyway?

When Autry came over the next afternoon, he noticed Marissa hanging back a bit, almost as if she was keeping watch. Assessing. Today he would focus on practicing for the competition and try to keep his eyes and thoughts off Marissa Fuller.

Ha. Like that was even possible.

Abby raced upstairs to get Kiera's remote control dog and Kaylee's jump rope, which was a bit too short, and then they all headed into the backyard. Marissa's dad got some rope and tied their two legs together. Each got a length of rope to use as a lasso, and with a little help, Autry had Abby lassoing like a pro. Well, like a nine-year-old pro.

"Okay, let the dog-calf go," Autry said.

With the robot on the move, Autry and Abby tried catching up to it, taking turns trying to lasso it. They failed miserably, mostly because they were both laughing so hard. Autry had to wipe away tears from how ridiculously funny it all was.

"Well, we might not come in first place in that challenge," Abby said, then doubled over in laughter.

Next they moved on to the raw egg in the cowboy hat while walking backward challenge, and neither dropped their eggs, so that was a plus. Tomorrow, Autry would be back to practice the hay-on-the-head challenge, where teams had to strap on a hat with a pound of hay, and whoever was fastest over the finish line with the most hay left won.

He was enjoying himself a little too much. It was time to go back to the Maverick Manor and regroup.

As he was leaving, Abby wrapped him in a hug. "You're the best, Mr. Autry."

He glanced at Marissa, who smiled warily. Her mom lifted her chin. Well, this was happening, so he'd see it through. And then he'd be in Paris. Far, far away from the Fullers. He'd miss them. That much he knew.

Later that afternoon, Marissa's dad offered to take Abby and her best friend, Janie, to Kalispell to see the movie they'd been talking about for weeks, and Marissa's mom was baking cookies with the little ones, so Marissa and her friend Anne Lattimore planned a girls' night out. A much-needed one—even if they'd both be home by eight thirty. They hadn't been able to talk in depth last week at the premiere of *The Great Roundup* at the Ace in the Hole because their table had been jammed in between others and they knew just about everyone in the bar. But tonight, episode two having aired yesterday, the Ace would be only moderately crowded.

When Marissa arrived, the Ace was only half-full. Anne sat in the back, her blond hair shining in the dim lighting. After ordering two beers and a plate of nachos with the works, the friends sat back, surveying the crowd.

"Every time someone comes into the vet's office, they ask me if I want to be fixed up with one of the five Dalton brothers," Anne said. "They're handsome, every last one of them, but I can't work up any interest in dating anyone. It's been five years since my divorce. What's my issue?"

"I think your issue looks a lot like my issue—tall, blond and blue eyed."

Anne laughed, then quickly sobered up. "Yup. I don't like to admit it. But when the boy you loved your entire life, from playing in the sandbox to high school, the boy you thought you'd marry, up and leaves town without explaining why... I guess it'll always feel unsettled."

Marissa felt for Anne. When Daniel Stockton was eighteen, his parents had died in a car accident, leaving seven children behind, most of whom were split up. Daniel had left town, breaking Anne's heart. And even though she'd married someone else, her heart had always belonged to Daniel Stockton. Autry's brother Hudson was married to Bella Stockton, one of the Stockton kids. She and her brother Jamie had been looking for their missing siblings for almost a year now.

"Sometimes I wish I could just ask him why," Anne said. "I know he was grief stricken over his parents' deaths. And I know his grandparents didn't think they had the money or the room to take in the older boys who were of age. But to just leave town? Leave his younger siblings?"

As Marissa squeezed her friend's hand, the waitress arrived with their beers and nachos. She and Anne clinked their glasses. As they did, Marissa noticed her friend's eye caught by a group of five men at the bar.

"Each of Phil Dalton's five sons is so good-looking," Anne said, upping her chin at the group of Daltons, who'd arrived in town last month with their father. Marissa noted that several single women were checking out Zach Dalton, with his longish dark hair and green eyes. "But you're right. I guess Daniel Stockton is standing between me and getting back out there. Maybe I should just start dating, force myself."

"I think you'll date when you're ready or when the right man presents himself. I certainly didn't think I was ready to date, but ever since I met Autry, it's like I'm led by my heart instead of my head. If he lived here permanently, I'd date him in a heartbeat."

"Any chance he'll stick around?"

Marissa shook her head. "He's not a small-town guy. Or a family guy. He's got Jones Holdings, Inc. in his blood and veins. Plus he's a jet-setter. He'd never be happy here."

"I've seen the way that man looks at you, Marissa. I think he'd be happy anywhere you are."

Marissa laughed and waved hand dismissively. "In my dreams, maybe."

"To dreams, then," Anne said, and they clinked to that and dug into the nachos.

Over the next few days, Marissa kept a bit of distance between herself and Autry. He came over every day to practice with Abby, and her heart squeezed even more every time he made sure the two little Fuller girls felt included, even though they were too young to participate in the event itself. On Friday night, as Marissa was tucking Abby into bed, her daughter sat up and wrapped her in a tight hug. She hadn't had one of those from Abby in a while.

"What's that for?" Marissa asked.

"Tomorrow I'm going to feel like everyone else for the first time in a long time," Abby whispered. "You know? I mean, Janie's mom and dad are divorced, but she sees her dad all the time and he's doing The Great Roundup Kids Competition with her. And now I'll have someone standing in as *my* dad."

Marissa touched her sweet, beautiful daughter's face. "That means a lot to you, huh?"

Abby nodded, then burst into tears. "Is that wrong?"

Oh no, what was this? Marissa pulled Abby against her and gently wiped away her tears. "Why would that be wrong, sweetie?"

But fresh tears streamed down Abby's cheeks. "Because I *have* a dad. Even though he's not here anymore. He'll always be my dad. Maybe he's watching from heaven and it's hurting his feelings."

Marissa held Abby to her, stroking her dark, silky hair. "Abby, your daddy is always watching over us. And I think he'd be very touched that Mr. Autry is going to be your partner in the competition. You know why?"

"Why?"

"Because it was nice of Mr. Autry to want to be your partner. And your dad would like anyone who was kind to you and our family. Your daddy wants you to be happy, sweetheart."

Abby thought about that for a moment, then nodded. "I think so, too, Mom." She smiled and settled back down in bed, her hands around the ancient Raggedy Ann doll that had been passed down from grandmother to mother to daughter. Abby's eyes drifted closed. "'Night, Mommy."

Tears stung Marissa's eyes and she blinked them away. "Good night, my sweet girl. I love you so much."

"I love you, too."

Before she could start bawling, Marissa tiptoed out of Abby's room.

Chapter Ten

"Listen, Dad, I have to be somewhere this morning—" Autry glanced at his watch "—in five minutes. So we'll have to continue this discussion later. Or preferably not at all."

"You listen to me, Autry," his father bellowed. "I want you on that flight this morning. My admin already booked it. Just have your hotel pack your bags and be at the gate on time. End of story."

Walker Jones the Second had called every night since Alexandra had tried to lure him home, screeching up a storm about how Autry had hurt Alexandra's feelings and that she'd reported he'd chosen "some country mouse" over her and wouldn't return home with her. Autry had told his father he would finish his vacation, that he was enjoying time with his brothers and getting to know their wives and he had zero interest in Alexandra.

"If you think I'm losing you to that hick town and '

some country mouse, you're wrong!" Walker the Second had shouted during last night's call.

"Dad, do you hear yourself?" Autry had asked. "And stop referring to Marissa as a country mouse. I won't stand for you insulting her."

"Ah, so the country mouse has a name," his father had said with a snort. "Marissa. She must be stacked."

Autry had hung up on Walker Jones the Second. The first time he'd ever done that.

Now, five minutes before Autry had to be at Rust Creek Falls Park for The Great Roundup Kids Competition, his father had called back, demanding to get his way—which was for Autry to fly home immediately.

Wasn't happening.

"Dad, you have an opportunity here to fix your relationship with Walker and Hudson," Autry said. "Why can't that be more important to you than business?"

"Our family and our business are synonymous," his father said. "That you don't understand that is mind-boggling."

Oh, Dad, Autry thought. *Please don't be the lost cause I'm thinking you are. Please give me hope that we can salvage this family.*

"Will you be on the plane home?" his father asked, his voice cracking. "I can't lose you, Autry. I just can't."

For the first time in maybe…ever, Autry heard anguish in his dad's voice, and it caught him off guard, to the point that he had to sit down for a second.

His head was spinning. Flashing in and out of his mind were images—his father, his mother, his four brothers at various ages. Karinna and Lulu and the nursery in his condo that he'd had someone come pack up and take to a charity. The offices at Jones Holdings,

Inc. in Tulsa. The view outside his window at Maverick Manor. The faces of the three Fuller girls, Kaylee, Kiera and Abby. And their beautiful mother, Marissa, who was no country mouse. Not that there was anything wrong with a country mouse.

He saw himself saying goodbye to them, the little girls wrapped around his legs. *"But you're like our daddy now,"* they said in unison. *"Abby said so."*

You're our daddy now. You're our daddy now...

The words echoed in his head until Autry could barely breathe.

"Autry, are you there? Can I count on you to come home today?" his father asked.

Autry didn't answer. But he didn't move, either, and he was now late for meeting Marissa and the girls.

You're our daddy now. This is what having a dad is like. I remember. It's just like this.

Just like this. Just like this...

Autry leaned back on the chair and stared out the window, unable to think, unable to move.

Abby woke up at the crack of dawn on Saturday, so excited she was practically hyperventilating, and Marissa planned on getting everyone over to Rust Creek Falls Park on the early side. But of course, Kaylee pressed an Oat Yummy in her ear, which Marissa had to carefully extract so as not to crumble it, and then Kiera stubbed her toe and sobbed for a full three minutes, and Abby, practicing walking backward while holding an egg in a cowboy hat, dropped said egg and burst into tears and had to be consoled that she wouldn't come in in last place.

Then Ralph couldn't find his lucky socks, the ones

with the Montana State University mascot, and Roberta was searching for the new tube of sunscreen she'd bought yesterday. Marissa soothed the little ones, found the socks and the sunscreen, drank two cups of strong coffee, got a decent breakfast in everyone, and finally, the Fuller-Rafferty crew was out the door and on the way to the park to meet Autry.

Autry, whose morning was nothing like Marissa's.

Autry, who didn't have to worry about crumbling Oat Yummies in small ears or getting a houseful of people out on time.

Autry, who was like a vacation in himself.

Take me away, she sang to herself with a smile, his gorgeous face floating into her mind.

As they turned the corner, they joined a crowd headed toward the park. Huge signs and banners were strung up at the entrance and the park was packed. She and Autry had made plans to meet at eight forty-five in front of the check-in table. She looked around but didn't see him. She glanced at her watch—eight forty-four. At least she wasn't late. But Autry wasn't here yet?

When her watch ticked to eight forty-five and she saw no sign of him, she stood on tiptoe and craned her neck. She saw his brothers and their wives with their extended family entering the park, but no Autry.

Eight forty-six. Eight forty-seven.

The competition began at nine sharp and Autry wasn't even here to check in.

"Mom, where's Autry?" Abby asked, looking all around.

"I'm sure he's here and just saying hi to his brothers," she said.

But she kept her eyes glued on the park entrance and he wasn't racing in.

Her stomach twisted. Had he changed his mind? Had the reality of what he'd overheard Abby saying to his sisters about how "this is what having a dad is like" scared him off? Was partnering with Abby in a dad-like team too much for him?

It better not be, she thought, anger burning in her gut. If he disappointed her child...

Autry might not have made any commitment to Marissa, but he sure as hell had made one to Abby, and there would be serious heck to pay if he let Abby down. Marissa had no idea what, but she'd let Autry Jones have it—an earful of her ire, at the least.

Eight fifty. Eight fifty-two.

Where are you? she thought, glancing around.

Abby had gone from excitedly standing on tiptoe and looking for Autry to biting her lip with an expression of sadness and worry.

"Abby, I thought you were in the competition," one of those not-so-nice girls said as she smoothed her own pinned-on entry number. She held her dad's hand, but he was busy talking to another dad behind him.

"I...I am," Abby said. "I'm just waiting for him."

"She's not in the competition," the other girl whispered. "Her father's dead."

"She asked someone to be her dad for the day," the first girl whispered back. "Oh my God, that is so sad. I'm so sorry, Abby."

Both girls made fake sad faces at Abby.

"I'm sure both of you have somewhere to be," Marissa snapped, and the girls tugged their dads' hands and walked away.

"I guess he's not coming," Abby said, tears filling her dark eyes. Her head dropped and Marissa's heart tightened.

"Not coming?" said a familiar, deep voice. "I never break a promise, Abby. Never."

Relief flooded Marissa to the point she almost fell over. Autry stood before them, slightly out of breath as though he'd run here from Maverick Manor. Or the airport.

"Autry!" Abby squealed, her face lighting up. He picked her up and swung her around, somehow managing not to bump her into the people around them.

"Sorry I'm late," he said, glancing at Marissa. "Tough call that was hard to untangle from. But I checked us in, so let's head over to the entrants' area." He handed Abby her number to pin on her shirt.

"Yay!" Abby said. "Wish us luck!"

The Fuller-Rafferty clan hugged Abby and assured her she'd do great.

Marissa was so exhausted from the emotional tailspin she'd just been through that she could barely speak. Luckily, her mother, always at the ready, handed her a foam cup of coffee from the urns the Jones family had set up for the event, along with juices and treats.

"I never break a promise," Autry whispered to Marissa, squeezing her hand. And then he was gone, running with Abby to the entrants' line.

But you will break a heart. Mine.

Abby did not drop her egg in the three-legged backward egg-in-the-Stetson competition—cowboy hats donated compliments of the Jones brothers. Luckily, that was the first event, and though they came in fifth place—which was saying something considering that twenty-two teams were participating—Abby was thrilled and pumped for the rest of the challenges. They came in first in the lasso competition, beating out a mean girl and her dad.

By the end of the three-hour event, Autry and Abby had a third-place ribbon, which they both proudly pinned to their T-shirts, and the entire family went to Buffalo Bart's Wings To Go to celebrate. Autry had arranged for Buffalo Bart to set up a wings, beer and soda buffet in the backyard for the family and whoever Abby and the Fuller-Raffertys wanted to invite. When Melissa's dad tried to pay, Autry mentioned he'd already taken care of the bill. Ralph tried to cover the tip, but Autry insisted he'd taken care of that, too. Her father seemed quite pleased.

"He's making up for almost being late," Roberta whispered to Marissa.

"Oh, Mom, have a wing. And try the tangy barbecue sauce."

Roberta raised an eyebrow but went off to the wings buffet and filled her plate.

Marissa glanced over at Abby, who was standing with her friend Janie and trying to talk and eat a wing at the same time. Her daughter looked so breathlessly happy that Marissa's heart pinged in her chest.

Autry was talking to his brothers and their wives by the beer taps, and though he was smiling, she could tell something was bothering him. Perhaps the reason he'd been late? She hadn't had a chance to talk to him one-on-one since he'd arrived at the park, and the yard was so crowded she wouldn't have a chance here, either.

He caught her eye and raised his glass to her, and

she raised her soda in return. But behind his smile she definitely saw conflict and something else she couldn't put her finger on.

Maybe she'd just have to sneak over to Maverick Manor tonight and find out what it was.

As soon as he could escape the festivities, Autry was gone, back to his hotel room. He had one more week in Rust Creek Falls, and instead of enjoying some time with Marissa, he felt like someone was stabbing him in the chest with a hot poker. Constantly. His father's plea had his gut all twisted. Abby's faith in him had his gut all twisted.

Marissa's acceptance of him had his gut all twisted, too.

Someone knocked on the door, and Autry almost didn't open it. It could be Alexandra again. Or his father. Marissa. The Fuller girls. Any number of people pulling him in opposite directions.

But it was his brother Walker. He was holding a folder.

"Need your signature on these for the preliminary Thorpe Corp. meetings in Paris," Walker said. "Dad's signed, I've signed, then you, and you're all set."

Autry took the folder, his heart so heavy he wouldn't be surprised if he broke a hole in the floor and crashed to the ground.

"Something wrong?" Walker asked.

"The water. The punch. Whatever it is. It got me."

Walker looked at him as though he had four heads, then realization dawned. "Marissa got you, you mean."

"Love got me. But how? I'm immune."

Walker laughed. "I thought I was, too. Then I met Lindsay."

"I'm going to Paris," Autry said. "I want to go."

"So figure out how to have both," Walker said.

"How? How can I fly around the world every few weeks and have a relationship? A relationship with a single mother whose kids would have expectations?" Autry shook his head. "Ridiculous. I'm not cut out for fatherhood."

He knew what happened when you thought you were, when you let your heart lead you. You got kicked in the head. Kicked to the curb.

"Autry, let me give you some advice from someone who's been there, done that. Someone who was raised by the same parents you were."

Autry looked at his brother. "I'll take it."

"You can try to lie to yourself, but the truth always outs. That's just the way it is. So first, work on accepting the truth. Then let that truth decide what you do."

"What am I lying to myself about?" he asked. "I just admitted to you that I have feelings for Marissa. That her kids matter to me."

"You have feelings. Her kids matter. You like chocolate ice cream. It's a nice day outside. Autry—I'm talking about truth, not spin."

"What do you want me to say? That I love Marissa?"

"If you do. Like I said, you can try to lie to yourself, but the truth always outs. Let the truth boss you around, Autry. Not Dad. Not what happened in the past. And not how you *think* you should feel."

Autry flipped through the papers. He'd read them carefully over the past couple of days and had just been waiting for the chairman's and CEO's signatures before he signed them. He brought the stack over to the desk and signed on the dotted lines. He was going to Paris; that was never in question or doubt.

He handed the folder back to Walker.

"You'll figure it out, brother," Walker said. "I did."

How? How would he possibly figure it out? He did have strong feelings for Marissa. Her kids did matter to him. He even adored her parents. But his job meant a lot to him, too, and he loved traveling the world, negotiating and wheeling and dealing.

Somehow, grilling steaks in a small-town backyard, playing charades, teaching Kaylee and Kiera how to play soccer, making pigs in a blanket, watching reality TV with a family and practicing for The Great Roundup Kids Competition had shown him he enjoyed that, too. More than he ever thought possible.

So fine—the truth would out. It was outing right here and now. But how could the worlds coexist?

Chapter Eleven

"You certainly snagged the most eligible bachelor in Rust Creek Falls," Helen Ganley said with a scowl as she marched up to Marissa at the reception desk in the sheriff's station. Helen lived in Anne's neighborhood and was the one who complained incessantly about dog walkers allowing their "mutts to pee on the edge of my property!"

Marissa felt her cheeks burn. Naturally, her boss was in his office and had likely heard every embarrassing word. Sheriff Christensen's two new deputies, a rookie guy and the very experienced Daniella Patterson, glanced up, the rookie wiggling his eyebrows and Daniella giving Marissa a thumbs-up.

God. Did everyone know her business? Yes. They did. Because this was a small town and she herself had paraded her business all over Rust Creek Falls.

"If you are talking about Autry Jones," Marissa said in a louder voice than usual, "we are just friends."

"Sure you are, hon," Helen said. "I want to file another complaint about the lady who lets her dog pee on my lawn."

"The very edge of your lawn?" Marissa asked. "Technically, that strip is public property, Helen."

"It's still *my* lawn," the woman said. "It's very bad for the grass! It dies!"

"Well, I personally have spoken to the lady in question and she has promised not to let her dog lift its leg on your property ever again."

"Good!" Helen snapped. "Finally."

"Helen, maybe it's time you adopted a puppy," Marissa said. "I heard the animal shelter just rescued a mother dog and her month-old pups from the woods."

Helen's face fell. "I don't think I'll ever be ready for another dog." Marissa knew that Helen's beloved miniature black poodle, Chumley, had died after sixteen years together, and the woman had gotten grumpier and grumpier ever since. But underneath that brittle exterior was a softy who needed something to dote on.

"I clock out at five," Marissa said, glancing at her watch. It was four fifty. "Let's walk over and just see them. I hear they're really cute. Black-and-white."

"Black-and-white?" Helen said, her face lifting a bit. "I suppose we could take a look."

A half hour later, Helen had signed on to foster all four pups *and* the mother dog, with the intention of adopting the mom and one puppy when they were ready. Marissa had a feeling that Helen would not be complaining about anything or anyone anymore.

After a day's work and a trip to the Rust Creek Falls Animal Shelter, all Marissa wanted to do was go home and soak in a bathtub. But it was her turn to cook, and Kiera wanted to practice her reading, and Kaylee wanted to learn to count to a hundred by tens. Wasn't that what older sisters were for? She'd put Abby on that. Except Abby wanted to redecorate her room, and Marissa had promised she'd help move the desk and bed and dresser around so that her father wouldn't throw out his back.

But when Marissa arrived home, Autry had not only rearranged Abby's bedroom and had Kaylee already working on up to fifty in the counting by tens, but was sitting on the sofa with Kiera, patiently listening to her sound out a tough word, her little finger on the page, her tongue out in concentration. *"Peh-oh-pel?"*

"Pee-pul," Autry said. "That's a toughie. Some words can't really be sounded out. You just have to learn them by sight."

"Like *house*," Kaylee said. "I learned that one."

"High five!" Autry said, hand up.

Kaylee beamed and high-fived him.

"Sorry I'm late," Marissa said. "I had an errand to run."

"Actually, it's good you're late, because dinner is just about ready. Two more minutes."

He cooks. He teaches kids to read. He teaches kids to count. He rearranges furniture.

He kisses...like he means it.

"I'll come help," she said, and Autry followed her into the kitchen. "I didn't know you were coming over tonight."

"I only have a week left. I want to spend as much time with you as I can."

"As friends."

He held her gaze. "As friends."

"Thanks for everything in there," she said, gesturing toward the other room. "I was swamped at work today, then I helped Helen Ganley turn her long-time frown upside down. And I thought I had a couple heavy hours of mom duty ahead of me. But then you were here."

"Autry Jones, at your service," he said, taking a bow. His smile almost undid her, sending a jolt to her knees.

God, she loved this man.

She froze, then felt herself tremble and took a step back.

What? She loved him?

Say something, she ordered herself. *Get that thought out of your head immediately!*

"So…what's for dinner?" she asked, her heart beating so fast she was surprised he couldn't hear it.

"My world-famous meatballs and spaghetti, with garlic bread and a green salad."

She grinned. "I may faint with happiness. So will my father. And the girls."

"Marissa, I did one more thing."

"You couldn't possibly have," she said. What was there left for this man to do?

"I know I should have asked, but the opportunity presented itself right then and there and I took it."

She tilted her head.

"A friend of mine bought eight tickets to a concert for his family, but there was a conflict, so he asked if I'd like to buy them and I did. I'd like to invite your entire family to go. You, me, your parents and the girls. And since there's an extra, maybe Abby would like to invite a friend."

"A concert? What kind?"

"It's 2LOVEU," he said. "With a certain dimpled lead singer named Lyle. Did I mention a backstage pass comes along with the tickets?"

"Oh my God. Abby might pass out. But I don't know, Autry. That's kind of out of our league."

"Not mine," he said.

"Let me talk to my mom."

"Does she like 2LOVEU?" he asked.

"Everyone does. I heard her humming one of their songs while folding laundry the other day. Abby plays their album so often that the ear worm has got us all. Even Kaylee knows half the songs by heart."

"I would love to take you all. The concert is in Seattle."

"Seattle?" she said. "But—"

"Private jet and a hotel for the night—you, your parents and the girls will have a large suite with three bedrooms, and I'll have a suite down the hall. If we're going front row at a boy-band concert, we have to do it right."

She laughed. "You really are from another universe," she said.

He held her gaze, his expression turning serious. "Except I'm right here in your kitchen, making spaghetti and meatballs."

Tears poked at her eyes and she quickly blinked them back. That was the problem. He was so close—and yet so damned far away.

And leaving in a week.

And she loved him. She loved Autry Jones.

As Marissa and her mom unloaded the dishwasher long after Autry had gone home, Marissa figured it was time to bring up the 2LOVEU concert. The conversation would go one of two ways. Either her mom would say "Oh, how generous and nice, what a wonderful family trip!" or "Absolutely not, that's too much, and setting up expectations for not only Abby but the younger girls, too."

Her eyes narrowed, her chin lifted, Roberta listened as Marissa explained the details of the big concert trip to Seattle.

"Marissa, that's very generous of him, but come on. Front-row tickets to the concert everyone is talking about. In Seattle. A private jet there. A hotel overnight. Backstage passes. This isn't us, Marissa. It's not our life. And it's not going to be our future. Autry is leaving in a week. Then life suddenly goes back to regular."

Marissa had to smile at how her mother managed to double up on what Marissa had figured she'd say. "So maybe a special once-in-a-lifetime event isn't such a terrible thing."

Her mother frowned and put the mugs in the cabinet. "I don't know, Marissa. Honestly, I'm just not sure. He's a good person, that much I know. He's genuine. He is leaving in a week, and yet he was here tonight, making spaghetti and meatballs, helping Kiera read, helping Kaylee count, rearranging Abby's bedroom furniture, going over Dad's stock picks and fixing the crazy font increase on my desktop that I couldn't figure out. He's doing everyday things. Family things. He's spent a lot of time here, Marissa, when he could have just taken you out on the town. So I can't say he's not a lovely, family-oriented person."

"He doesn't think he's family oriented," Marissa said. "It's part of the problem."

She thought about the woman who'd hurt Autry, the baby he'd lost all contact with. He'd hardened his heart against having a family for himself, against loving again, against expectations.

"For a man who came to town to visit his family and has been spending time with them and a family of three kids, two grandparents and a widowed mom, he's more family focused than he must realize."

Marissa nodded, taking out a stack of plates. "Do you think Abby will be hurt when he leaves?" she asked.

"I think Abby will be fine. Autry is kind of like Lyle from 2LOVEU to Abby. Sort of a celebrity, except she got to know this one a little. That he's leaving won't be a surprise, and you've prepared her well for that. I think it's *you* who'll be hurt."

Chapter Twelve

"AHHH!" four little girls—three Fullers and a Lattimore—shrieked as the Jones Holdings, Inc. corporate jet cleared the cloud cover and the Seattle skyline came into view. Ever since Marissa had told her daughters about the concert and the trip to Seattle, they'd been squealing and jumping up and down and happily shrieking in anticipation. They'd also already written Autry five thank-you cards each.

"Almost there!" Autry said.

Marissa, with Kaylee and Kiera seated between her and Autry, looked out the window. She'd never been to Seattle. She'd been out of Montana only once, come to think of it. But Autry Jones probably couldn't think of a city, state or country he hadn't been to.

This is a fairy tale and then this corporate jet will turn back into a pumpkin, aka my twelve-year-old car that needs new brake pads.

For tonight, she'd take the fairy tale. In a few days,

Autry would be flying off to Paris, and then life would go back to normal.

When the plane touched down, Abby and her best friend, Janie, started clapping and singing "Only You," one of their favorite 2LOVEU songs. Even Grandpa joined in, making everyone laugh when he knew the chorus, even if he was completely off-key.

By the time they arrived at their hotel, via a private car that had met them at baggage claim, Marissa was as starry-eyed as her daughters. The hotel was right across the street from the concert venue, and had an amazing fountain across both sides of the entrance. The Fuller-Raffertys craned their necks to look up at how high the skyscraper went—maybe forty floors. The lobby was as grand as the outside—marble floors and exquisite rugs and paintings and plush couches and chairs. Marissa counted two bars and two restaurants.

Autry took care of checking in and then they were going up in the express elevator to the twenty-eighth floor.

"I'm in this room," Autry said, as he walked past room 2802. "And I booked this three-bedroom suite a few doors down for you," he added, stopping in front of room 2810. He opened the door and they all gasped.

Wow. An entire wall of windows offered an expansive view of Seattle, including the famed Space Needle. A seating area of two sofas surrounded an entertainment center, and there was a desk and kitchenette. Three doors opened to three bedrooms. Two had king-size beds and one had four twin beds.

Each bedroom had its own private bathroom—of course—with fluffy white bathrobes, including kid-size ones for the girls, and slippers.

"Oh, is this going to be nice," Roberta said, smiling as she looked around the suite.

"Told you," Ralph whispered.

As the girls went racing into their room, flinging their overnight bags on their beds and pulling out the one stuffed animal that each was allowed to bring, Marissa smiled at Autry.

"Thank you," she said. "We needed this. All of us."

"I needed it, too. I just didn't know it until I met you."

She squeezed his hand, but really wanted to fling herself into his arms and kiss him.

"So who's hungry?" Autry asked. "We have an hour before the concert starts."

"Lines at the food stands can get pretty long," Ralph said. "We'd better head over now. A hot dog with the works for me!"

"And me!" Abby said.

"Can I have a corn dog?" Kiera asked.

Kaylee wrinkled her nose. "I just want a plain hot dog."

"Hot dogs?" Autry said, scratching his chin. "Sorry, guys. But I'm not sure if they're serving that to the fifty superfans who get to dine with the band backstage before the concert."

"What?" Abby shouted, tears streaming down her cheeks. "Ahhh!" She was jumping up and down and laughing and crying with her friend and sisters.

"Oh, Autry," Marissa said. "I should have figured."

He smiled. "Always figure."

"I'm learning."

"And who says money can't buy happiness?" Autry whispered.

Marissa glanced at him and could see that even he knew it couldn't. Because even though they had to-night, all the money in the world couldn't buy a fix for what stood in the way of their happiness.

Autry, surrounded by tens of thousands of squeal-ing, screaming, shrieking girls of all ages, almost wished he'd brought earplugs. But after a while, even he got into the boy-band music and enjoyed the show, which came complete with pyrotechnics and choreo-graphed dances and three encores. Abby had vowed she'd never wash her right hand again after Lyle, the lead singer, shook it when they met during the superfan dinner. She was speechless when he said hi and told her he liked her sparkly green hair band, and when she shrieked, he seemed very used to it.

About an hour in, Kaylee started showing signs of tiring. The music was just too loud for her, so Marissa's parents took her back to the hotel. Autry could tell they were ready to make their escape.

When the concert ended, Abby flung herself into Autry's arms. "I'll never forget this. Never in a million years, no matter what happens in my life. I'll always have this."

He hugged her tight and glanced at Marissa, and could see tears glistening her eyes. Her daughter's hap-piness meant so much to her, and he'd been glad to make this special night happen for and her bestie.

Five-year-old Kiera had managed to fall fast asleep, so Marissa was about to scoop her up from her seat when Autry did instead, easily picking up the girl and cradling her against him. Kiera didn't even stir. He looked down at the sleeping angel in his arms, and the old ache poked at his heart and gut. Once, he'd thought this would be his life. But he knew better now. Things didn't last. People changed, feelings changed, and the woman looking at him with such tenderness in her expression could slam a door in his face three months from now. A virtual door, since he'd still be in Europe in three months, but still... If he cracked open his heart even just a sliver and let these people in, really in, one day he'd wake up and find them gone, and in their place would be a gnawing void. Just the way it was when Karinna had dumped him and he'd lost Lulu.

The sooner he got back to the hotel and into his own suite, the better. Carefully holding Kiera, he headed into the aisle with the throngs of others, keeping Marissa, Abby and Janie in his sights. Kiera shifted and sighed, off in dreamland, and he couldn't help a little smile, despite how off balance he felt.

"Good job, Dad," said a man who was leaving with his daughter.

"No, I—" Autry started to say, then didn't bother correcting the guy.

Dad.

He was no one's dad and would never be. Couldn't be.

As Abby and Janie chattered on excitedly about every moment of the flight, the hotel rooms, the superfan dinner and the concert itself, Marissa glanced at Autry carrying Kiera. For all anyone knew, they were a family. A mom, a dad and their three daughters leaving the concert.

For a moment, she relished how it felt to be a full unit, even just in appearance. She hadn't realized how much she'd missed that, walking to the park with Mike and the girls, a family. But the past two years, one very important family member had been gone.

She glanced at Autry again, slightly rocking Kiera as he walked, smiling now and then at Abby and Janie's conversation, now focused on how cute Lyle, the lead singer of 2LOVEU, was and how neither of them were ever washing their right hands again, no matter what, unless their moms made them.

Marissa smiled.

They looked like a typical happy family. And as Marissa realized how much she wished they could really be one, her heart started beating really fast. She loved this man. And she'd have to let him go in just a few days.

Back in the hotel suite, Autry gently put Kiera on her bed, and Marissa tucked her in, careful not to wake Kaylee, who was fast asleep, her arm around her stuffed monkey.

Abby and Janie were both still too wired from the concert to head to bed, so Grandma and Grandpa let them talk their ears off about the parts of the concert they'd missed.

"Well, I'd better let you all settle down to bed," Autry said, heading to the door.

Abby and Janie both raced over to thank him profusely and hug him, and he seemed truly touched by their gratitude.

"You're very welcome, girls. It was my pleasure," he said.

When the girls ran into their room to change into the concert T-shirts Autry had bought all the kids, Marissa went to the door, wishing she didn't have to say goodbye for the evening. She didn't want him to go, didn't want to stop looking at that handsome, kind face, didn't want to stop being in his presence, which calmed her, comforted her and yet made her feel things she hadn't even thought about in years. Excitement. Romance. Sex.

Roberta got up, and as she passed them on the way to her bedroom, she said, "Why don't you two go have a nightcap at one of those fancy bars downstairs? It's time for bed for little ones and grandparents, but you two go enjoy yourselves. No need to rush back. Dad and I will hold down the fort."

Marissa almost gasped. Was her mother actually engineering a little one-on-one time with Autry involving alcohol and a hotel? It sure seemed that way. Or perhaps her mother was just wanting the two of them to get some time to themselves, since they'd been surrounded by shrieking kids for so many hours.

"I think that's a great idea," Autry said, extending his arm.

"Thanks, Mom," she whispered and took Autry's elbow.

"I keep expecting to have to cover my ears to escape a shrill scream of joy over a cute band member leaping onstage or something," Marissa said as they rode the elevator down.

He laughed. "I know. Sometimes I realize I'm talking too loud because I've been shouting to be heard for the past three hours." He leaned close and whispered, "Is this too loud?"

Every nerve ending in her body tingled. "No, that's just right."

She held on to his arm and he led the way to Bar 22.

It was elegant, low lit, with club chairs and couches and secluded corners. They chose a plush velvet love seat in one of those spots meant for two, and a sleek waiter appeared to take their orders.

"I don't feel dressed up enough for this place," Marissa said, glancing around at the women in cocktail dresses or stylish casual clothes. She was in a silky tank top and jeans, a light cardigan sweater tied around her waist, her usual silver ballet flats on her feet and her hair loose around her shoulders. In other words, dressed just right for the Ace in the Hole or a teeny-bopper concert.

"You look perfect and beautiful as always, Marissa," he said. "And I mean that."

She reached up to touch his face before she could think about it or stop herself. He so often said exactly the right thing, the thing that slipped inside her heart and kept adding check marks in the pro-Autry column. The con column had only one check mark in it: for the fact that he was leaving in a few days. There'd been another, the little business of him being from a completely different world, where private jets and super-fan dinners with the most popular band in America were no biggie, but Autry didn't act like he was from another galaxy. He acted like a regular person. Someone she could love. Someone she did love.

Someone who would poof away with all the magic, leaving her as Cinderella, but without a missing glass slipper. He would go his way and she would go hers, and they'd have their memories, but that would be that.

Marissa sipped her red wine. "Autry, I know I've said it quite a few times tonight, but I have to say it again. Thank you. For a perfect evening. For making my family so happy."

"What about you, though, Marissa? What would make you happy?"

"When my crew is happy, I'm happy." She smiled. "I guess it's hard to separate one from the other. It's been a long time since it's been just me, you know?"

He didn't challenge her, didn't keep asking, didn't push, and she could tell from the way he was looking at her that he was thinking about what would make him happy right then. To be upstairs in bed with her.

Which made *her* happy.

Oh God. She just realized that having sex with Autry Jones would indeed make her happy. It might break her heart later, but now, right now, she wanted nothing more. And later, she'd have her memories. Yes, she thought. Why shouldn't she allow herself just one night with Autry Jones? A perfect night to wrap up a perfect evening. Today was a fairy tale and it would end happily. Tomorrow she'd be back home, back in her regular life, looking for lost light-up sneakers and pulling Oat Yummies out of ears and doing load after load of laundry.

But while mopping the kitchen floor or scrubbing the upstairs bathroom, she could see herself stopping to think about her one perfect night with Autry, and the magic of it would sustain her.

Was she rationalizing? Maybe. But so be it. She was a grown woman.

"What would make me happy?" She paused and looked at him, and she was pretty sure her answer was written all over her face.

He sucked in a breath and leaned close and kissed

her. She kissed him back, grateful for their secluded corner.

"Just for tonight," she said.

"Just for tonight."

She kissed him again, her hands on his face, everything she felt going into the fierce kiss. "No strings attached," she whispered.

"That's always been the case," he said.

No strings. She'd shake on that again, but not on being friends. She couldn't be casual friends with Autry, not after this and certainly not after they made love.

"Maybe we should take this conversation upstairs," he said.

"I think we're done talking," she whispered and kissed him again.

They kissed all the way upstairs, prompting one giggled "get a room" from a couple entering the elevator as they exited.

Please let this night happen, he prayed to the universe. They'd been interrupted once before, in his room at Maverick Manor, and he figured he'd never have the chance again to have Marissa Fuller to himself, to explore every morsel of her amazing body, to show her just how much he wanted her.

"Shhh," Marissa whispered, her finger against her lips as they headed to Autry's room, which was thankfully several doors down from the Fuller-Rafferty clan's.

He smiled and unlocked the door, then kissed her inside, shutting the door behind them with his back. She unbuttoned his shirt and he let it fall to the floor.

As she undid his belt buckle, he sucked in a breath, barely able to stop himself from taking her right there on the probably-not-that-soft-on-the-back carpet.

The belt joined the shirt. All she'd taken off were her shoes.

They stood in front of the wall of windows, the Seattle city view barely visible through the filmy curtain. He liked that the lighting was dim in the room, romantic, but that he was able to see her. He wanted to see everything.

He slid off her silky tank top, his gaze rooted to the lacy white bra she wore. He let his hands explore her bare skin, her smooth stomach and sexy waist, and then he slid a finger underneath the straps of her bra and slid it down so he could savor every bit of skin as her beautiful breasts were revealed to him. His legs slightly buckled and he focused on unclasping the bra to keep himself from exploding—literally and figuratively.

He knelt in front of her and pulled down the zipper of her jeans, wriggling them off her sexy hips. *Mmm*, he thought, at the sight of the white cotton underwear. So damned sexy he again had to fight for control, counting to five in his head.

He picked her up and carried her into the bedroom and laid her on the bed, getting rid of his own jeans right afterward. He covered her body with his, tiny scraps of cotton and lace separating them. She kissed him passionately, her hands in his hair, and he couldn't wait another moment. He wriggled down her panties with a finger on each hip, his mouth exploring hers, then her neck, then her breasts, then her stomach and lower until she gasped and gripped the sides of the comforter. She let out a moan and he smiled.

When he felt her own hands on his hips, the boxer briefs sliding down, her cool, soft fingers touching him, he again had to count to five, then ten, to keep control.

Finally he ran out of numbers. He quickly put on a condom and then in moments was making love to Marissa, each thrust underscoring how much he wanted her, how badly he needed her, how deeply he loved her.

Oh hell.

There it was. He loved Marissa Fuller.

Shut up, Jones, he told himself. *Just lose yourself in this night.*

He took his own advice and pulled Marissa on top of him, reveling in the gorgeous sight of her naked, an expression of pleasure rippling across her face.

Finally, there was an explosion of sensation and Autry was gone, gone, gone into it, unable to think of anything but release and Marissa.

He pulled her close against him and trailed a finger down her cheek. "That was amazing. *You* are amazing."

"That was pretty damned amazing," she agreed, laughing between breaths, her hand entwined with his.

"Stay the night," he whispered.

"I wish I could. But I can't. You know I can't." She turned on her side to face him. "Thank you for this magical night, Autry Jones. Every last moment of it."

That sounded like goodbye. A final goodbye.

But they had a few more days. He couldn't bear to be in Rust Creek Falls and not see Marissa. But he was leaving. Love or not, he was getting on that plane to Paris.

You had no business getting involved with a single mother. With three kids.

But he had. And he didn't know which was scarier. That he loved her and the girls…or the idea of letting Marissa go.

Chapter Thirteen

In Autry style, he treated the group to breakfast in the hotel restaurant. Ralph was so surprised to see the size of his bacon, Swiss and tomato omelet that he took a photo of it, and Abby and Janie tried to teach him to how to upload it on social media. But of course, Ralph didn't have any social media accounts.

They ate, they drank their six-dollar glasses of orange juice and four-dollar cups of coffee, and then they were on the corporate jet again, flying back to real life.

This time, Marissa sat next to her mom, the two little Fuller girls across the aisle like "big girls" with their headphones on as they watched *Frozen* for the hundredth time. Abby and Janie also had their headphones on, but they were listening to 2LOVEU on their tiny iPod shuffles, Christmas gifts from Marissa and Anne last year.

Autry was a few rows up, next to her father, chatting about the stock market. Every now and then, Autry would turn and Marissa would get a glimpse of his beautiful profile, his strong, straight nose, that sculpted jawline and the sexy sweep of dark blond hair.

She sighed before she could catch herself.

"What was that for?" her mother whispered.

"What? Nothing. Just…a little tired."

"Uh-huh," Roberta said, eyebrow raised. "Maybe I was wrong, honey," she added. "Maybe playing it safe isn't the way to go."

"Of course it is," Marissa whispered. "That's the only way *to* go."

"But you're not escaping without a bruised heart."

"I also need to be realistic. He's who he is. I'm who I am. Our lives can't meet, Mom. How could they?"

Even that one had Roberta stumped.

"Autry loves what he does. He loves traveling for his family business. He might have very strong feelings for me, for all of us, but let's say he mysteriously and magically said he's going to stay in Rust Creek Falls for me. He'd be miserable. I know that and so does he."

Roberta covered Marissa's hand. "I guess so. Well, I have no doubt the two of you will figure it out."

"Or not," Marissa said, tears poking her eyes. "You know that annoying saying 'it is what it is'? Well, it is what it is."

"It's okay to admit that you're going to miss him," Roberta said. "And it's okay to be sad."

Marissa felt tears stir again. "It's not, though. I have the girls to think about. I have to be strong for them. Present for them. One of the reasons I don't date is so that I won't bring my crazy emotions into their lives. They lost so much. I just want to focus on raising them well and making sure they're happy."

"You're a good mother, Marissa."

"You taught me well."

Her mother pulled Marissa into a hug, as much as she could, given that they were buckled in.

"But you deserve happiness, too, sweetheart. Just don't forget that."

Marissa nodded and closed her eyes, but there was no way she'd sleep. She'd taken her ounce of happiness last night and it would keep her going through the lonely times, through the times she'd miss Autry. She had her girls. She had her parents. She had friends and a good job. She had a life in Rust Creek Falls and it was a good one.

She'd let Autry go because she had to.

Autry dropped off Janie first, Anne Lattimore ran to hug her daughter and thank everyone for taking her on the amazing adventure. Then the car headed to the Fuller-Raffertys', and Marissa wondered if this was the last time she'd see Autry, if this would be their final goodbye. She knew he'd never leave town without saying goodbye to the girls, but this was likely Marissa's last time alone with Autry.

Her parents ushered the kids inside, Roberta ensuring that Marissa had some time alone with Autry to say that goodbye, if that was what she wanted. It wasn't, but why prolong this for three more days?

"I can't be here in this town and stay away," Autry said as soon as they were alone, his hands gripping the leather steering wheel of his rented Porsche.

"There's no future for us," she said.

"I could fly in every few months and…" He sighed.

"This was supposed to be no strings attached, but we forgot that feelings are strings," he added.

She smiled and reached for his hand. "I know. So let's just cut them now. I need to take care of my family, Autry. I can't be lying in my bed, nursing a broken heart. I don't have that luxury."

"I know. Well, we have three more days. What's three more days of exquisite torture? It would be worse not seeing each other when I'm still here, Marissa."

Now it was her turn to sigh as her resolve went out the window. "Agreed."

"Your parents were champs during this trip. Let's give them a night out tonight. Send them to dinner and a movie. I'll cook for you and the girls and we'll play board games and charades."

"Now, that sounds like my life," she said.

"A life I want to be part of while I'm here."

"See you later, then, Autry Jones."

She could see the relief on his face that she hadn't said goodbye. But she had no idea if she was doing the right thing.

"Yay! Mr. Autry is here!" Kiera said when he arrived. She was standing in the doorway with her sisters.

He laughed. These girls had a way of making him feel like a rock star. "Yay! Kiera is here! And Kaylee! And Abby!" He growled like a bear and bent over, then charged in, scooping up each girl for a hug and kiss.

Good God, what was with him? One minute he was having arrows shot in his heart from the reminders of Lulu. The next minute, he had a three-year-old on his shoulders singing a song from *Frozen*.

Who was he turning into? *What* was he turning into?

It got me. And it's gonna get you, too... He remembered his brother Hudson's words. His brother Walker's words.

And his father's. *I can't lose you, too.*

As he headed into the kitchen with his grocery bag, he thought about the fact that he didn't want to lose himself, either. He knew who he was when he was doing things Autry Jones did. Bringing over gifts. Flying off to front-row seats to a sold-out concert. But this more homespun stuff, nice as it was, left him feeling just a bit...uncomfortable.

Maybe that was a sign. That he didn't have to worry about leaving his heart in Rust Creek Falls. Tonight was definitely a good idea. He'd have another "family" night, and he'd be itching to get to Paris, to trade his cowboy boots for his five-hundred-dollar leather Prada shoes. Though he'd been here at the Fuller-Raffertys', grilling, playing charades, practicing for The Great Roundup Kids Competition, and he'd had a great time.

Cripes.

"I thought I heard shrieks of happiness," Marissa said, coming into the kitchen. "I knew a celeb had arrived."

"They certainly make me feel that way," he said, pulling out a package of thin-sliced chicken breasts and four sweet potatoes. "I'm making my world-famous chicken fingers with honey-mustard dipping sauce and sweet potato fries."

"Yum. Sounds delicious. Need an assistant?"

"I've got this. Go relax."

As Marissa left, her father came in. "I hear I owe you one. Dinner and a movie? I could get used to this.

And luckily, the only good movie out right now is an action flick, so it's my night."

Autry laughed. "Have a great time."

When Marissa's father left, Autry got to work, grabbing what he needed from the cupboards. As he turned to the refrigerator, he was drawn to a photo of Marissa and a baby who had to be Abby. Marissa looked all of sixteen, but she must have been eighteen. Man, she was young. A mother since eighteen. Her entire adult life. And here he was, thirty-three and completely unencumbered, except for the way he felt.

There were family photos and colorful drawings all over the refrigerator and magnets holding reminder cards for dentist appointments and the water bill. This was home life. Family life.

The opposite of Autry's life. On his refrigerator door at his Tulsa condo? Nothing. Not much in it, either, since he was rarely there.

"Autry!" Marissa came rushing into the kitchen, a worried look on her face. "My friend Suzanne's fiancé just ended their engagement. She's beside herself. I need to go over there. Can you watch the girls? Or I could call my parents and have them come back."

He shook his head. "Don't you dare. Just go. Take all the time she needs. I've got this."

"You sure?"

"Completely. Go."

She threw her arms around him and whispered "thank you" in his ear, sending his pulse racing at the reminder of what she'd whispered in his ear last night.

Last night now seemed a million nights ago.

He heard Marissa telling the girls that Mr. Autry was in charge and they were to listen to him, be polite and behave themselves. Then he heard the front door close.

Three heads poked in the kitchen door. "Can we help?" Abby asked.

"Well, I'm actually looking for three assistants," Autry said. "Would any of you like the job?"

"Me!" three voices said, three hands shooting up and waving frantically.

"Perfect. You're all hired," he said.

Luckily, Abby reminded her sisters to wash their hands, because he wouldn't have thought of it. The two little Fullers took turns on the step stool, and then looked to him for instructions. *Ha.* If only they knew that he'd been busy on his laptop before coming over, looking up recipes and watching two cooking videos.

He put Abby on egg-cracking duty. Kiera was in charge of shaking the seasoned bread crumbs on a plate. And Kaylee's job was to put the chicken breasts in the egg wash.

Sixteen chicken fingers were created without a single one dropping on the floor or egg wash getting in anyone's eyes or hair. Granted, Kiera had bread crumbs in her hair, but all in all, it was a perfect cooking experience. He had Abby rinse the sweet potatoes and then he sliced them, and had Kiera brush them with olive oil and Kaylee sprinkle with salt. Then everything went into the oven, and Autry and the girls headed into the family room.

"Want me to teach you the lyrics to 'Only You'?" Abby asked as Autry settled on the couch, the three girls on beanbags.

"What makes you think I don't know them?" he asked with a grin. "Okay, fine, I know one line of the chorus.

'I'd travel to the ends of the earth for you-oo-oo,'" he sang, and the girls clapped, then started singing the rest of the song.

If his brothers could see him now. If his father could see him now. Autry had tried to put his dad out of his mind since their phone conversation the morning of The Great Roundup Kids Competition. Autry had promised nothing, but had made it clear he was staying in Rust Creek Falls until his flight left for Paris.

Just don't get married. For the love of Pete.

Autry had laughed, which had made his father feel better. Autry. Married. Come on.

Except it wasn't funny—that his father was pushing the single life, or at least the single life until Autry was back in his own territory. Walker Jones the Second really and truly didn't care if his sons were happy. And that was damned sad.

After the singalong, Abby got out Chutes and Ladders and they played a round—Kiera won—and then they played charades. The Fuller girls acted out the band 2LOVEU, which Autry would never in a million years have guessed correctly before last night.

Then it was time for dinner, so the girls went into the dining room and Autry served his chicken fingers and fries, which were a hit, even if Kaylee didn't like the honey-mustard sauce and Kiera didn't like the sweet potato fries.

"So, let's do our share," Abby said. "You first, Kaylee."

Kaylee put down her fork. "I'll share that I got to go on a plane two times."

"Me, too!" Kiera said. "That was my share. Oh,

wait. I have another. I got to go to the 2LOVEU concert yesterday! It was awesome!"

"Hey, that was my share," Abby said with a grin.
"But I have another. I have a few big dreams. One can't
come true. Ever. I didn't think the others would, either,
because they just seemed impossible. But I got to meet
Lyle from 2LOVEU. I got to shake his hand. He actually looked at me and told me it was nice to meet me."
She burst into tears. "That was the happiest moment
of my entire life."

Autry froze for a moment. "Are those happy tears?"

Abby laughed even though fresh tears were rolling
down her cheeks. "Yes! First I got to be in The Great
Roundup Kids Competition even though I don't have
a dad. And then I got to meet Lyle. How could two
dreams come true in a week?"

"Because Mr. Autry is magic," Kiera said. "Remember, that's what Kaylee said when she first told him
about us. He did magic tricks."

Autry smiled. He was magic for this family. It was
a good reminder that this wasn't real—this being-the-
family-man thing. Yeah, he was here. Doing it. But
it was temporary. And while this might be everyday
life for the Fuller girls, this was magic to him. This
house, this dinner, this conversation with these children. Magic.

After dinner they settled back in the family room to
watch the third episode of *The Great Roundup*, which
he was recording so Marissa could watch it later or
tomorrow. He wanted to shield three sets of little eyes
when Summer Knight, rodeo star, rode into the canteen in a push-up bra and a very low-cut tank top. She
flirted with Travis, who had an aw-shucks type of re-

sponse to her, which had Brenna leaping into action to keep her man away from "that woman."

Autry glanced over at Kaylee and realized she'd fallen asleep on her beanbag chair just twenty minutes in. Ten minutes later, Kiera was out. Autry covered them with throws.

"Just us left," he said to Abby, who was curled up on her own beanbag and munching on the popcorn he'd made in the hot-air popper.

Abby grinned, then her smile faded. "Autry?"

"Yup," he said.

"Are you and my mom a couple?"

It was a good thing he wasn't eating popcorn right then because he would have choked.

He didn't know if he should be saying anything. This seemed a subject Marissa should handle, to answer Abby's questions as she saw fit.

"I adore your mom. And the three of you. But I'm leaving for Paris this Saturday. And I'll be there for at least a year, maybe longer. My company will be buying a big corporation there and I'll be running it and looking into other businesses in Paris to add to our company's holdings."

"Can't you start a company here?" she asked. "Janie said she heard her mom talking and that your brother Walker did that. Now he lives here. You could do the same."

Oh hell. Now he was in trouble. "Well, Walker and I do different things for our family company. I'm the brother that flies all around the world and checks out new businesses we could invest in or buy."

"Oh," she said. "That does sound fun, flying all over the world. I was looking at 2LOVEU's world tour and they're going everywhere in six months." Her face lit up. "And just think, I got to see them while they were still in our country!"

"I'm really glad you had a great time, Abby."

The brightness dimmed a little. "Thanks, Mr. Autry. For everything."

Dammit, now it sounded like a nine-year-old was saying goodbye. She was too wise for her years.

The show ended, and Autry turned to Abby. "So what's next? A movie? We can make this a double feature."

"Ooh, can we watch *Brave*?" she asked.

"*Brave* it is," he said, finding it in their cable lineup.

They settled back to watch, and Autry was surprised to find himself liking the animated film.

"Ooh, this is my favorite part," Abby said, munching on the popcorn as she turned her attention to the TV and didn't make a peep for the next hour.

Saved by *Brave*. The irony wasn't lost on Autry. He was far from courageous. He didn't know how much more of the conversation he could handle.

He glanced at Abby's sisters, sleeping so peacefully on their beanbags, and felt his heart expand.

Which had to be his imagination. He'd seen *The Grinch That Stole Christmas* every year of his childhood. He wasn't a grinch, but he had let his heart shrink to barely nothing.

Until he came to Rust Creek Falls and met this family. This family that made him want to be what they needed.

He couldn't be the dad they needed. That was out of the question. He could handle a few hours here and there, but he was never opening the floodgates again.

He'd done that and got slammed against a brick wall, to be left bruised and battered. A little bit of playing house was one thing. Really doing it? Quite another.

That debate settled in his head—and what was left of his heart—Autry sat back and watched the animated movie heroine show a lot more moxie than he'd ever have.

When the movie ended, Abby was yawning like crazy. He carried Kaylee and then Kiera up to bed, tucking them in, his heart boomeranging all over the place. Kaylee curled up on her side and grabbed hold of her stuffed monkey. Kiera's little pink mouth hung open and one arm was flung dramatically over her head, and she looked so darned cute that he wanted to take a picture for Marissa, but figured the flash would wake her.

Then he walked Abby up to her room. She'd already taped the new 2LOVEU poster on her wall, this one featuring only Lyle.

"Isn't he just the best?" Abby said as she got into bed, pulling the covers up.

He sat down on the stool beside her bed and glanced up at Lyle with his dimples. "Seems that way."

Abby sat up. "Actually, I'd say there's a tie now. You're both the best with me." She held out her arms and he hugged her, barely able to breathe. Figuratively.

"That means a lot, Abby," he said, standing up. "Sweet dreams, kiddo."

"Autry?"

He turned back. Abby was lying on her side, her eyes closed, her arms around what looked like an ancient Raggedy Ann doll. "Thanks for making me remember what it's like to have a dad. It sure is nice."

He froze, unsure what to say, what to do. From Abby's steady breathing, it was clear she'd already fallen asleep.

He'd barely made it downstairs before he felt his collar tightening around his neck. He needed to get some air, but he couldn't leave because he was babysitting someone's children.

Autry Jones babysitting children. Reminding a nine-year-old girl what it was like to have a father.

I can't handle that kind of responsibility for a kid's feelings, he thought, something shuttering over his heart.

Abby had said something like that before—to her sisters. But somehow it felt different when she said it to him. As if she had expectations. As if he would hurt her by not fulfilling that role.

Stop it, he ordered himself. *She didn't say you had to be her father. She just said you reminded her what it's like to have a dad. And that it was nice.*

He sure wouldn't know.

A coldness settled around him, and he sat down in the kitchen with a cup of black coffee. The minute Marissa got home, he'd be out of there.

Marissa reluctantly left Suzanne's apartment over the drugstore once her friend's two sisters had driven in from Kalispell. Poor Suzanne. She'd been with her fiancé, Jared, for two years, and had only recently gotten engaged. They almost hadn't, because Jared could not and would not say that he wanted children, and Suzanne wanted at least two, though she'd settle for one. Jared didn't commit to that until Suzanne had said that maybe they wouldn't be happy together. So he had finally said the magic words: "One child sounds all right. Let's get married."

And now he'd admitted he really didn't mean it and just hadn't wanted to lose Suzanne. So she was in love with a man who didn't want something she wanted— a fundamental difference that had torn them apart.

Marissa couldn't help thinking of herself and Autry. A man who might have strong feelings for her, who might even love her, unless she was reading way too much into the way he looked at her, the way he held her when and after they'd made love in the Seattle hotel. But a man who didn't want to be a family guy, who didn't want a family, who'd closed his heart to family. A man who lived to travel and loved to travel.

A man whose life was at odds with hers.

She'd known this three weeks ago when they'd met at the Ace in the Hole. And she'd gone and fallen for the guy, anyway.

"Marissa!"

Marissa turned around. Helen Ganley, the woman who'd taken on the mama dog and her four puppies as fosters, was crossing the street with the mother dog on a leash.

Oh no. Was Helen going to complain again about the lady who let her dog pee on the edge of her lawn? Marissa had hoped that adopting a dog herself would open the woman's heart a little.

"Maria here is doing just great," Helen said, giving the pretty black-and-white dog a pat on the head and a little dog treat from her pocket. "I wanted to thank you, Marissa. You suggested I adopt a dog and you were right. Maria and her puppies changed my life."

"Aww, I'm so glad, Helen. She's a beauty." Marissa

scratched Maria behind the ears. She thought Maria
was a fine name for a pretty dog.

"And I should thank that big fish you caught," Helen
added. "It's thanks to him that Maria and her pups got
saved at all."

Huh? What did Autry have to do with it? Her expression must have asked the question because Helen
said, "Oh, I'm not surprised he didn't mention it. The
most generous people rarely toot their own horns. Two
week ago, Autry Jones donated a small fortune to the
Rust Creek Falls Animal Shelter and that's how the
shelter was able to buy more kennels and supplies.
They're going to expand even more now. I also heard
he started a fund with the PTO for programs for students with 'homes in transition,' meaning those who've
lost a parent or whose folks are separated or divorced."

Marissa sucked in a breath. "He did?"

"That's what I heard. My sister-in-law is the PTO
president—that's how I know. Don't let him get away,
Marissa. I'm a widow myself and I was alone too long.
Then my darling Chumley died and turned me grumpy.
All it took was something—five new somethings—to
love and care for, and I was back in business."

Marissa smiled. "I'm so happy to hear that, Helen."

As her neighbor continued down the street with
Maria, Marissa couldn't move. Autry had donated to
the animal shelter? He'd started a fund for school programs for students who'd experienced the death of a
parent, or divorce? How much more wonderful could
Autry be?

She got her legs to move and headed home. When
she opened the front door, the house was quiet. Autry

was in the kitchen, putting away the clean dishes from the dishwasher, and the room was spotless.

"Hey," she said. "Mr. Mom."

He barely smiled.

She bit her lip. "Everything go okay?"

He put the last plate away, then ran a hand through that thick, silky hair of his. "Everything went great. The girls are all asleep in their rooms. Kaylee and Kiera conked out pretty early, but Abby taught me the lyrics to every 2LOVEU song off the new album. Oh, and Kaylee doesn't like honey-mustard sauce and Kiera doesn't like sweet potatoes."

Marissa was so overcome with emotion that she rushed to throw her arms around him. "You're wonderful. Just wonderful. I'm very thankful I met you, Autry Jones, even though you're leaving in two days."

He gave her a quick hug, but then stepped back. "Me, too. It was a honor spending time with you and your girls." He glanced at his watch. "Well, I'd better get to the Manor. I have some papers to go over before a meeting with Walker in the morning."

Oh. Disappointment flooded her. She'd thought maybe he'd stay a bit longer and they could have coffee or some wine, talk for a little while. But he clearly wanted to leave. Maybe a few hours with the Fuller girls had shown him exactly what he already knew: that he wouldn't be up for this full-time.

She wrapped her arms around herself as a chill settled around her. If she was this affected by his leaving for the night, how was she going to feel when he left for *good*?

Chapter Fourteen

After tossing and turning all night, Autry stayed in bed longer than he normally would, then remembered he had a meeting with Walker at ten. The thought perked him up some; talking business with Walker was standard stuff, regular life—as opposed to his evening of babysitting Marissa's daughters. He hated how standoffish he'd been with Marissa when she'd gotten home last night. She deserved better treatment than that, but he'd had to get out there, had to breathe.

He got out of bed and took a long, hot shower, then had two strong cups of coffee. By nine forty-five he'd shaken off thoughts of last night and was completely focused on business and the upcoming Thorpe Corp. negotiations.

His phone beeped with a text. It was Walker. Meet me at Just Us Kids instead of home.

Oh hell. Kiddie central again.

He walked over to the day care, reminded of the first

day he'd arrived in Rust Creek Falls and had stood in this spot on the sidewalk, practically hyperventilating about having to go inside. Well, at least he could walk in calmly, like a normal person who wasn't scared spitless of little humans.

This time, Just Us Kids was a lot more crowded. A long table held a bunch of toddlers who were making something out of clay. On the far side of the room, a teacher was reading aloud to a small group, who sat on mats. Autry could see another bunch of kids on playground equipment in the backyard, and in a sitting area, two teachers held babies. Clearly, business was good at Just Us Kids.

"Autry, welcome!" his sister-in-law Bella said, getting up from the reception desk. Though she was the manager of the center, she often filled in when someone else was out for the day. "I'll lead the way to Walker's office. He's waiting for you."

Autry smiled at Bella and followed her to a small room in the back. Walker sat behind a desk, going over papers in a folder. He nodded at his brother. "Hudson's got a bad cold, so I'm handling business here today and tomorrow. Got the paperwork?"

Autry was getting used to seeing Walker in this environment, his usual Italian suits replaced by more casual clothes. Plus, the man had different-colored paint splotches on the back of his hands, which suggested he'd joined a few toddlers at their painting session.

Autry handed him the folder. "All signed and ready to go."

"Flight leaves day after tomorrow, right?" Walker asked.

"Yup. At 6:30 p.m. I have to admit, I'm going to miss this place. Rust Creek Falls, I mean."

Walker glanced up from the sheaf of papers. "So stay. Move here. Hudson says you're hot and heavy with Marissa Fuller. You going to walk away from her?"

Stab to the heart. "Yeah, I am. I care about her, but my life is a jet plane, Walker. I like it here, yes. I like Marissa. But I also like global travel. I like my job. I like negotiating deals for Jones Holdings. I like the history of the family business, the generations of Joneses behind it. I'm invested in the company's future. That means leaving."

Walker leaned back in his chair and observed his younger brother. "Huh. Guess the water or the punch didn't work its magic on you. Dad's influence is too strong."

Autry pictured his father sitting in his leather desk chair, imperious and impervious, his life about business and mergers and acquisitions. He wasn't like his dad. He knew people mattered more than business. But another difference between his father and Autry was that Autry hadn't made any promises to anyone in the form of vows or fatherhood to be there, to be present. He'd been straight up with Marissa from the get-go. No commitment. And she'd been the same. No strings. They'd had a good time. A magical time. But now that time had come to the end they always knew was waiting.

"It's not about Dad. It's about who I am. I like this town more than I ever thought I would. But I can't see myself settled down here, Walker."

"Maybe because leaving every couple of months is easier than building a life somewhere."

Autry shrugged. "Okay, Dr. Phil."

Walker laughed. "It's been great having you here, Autry. I hope you'll come visit in between countries."

"I definitely will," he said.

Walker stood up and the brothers embraced, and then Autry headed back out, stopping to smile at a little boy making faces at him through the sliding glass door to the backyard. Autry waved at the kid, who seemed disappointed that he wasn't getting chastised by the grown-up. Just then another boy called to him, and the two scamps went to play on a slide. Autry watched them giggle their way back up the ladder a second time, sending pebbles down the slide and chasing after them. Autry smiled; he could remember doing that with his brothers when they were kids. He could watch this kind of thing all day.

Wait. What? He could? The last time he'd been here, his collar had tightened on him to the point he was at risk of being strangled by his own three-hundred-dollar shirt. Now he was buoyed by the sight of an impish kid and a buddy racing around? *Eh, maybe it was a good sign.* That time really did heal all wounds. Spending these weeks with the Fuller girls had helped him overcome that old ache of seeing babies and toddlers and children, which had been a constant reminder of what he'd lost—little Lulu and who she'd become as she grew up.

Okay, so he could now walk into a day care without feeling the need to race out and find a kid-free zone. That didn't mean he was anywhere close to being a family kind of guy. Or else he wouldn't have been so torn up by what Abby had said last night.

Thanks for making me remember what it's like to have a dad. It sure is nice.

That old ache gripped him by the chest and squeezed. Autry frowned and slid on his sunglasses and left.

So much for change.

His cell phone rang—Marissa's home phone number.

"Autry, it's Roberta Rafferty."

"Roberta, this is a nice surprise. What can I do for you?"

"You could come to a going-away party for yourself tomorrow at five thirty. Ralph is doing the grilling this time. Your responsibility is just to have a good time and a wonderful send-off."

He didn't think he could take a whole evening with Marissa, knowing she'd be out of his life the next day, without imploding. "Roberta, that's very kind of you, but not nec—"

"After everything you did for my family these past few weeks, oh yes, it is necessary. I won't hear another word. We will see you at five thirty tomorrow. Don't bring a thing but yourself."

"Well, I can't promise I won't bring anything, but I'll be there."

"Good. See you then."

That was interesting, Autry thought, as he pocketed his phone. He hadn't thought Roberta was part of his fan club. Now she was throwing a party in his honor.

One thing was for sure when it came to the Fuller-Raffertys. He never knew what to expect.

* * *

As Marissa watched her daughters stack paper plates and plastic cups on the buffet table for Autry's bon-voyage party, she could swear that Kaylee was taller by at least an inch and that Kiera's hair had gotten very long over the summer and that Abby, who was teaching herself Spanish via a website so that she could learn 2LOVEU songs in two languages, was growing up way too fast. School was starting next week, and both Kaylee and Kiera were having firsts. Kaylee would start preschool and Kiera would start kindergarten.

And now that her younger girls would be in school a good chunk of the day, Marissa was going to talk to her boss about increasing her hours back to full-time. This way she could help her parents more financially and save up to send them on the Caribbean cruise they'd always wanted.

Maybe Marissa would even adopt one of Helen's little pups when the three available were ready. Abby had always wanted a dog, but Marissa hadn't been sure she could handle one more thing to take care of, and Roberta didn't love pet hair on her clothes. Anyway, it was just something to think about for the future.

She was thinking about anything and everything to avoid what was constantly trying to push its way into the forefront of her mind: Autry. When her mother had told her that the Raffertys were throwing a good-bye party for him, Marissa had been shocked—then not so shocked. Her mother had fallen under Autry's spell. It was hard not to. He was a great man. Kind, generous, warm.

And so damned sexy and great in bed that Marissa

could still feel every imprint on her body where his hands and lips had been.

She was glad they'd had sex. It wasn't a mistake and there were no regrets. She'd needed that night and she'd wanted him, and she'd taken what was being offered: one amazing night that she'd never forget and that would sustain her probably for years given just how earthmoving it had been. She smiled, but felt the smile fading. She would never feel his hands on her again after the perfunctory goodbye hug he'd give her after the party. She'd never feel his lips on hers. Maybe every couple years he'd come to town to visit his brothers and he'd stop by to say hello.

She wrapped her arms around her middle as a sadness crept inside her heart.

Then she lifted her chin and pasted a smile on her face. For the sake of her girls, especially for Abby, she'd act like everything was fine, that of course she'd miss Autry, but they always knew he was leaving, et cetera, et cetera. She'd put on a happy expression for the girls, then disappear into the bathroom or her room to cry if she felt tears coming. And she had no doubt they would.

At five thirty, her father had just put the burgers, marinated chicken and steaks on the grill with some veggie kebabs and corn on the cob in the husk, when Autry came around the yard, carrying two big shopping bags.

"I ordered that man not to bring anything," Roberta whispered in Marissa's ear.

Marissa smiled and felt the smile wobble, so she corrected it. Her girls were just a few feet away and watching her. How did Autry manage to look more handsome every time she saw him? He wore a dark blue Henley shirt and jeans and his AJ belt buckle.

"Mom! Mr. Autry is here!" Abby shrieked and raced over to him for a hug.

He bent over to wrap Abby in his arms, then scooped up the younger girls and swung them around. "Hey, Fuller girls," he said.

"What's in the bags?" Kaylee asked, peering in.

"Kaylee, that's not polite!" Abby chastised, also trying to peer inside. Marissa always appreciated when Abby did her work for her.

"Well, I might have a going-away present for my favorite three kids," Autry said with a grin.

Roberta leaned close to Marissa and whispered, "He's generous to a fault!"

"He's thoughtful," Marissa whispered back.

Her mom nodded. "That, too."

Kiera tilted her head, her long brown ponytail falling over one shoulder. "But you're the one going away, not us."

"Yeah. That's why *we* made *you* going-away presents," Abby said.

"What? Presents for me?" Autry touched his heart. "That's real nice of you, girls."

Kiera and Kaylee ran over to the table where they'd been working on the gifts and wrapping them this afternoon.

"Kaylee, you first," Abby said, like a little mother. "Then Kiera, then me."

Kaylee grinned and held out the gift she'd wrapped herself. The bright red sparkly paper didn't quite reach the back. Marissa held in a smile. Autry sat on the grass and gently opened it on his lap.

Marissa watched Autry closely; the man was clearly touched by the paper plate that Kaylee had decorated with feathers and glitter and wrote inside a big heart: Mr. Autry Is Nice.

"I love this," he said, giving her a big hug. "Thank you, Kaylee."

Next up was Kiera. Autry opened her gift, and for a second, Marissa wondered if he didn't like it. It was a photograph of him and the three Fuller girls that Ralph had taken during the last few weeks. They were in the backyard, under a tree, a soccer ball in Kiera's arms. She'd made the frame herself at an arts-and-crafts camp this summer.

"I'll treasure this," he said. "Thank you, Kiera."

Kiera beamed. "This way you won't forget us. When you go away."

He hugged her again. "I'd never forget you guys. Impossible."

"And now it's my turn," Abby said. "My present isn't something you can wrap. It's a song I'm going to sing."

Marissa watched her daughter bite her lip and stand back, as though the nine-year-old wasn't sure Autry would like her gift. Though Marissa had helped the younger girls make and wrap their presents, Abby wanted to do hers on her own. She'd spent the afternoon in her room working on it, so Marissa had no clue what the song was. But a song seemed a lovely idea for a send-off.

Abby walked over to the patio table bench and turned on her iPod and the speaker, and the tune of 2LOVEU's megahit "Only You" filled the air, but just the music, not the lyrics.

Abby cleared her throat. "I made up new lyrics to the song. Okay, here it goes."

Everyone quieted and sat down, excited to hear Abby's song.

"Oh, Mr. Autry, oh, oh, oh, at first you were just our mom's new friend," Abby sang, "but then you became our friend, too-oo-oo."

Kiera and Kaylee clapped, shaking their little bodies to the music.

Marissa glanced at Autry. He was smiling and she could tell he was deeply touched.

"You made us steaks and played charades…" Abby sang, "and even when you lost, you always smiled." The audience laughed and then the chorus swelled; Abby held her fist to her mouth as though it were a microphone. "And then you stepped in as my partner for the kids competition… Yeah, and I realized that only you could be our new dad. Ooh, yeah," she sang. "Only you-oo-oo. Only you."

Marissa froze and watched as Autry's face paled. She glanced at her parents. Her mother's expression was tight; her dad tapping his foot to the music as though he hadn't fully registered what Abby had just sung.

"Yeah, ooh, yeah, only you," Abby finished and took a bow.

Everyone clapped and Marissa watched Autry try to recover. Abby ran over to give him a hug and he hugged her tight.

"That was really nice," he said. "You have a great voice."

She waited for him to say more. Marissa recognized the look in her daughter's eyes from when Abby would ask Marissa for something, be told no and then wait for a change of mind.

Autry said nothing else.

Abby's smile was tight like Roberta's.

Oh God. Exactly what they'd been afraid of happening had happened.

Ralph announced that dinner was ready, and Marissa was grateful for the distraction. The crew headed over to the buffet table and filled their plates, then sat down. Ralph asked Autry all kinds of questions about Paris, and as Autry described all the exciting sights, like the Louvre and the famous *Mona Lisa* painting and the breathtaking Eiffel Tower, the Fuller girls, including even subdued Abby, were transfixed. Autry, who was just about fluent in four languages, spoke French to the girls, and they were delighted to hear that "I love hamburgers with pickles and mustard" sounded so fancy in that language.

Every now and again, Marissa would catch Autry looking at her, and she tried to keep her expression neutral and the conversation focused on his trip—not how she felt. Which was absolutely miserable.

She loved Autry. She loved him with all her heart. And tomorrow he was flying off to Paris.

After dessert of ice cream and fruit, her parents insisted on cleaning up themselves, no help allowed. Abby got a phone call from her friend Janie and disappeared with Marissa's phone into her bedroom. Marissa, Autry and the two younger girls played charades, Kiera standing up and holding up three fingers to indicate that her charade was three words. But then she glanced back toward the house. "Hey, wait. Where's Abby? I can't do this one if she's not here. It's 2LOVEU." She plastered her hand over her mouth. "Oops! I just gave it away."

Yeah, where is Abby? Marissa thought. She'd gone into the house with the phone at least fifteen minutes ago. Granted, the girl loved to talk on the phone to Janie, but it was unusual for her to stay away this long when Autry was over.

Marissa's parents came back out just then, and Marissa asked them to stay with the girls while she went to get Abby.

As she headed into the house, she realized Autry was right behind her.

"I think I should handle this," she said. "It's my fault." Tears poked her eyes but she blinked them back.

"Your fault? How? What do you mean?"

"I have a feeling that Abby is in her room upset about the reaction to the song. The lack of reaction, I should say, from you. I don't mean that you should have jumped up and said, 'Yes, I'd love to be your daddy.' Of course not. But…" She stopped, her heart clenching.

"But what?" he said flatly.

"My mother tried to warn me that Abby was the one who'd get hurt. But I let this happen, anyway. I let you come into our lives. I let you do The Great Roundup Kids Competition with her. I let you take us all on that dream trip to the 2LOVEU concert. I let her love you."

The tears she'd fought did come then and Marissa wiped them away. *I let myself love you.*

What had she done? Why wasn't she more protective of her children? Of herself?

Autry put his hands on her shoulders. "Marissa, I'm here now. And I'd like to try to fix this—somehow. Let me at least try to talk to her."

She sucked in a deep breath, torn in two. "Okay."

They headed up the stairs together, both silent.

Marissa knocked on Abby's door, then opened it. The room was empty. "That's weird. She's not here and we didn't pass her in the living room."

"She couldn't have gotten far," Autry said. "Let's split up and check the house and property."

"It's a big property. Over five acres. The girls don't go into the wooded area unless they're with us, and besides, we would have seen Abby come outside and head toward the woods. Where can she be?"

"We'll find her. I promise you."

Marissa's heart turned over. Where was her daughter?

Chapter Fifteen

While Marissa checked the house, Autry went to the front yard to see if Abby had gone outside. He glanced around at the big lawn, the huge trees dotting the property. In between the heavy green leaf cover of one, he could just make out a pair of orange sneakers with bright yellow laces dangling from blue-jeaned legs. Abby had climbed a tree and was sitting on a branch, not that high up, but higher than his eye level.

Be careful, he told himself as he walked over. He had no idea what he was going to say. He just knew whatever did come out of his mouth would come from his heart and would be the truth, whatever that was. The truth always did out.

"Hey," he called up, leaning against the trunk of the tree.

He noticed Marissa looking out the window from the living room and caught her eye; he gestured toward the branch and gave her a thumbs-up, then pointed to himself to let her know he had this. She nodded and stayed put, moving a bit out of view.

"Abby?"

He heard her crying, which turned into full sobs.

"Janie called to tell me that Lyle is leaving the band. Leaving 2LOVEU. Can you believe that? He's the lead singer! And my favorite." A fresh round of sobs ensued.

"I'm sorry to hear that, Abby. I know how much you like him. But, sweetie, why'd you come out here all by yourself? If you'd told your mom why you were upset, she could have made things better."

"No, she couldn't have!" Abby blurted out, anger lacing her voice. "Mom wouldn't understand at all. Mom is so strong and doesn't need anybody, but I do!"

Oh, Abby, he thought, his heart going out to the girl. "Sweets, everyone needs people. Everyone."

"Nope," she insisted. "I miss my daddy all the time, but Mom barely talks about him. And now you're leaving, too, and Mom is acting like she doesn't even care." She broke into more sobs. "Everyone always leaves. Everyone!"

Autry climbed up next to Abby, praying the branch would hold his weight. It seemed steady. He pulled Abby into his arms and let her cry it out, leaning his head on top of hers.

"I might be leaving tomorrow," Autry said, "but I will always be there for you, Abby. If you need me, text me. Call me. I'm a friend of the Fuller-Rafferty family, Abby, and that's what close friends do—they're there for each other."

"I can text you?" she asked. "If I want to tell you something?"

"You bet," he said. "Even if it's a bad joke. Or if you bomb a spelling test."

She laughed. "I'm a really good speller."

"Then text me about an A-plus on your spelling test. Bad news. Good news. That's what people who care about you are for. And I care, Abby. Even if I'm thousands of miles away. An ocean away."

"Too bad Lyle doesn't care," she said, rolling her eyes.

"You know celebs," he said. "But you know, you can still love listening to their music even if Lyle's leaving. There's always going to be change in your life, Abby. And you yourself will change constantly, too. That's what growing up is all about."

"My mom says growing up is full of ups and downs, but more ups."

"Your mom is one smart cookie. Life is amazing. I've had some downs, but look—here I am, hanging out with one of my favorite people in a tree. Pretty cool, huh?"

She laughed. "Yeah. It is."

"Should we go join the party? I hear your grandfather is making those lime rickeys I love so much."

Her face brightened and she wrapped her arms around him. "Thanks, Mr. Autry."

"Anytime," he said and kissed the top of her head.

As if he were her father. Or something like it.

Relief had flooded Marissa when Autry had indicated that he'd found Abby. Then anger. At herself. For letting him into their lives.

If it had been just her, just her heart that would be shredded when he left, fine. But she'd let her children experience the whirlwind magic of Autry Jones, and now her child was crying in a tree.

And hadn't come to her.

Marissa froze when the realization struck. Abby hadn't come to her. Why?

She peered out the window and saw Abby and Autry heading back toward the house, Autry's arm around her, Abby animatedly talking about something. Well, whatever he'd said had been the right thing.

They came in the front door, and her daughter ran into her arms.

"I'm sorry I just left, Mom. I was so upset because Janie called and told me that Lyle is leaving 2LOVEU. And that combined with Autry leaving... I just kinda lost it."

Marissa hugged her daughter. "I understand, sweetie. But next time you're sad about something, I hope you'll come to me, Abby. You can always tell me anything."

"Mr. Autry says you're a smart cookie. I already know that." Abby hugged her tight. "I'm going to help Grandpa make the lime rickeys. Mr. Autry loves those." She ran off toward the kitchen.

Marissa turned to Autry. "Thanks for talking to her. Whatever you said was obviously the right thing."

"I just let her know that I care about her and I'm here for her, even if I'm three thousand miles away. That if she needs a friend she can always text me."

Ah. Well, that was nice of him. Marissa wasn't sure how long that would last. Maybe the first couple weeks, he'd be charmed by a nine-year-old texting him that she was upset about a boy teasing her or something. But then he'd stop being so charmed and would take longer and longer to respond, until he stopped altogether. And then Marissa would have to deal with Abby's tears over that. So why prolong the inevitable?

"Marissa, I…"

And he still hadn't said anything about Abby's song. About how only Autry could be their new dad. He was ignoring, avoiding it. Because he couldn't be their dad. Wouldn't be. Didn't want to be.

And, hell, was Marissa ready for someone to step into their lives just like that?

Whatever. He wasn't asking to stay, anyway. He wasn't asking to be her children's father.

"I care about all of you, Marissa. You know that. I wish things could be different."

Right. If wishes…

She lifted her chin, ignoring the stabbing sensation in her chest. "After the lime rickeys, I think you should go, Autry. Give everyone a hug goodbye and then…go. Tomorrow, just leave. No stopping over, no calls. Tonight is it."

He sucked in a breath and ran his hand through that sexy dark blond hair. "Marissa—"

"There's nothing to say, Autry. I thank you from the bottom of my heart for a magical three weeks. But even if you were the small-town type, which you aren't and never will be, who says *I'm* ready for a relationship? I wasn't ready to date when you sauntered into town. I'm still not. There's just too much to consider and too much on my plate, like my daughters' lives and hearts. So these weeks were all we'd ever have, anyway."

For a moment before he walked away, he'd held her gaze, and she wished she were a mind reader. She knew he didn't love her. Maybe if he did he'd fight for them.

But what was there to fight for? He was leaving. To-morrow.

"Mommy! Mr. Autry is handing out presents!" Kiera called.

She closed her eyes, grateful for the privacy of the foyer. Bracing herself, she forced herself into the back-yard. Abby was modeling her new school backpack, her initials embroidered across the pocket in hot pink. Inside were school supplies, everything she needed, which meant he'd actually gone on her school website and looked up the list for the fourth grade. He'd even managed to find a 2LOVEU pencil case.

"Lyle might be leaving 2LOVEU but that doesn't mean I can't still love their music," she said. "And I got to see them before they broke up!"

Kiera had a new backpack, too, her very first, with her initials embroidered in her favorite color, royal blue. Inside was a monkey key ring holder to chain on the outside loop and school supplies for the kin-dergarten class.

And Kaylee, starting preschool, had brand-new light-up sneakers in her favorite color, purple. She was jumping around the yard, showing them off.

The Raffertys received a voucher for a cruise around the Caribbean islands anytime in the next year. Ralph was still gasping, and Roberta had tears in her eyes.

"You all have given me so much, you have no idea," Autry said. "I came to Rust Creek Falls a different per-son. I'm leaving a changed man. Thank you."

The three Fuller girls fell on him, crying and hug-ging and laughing.

And then Marissa walked Autry to the door.

"Last but not least," he said, handing her a small wrapped box.

"I don't think I should," she said.

He tilted up her chin with his finger. "Please."

She took the gift and unwrapped it. It was a light blue box she'd recognize anywhere. She opened the lid. Inside was a heart-shaped locket. She opened the locket and there was a tiny photo of her and her three girls. On the back was engraved: *You changed my life. AJ.*

Don't cry, don't cry, don't cry, she told herself.

"Thank you, Autry."

He took the box and set it on the hall table, then fastened the locket around her neck. Then he took her face in his hands and kissed her. One more time.

One last time.

And then he was gone.

Passport, check. Boarding pass stored electronically, check. Tablet, phone, Thorpe Corp. folder for the flight, check.

Autry checked and rechecked his carry-on bag in his room at Maverick Manor, anything to avoid thinking about the house he'd left a little while ago. The family he'd said goodbye to.

He wasn't a small-town guy—that was true. And he'd never be. That was true, too. But he was a Fuller-Rafferty guy. His brothers had found happiness settling down here, so why did the idea of it fill Autry with a sense of dread?

Because it's not right for you. No matter how much you love Marissa.

He did love her.

And he loved her kids.

But he knew where that led, and maybe that was why he couldn't imagine settling down here. Maybe it wasn't so much that he wasn't a small-town guy as he wasn't a settling down guy. He wasn't a family guy. He might have become pretty good at soothing tears and choosing gifts and playing charades, but that didn't mean the life was for him.

You loved and you got stomped on. That's what he knew for sure. That had been the case in his life ever since he was a kid. His father had disappointed him time and again. His mother had forgotten his and his brothers' birthdays several times as they'd grown up. Maybe with five kids that happened.

Autry doubted that. If Marissa had ten kids, she'd know their birthdays.

But then he'd finally let love in and Karinna had taken a bat to his heart. He'd lost her and Lulu. And now he'd let in Marissa and her three girls. Hell, he'd let in her parents. And someday, Marissa would prob- ably realize that he'd been her rebound guy, her entrée to dating, and she'd find the guy she really loved, the guy she was supposed to be with. Not some jet-setter whose life she didn't understand.

He thought of his father, and how he'd failed to bring Walker Jones the Second closer to Walker the Third and Hudson. He'd had three weeks, and all his attempts to make his father see reason, see love when it was right in front of him in the form of his happy sons, had been fruitless.

He was giving it one more try.

He pulled out his phone and pressed in his dad's number.

"Ah, good, Autry," his father said. "Did you convince those brothers of yours to see reason and move home?"

Autry shook his head, literally and figuratively. "With or without their wives?"

"With, of course. Once they see Tulsa, both women will never want to go back to that dot on the map. Is Rust Falls Creek even on the map?"

"*Rust Creek Falls*, Dad. And doesn't it mean anything to you to know that Walker and Hudson are happy? Truly happy?"

"Of course. But I don't see why they can't be happy in Tulsa."

"Is that Autry, dear?" he heard his mother say. "Let me talk to him."

"Autry, honey, I hope you'll be a better influence on Gideon and Jensen than Walker and Hudson have been on you and your younger brothers. You are leaving for Paris tomorrow, right?"

Autry could only hope his two younger brothers were as lucky as Walker and Hudson some day. "I am leaving tomorrow. But Mom, you and Dad are being unfair to Walker and Hudson—and their wives. They're happy. Truly happy. I wish you could understand that."

"We do, dear. It's difficult to understand how they could be happy in that town, but if they are, they are."

That was the best he was going to get. Resignation and acceptance. Unbelievable.

"Well, your father and I are off to a fund-raiser. Best to your brothers. Bye, dear."

He'd tried.

When he thought of the differences between his

family and the Fuller-Raffertys, it was almost comical. Polar opposites.

He sat on the edge of his bed and pulled out the antique pocket watch he'd bought in the Rust Creek Falls thrift shop. Twenty bucks and he loved it. The minute he'd seen the old bronze cover with a compass symbol on the front, he'd known he had to have it. And he'd printed out another copy of the photo he'd put in Marissa's locket and put it on the left side of the pocket watch.

He clicked it open now and there they were. Marissa and her daughters.

The family he was walking away from.

His heart heavy, he closed the watch and put it in his carry-on, then went out to say a final goodbye to the town, the general store and the doughnut shop and the Ace in the Hole. He wanted to stop by all the places he'd visited while in town. And then tomorrow night, he'd be on a plane, headed toward the future.

For a moment he let himself imagine staying here. Moving here. Shipping the contents of his office to the Jones Holdings, Inc. in Rust Creek Falls. He and Walker would probably order in from the Ace all the time. He smiled at the thought.

Except he didn't want to move to Rust Creek Falls. He didn't want to work out of this town. He wanted to go to Paris. He'd be there for at least a year.

And all he'd have to remind him of Marissa? Her picture in a pocket watch.

He'd said goodbye. She'd said goodbye. And reminded him that she wasn't up for a relationship, anyway. Not a real one. Three weeks when she knew he was leaving—that was one thing for a widow with a lot on her plate and three young lives to manage. A real, in-person, constant relationship with a man was something else. She hadn't been planning on that.

So that was that.

His heart breaking, Autry headed out to say goodbye to this town that had slipped inside his heart when he wasn't looking.

Chapter Sixteen

Autry woke up at the crack of dawn. The sun was just peeking over the horizon. He'd barely slept, his hand wrapped around his phone, the need to call Marissa and hear her voice so strong it took everything in him not to press in her number. Last night, when he'd walked around Rust Creek Falls, saying his mental goodbye to this special town, everything had reminded him of her and the girls. He'd been about to swing by the Ace in the Hole and have a draft when a pang hit him so hard he'd avoided Sawmill Street entirely. He would never forget looking around the crowded bar and the entire world falling away except for that brunette beauty's lovely face, the twinkle in her dark eyes, the way her silky brown hair fell over her shoulders. A single mother in a T-shirt and shorts, though of course he hadn't known she was a single mother then.

I didn't know you were a single mother... I wouldn't have approached you...

He remembered the look on her face when he'd said those cruel words. At the time he'd thought the truth was all that mattered, and, yeah, the truth always mattered. But he didn't have to say that. You couldn't fix some things to make other things work, but nothing would change the fact that Marissa Fuller was a single mom.

Except if you married her, he could hear his brother Hudson saying as a joke, with a Groucho Marx wiggle of his eyebrows.

A new truth? Autry could see himself married to Marissa. He could see himself as a father to her daughters, the three girls he'd come to love despite all his trying not to. He smiled, thinking about how easy it was for the Fuller family to get inside his heart. Just by existing. By being themselves.

But then there was another truth—that Marissa lived here in Rust Creek Falls and he was about to leave for Paris for a year. He was going to Paris; there was no getting around that, and he didn't want to get around it. This trip was important to him, to the family business. And Marissa and her daughters were important. But they lived here.

Problem.

Autry pulled a fluffy down pillow over his head and groaned. He chucked the pillow aside and got out of bed and took a hot shower. Under the spray of the water he realized that maybe he should go say goodbye to the Ace in the Hole. Maybe doing so would give him some closure. He'd see the place where it had all started, acknowledge it and accept that this was just how it was, and then he'd board his corporate jet for France.

It was barely six o'clock in the morning and the Ace

wasn't open, but he figured he could just peer in the windows. Except as he approached, there was a light on inside, a dim light over by the pool table. A sign on the door said the bar's hours were noon to 1:30 a.m., so the place definitely wasn't open. But he could see two people inside, talking and hugging and sipping something from mugs. Maybe they wouldn't mind if he came in and just took one last look around?

He tried the door and it opened. The couple, a man and a woman, started, clearly not expecting anyone to be coming into the bar at 6:00 a.m.

"Sorry to barge in on your—" he began to say, then froze.

Whoa. He was pretty darn sure that Brenna O'Reilly and Travis Dalton, of *The Great Roundup* fame, stood not two feet in front of him. He'd seen them around town over the past few weeks but hadn't had an opportunity to meet either of them since both were always surrounded by friends and family and fans. Brenna's long red hair was up in a bun or something and hidden under a hot-pink cowboy hat, and Travis wore his dark brown Stetson low over his forehead, but the dark hair, bright blue eyes and confident expression was unmistakable. He had no idea why they were here at the crack of dawn but that was none of his business.

"—private something or other," Autry finished. "I just wanted to take a look around for old times' sake."

"Old times' sake?" Travis said. "Look, I'd know a Jones brother anywhere, and you are definitely a Jones. You have the face and the four-hundred-dollar shoes. But how could there be an old times' sake for you here in Rust Creek Falls? Aren't you from Oklahoma?"

He laughed and extended his right hand. "Autry

Jones. I've been here for a few weeks visiting Hudson and Walker. And I met someone here, someone pretty special."

"Ah. Love. Got me, too," Travis said, grabbing Brenna around the waist and pulling her close.

"Yup, a Jones, all right," Brenna said, studying him as she shimmied out of Travis's hold. "I'm Brenna Dal—O'Reilly," she added fast. "And this is my—this is my fiancé, Travis Dalton."

"The two of you need no introductions," Autry said. "I've now seen three episodes of *The Great Roundup*. Great job on that button-sewing challenge, Brenna."

Brenna beamed. "Thanks. So this special person you met here. Why isn't she with you?"

Autry sighed. "I'm leaving the country on business today. For a year. And Marissa lives here."

"Marissa? Marissa Fuller?" Brenna asked. "We went to high school together—well, I was a year behind her. I always looked up to Marissa. She knew what she wanted and nothing stood in her way, you know? She had a life plan. I was more a wild child—until this guy made it easy to settle down. Okay, fine, I've loved Travis Dalton since I was a kid."

A life plan. Marissa's life plan had gotten a left hook to it. That was how it was, though. Who was it who said that life happened when you were making other plans?

Autry smiled. "You two are lucky."

"You could be, too, man," Travis said. "If you want this woman, go get her. That's all there is to it. If you can walk away, then do that. That's how you'll know. You're either going to break down her door—though I wouldn't recommend that, since I know Marissa and her kids live with her parents, and you don't mess with

Roberta Rafferty—or you're going to catch a plane to wherever. So which is it gonna be? You don't have to answer that now."

Good, because Autry didn't have an answer.

"I'm sorry I barged in," he said. "Looks like you two are having a little private remembrance of your own."

"No problem," Travis said. "We sneaked in for some time alone in one of our favorite places. Since the show's aired, we get mobbed. If we want to make out and slow dance, we have to do it at 6:00 a.m. in a closed bar."

Brenna laughed. "I like all the attention, though. Filming on location was exciting, but there's no place like home, and Rust Creek Falls is home. I used to think I couldn't wait to leave this small town, but I was sure wrong."

"Thanks to me," Travis said, swooping her into his arms. "You would never have left town or Bee's Beauty Salon with me still here, and you know it."

"Darn tooting I wouldn't have," Brenna said, winking. "And now you're mine."

They started making out, so that was Autry's cue to leave. He took one last look around, his gaze stopping on the table where Marissa had sat with her friend Anne. His heart had stopped in that moment he'd first seen Marissa. And restarted—without him realizing just how restarted it was.

You're either going to break down her door...or you're going to catch a plane...

The problem was, he wanted to do both.

Marissa glanced at the alarm clock on her bedside table. It was 6:20 a.m. and she hadn't slept a wink.

She'd tossed and turned, Autry Jones's face flashing in her mind all night long like a blinking neon sign. She'd heard his voice, seen him hugging her girls, talking for hours with her dad about stocks and fishing. And then she remembered their night in Seattle in his hotel room, where they'd finally made love.

Would that be enough? One amazing night with Autry to remember him by?

It wasn't like she had a choice. She had to let him go.

She reached into the bookshelf below her bedside table and pulled out one of the photo albums she kept there. Sometimes, when the girls couldn't sleep and would come tearfully into her room, talking about monsters and bad dreams and sore gums, she'd lie with one or two or all three Fuller girls and pull out the album and show them pictures of themselves as babies, their father holding them. And they'd quiet down like magic, loving to look at their dad and see what they couldn't remember. Abby could, of course; she'd been seven when they lost Mike Fuller, and one of the last things he did was teach her to ride a two-wheeler. Marissa had photographic evidence of her wipeouts, of Mike holding the back of the bike as she pedaled along, of Abby soaring down the side-walk, Mike pumping his fist in the air. Abby loved that photo.

On the first page of the album were pictures from high school, Marissa and Mike holding hands, kissing under the bleachers on the baseball field. And of prom night, when Abby was conceived. Then there were the wedding pictures, the reception in the Raffertys' back-yard and the tiny first house they'd rented in town, new parents at eighteen.

This is your life, Marissa Fuller, she thought, flipping the pages, smiling, a tear coming, her heart comforted. *This was your life. But you'll always have your memories and Mike will always live on in your daughters.*

She was saying goodbye, she realized. To who she used to be. And she was ready to be this new person. Not a woman in transition. But a new Marissa.

Autry had helped her become that new person. And for that, she would love him forever. Even though she'd have to do it from thousands of miles away.

"Mr. Autry is so lucky," Kiera said as Marissa put two "face" pancakes on each girl's plate. She'd made eyes with blueberries and a smiling mouth with cut-up strawberries.

Marissa eyed the clock on the wall. It was 8:30 a.m. She was exhausted from not sleeping and from getting up so early, but she felt like the new person she'd claimed to be. Today was the first day of the rest of her life. She wasn't going to mope about Autry. She was going to be this new Marissa, one who'd loved and lost—twice—but who relished memories and learned from her mistakes and kept putting one foot in front of the other. Her heart was open. That was the key. She was ready to accept new people. New experiences. New ideas. That was the kind of mother she wanted to be for her girls. Someone who took risks—well, the right risks. Falling for Autry had been the right risk. Yes, she was losing him today. But he'd been worth it. Everything about these three weeks had been worth it.

"Why is Mr. Autry lucky?" Kaylee asked, taking a strip of bacon from the platter in the center of the table.

Abby poured maple syrup on her pancakes. "Yeah, why?"

"Because he's gonna live where the little cute rats are the cooks," Kiera said. "Paris is where Remy lives, right? I would love if a funny rat in a chef hat made my pancakes."

"What?" Marissa asked. Rats? Working in restaurants? And who was Remy?

Thank heavens her parents had gone out to breakfast with their friends. Her mother did not like rats. And Ralph would get the broom out at the very mention.

Abby laughed. "We woke up kinda early this morning and I was saying I was gonna miss Autry and suggested we watch the movie *Ratatouille* because it takes place in Paris—where Autry is going."

Marissa raised an eyebrow. "Ratatouille? Isn't that a vegetable stew?"

Kiera laughed. "Mommy! The rat is the cook who makes stew. And other yummy stuff."

Abby nodded. "Mom, don't you remember the movie? Remy's the rat who wanted to be a real chef, so he started helping out the restaurant worker guy who couldn't cook? The guy got all the credit, but Remy was happy just cooking."

Marissa shivered. "I vaguely remember. Rats, even cartoon rats, freak me out a little. I don't think I'd want a rat making my dinner."

"But Remy was so cute!" Kaylee said.

Kiera nodded. "I wish I could have a pet rat."

Oh no. Not happening.

"I'll bet the most amazing things happen in Paris," Abby said, her eyes all dreamy. "Thinking about Paris helps me not think about Lyle. I still don't know how he could leave 2LOVEU. But Autry was right. Change is part of life."

Change was definitely a part of life, Marissa thought, Autry's handsome face coming to mind. She wondered what he was doing. Packing, probably. Having his last breakfast in Rust Creek Falls with his brothers and their wives.

"We've been through lots of changes," Kiera said, popping a blueberry in her mouth.

Kaylee looked at her big sisters. "I have a change. I want to change to eating bacon now."

Abby laughed and passed her little sister a strip of bacon.

"Maybe we could learn French," Abby said. "Mom, I was studying Spanish so I could learn 2LOVEU songs in two languages, but now I want to switch to French. I wonder how you say hello in French."

"I think it's *bonjour*," Marissa said, slugging down her coffee. "I think it translates to *good day*." The last thing she wanted to talk about was Paris. And Autry. But the girls needed to and so she would.

"How do you say goodbye?" Kiera asked.

"I'm pretty sure it's *adieu* or *au revoir*," Marissa said, her appetite waning.

"We had to say adieu to Autry," Kiera said. "I miss him already. I wish he could have breakfast with us." She frowned and put down her fork.

"Me, too," Kaylee said. "He's nice. I love my new backpack."

"Me, three," Abby said. "It doesn't feel right not to say goodbye the day he's leaving."

Three girls turned their gazes on Marissa.

Au revoir. Adieu. Goodbye. They'd said their good-
byes yesterday.

And today was the first day of the rest of her life.
Wasn't that what she'd said for the past two hours? She
was a new person thanks to Autry, and she would start
being that new person by letting him go. Because she
didn't have a choice.

Right. She had no choice. He was leaving. But...

But she could tell the man how she felt about him.
*You told him you weren't ready for a relationship. But
you're ready for him. Autry Jones. The man you love.*

*Tell him. Just tell him. He'll go to Paris and you'll
be here, but at least you'll have said it.* The new Marissa said what was on her mind. And in her heart.
She didn't hide her feelings. She didn't pretend she
had no feelings.

As the girls realized she wasn't answering, they
went back to eating their breakfast, if a little more
glumly than a minute ago.

Phone in hand, she went into the living room for
a little privacy. She tried Autry's room at Maverick
Manor, but was told he'd checked out a half hour ago.

No. No, no, no. She'd missed him? She tried his cell
phone, but it went straight to voice mail.

He wasn't leaving Rust Creek Falls without knowing
how she felt. That she loved him. That he'd opened her
eyes, opened her heart. She loved him and she'd scream
it from the rooftop of the Ace in the Hole if she had to.

So do it. Go scream it.

An idea started forming in her head. Could she?
Would she?

"Girls, put on your sneakers."

"Why? Where are we going?"

No, they weren't headed for the Ace in the Hole so she could climb up onto the roof and shout "I love Autry Jones!" for all the town to hear. Though she was so crazy in love she just might, if it came to that.

"Where are we going?" she repeated. "To the airport, even though it's a very long drive. We have a man to say goodbye to." The airport was three hours away, but it would be worth every mile.

"Yay!" Abby shouted. "Oh, Mom, I knew yesterday couldn't have been our final chance to say goodbye. Not when we have this morning."

What was that famous movie line? From *Casablanca*. "We'll always have Paris." She and Autry wouldn't, but yes, they'd have this morning. In the airport. Though by the time they got there, it would be afternoon. Closer and closer to his six-thirty departure.

Kiera and Kaylee raced to the hall closet and stuffed their feet into their sneakers, Kaylee wearing her brand-new light-up ones, her gift from Autry.

Marissa glanced in the hall mirror. No makeup. Her hair all messy. She smoothed it best she could and yanked down her long T-shirt over her black leggings. Well, if this was how she was going to look to tell Autry she loved him, so be it. This was who she was. A woman in flip-flops. Some things really would never change.

"Let's go, girls!"

Marissa pulled open the door.

Autry was standing there, his hand raised to knock.

She gasped. She looked at him, six feet plus of gorgeous, sexy Autry, a millionaire with a heart she'd never imagined such a man could have. Autry would give you the shirt off his back, even if he was penniless and had nothing. She knew that. Autry would soothe an upset child with the right words—not platitudes or what he thought Marissa might want to hear him say, but what a nine-year-old girl needed to know. Autry bought school supplies and pencil-cap erasers in animal shapes. And he made delicious spaghetti and meatballs. He'd even sat through a handful of animated movies. He was pure gold.

He stared at her, then smiled at the three little Fullers crowded behind her. "I have something to say to you, Marissa."

She lifted her chin. "I have something to say to *you*."

Question was, should she go first and risk sounding like a fool? He should go first. But what if he said he'd only come to say a final goodbye, that she was right that there was no future? Then she'd feel stupid for telling him she loved him.

She should go first. She should say how she felt, no matter what. That was what she would teach her girls. To speak their truth. To risk. To put themselves out there.

"You first," he said.

Oh God.

Autry stood on the porch, waiting to hear what Marissa had to say. Goodbye, he figured. And he wasn't ready to hear it. His plane wasn't leaving for hours. He had time to prolong his agony. But at least he'd be in agony while looking at Marissa's beautiful face.

"But first," he said, "where were you all going in such a hurry?" He smiled at three-year-old Kaylee, who was still in her pajamas.

"Look, Mr. Autry," Kaylee said and she stomped

the porch, her sneakers lighting up. "Thank you for my sneakers. Thank you for being so nice."

Autry knelt down. "Thank you for your being such a great three-year-old." He pulled her into a hug.

Kiera pushed past her mom's leg. "Thanks for my new backpack," she said, tears glistening. "And my monkey key ring."

"You're very welcome, Kiera." He wrapped her in a hug.

Abby stepped forward. "I'm not going to cry. I made myself a promise, so that I wouldn't ruin the goodbye by being a blubbering mess."

Autry laughed. "You can cry. I'm going to cry."

"You cry?" Kaylee asked. "But you're a grown-up."

"Well, sometimes grown-ups cry when they get really sad. And leaving you guys, well, that makes me really sad."

"But you have to," Abby said. "Because you're going to Paris."

He nodded. "I am going to Paris. In just several hours. But where were you guys headed just now?" He realized he'd never gotten an answer to that question.

Marissa crossed her arms over her chest. In a protective gesture? "To find you."

"Why?"

She glanced at her daughters, who were all staring at her. *Well, go ahead. Say it. Speak your truth.*

"Because I love you, Autry Jones. And I couldn't let you go without telling you."

She felt her daughters staring at her. Out of the corner of her eye she could see their mouths hanging open, then glee light their faces.

"You love me?" he asked.

"I love you," she said. "I didn't think I had any room left in my heart. But I was wrong."

Kaylee stepped forward. "I love Autry, too. He's really nice. He makes really good steaks. And I love my new backpack."

Kiera said, "I love you, Mr. Autry, because you're really good at charades."

"I guess it's my turn to tell Autry that I love him and say why," Abby said. "But I'm keeping it my own special secret. Is that okay?"

Autry knelt in front of Abby. "Of course it's okay. But one of the reasons I came here this morning was to tell you that you were right."

Abby tilted her head. "Me? Right about what?"

"Remember when you sang me your own version of 'Only You'?"

"Of course," Abby said, glancing at him with half shyness, half anticipation.

"You were right that only I can be your new dad," Autry said.

Four gasps filled the air.

"And your dad, and your dad," he said to Kaylee and Kiera. He stood up and looked at Marissa, taking her hand. "I love you, too, Marissa. I love you with everything I am. I love all of you."

"Oh, Autry," Marissa said, and launched herself into his arms.

Their audience cheered and clapped.

"But you're leaving tonight! You're going to Paris."

"Not if I'm going alone," he said. "Not without the four Fullers who've become my family."

She stared at him. "What? What do you mean?"

Autry held her gaze and reached out a hand to touch

her beautiful face. "Come with me. All of you. Come to Paris."

"What?" she said again, her head spinning.

"This morning I ran into Travis Dalton and Brenna O'Reilly. I hadn't had a chance to meet them before, so it was nice that I got to before I left. Travis said something that really got to me."

"Oh my God, you met Travis!" Abby squealed. "I knew him before he was famous, but you met him after. How cool is that?"

Marissa ruffled Abby's hair with a smile, then turned to Autry. "What did Travis say?"

"He said, 'If you want this woman, then go get her. If you can walk away, then do that. That's how you'll know.'"

"Huh," Marissa said with a grin. "I wouldn't have taken Travis for a love guru, but I guess Brenna has changed him."

"I can't walk away from you, Marissa. Or from your daughters. I love you. But yes, I'm going to Paris for a year, maybe longer. I want you and the girls to come with me. Not today, of course—I'm assuming none of you have passports and you'll need to apply and wait for them to arrive. Then we'll need to look into schools and a bigger home than the one I'm renting for the year. Oh, and of course the Raffertys are welcome to come, if they'd like."

Marissa looked slightly dazed and he smiled. "But... but we don't speak French," she stammered.

"We do!" Abby said. "We know *bonjour* and *adieu* and the other word for goodbye!"

"Au revoir," Autry said. "Don't make me say it for real."

"We want Paris! We want Paris!" all three girls started chanting.

He watched Marissa's face. He could see the emotions racing across. Excitement. Fear. Hope. And the word *but*. He saw the word *but*.

"I need to think," she said. "Excuse me for a moment. Girls, will you stay out here with Mr. Autry?"

His heart plummeted. She was going inside to have the space to think, without the girls' hopeful faces. Without his hopeful face.

She was going to come out and tell him no.

Marissa closed the door behind her, her eyes wide like saucers, her heart beating like mad.

Was she going to uproot her daughters? Herself? Change her entire life to move to Paris?

Yes, dammit. She was. Hadn't she said that today was the first day of the rest of her life? Hell yeah, she had.

She was doing this. Small-town gal Marissa Fuller was moving to Paris with her daughters to be with the man she loved. The father they all loved. And they were going to be a family.

Except... Wait.

She frowned, biting her lip. He hadn't said anything about marriage.

She wasn't uprooting her children and moving to a foreign country without a ring on her finger, that was for sure. No commitment, no France.

Her chin lifted, she opened the door and stepped back outside. Her daughters were staring at her. Abby was biting her lips so hard Marissa was afraid she might draw blood, and the girl's hands were in prayer formation.

Autry smiled—that captivating smile that always made her knees weak. "It's four against one, Marissa. You're outnumbered and overruled."

"Oh, wow," Abby said, jumping up and down. "I just realized I'll get to be a bridesmaid at my own mother's wedding!"

Marissa felt her cheeks burn. Well, at least the subject had come up! "Honey, Autry didn't say anything about us getting married. He just invited us to move to Paris with him."

And told her daughters he was their new father. He wouldn't have said that unless—

"I didn't say anything about marriage?" Autry asked. "Well, of course I didn't. How could I say anything about marriage without getting down on one knee?" He did just that and took a small velvet box out of his pocket.

Marissa gasped for the tenth time that morning. So did the girls.

"Marissa Fuller, will you do me the honor of becoming my wife?" he asked, opening the box to reveal a gleaming, twinkling diamond.

"That is some rock!" Abby shrieked.

Marissa's eyes widened. A certain little girl was growing up way too fast. Either Abby was listening in on Grandma's viewing of her guilty-pleasure TV show, *Real Housewives*, or the gals at Bee's Beauty Parlor forgot themselves when little ears were around. She smiled at Autry.

Then it hit her. The man had just proposed to her!

"Oh, Autry," she said, unable to say anything else,

unable to speak. The air had whooshed out of her body. She took a breath and looked at the man she loved so much. "Yes!" she shouted. "Yes, yes, yes! I will marry you!"

Autry stood up and slid the beautiful diamond ring on her finger.

She was so overwhelmed for a moment that she covered her mouth with her hand, then turned to her daughters. "Girls, we're moving to Paris!"

"Today?" Kiera asked, clapping.

"Not today," Marissa explained. "When you go to another country, you have to have something called a passport. So we have to get those and make arrangements. But in about a month, we'll be joining Autry in Paris."

"Yay!" Abby shrieked. "This is more exciting than if Lyle rejoined 2LOVEU! Oh, and you two can get married at the Eiffel Tower!"

"Or here," Autry said. "Whatever would make my bride-to-be happy. If you want to get married at the Ace in the Hole, that would be fine with me."

Marissa laughed. She couldn't see Autry Jones saying I do beside the pool table and dartboard. Or maybe she could. He'd changed. She'd changed. And now all their lives were changing.

"I don't care where we get married as long as we do," he said. "And I want us to become a family as soon as possible." He pulled Marissa into his arms. "I love you."

"I love *you*."

"A kiss to seal the deal?" he asked Marissa.

The girls giggled. "Ooh, la, la," Abby said.

Autry took her face in his hands and kissed her so passionately that she felt her toes curl.

"Bonjour!" Kiera said and they all cracked up. Out of the mouths of babes.

As Marissa gazed into the gorgeous blue eyes of her fiancé, she vaguely heard her daughters planning a Euro Disney wedding with Mickey Mouse as the officiant. The future was theirs—as a family.

Epilogue

Autry took a photo of Marissa and the girls sitting on the low stone wall along the Seine, Abby holding the baguette they'd just bought from a café.

"We're in Paris. I still can't believe it," Marissa said, touching the charming, very Parisian silk scarf she'd purchased from a little boutique. Her daughters already looked like French schoolgirls. They had started at the American school last week and were fitting in well. All three were enchanted with Paris, and Abby and Janie were texting away, sharing photos of home and France.

A few months from now, she and Autry would say "I do." Nope, not in Paris, their adopted city. In Rust Creek Falls, in the Ace in the Hole, where they'd met. Where a man who didn't date single mothers first fell for a single mom. And where a widowed mother of three who didn't think she'd ever find love again, found it.

Marissa's phone beeped with a text. Her mom and dad texting their first selfie at the railing of the *Caribbean*

Star cruise ship. Her mother's big smile and her dad's rested expression made Marissa so happy.

"I love you, Marissa," Autry said, standing behind her and wrapping his arms around her.

"I love you, too," she said.

"Je t'aime aussi!" Kaylee said.

Marissa and Autry stared at the little girl, their mouths agape.

Marissa turned to Autry. "Did my three-year-old just say 'I love you, too' in French?"

"She most definitely did," Autry said, picking up Kaylee and kissing her on the cheek.

"Ooh, la, la," Kiera said. It had become one of her favorite phrases. *"Je t'aime, je t'aime!"* She twirled around and Autry picked her up with his other arm, two little Fullers caught for hugs.

Just then, a little stray dog came and swiped the baguette right out of Abby's hand and ran off.

"There are many more where that baguette came from," Autry said.

Marissa laughed. "To Paris. And to us."

"To all of us," Autry said, as Abby came rushing over for the family hug.

* * * * *

*Don't miss the next installment of the
new Mills & Boon Cherish Continuity*

**MONTANA MAVERICKS:
THE GREAT FAMILY ROUNDUP**
*Zach Dalton is in search of the perfect kid-loving,
pie-making bride. Lydia Grant is anything but
perfect! She knows zilch about babies, and can't
bake to save her life! She's got nothing
Zach wants—but what if she's really everything
the lonely cowboy needs?*

Look for
THE MAVERICK'S BRIDE-TO-ORDER
by
USA TODAY *bestselling author*
Stella Bagwell

*On sale September 2017,
wherever Mills & Boon books and ebooks are sold.*

MILLS & BOON®

Cherish™

EXPERIENCE THE ULTIMATE RUSH OF FALLING IN LOVE

A sneak peek at next month's titles...

In stores from 10th August 2017:

- **Sarah and the Secret Sheikh** – Michelle Douglas *and* **Romancing the Wallflower** – Michelle Major
- **A Proposal from the Crown Prince** – Jessica Gilmore *and* **A Wedding to Remember** – Joanna Sims

In stores from 24th August 2017:

- **Her New York Billionaire** – Andrea Bolter *and* **The Waitress's Secret** – Kathy Douglass
- **Conveniently Engaged to the Boss** – Ellie Darkins *and* **The Maverick's Bride-to-Order** – Stella Bagwell

---

Just can't wait?
Buy our books online before they hit the shops!
www.millsandboon.co.uk

Also available as eBooks.

7/23

MILLS & BOON®

EXCLUSIVE EXTRACT

Artist Holly Motta arrives in New York to find billionaire
Ethan Benton in the apartment where *she's* meant to be
staying! And the next surprise? Ethan needs a fake
fiancée and he wants *her* for the role…

Read on for a sneak preview of
HER NEW YORK BILLIONAIRE
by debut author Andrea Bolter

"In exchange for you posing as my fiancée, as I have
outlined, you will be financially compensated and you will
become legal owner of this apartment and any items such
as clothes and jewels that have been purchased for this
position. Your brother's career will not be impacted negatively
should our work together come to an end. *And…*" He
paused for emphasis.

Holly leaned forward in her chair, her back still board-
straight.

"I have a five-building development under construction
in Chelsea. There will be furnished apartments, office lofts
and common space lobbies – all in need of artwork. I will
commission you for the project."

Holly's lungs emptied. A commission for a big corporate
project. That was exactly what she'd hoped she'd find in New
York. A chance to have her work seen by thousands of people.
The kind of exposure that could lead from one job to the next
and to a sustained and successful career.

This was all too much. Fantastic, frightening, impossible…
Obviously getting involved in any way with Ethan Benton

was a terrible idea. She'd be beholden to him. Serving another person's agenda again. Just what she'd come to New York to get away from.

But this could be a once-in-a-lifetime opportunity. An apartment. A job. It sounded as if he was open to most any demand she could come up with. She really did owe it to herself to contemplate this opportunity.

Her brain was no longer operating normally. The clock on Ethan's desk reminded her that it was after midnight. She'd left Fort Pierce early that morning.

"That really is an incredible offer…" She exhaled. "But I'm too tired to think straight. I'm going to need to sleep on it."

"As you wish."

Holly moved to collect the luggage she'd arrived with. Ethan beat her to it and hoisted the duffle bag over his shoulder. He wrenched the handle of the suitcase. Its wheels tottered as fast as her mind whirled as she followed him to the bedroom.

"Goodnight, then." He placed the bags just inside the doorway and couldn't get out of the room fast enough.

Before closing the door she poked her head out and called, "Ethan Benton, you don't play fair."

Over his shoulder, he turned his face back toward her. "I told you. I always get what I want."

Don't miss
HER NEW YORK BILLIONAIRE
by exciting new author
Andrea Bolter

Available September 2017
www.millsandboon.co.uk